THE MALEVOLENT SEVEN

Also by Sebastien de Castell

THE
MALEVOLENT
SEVEN

Sebastien de Castell

Jo Fletcher
BOOKS

First published in Great Britain in 2023 by

Jo Fletcher Books
an imprint of
Quercus Editions Ltd
Carmelite House
50 Victoria Embankment
London EC4Y 0DZ

An Hachette UK company

A CIP catalogue record for this book is available
from the British Library

HB ISBN 978 1 52942 277 1
TPB ISBN 978 1 52942 278 8
EBOOK ISBN 978 1 52942 280 1

10 9 8 7

Typeset by CC Book Production
Printed and bound in Great Britain by Clays Ltd, Elcograf S.p.A

Papers used by Jo Fletcher Books are from well-managed forests
and other responsible sources.

For Dirk Henke, a musical wonderist
who put together some truly killer bands.

Contents

CHAPTER 1

Real Mages Don't Wear Funny Hats

Picture a wizard. Go ahead, close your eyes if you need to. There he is, see? Old, skinny guy with a long scraggly beard he probably trips over on the way to the bathroom in the middle of the night. No doubt he's wearing some sort of iridescent silk robes that couldn't protect his frail body from a light breeze. The hat's a must, too, right? Big, floppy thing, covered in esoteric symbols that would reveal to every other mage which sources of magic this moron relies on for his powers? Wouldn't want a simple steel helmet or something that might, you know, protect the part of him most needed for conjuring magical forces from being bashed in with a mace or pretty much any household object heavier than a soup ladle.

Yep. Behold the mighty wizard: a stoop-backed feeb who couldn't run up a long flight of stairs without giving himself a heart attack.

Now, open your eyes and let me show you what a *real* war mage looks like.

'Fall, you pasty-faced little fuckers!' Corrigan roared as our contingent of wonderists assaulted the high citadel walls our employer had sent us to bring down ahead of his main forces. 'Fall so that I can rip your hearts out with my bare hands and feed you to my favourite devil as an appetiser before he feasts on your miserable souls!'

Yeah, Corrigan was a real charmer all right.

Big man, shoulders as broad as any soldier's. I stood maybe half an inch taller, but in every other dimension he was my superior. The muscles on Corrigan's forearms strained against the bejewelled gold and silver bands he always negotiated into his contracts. Tempestoral mages of his calibre have no particular use for precious metals or gemstones, but when it comes to selling his services, Corrigan likes to – in his words – 'Remind those rich arseholes who needs who.'

'Watch this one, Cade!' he shouted to me over the tumult of battle all around us. Our employer's foot soldiers and mounted cavalry were fighting and dying to keep the enemy troops busy while we wonderists did the real damage. Corrigan's eyes glowed the same unnerving indigo as the sparks that danced along the tightly braided curls of his hair and beard. Tendrils of black Tempestoral lightning erupted from his callused and charred palms to sizzle the air on their way to tear at stone and mortar like jagged snakes feeding on a colony of mice. He grinned at me, his white teeth in stark contrast to the ebony of his skin, then laughed as each of his fists closed around one of his lightning bolts. He began wielding them like whips, grabbing hold of the stalwart defenders atop the walls and sweeping them up into the sky before shaking them until their spines snapped. Several other poor bastards leaped to their deaths rather than waiting for Corrigan to take an interest in them.

'We don't get paid extra for making them shit their pants, you know,' I reminded him, my fingers tracing misfortune sigils in the air so that the volleys of arrows the enemy fired at us missed their targets. 'Our job is to convince them to surrender, not commit suicide.'

'*Our job?*' The indigo braids of Corrigan's beard rustled with the same enthusiasm his lightning snakes showed as they destroyed in minutes the gleaming, high-towered citadel that had taken hard-working masons decades to build. 'Our job, Cade, is to make what we in the trade call *an impression.*'

I suppose I couldn't argue with that. Our employer was an Ascendant Prince – self-declared, of course – who'd been having some difficulty convincing the local ruling archons of his divinely sanctioned rule. Sending a coven of mercenary wonderists to wage mayhem and murder (I never lied to myself by calling it 'war') wasn't likely to convince anyone of Ascendant Lucien's holiness, but as his Magnificence had explained it to me, 'Kill enough of the brave ones and the rest will pray to anyone I tell them to.'

He might be a complete fucking moron, but Lucien was right about that much, at least.

The crossbowmen atop the walls stopped firing their bolts at us, no doubt tired of watching the wooden shafts splinter against the rocks as the ill-luck spells I'd kept around our division meant each and every one of them missed their mark. Meanwhile, Corrigan and a couple of the others got on with blasting their brethren to pieces with impunity.

Corrigan lightened up on his thunderous assault and motioned for a nearby echoist to spin a little sonoral magic to amplify his voice as he called out to the citadel's terrified defenders, 'There now, my little ducklings, no need to jump. Just open up the gates for Uncle Corrigan and we can all have a nice cup of tea before supper.' He glanced back at me. 'There. Happy?'

'You really are a prick, you know that?' I took advantage of the momentary distraction among the archers to give my fingers a shake before renewing the shield over our squad of eleven wonderists.

Corrigan shrugged. 'What do you expect? I conjure rampant fucking devastation from the Tempestoral plane for a living so that one group of arseholes can conquer another group of arseholes – and then a couple of years later, that second group of arseholes hires me to kill off the first lot. That can't be good for the soul.'

3

Truer words had never been spoken.

'Enemy wonderists!' one of our comrades shouted.

Up on those high walls, the tell-tale shimmer of Auroral magic (that being the 'nice people' kind) appeared: Archon Belleda had finally sent out her own contingent of wonderists to kick our arses.

When Corrigan got a look at the silk-robed, grey-bearded scarecrows standing up there, he was pissing himself laughing so hard his tendril spell almost collapsed.

'Look,' he shouted to the rest of us, 'real live Auroral mages have come to cast our souls to the pits! Kneel before these noble miracle-workers and weep for mercy, for surely the judgement of the Lords Celestine is at hand!'

The rest of us didn't laugh. We focused on our jobs, which now included sending those dignified old men and women to their graves. It wasn't Archon Belleda's fault her defenders couldn't beat us. They were locals, patriots fighting for a noble cause, while we were mercenaries, motivated by greed and lousy upbringings, loyal only to the fees our employer had promised us.

The poor bastards never had a chance.

One of the enemy wonderists, a silver-haired woman already dripping with nervous sweat, took the lead. Blood seeped from her eyes as she cast a sorcerous incantation we in the business call a 'heartchain', because it pierces right through defensive spells to burst the enemy's blood vessels. It's not the sort of thing any of us would use because it's a conjoined sympathy spell, which means a heartchain also kills the person casting it. I marvelled at the old codger's redoubtable courage and sacrifice as the thread-like silver tether stretched across the two hundred yards between them to bind her heart to Corrigan's.

The big brute's eyes went wide as his thick fingers clawed at his own chest. He turned to me, but no sound came from his lips as he mouthed my name.

Corrigan Blight was a monster, no doubt about it. He killed people for money, and he did it without ever questioning whether such acts could be justified. Any time I'd asked whether perhaps there was a better way to earn a living, he'd slap me across the head and proudly declare, 'Didn't make the rules, don't plan to break them.' If you stuck him next to the old lady on the wall and asked a hundred people which one of them deserved to live, not one of them would say Corrigan.

Well, except me.

Corrigan was my friend, which was a hard thing to admit to myself and an even harder thing to find in this profession. He'd saved my life more times than I'd saved his, and I know that doesn't justify the choice I made in that moment, but maybe it explains why, without giving it a second's thought, I conjured a poetic injustice.

Beneath my leather cuirass, a set of three intertwining sigils etched into my torso began to smoulder, then the sigils appeared in the air before me as floating scrawls of ebony ink, curves and edges glimmering. I could feel the seconds counting down towards Corrigan's heart bursting in his chest.

He clutched at my shoulder in panic, or maybe searching for a final moment of human connection. I shrugged him off; I needed to concentrate.

I placed my right hand above the first sigil, which looked like a distorted stick figure crowned in seven rays; it represented the enemy spellcaster. When I moved my hand upwards, the sigil followed, and I placed it in a direct line between myself and the Auroral mage casting the heartchain.

The second sigil, a gleaming black circle with a second, smaller half-circle overlapping the top of it, looked almost like a padlock. It moved of its own accord, floating silently up to Corrigan's forehead, which would have unnerved him no end if he'd not been too busy dying to notice.

The particular forms of magic I work manifest a kind of elementary consciousness within them, which meant that the spell knew Corrigan was the target of the Auroral mage's heart-rending invocation. I quickly placed three fingers atop the locking sigil, then moved it between me and the enemy wonderists atop the citadel walls, looking for my target.

This is where casting a poetic injustice gets tricky. Altering the binding on someone else's spell requires finding someone to whom they have an already strong emotional connection, which would usually require time and research, neither of which we had to spare. But these idiots had made it easy for me. Beside the Auroral mage stood a fierce-eyed old gentleman holding her hand. I might not be the world's most sentimental guy, but even I could sense the love between them. I quickly tethered the targeting sigil to him.

Now for the third sigil. With the thumb and forefinger of each hand, I grasped the two-headed coiled snake, ignoring the ink-black tongues that flickered menacingly at me, pulled the spiral straight and attached a head to each of the other two sigils.

The thin silver thread binding the Auroral mage to Corrigan snapped away from him, whipping through the air with blinding speed before attaching itself to the old man next to her. Even when he saw the heartchain coming for him, he didn't make a move to abandon her. Maybe he was her husband and such a cowardly thought never occurred to him.

Till death did they part, as no one with a conscience might say.

Corrigan painfully sucked air into his lungs, giving me just the barest nod of acknowledgment, then, smiling with smug self-satisfaction, renewed his attack on the walls with just as much vigour and twice as much pleasure as before.

I had to lean against him just to keep from collapsing to the ground. Poetic injustice spells are hard on the body. And the soul, I guess.

In case I hadn't made this clear already, we're not exactly the good guys.

But don't worry – by the end of this story, me, Corrigan and the five other wonderists who would come to be known as the Malevolent Seven would definitely be getting what was coming to us.

CHAPTER 2

And the Walls Came Down

Watching the walls of a once magnificent citadel being torn down isn't pleasant. The rumbling, crumbling, thunderous collapse of stone, wood and mortar is soon followed by the screams of those unfortunate enough not to have died instantly in the fall. Thanks to a few time-delayed eruption spells, ingeniously placed with the help of engineers who ought to be building things rather than figuring out how to blow them apart, a magnificent feat of architecture that once made people believe the world could be a safe, civilised place was now proof of the opposite.

Cheers rose up from the foot soldiers on our side. Men and women who hours before had been glaring resentfully at us because we got better pay, better tents and better prostitutes than they did were now slapping us on the back and praising our achievements to the heavens.

I doubted anyone up there was pleased.

My part in this accursed endeavour left me sick to my stomach. It wasn't just the spells themselves, which were vile enough. It was the thrill all this devastation produced in everyone around me, a pleasure I couldn't seem to keep from slithering inside me until I was cheering right alongside them. Maybe it just felt good to be part of a team again.

'Silord Cade! Silord Cade Ombra, I need to see you!'

The voice calling out my name was young, enthusiastic and exasperating. When I'd first met the gangly, witless teenager, I'd assumed he was some camp follower looking to worm his way into my tent. Turned out he was an amateur luminist hoping to apprentice himself to a war mage. I should've sent him packing when he'd first suggested the idea; it would have saved me having to constantly resist the urge to slap him senseless.

'What did I tell you last time?'

'Silord?'

Okay, this time I *did* have to belt him – as much for his own safety as my satisfaction. Silord, a portmanteau of 'sir' and 'lord', is, technically, how one should address a war mage, since in terms of rank we sit somewhere between a cavalry officer and a minor noble.

However . . .

'Our employer – *your* employer, in case you forgot – doesn't approve of that particular honorific,' I reminded the boy. *Again.*

Corrigan whispered conspiratorially to him, 'Ascendant Lucien feels such titles risk confusing the peasantry about who the gods love and who they just sort of put up with.'

'But Sil—' He caught himself just in time to avoid a black eye. 'Master Ombra—'

'Ascendant Lucien doesn't like hearing people refer to his subordinates as "master", either,' I told him. 'Nor, by the way, do I appreciate you using my fucking real name in front of other people when there could be spies about taking stock of who should be on the receiving end of a sharp blade should the opportunity present itself. For the duration of this engagement, you will refer to me as Brother Cerulean. You will refer to our big friend with the ridiculous violet-blue hair' – I gestured to Corrigan, who was practically glowing from the admiration of the crowd of soldiers and camp followers flooding around him – 'as Brother Indigo.'

'And what should I call myself?' asked the boy.

'You are Cousin Green.'

And never was there a name more apt.

Corrigan whistled through his teeth and shoved his would-be admirers away. I knew without having to look around that this meant our employer was approaching.

'Ah, Silord Cade, Silord Corrigan,' Ascendant Lucien said graciously.

I shot Green a look so he'd know this wasn't a contradiction of my earlier injunction. Lucien was just showing us how magnanimous he could be. By nightfall, you could be certain one of the soldiers would have mistakenly referred to us as 'silords' and Lucien would have them crucified for it to make sure everyone remembered the rules.

'Your stratagem worked just as you predicted, Ascendant Lucien,' I said, swallowing the bile engendered by having to compliment this silver-haired, alabaster-faced moron who couldn't plan his way out of a privy. On the other hand, a little arse-kissing after a victory does help loosen the purse strings.

Lucien gave me that smile of his – the one that had already kept me up several nights during this campaign contemplating murdering him and switching sides. I might have, too, but there are rules to the game we play. Breaking a contract can damn your soul faster than razing a dozen villages.

'And you executed the plan flawlessly,' Lucien enthused, always determined to best me, even in flattery. 'Such skill and loyalty deserves recognition . . . and reward.'

A dozen of his private guard – who were, so far as I could tell, just regular soldiers wearing shinier armour beneath their gaudy white-and-gold tabards – marched smartly up to us in two columns, escorting a group of what any decent person would have to call boys and girls. They were clean and well-dressed in fresh silver-white gowns, which made me feel sick, because it meant they were here for a purpose.

'For my wonderists!' Lucien declared, drawing *oohs* and *ahhs* from hard-bitten soldiers who were in no way impressed by this act of perversity.

The boys and girls smiled at us with every part of their faces but their eyes, which betrayed them. I grinned as wide as I could without letting what was left of my integrity spew from my mouth.

Corrigan put a collegial hand on my shoulder and squeezed hard enough to make the bones creak. This was his way of keeping me from throttling our beloved employer then and there.

The Lords Celestine, benevolent rulers of the Auroral realms, rely on their human worshippers to enact their policies upon the Mortal plane. Some of these agents act as judges to punish heretical crimes; others, like Lucien, 'spread the Auroral song of devotion and self-sacrifice'. Some are even raised in monastic institutions to believe that their own spiritual fulfilment can come about only by giving themselves utterly – in *every* sense of the word – to whomever they are gifted by their religious leaders. These lucky boys and girls are known as the *sublime*. It's said there's nothing you can do to a sublime – not even murder them – that won't fill them with righteous bliss. It's all consensual, of course, as long as you're a piece of human garbage who thinks teenagers dream of becoming your playthings.

'The Ascendant's cunning in battle is rivalled only by his generosity,' I said, and though I doubted I managed to keep the disgust and nausea from my voice, Lucien nonetheless nodded graciously.

'One each,' he said, wagging a finger at the others among our little cadre of mercenary wonderists, 'but for my captains, my *chancer* Cade Ombra and my *thunderer* Corrigan Blight, I offer two!'

While a centuries-old citadel fell behind us, crushing men and women who, if not innocent, at least deserved something better out of life than being squashed to death beneath the rubble, those on our side clapped daintily as if we were at a tea party and His Most Gracious Ascendancy had just given a toast.

My fellow wonderists made their picks of the most comely, except Corrigan, who, noting my glare, gave me a slight nod to acknowledge that whatever pleasure he might have taken wouldn't be worth the consequences I would dish out later to any among our number who sampled too deeply of our employer's magnanimous 'gift'.

Unable to risk giving offence by turning down the generous gesture, I chose the two most frightened of the group: a young boy of about eleven – who Lucien kept leering at – and the girl of seventeen hugging him protectively as if that would do either of them any good.

Ascendant Lucien shot me a curiously satisfied look, which I met with one of those smiles men like him recognise as the enjoyment of terror over beauty.

'Excellent choices,' His Ascendancy said to me. Then he raised his arms wide to the others. 'Revel tonight, my loyal followers, for tomorrow, we burn every last one of the false Archon Belleda's followers on the stake!'

'But Your Ascendancy,' I said, probably louder than I should have, 'our contract was to induce Archon Belleda's people to *capitulate* to your rule, not kill them – already they raise her flag upside down to signal their surrender.'

Lucien's shoulders rose and fell wearily, as if to say he was just as disappointed in this recent development as I was. 'Alas,' he said, turning to leave. 'They waited too long.'

This was my cue to shut up, but I made one last appeal. 'They worship the Aurorals, as do you. Surely the Lords Celestine would nev—?'

'The Lords Celestine have sanctioned my ruling in this matter,' Lucien informed me, adding a gravel to his voice which hadn't been there a second ago. 'Do you wish to question *their* judgement? Perhaps you have some special relationship with the Aurorals that gives you a deeper insight into their wishes?'

'Of course not, Ascendancy,' Corrigan said, casually driving the second knuckle of his forefinger into my spine. 'Cade here's just addled from the battle. All that Fortunal magic, you know. Makes him forget himself – but only temporarily.'

Lucien gave a gracious chuckle before leading the procession of happy soldiers, wonderists and soon-to-be miserable sublimes on their way, leaving me and Corrigan standing there listening to the cries of the dying behind us.

'Don't fucking say it,' I warned him.

He kept his mouth shut, but his expression made it clear that this wasn't our fight, and that if I couldn't summon the self-discipline to keep my mouth shut, he'd do it for me. We were mercenaries, not heroes. Wars almost always end with a good old-fashioned massacre, whether by steel or by spell.

I returned him a look that said I understood completely, would heed his warning to keep quiet, but also that Ascendant Lucien was going to meet with an unfortunate accident tonight, and so would anyone who tried to get in my way.

CHAPTER 3

Necessary Cruelties

Those who wage war for a living see the world around them as territory. The most breath-taking landscape, the most heart-rending scene of devastation, both are merely lines on a map to be erased and redrawn with pen and ink when diplomacy served, or with swords and blood when it did not. It should be no surprise, then, that Ascendant Lucien's camp was a moveable nation, with tented cantons and districts arranged according to his own design. Just as in any city, location was a marker of status easily understood by those who lived nearby.

'Your tent is like a palace!' the boy – Fidick, he'd said his name was – declared.

'Have you ever been inside a palace?' I asked.

He gave a light, nervous laugh. 'No, Silord. Never.'

'Then what the hell do you know?'

The girl, who'd told me her name was Galass, gave the boy a quieting glare and me something more akin to a snarl. She so obviously saw herself as his protector that I almost pitied her the heartbreak for which she was surely destined.

Galass was on the cusp of womanhood, dark-haired and pretty in that way that waxed and waned depending on her expression, but Fidick was something else entirely. He was possessed of a luminous beauty that would make great artists want to lock him away so that

14

no one but they could capture his golden curls and cherubic features. Others would want to lock him away for far worse reasons.

Someday soon Galass would be cradling Fidick's trembling body, wiping away the blood and filth emanating from every orifice, whispering to him that it was all right now and he should just put the recent atrocities done to him out of his mind. And when Fidick finally slept, she would contemplate the ways in which she might, with sublime kindness, cause him such permanent disfigurement that he would for evermore be an object of pity and disgust rather than desire.

The worst part of it all? That nonsense about spiritual bliss they'd been filled with at whichever monastery Lucien had acquired them from would be the only retreat from the misery of life available to them. Sometimes a lie really is more comforting than the truth. I should know.

There was a small stool outside my monstrously spacious tent of dyed blue canvas featuring front flaps painted with golden esoteric sigils (which did nothing, but whoever Lucien had in charge of our accommodation had taken some artistic license with the design). I sat down and wiped the muck and grime from my trousers and boots with the towel left there for that purpose, then handed it to the boy. 'Clean your feet, both of you. I don't want you tracking mud into my "palace".'

They did as they were told while I undid the spell knots from the cords fastening the tent flaps, trying not to breathe in the stink of putrefied flesh emanating from the recently charred canvas. Some curious individual was now walking around camp with a couple of missing fingers.

'Where are the tents of the other wonderists?' Fidick asked, glancing around. 'Aren't you friends with them?'

'Fidick!' Galass hissed.

'It's fine,' I said, only because I didn't want her thinking she could decide what was or wasn't discussed under my roof. 'His Ascendancy prefers that his wonderists be spread out in case one of us is urgently needed to fend off an unexpected magical attack.'

A more truthful answer would have been that Lucien didn't like the idea of a coven of wonderists nestled together in the bosom of his encampment where they might be tempted to talk late into the night, drinking, imbibing various pleasure drugs and wondering aloud why those whose magic was crucial to winning the war shouldn't be the ones to rule over what was left when said war was over.

Was that why he'd ordered us to slaughter Archon Belleda's troops in the morning? Did Lucien want to make such monstrous villains of his wonderists that no one else would ever trust us? Why would the Lords Celestine, those beneficent guardians of morality, sanction such a massacre in the first place?

'Your domain is magnificent, Silord,' Galass said as she stepped inside.

The tent was indeed glorious, the rough canvas barely visible from inside, hidden as it was by long lengths of gleaming azure silk hanging from hooks attached to the very top and draping over the ten-foot-long mahogany poles holding the shape. The light of half a dozen bronze oil lanterns twinkled off the precious threads woven into the thick carpets covering the ground, each one depicting some of Lucien's *many* victories – most of which hadn't actually taken place yet, but it's never too early to be thinking about commemorating one's glorious legacy.

Walk into the average soldier's tent and you'll be hit with the odours of musk, sweat and stale beer. Mine was scented with fresh flowers and baskets of pine needles, which Lucien's overworked retainers would refresh each morning before battle. Every evening they would deliver a cask of wine from the Ascendant's own vineyards three hundred miles away, as well as a variety of delicacies utterly unlike the swill afforded his hard-fighting troops.

War is hell, just not for everybody.

The ostentatious accommodations were more for Lucien's benefit than mine; he wanted those among his officers who might be contemplating their own advancement to be aware that *he* was the one who commanded the deadliest wonderists in the country. As petty acts of self-aggrandisement went, this was one I didn't actually mind.

I removed the preposterous golden cape Lucien insisted we wear in battle and hung it inside the polished oak armoire next to my silk-sheeted bed. Fidick and Galass were still standing at the entrance, waiting for my commands.

'Get in here. Make yourselves . . .'

I was about to say *at home*, but that would have been dishonest. They wouldn't be here more than a single night. My hesitation confused Galass and Fidick in the worst way possible: they began disrobing.

'Stop—' I said, too loudly and forcefully for anyone's good.

The pair of them froze, hands on the hems of their silvery-white gowns. Fidick's glance flitted around the tent, clearly worried I'd changed my mind and was about to banish them from this temporary but welcome opulence.

'Have we displeased you, Silord?' Galass inquired, using pretty much the same inflections I use when asking, *'What the fuck is your problem, arsehole?'*

I began unclasping the bronze bindings of my leather cuirass. 'Forgive my outburst,' I said. 'The two of you are welcome to stay here for the night – as long as we come to certain agreements about what you will and won't see here. Either way, I give you my word I won't lay hands on either of you.'

Fidick's breath came out in a whoosh and he looked so relieved I thought he might faint with joy. Then his eyes caught something to my right and his face lit up. I followed his gaze to a bowl of red and purple plums on the far side of the bed. You don't generally find much in the way of fresh fruit in army camps.

'Help yourself,' I said, then thought better of it. 'You may have one now, and another in the morning.' Those unaccustomed to such luxuries invariably overindulge, and I don't know any spells for getting diarrhoea out of my carpet.

The boy gingerly stepped past me to begin a careful tour of the fruit bowl, never touching anything, just sweeping his gaze over every inch of its contents in search of the perfect choice.

Galass folded her arms across her chest. 'Why?' she asked.

'Because it's too sweet if you're not used to it,' I replied. 'I don't want either of you—'

'No, I mean, why do you have no intention of making use of our bodies?'

Making use of our bodies.

I liked her bluntness, but the fact that this was the third time she'd been belligerent suggested that her perceptiveness could be dangerous to both of us. She read in my words and deeds a weakness that suggested I committed acts of violence for money but lacked the stomach to do so for pleasure – and she was right, after a fashion, which was a problem because it might require me to prove her wrong.

'I have no taste for the flesh of unripe fruit,' I said.

She snorted at my attempt to be clever. 'You mean you won't violate those who don't desire you,' she corrected.

What the hell was wrong with this kid? Did she have a monumental death wish?

I finally got the damned leather cuirass off and let it fall to the ground. My sweaty, grimy shirt followed. I don't usually like anyone to see me unclothed, but neither of these two were likely to recognise the black and silver markings burned onto my chest, arms and back, and in any case, most people get nauseous if they stare at the sigils too long.

I grabbed a jug of water and a clean towel and began wiping myself down. 'All that bullshit your teachers told you about how spiritually rewarding it is to sublimate your will to that of another aside, I prefer the companionship of those who enjoy my attentions,' I replied.

My response appeared to annoy my unwelcome guest, which irritated me in return. It's not like I was asking for gratitude – I wasn't nearly so foolish as that. But did she have to keep needling me like this?

'You haven't asked,' she said.

Fidick looked up from the plum he was half devouring and half dribbling down the front of his gown, his eyes going from the girl to me.

I squeezed out the filthy towel and soaked it a second time. 'Asked what?'

'You haven't asked if Fidick or I desire you. So how do you know? Perhaps I want you right now, Silord.' She began playing with the loose collar of her silvery gown.

I wasn't fooled. She was goading me, though I had no idea to what end. 'Maybe I just find you ugly,' I said.

'Is that so?'

She stripped me with her eyes. Unlike Fidick's almost perversely innocent beauty, Galass knew exactly how to wield her looks for maximum effect, which made her infinitely more attractive – and dangerous.

'You're lying again, Silord,' she said, arching her back just so and causing the strap of her silvery gown to slip off one shoulder. 'You don't find me ugly at all. Here I am, gifted to you by the Ascendant himself, my duty as clear to me as it is to you, yet you pretend indifference.' She took a step closer. 'You can't hide your desire for me, Silord.'

I raised my outstretched hand. 'Do you also see this? Because in about five seconds you're going to see the back of it close up if you don't stop taunting me.'

She stepped back, but smiled as if she'd just won the game. 'And still you haven't asked.'

'Asked what?'

'Whether I desire you.'

'Why the fuck would you?'

'Because you're right about what they beat into us at the monastery, Silord. The "ecstasy of spiritual submission" is – how did you put it? *Bullshit?* – but if the Ascendant discovers we've failed to please you, Fidick and I will suffer a fate far worse than anything you can imagine.'

Which suggests Lucien specifically wanted these two for me. But why?

'He won't find out from me, so if the two of you can keep your mouths shut—'

She raised her chin. 'You assume lying comes as easily to us as it does you. You denigrate any pride a sublime might take in the pleasure we give others as beneath you, but it is all the pride I have. For all your pretences at nobility, you don't actually care whether I desire you. You simply believe such pathetic creatures as Fidick and I are incapable of our own desires.'

It had been a long time since a sublime had schooled me in philosophical incongruity. I was looking forward to being rid of this one as soon as possible.

I walked to the armoire, found a clean shirt, slid it over my head and said, 'You want to talk about *my* "pretences at nobility"? Let me tell you, sister, only rich lordlings and sublime obliviates are stupid enough to believe a slave can desire her oppressors any more than a man dying of thirst *desires* a glass of water!'

Her head rocked as if I'd struck her across the jaw.

Fidick, still sucking on his plum, ran to her side.

For reasons I can only attribute to my imminent participation in the slaughter of the defenders of Archon Belleda's citadel, I actually felt guilty. 'I'm sorry,' I said. 'I didn't mean to insult you.'

Galass shook her head. 'A necessary cruelty, Silord. I am grateful for it.' The blue eyes went icy. 'Allow me to repay your generosity in kind and suggest that the difference between you and me is not that I am a slave and you a mercenary. What separates us is that I *know* I am a slave, and you still harbour the illusion that you have free will, as if Ascendant Lucien *asks* you to do his bidding, or more laughably, *negotiates* for your services. The coin with which he pays you affords you the self-deception denied to us.' She held up her wrists. 'See? No chains here either, but I feel their presence.' She walked to the centre of the tent, grabbed my wrists, and held my hands up between us. 'Can you see your chains, Silord Cade?'

It was a mad thing to do. Wonderists aren't known for their appreciation of those who lay hands on them without permission. But somewhat to my surprise, I found myself laughing.

So this is why she keeps goading me. She thinks if she gets a rise out of me, whatever vile abuses I'm secretly intending for the two of them will be directed at her, not Fidick.

I was about to call her on it when I heard a yipping sound, followed by a low growl. There was a dog in my tent – a jackal, actually, with tall ears, a long, sharp snout like that of a wolf, and a face I doubted even its mother could have loved.

'Mister Bones!' Fidick said excitedly, looking around for the animal.

My eyes narrowed as I spotted the beast near the entrance. I studied it, searching for any spell or charm that would explain how he'd got into my tent without permission. Galass must have mistaken my look of irritation for impending violence because, for the first time, she looked anxious.

'Please, Silord!' she cried and rushed to take hold of the jackal. 'He means no harm. He follows Fidick and me around everywhere. I'll send him away – or if you must kill him, I beg you, do so quickly. Do not—'

'Why are you so convinced I want to kill this mutt?' I asked, then remembered the rumour going around camp that one of my fellow mages sacrificed dogs as part of his ritual preparations for each day's battle.

I knelt down and held out my hand for the jackal to sniff.

The ugly little beast padded closer, putting himself between me and Galass. His little dog-like head hunched forward, nostrils flaring, before showing me his teeth. The grey-brown fur bristled, the stripes at the tip of its tail somehow sharpening, as he looked poised to go for my throat at any moment – then he finally sniffed at my hand and let out a slightly more companionable snarl that nonetheless conveyed that there would be trouble if I crossed his favourite humans.

Even the dogs were telling me my business lately.

'Let's get something straight, Mister Bones,' I said, deliberately sticking my finger between his teeth. 'You can stay here tonight and protect your charges, but if you pee on *anything* in this tent, I will transform you into a three-legged cat.'

'You can do that?' Fidick asked.

'Better for all of us that you never find out.'

'Thank you,' Galass said, grabbing the jackal and cuddling it. 'You are . . . kinder than the others.'

I could almost believe her this time, which only made me angrier. 'I'm *not* kind, you idiot child! I'm not noble, honourable, decent or compassionate. I'm barely fucking human. I'm . . .' Why was I trying to explain myself to this kid? 'I'm a mercenary, that's all, halfway to a monster as bad or worse than Lucien, if you want the truth. I'd rather not travel farther down that road, that's all.'

I rose up and strode to the small chest next to my bed, traced a pattern in the air with my ring finger while whispering the words that would restrain the curse as I opened the lid long enough to fish out two coins. I turned back to Galass and Fidick and held one out for each of them. 'Do you have the means to keep these hidden? Have you some place where you can be sure no one will find them?'

Galass nodded, while Fidick stared at the sheen of gold, fingers reaching out of their own accord. I held the coins up out of his reach.

'Here's the deal,' I said. 'You'll stay here tonight. I'll see you fed and kept safe until morning. When you leave, you'll have these. If you're smart, you'll wait until the battle begins tomorrow and run from the camp while the army is still revelling in the carnage. They'll leave some of the defenders alive to play with, which will keep them sufficiently occupied that no one will be paying attention to you. Head back the way the army came. Find the least ruined town left standing and set yourself up with a place to live and an apprenticeship. I recommend a tannery. The pay's good and the stink's no worse than corpses on a battlefield – assuming you're clever enough to keep someone from taking the money away from you.'

'And the price?' Galass asked. She was watching me, not the coins.

'You let me cast a memory binding on you.'

She shook her head and stepped away. The jackal growled. 'No,' she said. 'No mage's curse for me.'

'But Gal,' Fidick cried, 'this could be—'

'I told you before, wonderist,' she said, holding up her arms, 'I'm not blind to my shackles. I'll not add your foul magic to harden them further.'

'It's not that kind of binding,' I insisted. 'I just need . . . there are things I have to do now – things I don't want any of my fellow mages to learn about. I can't risk you telling them, or them drawing the memories from you by some other means, so I'll need to . . . tamper with your recollections.'

'We'll forget what you did to us?' Fidick asked, sounding suspicious for the first time.

I shook my head. 'You'll remember what you saw in this tent, but should anyone ever ask, or should you try to speak of it – or even if someone uses magic to pull the memories from your mind – you'll suddenly remember it differently.'

'And what will we remember, should that occur?' Galass asked.

I wondered if she knew how prescient that question was. Implanting false memories is tricky. I'd have to imagine a series of events between us that people like Ascendent Lucien would find believable, and that was something I very much *didn't* want to imagine. 'You'll remember me as a cruel – though not excessively so – user of your bodies and tormentor of your psyches. You'll recall me being arrogant, mean-spirited and, in the end, dismissive.'

'That's no different than any other night,' Fidick said, with a faint smile.

How the kid could live the life he did and joke about it, I had no idea.

'We accept the bargain,' Galass said. 'But I must warn you, Silord, that no magical trickery will prevent me remembering every detail exactly as it occurred. I'm not so easily glamoured as some you may have met in the past.'

Everyone says that. Even me.

'Nonetheless,' she went on, 'you have my oath that I will never repeat anything that takes place inside the walls of this tent.'

'Your oath?' I asked.

I guess my tone was off.

'Yes, *my oath*. Is the oath of a sublime a matter of amusement to you?'

'The only thing I find funny about you is that you seem to think I value one person's oath over another's.' I handed each of them their coins. 'I'm going to cast the spell now. Are you ready?'

They looked at each other first, which I liked, then nodded.

The spell itself wasn't complicated – it's not even especially powerful. The mind doesn't have 'memories' in the way we think of them, just fragments from which it reconstructs events after the fact. I watched the looks of all-too-familiar discomfort on Galass and Fidick's faces as I fiddled with glowing black sigils in the air between us and pushed my unpleasant imaginings into their minds.

If pressed, they'd remember this night as no different from just about any other.

The world is an awful place sometimes. Better people than me have failed to rise above its ways.

'What now?' Galass asked, holding on to the bed post for balance. 'What are we about to witness that so damns you it must never be revealed?'

I went back to my chest, unspelled it again and took out a brazier and two small leather pouches, one dark blue, the other a faint pinkish hue. I returned to the centre of the tent, opened the darker pouch and poured the glinting azure sand into a three foot circle which I then surrounded by a larger, four foot circle. After making sure there were no gaps in either, I opened the second pouch and used the pale salmon-coloured sand within to create a thinner circle between the other two. 'I'm going to summon a demon.'

They both gasped, and I suddenly realised I hadn't sealed the tent to keep them from running away – but whether from fear of my retribution or some perverse sense of honour, neither of them fled.

'A demon?' Galass demanded. 'The Ascendant called you a chance mage – isn't that one whose spells are drawn from the Fortunal plane? Does this mean you're really a servant of the Infernals who traffic in thrice-damned conjurations condemned by the Celestines themselves?'

I chuckled at that, which was cruel given how terrified the two of them looked. I wasn't trying to be mean; I just find it funny the way regular people talk about the Infernals. 'Don't panic,' I said as I prepared the summoning, 'as demons go, he's actually kind of a nice guy.'

CHAPTER 4

Everything Comes
With a Price

Magic, like booze, comes in all different flavours. Amateurs talk about colours – black magic, white magic, grey magic. I once met a guy who insisted he only invoked turquoise magic, whatever the hell that was supposed to be. Really, though, what defines magic is not colour, but where the power comes from – or more specifically, where the *rules* come from.

All spells are, by definition, violations of the natural order: you want lightning to appear out of a clear sky? You're messing with everything from temperature to humidity to the pressure of the air itself. Want a tree to grow faster? You have to start by screwing with the fundamental elements of life. The easiest way to do this isn't by trying to force nature to conform with your will, but rather, to allow the physical laws of a *different* reality – say, one where freaky red and black lightning often appears out of a clear sky, or somewhere plants grow faster than they do here – to momentarily interfere with our world.

That's magic.

The mechanics work differently depending on the particular form of spellcraft used to bring those rules into one's present location, but whether it's through incantations or charms or ritual desecrations, all spells rely on the same phenomenon: you have to trigger a breach between the Mortal plane and one more conducive to your needs.

Of course, that's where the problems begin, because not all of those other planes of reality are uninhabited. Some are dominated by conscious entities with their own desires and plans, and without them, you can't make their brand of magic work. Oh, and the vast majority of those metaphysical beings are not exactly nice people. That's why magic, like booze, always comes at a price – and it's never good for you in the long run.

'Cade! How's my favourite client?' asked Tenebris cheerfully.

As demons went, my Infernal agent wasn't a particularly imposing figure. He stood maybe five foot six when he wasn't floating in the air. His skin was paler than mine, almost ivory, and textured like leather with a disturbing herringbone pattern to it. The fore horns sticking out from above his eyebrows were short, two inches long and spiralled like a goat's. A second pair, curled like ram's horns, came out on either side of his skull. I had the sense that among his kind, those ram's horns were considered quite debonair, because I often caught him tracing a finger around one when he was bragging or excited. He was also something of a dandy, favouring long brocaded crimson coats that looked like silk but were probably made of the skin of the damned or something equally gruesome.

When Tenebris looked down at the floor and saw the three concentric rings of coloured sand surrounding him, he shook his head sadly. 'Oh, Cade. This is the gratitude you show me after I got you this sweet gig?' Gleaming red eyes glanced meaningfully around the tent. 'I mean, look at the high life you're living, buddy! Almost makes me wish I could cross over and hang out a while.'

Fat chance of that. Despite the more exuberant visions you might have seen, generally painted by delusional artists in the throes of religious ecstasy, dwellers of the Infernal demesne can't actually walk through a portal into your village to start eating you and your neighbours. Something about the Mortal realm makes most Infernals horribly sick – I'm talking full-on, fall-to-the-ground-coughing-up-internal-organs sort of sick.

The effects are different on beings from other realms. Auroral angelics, for example, can transition to the Mortal plane without too much suffering, but it's a one-way trip for them, so they never do. The more powerful entities, like the Lords Devilish or the Lords Celestine, can't cross over at all, which is why both use intermediaries to perform their dirty work on our plane of existence.

The rituals for conversing with extra-dimensional beings therefore require both an inner circle to open a passage between the two realms and an outer circle to erect a barrier that protects the summoned entity from the unpleasant effects of our 'disgusting shithole of an existence', as they generally refer to our human plane.

All of this is well-documented in any number of occult texts, but *my* particular innovation was the devising of a set of interlocking symbols forming a middle circle that acts as a very limited bridge between the barrier and the portal. See, a couple of years back I found a peculiar azure-coloured sand that turned out to be the only mundane matter that can pass through the bridge.

What good is sending sand through an Infernal portal, you may ask?

I flicked a single grain in the air. It passed effortlessly through both the outer and middle circles – and Tenebris flinched when the tiny particle produced an eruption of angry pink sparks across his pale, leathery flesh.

'Son of a bitch!' he yelped. 'What's with the aggression, Cade?'

'That was my expression of gratitude for this "sweet gig" you tricked me into signing up for, *old buddy.*'

Tenebris shot me a hurt look. 'Hey, how was I to know Lucien would turn out to be such a homicidal prick?'

In purely spiritual terms, Ascendant Lucien was a servant of the Aurorals, so his crusade was blessed by them. Unfortunately, the Lords Celestine tend to be far more concerned with outward displays of devotion and sacrifice than, you know, actual ethics. The Lords Devilish for whom Tenebris works, on the other hand, find religious hypocrisy tremendously entertaining and will, on occasion, lend material support to someone like Lucien so he can go off and slaughter as many innocent human beings as possible before the Lords Celestine finally figure out they bet on the wrong horse.

Which was how I wound up as co-captain of a squad of wonderists charged with massacring a citadel full of people in the morning, even though they'd already surrendered and were, most likely, devotees of the Aurorals themselves.

'Cade, old pal,' Tenebris said, holding up his hands in mock surrender, 'if you want to walk away from the job, no problem. You can even keep the spells I gave you.' He gave me a disturbingly exaggerated wink. 'Those other wonderists still buying you being just a friendly neighbourhood chancer?'

I heard Galass gasp behind me. I guess she'd hoped I really *was* a Fortunal mage. I would have turned to glare at her, but I was rather keen that Tenebris not be introduced to a pair of sublimes.

'What was that?' he asked.

I flicked another couple of grains of sand through the circles and set his new coat to smouldering. 'I farted. Can we get down to business?'

You hear the word 'demon' thrown around a lot when speaking of the Infernals, but it's more an umbrella term for a whole host of beings with whom certain *accommodations* can sometimes be made. What most people think of as a demon is more correctly referred to as a *demoniac*. They're your run-of-the-mill thugs, mostly used as warriors and assassins by the Lords Devilish who wage perpetual war over the Infernal territories in preparation for the Great Crusade. That's when a single Lord Devilish will take command of the united

Infernal hordes to engage the equally bloodthirsty Auroral armies in a final battle for supremacy – assuming the two sides ever find a battlefield where they can both exist. Which, trust me, isn't going to happen any time soon.

Anyway, back to Tenebris. He's what we call a *diabolic*, which is sort of like an Infernal diplomat. Actually, he's more like a carnival barker crossed with a conman. His job is to convince suckers like me to get embroiled in the schemes of various Lords Devilish who probably don't realise that he's working for more than one of them at the same time.

'You really are an uptight arsehole sometimes,' he complained, wiping the smouldering embers from his coat. 'Besides, what do I keep telling you? You're a tough sell to my people, Cade. The Lords Devilish don't hand out spells to charity cases.' He rubbed the claws of his thumb and forefinger together. 'You've got to show me some love, brother.'

I hoisted up the small bronze casket at my feet and opened the lid to reveal the trove of silver coins inside. Tenebris peered through the barrier at them and involuntarily licked his lips.

Now, I know what you're thinking: why would the rulers of an Infernal realm care about bits of metal currency from ours when the coins can't pass across the dimensional veil anyway? The answer is complicated, but the short version is this: that which humans value, worship or even despise contains *ecclesiasm* – it's a sort of spiritual juice that becomes attached to physical objects. While you can't hand a demon a pile of cash, you *can* destroy those objects in the space between the outer and inner summoning circles, which releases the ecclesiasm and allows it to pass through to the Infernal demesne. There, it transmutes into living *ecclesiasters*, which look like tiny glittering butterflies.

And the Lords Devilish *love* the taste of ecclesiasters.

Tenebris gave me a look that tried and failed to hide his desire for what he was feeling coming off those coins. 'I'm not saying I'm buying, but you've got me curious. Where do these come from?'

'These coins recently belonged to an order of nuns devoted to the Celestine of Chaste Adoration.'

'Chaste Adoration? You mean the . . .'

'The kind *without* any fucking involved.'

The diabolic's interest was piqued. 'You actually stole from the *huggers*?'

'Tenebris, this money was meant to be used to pay for the construction of a Redemptive's Tower.'

'And now?'

'No sacred retreat for wayward souls. The nuns lost the site to a guy who's going to build a brothel.'

The diabolic grinned. He's got way too many teeth to do that without making you feel a little queasy. 'Oh, I like that.'

I pushed the brazier for melting the soft silver coins with my foot towards the outer circle. 'Then we've got a—?'

'Hang on,' Tenebris said, studying me suspiciously. 'How exactly did you come by this stuff?'

'Who cares? These coins are *hot*, Tenebris.' I touched one with my fingertip and pulled it back as if stung. 'You can practically feel the waves of spiritual unease coming off them.'

Maybe I'd overdone it with the burning finger thing. Tenebris' eyes narrowed to slits. 'Yeah, only, why am I beginning to suspect that you didn't so much *steal* these coins from the huggers as you received them in payment for some mission you performed for them? Come on, Cade, you can tell me. What, did you rescue some kidnapped nun? Recover a lost holy artefact?'

'Why do you care?'

'I don't, but my customers can tell when the ecclesiasters have been tainted by generosity or self-sacrifice.' His frown deepened. 'Besides, why are you trying to hawk this junk, anyway? I advanced you two dozen spells for use in the Ascendant's crusade. Don't tell me you've used them up already?'

'Lucien likes to show off. He's got us using spells like we're setting off fireworks at a parade because he thinks it makes *him* look powerful. Half the time it's his own supporters we're terrorising.'

It occurred to me that Tenebris had almost certainly predicted as much, which was why he'd been so unusually generous with the advance in the first place. The consoling look he gave me was entirely unconvincing. 'Listen, man, I had no way of knowing Lucien was playing both sides. Maybe he's auditioning for a position among the *Profane* just in case the Aurorals turn on him?'

Now there was a disturbing thought. The Profane were those humans so attuned to the Infernal realm that the Lords Devilish would recruit them as high-ranking servants. Lucien would have been an excellent candidate for such a position, were he not destined to die tonight.

'Tell you what,' I said, holding up the open casket, 'trade the ecclesiasm from these coins for the spells I need and I promise to use them in the commission of a particularly brutal murder tonight.'

Tenebris started stroking one of his horns. 'Anyone I know?'

'Ascendant Lucien. Give me the tools I need and I'll make sure his suffering is the stuff of legend.'

I probably shouldn't have made my intentions sound so vile, because this time Fidick and Galass *both* gasped. Tenebris tried to peer around me to see them, but I blocked his view. 'Who's that hiding in the shadows?' he asked.

'Nobody. Let's get back t—'

'Forget it, Cade, no Lord Devilish is going to trade you spells so that you can murder the most bloodthirsty, homicidal Ascendant those idiot Lords Celestine ever blessed. We *like* that guy!'

'Well, too bad, because by morning he's going to be ashes.'

'Then I'll need something big in return.' He gestured past the tent post. 'I'm getting some very enticing vibrations off whoever you've got back there, Cade.'

'Back off. *Now.*'

He ignored the threat. 'Hey, little ones, why not come out and play with Uncle Tenebris?'

I'd warned the pair of them to stay out of sight, but Fidick, drawn perhaps by that Infernally seductive quality diabolics have about them, crept forward.

'Oh, my,' Tenebris cooed. 'Aren't you handsome? Positively angelic. Practically radiating ecclesiasm and spiritual purity.' The diabolic turned back to me. 'If the kid's on the table, I can get you whatever you want. *Anything.* I mean it, Cade. I'll give you stuff that will fuck up Lucien so bad the grandchildren he'll never have will feel his pain.'

'I'm not—'

'Back to the pits with you!' Galass shouted, striding towards the ritual circles brandishing a short but obviously sharp blade she'd probably been considering using on me earlier. 'I'll flay the skin from your accursed body and use your flesh as a winter coat if you so much as look at Fidick again, you devil!'

'Diabolic,' Tenebris corrected, then muttered to me, 'Don't your species have schools so young people can learn these things?'

'I'll take it up with the authorities,' I said.

'Please do.' The diabolic began stroking one of his curved horns again. With his free hand, he pointed to Galass. 'Now, this one I like. A lot. Not so much on the spiritual purity, but would she consider becoming one of *my* Profanes? Because if so, I can get y—'

'The girl's not on the table either.'

'Are you sure?' Tenebris asked, positively *oozing* disappointment. 'She's just the type, and I've got a couple of Lords Devilish who are seriously sick and tired of our side getting whupped in the human-servant department. Those fucking Celestines recruit more and more *Glorians* every year, but it's like pulling teeth for us to enlist anybody these days.'

I didn't bother reminding him that this imbalance was because humans tended to see the Aurorals as forces of good and the Infernals as evil. He always had trouble getting his head around this fact. To be fair, I did too, sometimes.

'Speaking of servants,' Tenebris went on, a sly grin coming to his face, 'I was tempting a fallen Glorian Justiciar the other day and we got to talking about you.'

'Why would you—?'

'You know, on account of how the justiciars are always trying to kill you? Funny thing, though: this guy claimed the reason they've got it so bad for you is because you used to—'

I dropped the casket, letting the coins spill out onto the floor, then reached into the bag of cursed sand and hurled a handful into the circles. The explosion of sparks set Tenebris' coat on fire. Within seconds, the crimson brocade was in cinders and the ivory flesh underneath was beginning to char. Tenebris yelped, batting away at the flames before they could spread. 'All right, all right!' he yelled. 'I was just having a little fun! No need to get huffy.'

I kicked the pile of coins with my foot. 'No more screwing around, Tenebris. You're supposed to be my agent. A lot of friendly-but-not-too-friendly nuns went to a great deal of trouble to acquire these coins. What can you get me for the lot?'

The diabolic knelt down and held out a hand towards the edge of the middle circle, palm down, tilting left and right as he weighed the spiritual resonances coming off the coins to determine how much value they'd hold for the Devilish with whom he traded. 'For my favourite client? I can probably get you a couple of those poetic injustice spells you like. Maybe throw in a dire wilting if you want to wreck somebody's crops.'

'I need a hellborn conjuring.'

Tenebris whistled through pointed teeth. 'That's serious magic, man. Can't make that deal for you . . . unless—' He tilted his head towards Fidick and Galass, whispering conspiratorially, 'Either one will do, Cade. For both, I can get you something *really* exci—'

I showed him the sand I still had left in my bag. 'Ask me one more time about those two, Tenebris. Go on. I dare you.'

'Fine,' he grumbled. 'Then it's the coins for the poetic injustices and maybe a couple of weeping arrows. I'll even see if I can throw in a nightmare bloom. Best I can do.'

There was no way I was going to kill someone as highly guarded as the Ascendant with a couple of lousy distraction spells and an incantation that gave people waking nightmares. On the other hand, I was running short-handed as it was. Even if I abandoned my own plans and went along with Lucien's attack tomorrow, I'd need *something* to work with.

'Deal,' I said at last, and kicked the coins into the gap between the outer and middle circles. I was about to cast a ruination spell on them when Tenebris stopped me.

'Please, allow me,' he said. His eyes lost all their colour – no idea why that happens to diabolics when they use magic, but it always looks impressive. A moment later the silver coins were charred slag and a cloud of glittering silver and blue butterflies fluttered about Tenebris' head as if each one were intent on kissing him.

I stood there contemplating the fact that an Infernal had taken pity on me to save me using the last of my spells.

'Always a pleasure, Cade,' he said cheerfully. He gestured to my chest, which was already itching painfully. 'You should see the markings in the morning. Don't use 'em up all at once.'

The tell-tale wisps of smoke that signalled his departure began to swirl around the diabolic, only to suddenly fade away, leaving him still there.

'What is it?' I asked.

He bit his lower lip, which, I can tell you, doesn't look in the least bit endearing on a demon. 'I wasn't going to suggest this, because I know it's not usually your thing, but you look like you've fallen on hard times and I hate to see a friend suffer.'

'Tenebris . . .'

Here's the thing with diabolics: they're patient. Whatever my lousy agent was about to propose, he'd kept it in his back pocket the entire time. This wasn't an afterthought; this was the show.

Tenebris put his hands up in mock surrender. 'Look, I've got a gig – a big one. I'm talking premium spells up front, anything you need, and a massive pay-out at the end. It's a seven-mage job, but I'll put you in charge. You can write your own ticket.'

'Not interested.'

He drifted in the air closer to the edge of the middle circle – a dangerous move for him if I decided to toss the entire bag of cursed sand at him. 'I'm telling you, this job is a gift! There's this town up north, beautiful little place. Fine people.'

'What's it called?'

'Hmm?'

'The town, Tenebris. What's it called?'

'Uh, yeah, the town . . .' He looked up and off to my left, squinting one eye as if he were struggling to recall such a trivial detail that obviously had no bearing on our conversation. 'Something like May-Just-Gave or—?'

'Mages' Grave?'

Here's a sight you never want to see: a diabolic looking sheepish. 'I know, I know. Who wants to travel through the Blastlands, right? I mean, all the devastation, that red haze that never goes away, the barren soil that grows nothing but those ugly poppies with the creepy texture that feels like skin?' He gave a pretend shiver. 'Gross.'

'Yeah, that's a real prime vacation spot you're trying to get me to visit.'

'Oh, quit being such a baby. I'm telling you, this job's a breeze. There's this baron, nasty fellow – oppresses his people, eats their babies, you know, the usual human stuff you all do to show you're in charge.'

'That's *not* the usual "human stuff"! This baron of yours sounds like another Lucien, which is a problem I'm already trying to solve, thanks to you.'

'*Puh-lease.* This guy makes Lucien look like a tactical genius. He's already getting his arse handed to him by the locals. You'd like these folks, Cade. Brave mommies and daddies fighting a maniacal fiend to protect their children.' The diabolic put a hand on his chest where his heart would be, if he had one. 'Heroes, one and all.'

The thing about Tenebris is, he likes to set up the joke and have you deliver the punchline.

'Let me guess, you want me to beat up those brave mommies and daddies?'

He grinned from horn to horn. 'It's a good gig, man. Two weeks, tops. Turns out a band of wonderists calling themselves the Seven Brothers have come along to help the rebellion. They're *really* pissing off the baron, so we need you to round up a few of your pals and go and murder them real good.'

I opened the ties on the bag of cursed sand all the way. 'Thanks for the spells, Tenebris. Don't let the ethereal door hit you on the arse on your way out.'

The wisps of smoke rose up once more, this time enveloping him. 'Oh, and I almost forgot about the grand prize . . .'

'The grand what now?'

The fog inside the spell circle was so thick that all I could see were the diabolic's red eyes and the toothy gleam of his smile. 'The baron's got hold of a certain artefact that would come in real handy for you, Cade . . . something he'd be willing to part with if you could get these Seven Brothers off his back. No joke, buddy. This thing would be worth more to you than all the spells in hell.'

'And just what is this artefa—?'

I stopped myself. I was falling right into the trap, letting myself get sucked into whatever long con he was setting me up for. So I took up a handful of my nasty spell-sand and started flicking the grains into the circle.

The diabolic cried, 'Fine, fine. You don't have to be such an arse-hole!' Tenebris left me with one final entreaty before he disappeared. 'Look, take the day to think about it. When you change your mind about the job, give me a shout. This is the deal of the epoch and I'd hate for it to go to someone I like less than you.'

This is what my life has come to: the person most concerned about my survival is an Infernal diabolic huckster with a lousy sense of humour.

When I turned back, Galass was staring at me, still holding the knife in her hand. 'So it's true? Your spells . . . they really come from the Infernal demesne?'

'All magic comes from somewhere.'

'But not everyone draws upon the Infernals for their power.'

'Not everyone,' I conceded.

Her hand was shaking. She was holding the little blade so tightly I was pretty sure I was going to see blood seeping out between her fingers.

'I am glad you placed your foul binding on our memories,' she said, and turned to put her arm around Fidick and lead him as far away from me as they could get without actually leaving the safety of the tent. 'I prefer to remember you as a pig who violated our bodies rather than a decent man who debased his own soul.'

CHAPTER 5

The Bat

I left my two guests alone in the tent. They'd rest easier without me there, and I doubted I'd be doing any sleeping myself. Dozens of soldiers and camp followers saw me leave, but I wasn't concerned; even without the wards I'd placed on the tent, uninvited folk generally don't risk sneaking into a war mage's accommodations. We tend to be prickly about trespassers.

I made it about fifteen feet before a bat landed on my shoulder and tried to bite my neck.

'Don't you fucking try it,' I warned.

The bat gave a distressed squeak before making a second, more tentative attempt.

'I'm not kidding,' I said, letting the black wisps of a bewilderment fog swirl around the fingertips of my right hand. I've always had a fondness for that particular piece of magic. Unlike most confounding cantrips, you don't have to use it up all at once. It's basically this big barrel of confusion you can draw on a bit at a time until it runs out.

'Bats don't do so well without their sense of direction,' I said. 'It'd be a shame to watch you flying into tree trunks over and over until you broke your nose.'

The bat leaped off my shoulder to flutter awkwardly in the air before me. It squeaked mournfully, abandoning whatever sense of shadowy menace it had probably spent its whole life perfecting.

'Tell the arsehole to send a note like a normal person.'

The bat followed me as I strode through the camp. Regular soldiers paused in doing the things regular soldiers do between trying to kill their fellow regular soldiers on the other side long enough to gape at the sight of me arguing with a bat. I couldn't say for sure, but I rather thought the bat was even more embarrassed than I was.

'Oh, fine,' I said at last, stopping to extend my arm out. 'But just the wrist – and not hard, either, or we'll see just how well bats can fly with their heads jammed up their own arseholes.'

The bat looked offended, but nonetheless landed on my forearm before leaning down to bite the vein on my upturned wrist.

Totemic magic annoys the hell out of me. Supposedly serious wonderists going around tapping realms of animistic symbolism to forge inexplicable mystical correspondences between the mage and whichever type of beast or bird they're most attuned to? That's how you end up with all these idiot felinists, avianists, lupinists and – gods save us all – chiropteranists, prancing around in animal costumes casting spells that make no sense and regaling you with how their chosen beast is the most noble of all. It's embarrassing.

I guess I should be grateful he hasn't started working with rat mages. Those guys are seriously nuts.

The first few seconds of having enchanted bat saliva mix with your blood are the worst. My senses were overwhelmed, flooded by the bat's experience of the world all around it. Everything was high-pitched and hollow-sounding. I could smell things I'd never wanted to smell and taste my own blood on the creature's tongue. The effects passed slowly, but after a few uncomfortable seconds, I was back to perceiving the world through my own eyes and ears. I resumed my march through the camp, this time while being lectured to by a fruit bat.

'Don't be an arsehole, Cade,' the bat said with Corrigan's voice.

I wondered how much he'd paid for the animism charm he must be using up right now. 'The other wonderists are expecting you – Green's been asking about you for *hours*.'

I peered into the bat's eyes. I couldn't see Corrigan in there, but I had no doubt that wherever he was, he could see me. 'Tell them to have a drink on me. Or better yet, on you. I've got better things to do than sit around placing bets on how many people I'm going to murder tomorrow.'

'It's *tradition*,' Corrigan insisted, as if such things mattered. 'Tomorrow, Green's joining the battle. It's his first time. He could die.'

'Archon Belleda's troops already surrendered. It's not a battle, it's a massacre. Anyway, I'm a little busy right now, *Indigo*. I'll join you and the others later.'

While the soldiers nearby couldn't understand what the bat was saying, they could hear me. I'm not sure why it's such a superstition among wonderists to never use our real names in front of regular people, but superstition is a close cousin to paranoia, and over the past few years, I'd developed a definite fondness for paranoia.

The bat gave me a withering glare – at least as withering as its batty face could achieve. 'You're not fooling anyone, Cade. The other wonderists know you aren't partaking of the Ascendant's . . . treats. And they've started to notice the way you avoid killing. It's making them uneasy.'

'Did they not notice me murdering an Auroral thaumaturge *and* her elderly husband today?'

The bat shook his head dismissively, which was also an unnerving thing to witness. 'That was different. You were saving my life.'

'How stupid of me.'

The bat spread its wings and then flopped them down again. I guessed it was meant to be a shrug. 'The bottom line is that the others have started questioning your sympathies.'

'You're saying they don't trust me?'

'I'm saying there's chatter about maybe needing to eliminate you just to be on the safe side.'

'And you?'

The bat looked offended. 'Me? I just figure you're hiding being an even bigger pervert than the rest of us and the rituals you use to fuel your spells are so disgusting it's better if I don't have to see them up close.'

I smiled menacingly at the bat. 'You've got me all figured out, Indigo. Now, if you could just point me to the barn with the sluttiest sheep in camp, I can go about my "rituals" in peace.'

The bat tried to speak, then gave a squeak I could no longer understand before batting its eyes at me plaintively.

'Oh, fucking hell. Fine. One more and that's it.'

The bat bit me again, gave a little cough, and said, 'Right. Look, Cade, I didn't want to bring this up before we talk in person, but there's something you, me and a couple of the others need to discuss.'

The prospect of being in an enclosed space with a group of wonderists who needed to 'discuss' something with me was not appealing.

Corrigan must've caught my expression through the bat's eyes. 'Don't be like that. This is a good thing, I promise. The Ascendant's war will be over soon and I've got word of a job up north that could make us all filthy rich. All we have to do is deal with a few do-gooder wonderists sticking their noses in some evil prick's business. In and out in two weeks, lots of money, lots of spells and—'

'Lots of the things people like us always want in exchange for murdering do-gooders. I turned that same job down half an hour ago. I'm even less interested now.'

'Oh? And did you hear about the artefact?'

Artefact. Relic. Celestial Bidet. There's always some 'supreme mystical treasure' offered as a bonus for taking on a particularly suicidal job, and it's always bullshit.

Corrigan must've caught my look of disdain through the bat's beady little eyes. 'This one's for real, Cade! This guy, this "Baron Tristmorta", somehow got hold of the Appa—'

'Not interested.'

I was, however, tempted to ask how Corrigan, who didn't traffic with Infernals, had heard about the job. Then I remembered that I didn't care. I tried shaking the bat off my wrist to end the conversation, but the little beast clung there with its claws, then reared up to glance around the campsite before its head swivelled back to glare at me. 'Where are you going, Cade?'

'Bugger off a while, will you?' I tried shaking off the bat again, with exactly the same result. 'I'll come down to the village later and you can tell me all about this dream job.'

'Looks like you're headed towards Ascendant Lucien's pavilion,' the bat said.

'Pure coincidence. Just out for a stroll.'

The bat's claws squeezed my wrist tighter. 'Whoa, Cade, stop. You're angry that Lucien lied about ending the battle as soon as the citadel forces surrendered. I get that. He's a nasty piece of work, okay? You think Archon Belleda isn't? If the situation were rever—'

I stopped and brought my forearm up so the bat's face was just inches from mine. Their vision isn't the best and I wanted Corrigan to see me clearly. 'You know exactly what I'm about to do, *Corrigan*,' I said, using his real name to emphasise how done I was with this conversation. 'You knew it before you sent this bat of yours to suck my blood and piss all over my plans.'

The bat gave a sigh, which made the little fella almost cute for a second. 'Yeah, I guess I did. This kind of thing is exactly what makes the other wonderists nervous about you, Cade.'

'Don't worry about it. Everybody got paid in advance for the job. I'll make sure none of this blows back on you.' I lowered my voice so no one nearby could hear me. 'You've been a good friend to me,

Corrigan. Especially considering what an arsehole you are to the rest of the world.'

The bat looked up at me and tried to smile. It didn't work – the creature's mouth just wasn't made for such things. 'I feel the same about you, Cade. I mean, you're a moralistic prick who's never once confided in me as to why you do the things you do, but who knows? Maybe that's why I look out for you.'

'Don't get all soft on me now, Indigo.'

'Hold off on Lucien,' Corrigan pleaded. 'Come for a beer and let's talk. Maybe we can figure out how to convince him to back off on this massacre thing. Besides, if you kill him now, we'll just end up with some new piece of shit taking over.'

'I'm betting I'll like that piece of shit better. Sorry you wasted a bat charm on me.'

The Ascendant's tent was just ten yards away and I could see half a dozen of his precious *sanctifieds* standing out front in their gleaming armour, holding their smart, overdecorated swords and crossbows. One guy had a pistol so engraved with holy symbols that I'd lay odds they just ruined the balance. Lucien would have several more guards inside his massive pavilion, of course, along with a pet mage or two – not ours, of course; dumb as Lucien was, he knew better than to put his trust in a mercenary wonderist. Too bad he wasn't smart enough to have known not to screw with the terms of a mercenary wonderist's contract.

Infernal magic comes at all kinds of costs, and it's absolute crap for things like growing crops or healing wounds. But even with the limited spells I still had on me, if I played my cards right, I had more than I needed to kill Lucien and anyone who got in my way.

Here ends the reign of Lucien the First, Ascendant Prince of the Celestine Orders, I thought. *Too bad your Auroral bosses never gave you the gift of prophecy.*

'Cade?' the bat said.

I kept my eyes on the tent. 'Yeah?'

'It was two.'

I froze. 'What?'

The bat tried to speak again but the words got garbled as the blood fuelling the spell faded. With what I thought was admirable dedication, the little beast flapped to my shoulder and managed to cough out Corrigan's parting words into my ear. 'I wasted two charms on you.'

I never even felt the bite on the back of my neck, just the warm, soothing tingle as its bile mixed with the magic Corrigan's second charm had imbued it with and knocked me unconscious.

CHAPTER 6

The Hanged Man

I awoke – if you could call the nauseous cesspool that constituted my present mental state 'awake' – hanging upside down with my hands bound behind my back. The headache was easily explained by the blood rushing to my head, the sharp pain in my right knee the result of being suspended by my ankle. I could see no shackles, but there was the faint shimmer of a tethering spell.

My vision was coming back in blurry waves, and after a moment or two, I could make out the dirt floor beneath me and the wooden walls and ceiling. Half a dozen rustic tables and benches filled up most of the room; the rest was taken up by the bar, behind which huddled a very frightened-looking woman of middle years who was washing the same mug over and over while mumbling prayers to what I assumed was every single Auroral and Infernal deity she could name and a few she was probably making up on the spot.

'He's awake,' said a voice that sounded like shards of glass crunching between someone's teeth.

That would be Narghan, a professional incarcerationist whose pride and joy was his unhygienically long facial hair which he tied and waxed into dozens of intricate knots as advertising for his area of specialisation. He called it 'custodial wizardcraft' and could detail its rich history, complexity and tactical advantages at tedious length. The rest of us just figured he liked to tie people up with magic.

'I can put him back to sleep,' suggested a feminine voice smelling of those sour, cloying herbs she chewed for her particular brand of magic which were enough to make me all in favour of her proposal. She always introduced herself as Somaka, which means 'aroma of spirit' in some language nobody speaks any more. Just about everyone else called her 'Lady Smoke' because her spells manifest through the exhalation of misty fumes that could produce any number of unpleasant effects on the world around her. She was raven-haired and ebony-skinned and didn't bother with clothes because the ever-present fog surrounding her protected her from both the elements and unwanted stares. When she wasn't in earshot, Corrigan called her 'Lady Farts'.

Lady Farts – yeah, I called her that, too – added something garlicky to the mixture she was mashing between her back teeth. 'This concoction will give him nightmares so fierce he'll spend his final hours lying in a ditch, a mumbling, impotent wretch snapping his own finger bones one by one.'

Somaka was considered by many to be a great beauty. I mention this because my old mentor used to insist that you should always find something nice to say about people, even when they're planning to kill you.

'Why bother wasting time on him?' asked a third voice. Nobody knew if 'Locke' Fandaris was his real name, but if it was, then the universe loves coincidences, because all of his magic came from the bandolier of intricately shaped keys he wore across his chest. Each one could open a door in the air that led to some far-off place. Of all my fellow wonderists, Locke Fandaris was the only one whose magic made me jealous. Also, I think he had a crush on me.

'I'll just open a door to a lava pit and we can push him through and be done with him,' said Locke.

Okay, maybe it wasn't so much a crush as slightly less antipathy towards me than the others.

'We should make an example of him,' Narghan insisted. 'I'll float him to the centre of camp, slit his throat and we can each perform a ritual desecration on his corpse.'

'Why would we go to all that bother?' asked Lady Smoke.

'Because it will show the Ascendant that he can trust the rest of us,' replied Narghan. 'Also, it'll be fun.'

Several other voices piped up with their own opinions on the matter. It sounded like there might be a dozen people in all, so I guessed Corrigan must have assembled every wonderist in Lucien's war coven for this little trial. My colleagues were enjoying themselves, discussing the possible sentences to punish me for a crime I hadn't yet committed. I still couldn't believe Corrigan had sold me out.

I was getting increasingly dizzy hanging there. The tether spell behaved a lot like regular rope, which meant I couldn't stop myself constantly swinging around. When I finally managed to catch Corrigan's eye, I whispered, 'You ratted on me to the others before I even got to him.'

'This isn't about your little temper tantrum,' he whispered back furiously. 'So keep your mouth shut, try not to panic and pray I can get you out of this with a couple of your limbs intact.'

He turned to the others and unleashed his big booming baritone on them. 'Listen, brethren, nothing's happened yet. For all we know, the Glorians are just here as insur—'

'Glorians?' I blurted out. Now I *was* panicking.

'Eleven of them,' Skanda confirmed.

Skanda Ruzik was the chiropteranist who'd likely traded Corrigan the bat charms he'd used to lure me here. She was short and stocky, with a pretty smile and green eyes that were entirely captivating – so long as you could ignore the huge bat-head cowl she wore over her grey fur coat. This is what I mean about Totemicists being weird.

'One of Skanda's familiars was flying the perimeter of the camp when it noticed a band of white-cloaks camped out a mile to the south,' Corrigan explained.

Now I understood why he was so pissed off at me, why he'd wanted to make sure I didn't get the chance to murder Ascendant Lucien. The Glorians are to faith and duty what wonderists are to not giving a shit about anyone but themselves. Their magic is entirely Auroral in nature, which isn't all that unique, as many wonderists draw on a little Auroral magic here and there. But the Glorians are different: their minds are transfigured and transmuted by their devotion to a single Lord Celestine. They're kind of like the preachy neighbour you avoid at parties, assuming your neighbour would burn you at the stake for offending his religious views – you, along with your extended family, including the third cousins you barely knew existed.

'Which order?' I asked.

Please say the Glorians of Mercy. Please say Glorians of Mercy.

'All my bat could catch was muttering, lots of muttering, which I assume were prayers,' Skanda replied. She closed her eyes as if trying to draw on someone else's memories. 'Oh, but they all had golden gloves attached to their right shoulders, like funny epaulets. Does that mean anything?'

Yeah, I thought. *It means I'm well and truly screwed.*

The Glorian Justiciars are the order devoted to the Celestine of Law. They're incredibly powerful, inhumanly disciplined, and when called to investigate a crime that violates one of the Celestial Edicts – like, just as an example, trafficking in Infernal magic with a diabolic – they always, *always* get their man.

Corrigan, clearly intent on keeping everyone calm, said, 'We figure Ascendant Lucien must be keeping them nearby in case any of us get out of hand. He's always been paranoid about wonderists, no matter how badly he needs us to do his dirty work.'

'*You* figure that,' Narghan said, fingers playing with the waxed knots of his beard. 'The rest of us are wondering why any time we do a job with Cade Ombra, the fucking justiciars come sniffing around.'

Eleven Glorian Justiciars – that's enough for a Court Auroral, enough to conduct a trial for heresy and be damned sure they had the firepower to enforce the verdict, no matter how many friends the accused had willing to fight on his behalf. Not that that was looking like it would be much of a problem in my case right now.

'Look at him,' Narghan sneered. 'The sneaky bastard knows he's to blame for this.'

Corrigan was trying to keep himself between the others and me. 'Back off, Narghan. We don't know if Cade's to bl—'

'Quit protecting him, Corrigan.' The incarcerationist sidestepped him, got in close and jabbed a finger against my forehead, surreptitiously hitting me with a minor clenching cantrip that caused my tongue to curl back painfully into my throat. 'You think they won't use whatever crime he's committed as an excuse to condemn us all?'

The clenching cantrip was making it hard for me to breathe, and dangling upside down was making me so dizzy I couldn't summon the concentration to counteract the spell. Maybe Narghan was hoping I'd asphyxiate and save everyone the trouble of a formal execution.

Here lies Cade Ombra, who had been planning on delivering a scathing eulogy over Ascendant Lucien's corpse and instead ended up choking to death on his own tongue.

My vision was seriously starting to blur when I felt Corrigan's thick fingers pry my mouth open and forcibly uncurl my tongue. Air rushed into my lungs and I would have been even more grateful to him if his fingers hadn't smelled of the bat guano he'd needed to activate Skanda's charm.

The others had already resumed the debate over the extent of my blame for the presence of the justiciars and how best to punish me. Their suggestions ranged from 'utterly horrific' to 'utterly horrific with more than a dash of perverse sexual abuse thrown in'. It's amazing what you can learn about your co-workers in a situation like this.

I passed the time gathering my wits and contemplating who I'd need to kill to make the others think twice about having their wicked way with me. Not that I had any real expectation of freeing myself – a guy like Narghan spends his whole career mastering a single form of magic because being the best at something is how you attract the attention of the highest-paying employers. He wasn't alone in that, either. Smoke and Locke and several of the others were similarly expert in their respective disciplines, while I've always been more of a generalist. I like to have as wide a range of spells at my disposal as possible, which Corrigan wrongly maintains is conclusive evidence that I have commitment issues.

Whatever the truth, I wasn't going to be pulling off any daring escapes any time soon. The trick to surviving the wrath of a coven of wonderists – other than by not making them angry in the first place – is to have your ploy worked out well ahead of time, ideally by laying traps for them before they even walk into the room. Corrigan, despite looking for all the world like a big, dumb, piss-drinking brute, was always better at forward planning than I was, which explained why he'd had that second bat ready. I, on the other hand, had been heading for Lucien's tent with no particular plan other than to improvise a way to murder the Ascendant when I got there.

I concluded that my best hope was to catch Corrigan's attention again and appeal to our friendship, however transactional it might be. Unfortunately, what I saw when I swung back around was Zyphis' gangly silhouette slinking towards me.

Ugh. Why does it have to be Zyphis?

He was an interrogationist: his spells supplied the most effective ways to terrify and torture his targets. I'd been told he was barely twenty years old, but with his wrinkled bald head and sagging jowls, he looked more like a youthful corpse. The way he walked was what bothered me most, though: his limbs moved with an awkward jerkiness, as if his joints had been attached backwards. His fingers were the longest I'd ever seen – and you only needed to watch those filthy nails of his slither into human flesh with both ease and enthusiasm once to know you did not ever want to be the object of his interrogation. Zyphis was the only person I'd ever met who appeared to take genuine pleasure in the looks of disgust everyone else gave him. He and Narghan adored each other.

His nails clacked as he approached. I was pretty sure that while the others were still arguing over what to do with me, Zyphis was going to cast a quieting spell on me, kneel down so he could get his face right up close to mine, reach down my throat with one of those long, skinny arms and dig around my internal organs for a snack.

I screamed before he got within three feet of me.

'Zyphis . . .' Corrigan warned, and I was pleased to hear in that one word enough to convey a host of very logical arguments as to why my premature evisceration was a bad idea, let alone the implication of an *extensive* list of punishments that would be inflicted on the skeletal creep should he refuse to back off.

Zyphis hissed at me – actually *hissed.*

I really have to get out of this business.

'All right, look,' Corrigan said, taking charge once again. 'Until we know what the justiciars are planning, we can't risk killing Cade. None of us know their rituals. What if they want to torture him before the execution? We'll have lost our one bargaining chip.'

When I mentioned earlier that Corrigan and I were friends, I was using the term loosely. We were more like casual acquaintances who appreciated the same jokes.

Lady Smoke piped up, 'No matter his other crimes, Cade's been keeping secrets from the rest of us – he's always sneaking off to his tent, refusing to tell anyone what he's been up to. I don't trust him.'

'Yeah,' Locke agreed, 'and the dumb fucker keeps getting in Ascendant Lucien's face every time he issues an order Cade doesn't agree with.'

Zyphis hissed again. 'Give him to me. I want to feel the vibration on my tongue as he screams while I suck upon his intestines.'

Somebody in the back chimed up, 'What about his wages? Shouldn't we see if we can get his back pay from the quartermaster before we kill him?'

Meet my brothers-in-arms, folks.

There was a thunderclap as Corrigan slammed his hand on one of the tables. 'Enough! I'm captain of this misbegotten troop and I'm telling you there won't be *any* executions tonight.' He turned to me and I thought I saw something approaching remorse peeking out behind the braids of his indigo beard.

'What, then?' Lady Smoke asked. 'You expect us to just *forgive* him?' She said the word like she'd had to look it up in a dictionary first.

Corrigan looked over at me. 'No. Cade's been keeping too many secrets and taking too many risks pissing off Lucien. He needs to be reminded who his friends are. I've known him longest, so I'll take point. A few burns, a few bruises, a couple of broken bones – I'll make sure he can still cast his spells, mind – and tomorrow' – he turned me around to face him – 'tomorrow Cade will prove his loyalty to us and to the Ascendant by leading the massacre of Archon Belleda's people.'

'You would exalt the traitor by putting him in the vanguard of the destruction?' Lady Smoke demanded, and several of the others grumbled along in agreement.

I could see Zyphis, however, grinning so wide you could count on his teeth just how many years it had been since they'd been cleaned. 'I like it,' he said. 'I can see how his spirit withers at the mere thought of such a massacre of innocents. His soul will truly be burned by this, never to recover.'

'All right, then,' Corrigan said, sounding eager to get this over with. 'We have an agreement.'

Narghan's tether kept me turning so I was now facing the wall. I couldn't see what the others were doing but I heard the heavy thump of Corrigan's boots moving closer. 'Sorry, Cade. Going to have to work you over some. Nothing personal.'

'Nothing personal,' I agreed.

I resolved to be a better friend in future. I'd kill Corrigan quickly once the massacre began tomorrow. Well, quicker than I was going to kill Zyphis, anyway.

I was just tensing up in anticipation of the first blow when the sudden crack of a door bursting open was followed by a cacophony of preparatory incantations, arcane objects being whooshed from pockets and Zyphis hissing again. That guy never shuts up.

'Silord Wonderists! Silord Wonderists!' shouted the frantic, youthful voice of Cousin Green, the kid who was supposed to be formally joining the company tonight. 'I bring terrible news!'

'Get out of here, Green,' Corrigan roared. 'I told you this was a private meeting!'

'But Silord Indigo, there has been a—'

'Out!' Corrigan snapped. 'Before I roast your insides!'

'Oh, let him speak if he must,' Lady Smoke said. I didn't understand why, but she'd always had a soft spot for the kid. Maybe his naïveté and innocence attracted her. Perhaps she wanted to handle his inevitable corruption personally.

When Green next spoke, his words crashed down on us all with the force of an Infernal conjuration, which turned out to be a regrettably apt metaphor.

'The Ascendant has been murdered in his own tent,' he told the assembled wonderists. Then he pointed to me. 'With one of Silord Cade's spells.'

CHAPTER 7

A Nasty Way to Die

Righteous moral outrage can spread through a coven of wonderists faster than a wildfire when they find out they're not going to get their bonuses. Death and destruction are never more than a few ugly syllables and a twitch of the fingers away, so keeping temperatures cool through calm and diplomacy takes on tremendous urgency.

'Everybody shut the hell up before I blast each and every one of you dumb fuckers to oblivion!' Corrigan roared over the din.

Cousin Green's panicked revelation of Ascendant Lucien's murder had got everyone in a frenzy, which struck me as an excellent time to begin wriggling out of Narghan's abominable tethering spell. Corrigan must have come to the same conclusion, for he spun on his heel before driving his fist into my stomach with so much malice that I wondered if I'd ever draw a full breath again.

'Finally!' Zyphis cheered, the hollow-cheeked bastard grinning so wide his tongue slithered out from between his teeth. He tried to get past Corrigan, but the broad-shouldered thunderer shoved him away before turning his ire on the hysterical Cousin Green.

'You,' Corrigan said, jabbing a finger at the teenager, who was wiping his sweaty hands on his chartreuse wonderist's coat. 'Tell us what happened.' Then he stopped himself. 'No— You're some kind of luminist, right?'

'Yes, Silord. I mean, sort of. I studied luxoral magic for several years under—'

'Don't care. Show us all what you saw.'

Green started to stutter. 'I . . . I didn't actually *see* the murder, Silord. I was—'

'The kid doesn't know shit,' Locke Fandaris interrupted, scratching the patchy grey stubble of his jaw. 'Probably heard a few screams before running off like a chicken with its balls cut off.'

'I *did* run when I saw what was left of the body,' Green confessed. The others mocked his cowardice a while, then fell back on debating the best way to flee the justiciars. But the boy swallowed, wiped the back of his hand across the sweat-soaked muddy brown hair matted to his forehead and called out, 'But not before I grabbed a handful of dirt from right outside the Ascendant's tent.'

The room went dead quiet.

'You got *actual* soil from outside Lucien's *actual* tent?' Corrigan asked.

Green nodded.

'Soil that no one touched, no one trod on, no one so much as spat on?'

Green took the black velvet glove dangling from his belt and slid it over his palm. It hadn't occurred to me to wonder why he'd taken his gloves off in the first place, but now I understood he hadn't wanted the sweat on his hands to permeate the velvet and thus pollute the evidence when he removed it from the pocket of his coat.

'Dust from inside the tent would have been better,' Lady Smoke said, the blanket of fog surrounding her drifting towards Green as she approached him, readying herself to apply her particular abilities.

'Candlewax is best for such work,' Smoke said, offering Green an encouraging smile. 'I will awaken the ecclesiasm inside the dirt, but you must perform the backwards gaze to go with the temporal visualisation. Can you manage both?'

'I can, my Lady. I will.' With his jaw set that way, Green was looking almost heroic. Shame he ruined the effect when he asked sheepishly, 'Does . . . does anyone have a purified hourglass handy? I left mine in my tent.'

Amateur, I thought. Everyone else said it out loud.

The first thing a war mage does when the situation gets ugly isn't to run around proclaiming doom and destruction. It's to get their gear together. Otherwise, half your best spells are just nice ideas in your head that won't do you any good when the mayhem starts.

'I've got an hourglass, of sorts,' Zyphis said.

It was unusual for the creep to offer, but I guess he was keen to watch a murder up close. His bony hand slithered into his filthy rags to pull out a small hourglass, maybe three inches tall, trimmed in blackened iron.

Green took the object from Zyphis gingerly – as one should do with anything that wretch offers.

'This isn't sand inside the glass,' Green said, holding it up to his eye. 'It moves . . . unnaturally.'

'Desiccated blood,' Zyphis explained, 'among other bodily fluids. I've formulated the mixture to pour at the same rate as sand.'

Green muttered an unconvincing thank you for Zyphis' generosity, then held the hourglass between his thumb and forefinger while with his other hand, he poured out the soil.

I heard whistling, like steam escaping a boiling pot, as Lady Smoke uttered the first incantation. The grains of dirt in Green's palm began to twitch and crackle like paper held too close to a candle flame.

In our realm, ecclesiasm isn't visible to the naked eye, but it's hard to mistake the queasy feeling it produces in your stomach when you're too close to it.

'Quickly now,' Narghan urged Green, 'before it dissipates into the aether.'

Green steadied himself against a table as he began the second incantation.

The backwards gaze is a tricky spell to perform, especially when you're nervous. The first syllables have to be uttered slowly, at a plodding pace, but by the second verse, you have to start speeding up, and by the third verse, the words should be tripping off your tongue so quickly that no untrained mouth could form the syllables accurately enough.

Green must have had a decent teacher, because soon the tiny flecks of dried blood in Zyphis' hourglass were floating above the bottom, moving synchronously with the grains of dirt in Green's palm. After a moment, the individual flecks of blood began drifting upwards, back into the top half of the hourglass.

'Hold her close now,' Locke advised, putting a hand on Green's shoulder. 'Time may be your mistress here, but you are not her master.'

'Don't coddle the boy,' Corrigan said. He kept one eye on Green and the other on me to make sure I wasn't in danger of escaping. 'Let's get on with this, shall we? We all need to see what happened to Lucien.'

Luxoral magic isn't widely respected among those in our profession; someone who conjures images in the air is about as impressive to us as a decent ventriloquist. When Green had first shown up in the camp begging to join our company of wonderists, the others had refused him. The universe having a perverse sense of humour, I'd felt bad for the boy; it was me who'd convinced them to give him a chance – after all, we all have to start somewhere.

With Lady Smoke splitting the raw ecclesiasm from the mundane soil and Green's backwards-gaze spell shifting the direction of the sensory impressions it held within, he was finally set to do the easy part: cast a luminist spell to show everyone in the tavern what they would have seen if they had been standing on that same muddy mound when death had come for Ascendant Lucien.

Green carefully spread the dirt across a tabletop. All the lantern lights dimmed at once, shrouding us all in darkness – save for the thousands of stars, just pinpoints of light, that had appeared above our heads and the flickering light of a fire leaking out from between the flaps of Ascendant Lucien's gaudily decorated tent a few feet away.

'I don't see anything happening inside,' Narghan complained, leaning forward, trying to peer through the gap in the ghostly tent flaps.

'Green hasn't got the timing right,' Lady Smoke said, softening her whistle to keep from burning up all the ecclesiasm emanating from the soil. 'We're too far back.'

Green began tilting the iron-banded hourglass clockwise, a fraction at a time, and as he did, the events that had transpired an hour ago played out for us all to see.

'There!' Zyphis hissed. He jabbed a finger towards the back end of the tavern behind us. 'It's coming for him!'

When the others turned to follow where he was pointing, I followed suit, twisting my head uncomfortably to see past Corrigan's crimson leather-covered buttocks. Travelling through the landscape of Green's illusory spell, heading for the Ascendant's tent, was a shadow.

'Who is that?' asked Narghan. 'I can't make out a face.'

'That's because it has no face,' Zyphis said with delight. 'The shadow is cast from elsewhere. We are witnessing a hellborn con-juration: a demoniac's spirit, shredded from its physical form on its own realm and then squeezed through the nether planes until it can manifest on ours. It won't survive long that way. Watch as it slithers between the substrata of reality, its very existence a violation of laws both natural and divine.'

'Nobody asked for a fucking poem,' Corrigan said. 'What does it do?'

'Just watch,' Zyphis replied unhelpfully, ignoring his glaring colleagues.

He was right about the spirit, though. The shadow twisted, writhing against the unnatural physics of our realm that couldn't bind it into earthly matter. It slithered along the ground like a snake, then split apart into twin black serpents that reared up, the two heads coming together as if in a kiss – and from that kiss bloomed a shadowy torso which shook itself until arms grew on either side. It didn't bother with a head. The quavering black emptiness entered the Ascendant's tent, stepping effortlessly across magical wards that would have torn any war mage's conjurations into a thousand pieces. It devoured Lucien's protectors before moving on to the main course.

It's usually almost impossible to keep a troop of wonderists quiet, but everyone in that tavern bore witness to what happened next in horrified silence. Most of us would have rather clawed our own eyes out than to watch what transpired next.

I'd never believed that one way to die was any better than another. There are gradations of pain, of course, and levels of personal desecration, which is its own type of pain, I suppose – but death? Death itself is nothing but a final tick of the clock wound inside us by our unwitting mothers the moment they gave birth, counting down from our first breath to our last. There are no 'good' or 'bad' ways to leave this Mortal realm. We simply . . . *end*.

Turns out I'd been wrong about that, though, because the death suffered by Lucien the First, Ascendant Prince and Beloved of the Lords Celestine, revealed to us in brief snatches between the rustling flaps of his tent as his body contorted and danced in hideous torment, was worse than any I could have imagined. His screams echoed continuously around the tent, each cry magnified and repeated sevenfold, as the hellborn took Lucien apart, piece by piece, before moulding him back together, constructing a body perfected in its ability to know pain and misery, blind to all sensation but that of its own damnation.

At the end, the hellborn finally showed mercy, tearing Lucien's head from his body. It placed the bleeding skull atop its own shadowy shoulders and danced a jig before finally losing its battle with the natural forces making up our own plane of existence.

Lucien's severed head fell to the ground, the empty sockets where his eyes should have been staring out at a world now proven to be beyond redemption.

Zyphis, the most deranged and perverse lunatic I'd ever met, chose that moment to find his sanity. 'We're all fucked,' he said.

The death of a patron or employer isn't exactly unheard of in our business. Jobs go bad all the time, and when they do, often as not, the boss gets it first. In such unfortunate circumstances, there are typically three possible outcomes.

First and most common is simple enough: someone new takes over. It's generally a trusted lieutenant (who, half the time, is responsible for murdering their boss in the first place) or a close family member (they account for the other half) who steps up to take command. Mercenary wonderists become especially valuable at times like these, because it's a lot easier to consolidate power if the rank and file of your troops have a reason not to question the legitimacy of your precipitous rise to power. In those situations, our jobs basically go on as normal – well, other than the customary change-of-boss surcharge added to the bill.

The next possibility is that after the boss dies, the job falls apart. There's chaos and looting, a few acts of judicious revenge. When that happens, mercenaries like us steal what we can and get out of town before the whole place turns into one hellish blaze of sadistic carnage.

Lastly, there's the situation where the wonderists are presumed responsible and a posse is put together to capture and kill us. I really don't blame people for jumping to the conclusion that everything must be our fault. I mean, it's hard for regular folks to wrap their heads around the various forms of magic or to understand our limits;

they generally have no idea what is or isn't possible. Why wouldn't they assume that if things went badly, it must have had something to do with us? To protect themselves from our spells, they assemble whatever artefacts they can lay their hands on for such occasions, and basically hunt us down like rabid dogs.

It's a hazard of the job. No big deal.

This, though? This wasn't that.

What had happened to Ascendant Lucien was end-times kind of stuff. This was everything that made people fearful and resentful of wonderists all coming together at once. This was 'whatever our personal disputes – be they who ought to rule the country or who murdered whose children – surely we can all get behind the idea that what *really* matters is capturing those fuckers and disposing of them in the worst way possible – well, whichever "worst" way is left over after what they did to the Ascendant'.

The response to such reasoned argument would inevitably be, 'Well, my good man, I despise you and your entire lineage, but damned right, we've got to kill those bastards.'

I wouldn't have been in the least bit surprised if outrage over what had happened to Ascendant Lucien couldn't bring about world peace, however temporary that state of affairs might be.

I can only blame what came out of my mouth next on the fact that I'd been dangling by my ankle from a tethering spell for rather a long time and the blood had rushed to my head. It's well known that this has been known to cause any number of cognitive impairments and induce even the most rational of individuals to say things that are patently insane.

'Let's not panic,' I said.

Green, who was looking more and more like the name we'd saddled him with responded to my call for calm by turning the iron-rimmed hourglass a fraction more, advancing events second by second until we saw Lucien's guards and retainers first rush into his tent and then run back out again, moving twice as fast while screaming at the tops of their lungs.

We all heard them crying, 'The wonderists have murdered Ascendant Lucien! Seal every exit from the camp! Kill any you find!'

And then came the worst part. 'Summon the Glorians!'

'That's not good,' Corrigan muttered. He reached out a hand and put it on Green's, making him turn the hourglass forward a bit more.

There they were, eleven men and women, tall and majestic in shining steel armour, their gold-trimmed white cloaks fluttering elegantly in the night breeze. On each right shoulder was strapped a golden gauntlet, representing the hand of a Lord Celestine guiding them towards the path of virtue and necessity. When it was time to begin the interrogations, torture and executions, the justiciars would put on those gauntlets, so that all would know their verdicts were not personal; they were being administered by the hands of the Celestines themselves.

One of them standing outside the entrance to Lucien's tent turned around, almost as if he could see us watching him, even though these events must have taken place at least half an hour ago. The blessings granted to the justiciars by their chosen Celestine lends their skin a warm, beneficent glow that could almost make you believe they're the good guys.

The one who'd turned was about my height, maybe a little broader, thanks to his armour. Dark hair like mine in a military cut made him look almost dashing. His gaze was pure Glorian Justiciar: piercing, commanding and filled with the righteous determination that someone nearby was deserving of punishment.

I could have sworn he was looking right at me.

CHAPTER 8

Better a Big Betrayal
than a Small One

'It wasn't me,' I yelled, not quite sure if I was shouting at the apparition Green had conjured or the assembled company of panicking wonderists, all of whom were pretty sure their cushy lives as war mages for a successful and generous Ascendant had come to an abrupt and very messy end. They were in no doubt whatsoever over the question of who to blame.

'I had nothing to do with summoning the hellborn!' I shouted again.

I was feeling *extremely* grateful that Tenebris had set the price for the conjuration higher than he knew I could afford – but that, alas, left a nagging question rattling around in my already throbbing skull: which of the other wonderists happily letting me take the blame for this disaster *had* met the price?

Corrigan backhanded me across the face, which somehow hurt worse because I was hanging upside down. When Narghan's tether spun me back around, Corrigan was holding up three fingers in front of my face. I thought he was about to blast me with some Tempestoral bolt of ouch-my-flesh-is-burning-away that I hadn't seen him use before, but it turned out he was only using his fingers to count off his assessment of my innocence. 'First, I don't care. Second, I don't believe you, and third, it makes no difference now.'

The others were shuffling about like children needing to pee, muttering to themselves, hands rifling through their own pockets as if maybe they'd find some magnificent spell they'd forgotten that would instantly solve all their problems.

Locke Fandaris had taken off his bandolier of keys, examining each one, no doubt wondering which would get him far enough away not to have to worry about the Glorian Justiciars catching up to him – or whether, perhaps, he should just drop himself in the lava pit he'd originally planned for me.

Lady Smoke was so anxious the murky smog surrounding her had started dissipating like fog burning away beneath a rising sun. This was one of those times when wearing actual clothes would have come in handy to protect her modesty. Not that I looked, of course – I'm a gentleman in that regard.

'Can we not fight them, Silords?' Green asked in that way the young and inexperienced do when they have this inkling that perhaps they're about to deliver their first stirring speech, one assured to launch them into a grand career as a hero. Seeing the reactions of his fellows, he added, much more sensibly, 'Or maybe we should run away?'

Not even Zyphis laughed at that.

There's actually no such thing as 'getting away' from a court of Glorians. Kill one, and the rest will hunt you down with even greater determination. Justiciars can't be bought, and they never give up. They're sometimes called the 'Twice-Blessed' on account of the two benedictions granted them by the Celestines: the first makes them immune to non-Auroral forms of magic, so wonderists like us can't blast them, curse them or so much as give them a nasty itch in their crotches.

But what about spells that don't target them directly, you may ask? What about, you know, causing an earthquake beneath their feet or setting the countryside around them on fire?

That's where the second benediction comes in. That lovely shiny armour the justiciars wear isn't plain old steel. The alloys from which the plates are forged have been infused with the sentience of dead angelics, which, somewhat ironically, makes the armour alive and aware. Crumble the ground beneath an armoured justiciar and they won't actually fall. Catch one asleep in a barn and set the hay on fire, and their angelic armour will keep them beautifully cool until they have time to finish their nap and enjoy a hearty breakfast before coming to chop off your hands for having the temerity to attempt – not *succeed*, mind you, just to *attempt* – to interfere with their righteous repose.

Oh, and when they *do* round you up? They'll uncover every crime you've ever committed, however minor, even if unrelated to their current investigation. Then they'll make you pay for each and every one, to the fullest extent of Auroral Law.

'There has to be some way to escape!' Green insisted.

Teenagers. They never appreciate the fundamental unfairness of existence.

Actually, there is one way to evade the justiciars, which is to abandon the guilty party, leaving them to keep the bastards occupied while you run away as fast and as far as you can. The only problem is that it doesn't usually take the justiciars long to extract a full confession from their victims, which invariably includes the names of all their associates. That's why you never leave them a living body, and why my fellow wonderists had all turned to watch me as I dangled in the air by my desperately aching ankle.

'There can't be anything left of him but ashes,' Narghan said.

'And we must burn away all traces of ecclesiasm,' Lady Smoke added.

She was absolutely right about that; anyone can burn a body. Destroying the evidence of a soul? That takes far more potent magic.

'Aetheric lightning will do the job,' Corrigan said. He stared down at me and shook his head with disgust. 'I'll take care of it.'

'Such a spell requires preparatory rituals, does it not?' Zyphis asked. 'Don't think the rest of us are going to walk out of here and just trust that you'll do him. Everyone knows you've got a soft spot for Cade.'

'No preparation required,' Corrigan replied. 'I got everything ready before the rest of you arrived.' Once again, he glared down at me. 'You stupid shitbag. This was a great gig until you fucked it up.'

'It was a lousy gig, working for a spiteful arsehole,' I reminded him. 'And was nobody listening when I mentioned I'm *not* the one who summoned the hellborn?'

Lady Smoke glided towards me, those mists of hers writhing closer as if they meant to throttle me. 'Everyone here knows you use Infernal magic, Cade. You pretend it's Fortunal, but we recently learned the truth about you.'

Great. That was the one thing I really *was* trying to keep secret. I wondered if one of those kids, Galass or Fidick, had run off and ratted me out. It was hard to imagine either of them wanting to get near another wonderist, though.

'I'm pretty sure I've caught you casting an Infernal cantrip or two, Somaka,' I countered, 'and Zyphis practically oozes the stuff!'

The wraith-like, wrinkled youth spat at me. 'Not the kind you use, you pervert! Your conjurings don't just draw on the laws of the Infernal plane, you actually *buy* spells from a diabolic, don't you? You make deals with the Lords Devilish! No wonder the fucking Glorians show up wherever you are, just waiting for our employers to give them the go-ahead to rip us all to shreds for whatever it is you did to piss them off!' He turned to Corrigan. 'Time's running out. Either you obliterate him or I will.'

Zyphis' little tirade elicited indignant grumbles of agreement from the others. There was something funny about the fact that in this room filled with merciless killers, *I* was the one whose practices offended their delicate sensibilities.

'I'm telling you all, for the third time, I did *not* buy the hellborn conjuration,' I insisted. 'The price was too high. If you haven't any faith in my integrity, maybe you could at least give me credit for being cheap.'

The assortment of faintly dubious and outright bloodthirsty scowls I got in response wasn't exactly reassuring.

'Well, Corrigan?' Narghan asked.

My erstwhile best friend made a sign to the woman behind the bar, who had finally stopped pretending to polish her mugs and was instead sobbing quietly, her hands clasped together in desperate prayer. She got the message and without a word, ran as fast as she could out of the back door. Corrigan turned to Locke. 'Does one of those trinkets on your bandolier open a door to somewhere very far away from here?'

The key mage nodded. Holding up what looked like a rod with a set of wolf's fangs on one side, he said, 'Won't be especially pleasant. Are you sure you can pull off enough aetheric lightning to destroy his ecclesiasm?'

'Yeah,' Corrigan replied. 'Like I said, I prepared the spells before the rest of you got here. Somehow I just knew Cade's stupidity was going to wind up with us needing to burn the evidence.'

Like I said before, he may look like a big, hairy, ill-tempered brute, but the truth is, Corrigan's always been better at advanced planning than most wonderists. For the third time in as many minutes, he glared down at me with such consuming disappointment that I almost felt guilty that he felt he had to eradicate me from existence. 'This was your fault, Cade.' I saw the first tell-tale smouldering of the air around his right fist as he prepared to summon the lightning. 'Anything you want to say to the others before it's all over?'

'Yeah,' I said, oddly grateful for the opportunity to unburden myself. I took a deep breath, and as politely as I could, said, 'You're all a bunch of unconscionable pricks and I wish I'd killed a few of you before my own time came.'

Zyphis hissed out a laugh, Lady Smoke rolled her eyes and Locke shook his head in dismay. Apparently, my speech-making skills needed work.

Corrigan's fingers twitched, flicking out to all four corners of the tavern as he activated his aetheric lightning spell. I'd never seen him cast this particular variation before, but as I prepared for my no doubt richly deserved death, I thought absently how odd it was, because his explosive spells usually involve first delineating the area where the lightning would strike. I couldn't stop myself wondering if setting the boundaries to all four corners of the tavern might not cause it to—

Someone swore aloud, but they were too late, for Corrigan had spun around and was hugging my upside-down body in a way that would have been awkwardly intimate were the air around us not suddenly igniting as bolt after bolt of black and gold lightning struck every inch of the tavern – and everyone inside except us. Most thunderers' spells come in two parts: the first bursts open a portal to the Tempestoral plane, which unleashes its particularly destructive physics into our own, while the second protects the caster from their own summoning. By grabbing onto me, Corrigan was keeping me inside his protective sphere, safe from the lightning strikes. I didn't think this was the time to complain about body odour as I hung upside down, my head just below his crotch, watching the endless cascades of lightning striking our fellow wonderists, turning both bodies and souls to ash. I caught the look on Green's face as he searched for an escape. His eyes met mine as if to remind me that he was young, that he'd committed no great crime save that of wanting to be one of us. I fear the look I returned him said that was crime enough.

As the flesh and spirit that had once been Narghan was destroyed, his binding spell disappeared and I fell to the ground, twisting to avoid smashing my skull open as I hit the floor. The storm ended abruptly as I lay there, staring up at the scorched ceiling, my eyes barely able to focus. Corrigan's big head loomed over me, gold sparks still dancing across his indigo hair and beard. When he spoke, I couldn't hear what he was saying over the thunder echoing in his voice. Didn't matter, though. I got the message anyway.

'Sure,' I said. 'I'll be happy to take that job up north with you.'

CHAPTER 9

Military Indiscipline

My ankle hurt. What a strange thing, that such a trivial, mundane sort of pain should catch my attention, given all the death and destruction I had witnessed only minutes before, not to mention the chaos and bloodshed that was surely still to come.

I stumbled through the encampment behind Corrigan as he blazed a trail through the haze of dust stirred up by the distinctly un-military disarray that had taken over Ascendant Lucien's once great crusade. Real armies are led by generals with ordered chains of command. They have neat and tidy divisions of cavalry, infantry, and artillery full of archers or cannon or whatever the hell people use to rain destruction down on each other when they don't have wonderists at their beck and call. Lucien's army might *look* magnificent when it came marching up to your fortress, citadel or impoverished village, but in disciplinary terms, it was basically a well-dressed mob whose primary function was to pick up the scraps after Corrigan and I – and the rest of our recently deceased brethren – had made the enemy shit their pants and throw up their hands in surrender.

Without Lucien's charismatic leadership, not to mention the ever-present threat of him ordering his own troops crucified, his 'grand campaign' was what any proper military strategist would refer to as a 'shit-show on wheels'.

The once orderly camp had disintegrated into anarchy. Soldiers, staff and camp followers alike were scurrying about madly, some following orders given them by equally panicked superiors, others just trying to keep moving, terrified about what might happen if they stopped. The looting had started, with idiots getting into fights over the goods they were stealing, the women they were leaving or the bitter old scores they were settling before the whole place went up in flames.

Corrigan was delighted. This chaos would put a serious crimp in the Glorian Justiciars' efforts to hunt us down.

'We'll leave tonight,' he said, leisurely shoving aside two men about to come to blows with no regard for the weapons they'd left in an untidy heap beside them. 'Two hundred and fifty miles in ten days is easy enough, but we'll need to pick up a few more wonderists along the way. Apparently, the reason this Baron Tristmorta is getting whupped so bad is because these seven wonderists – brothers, if you can believe it – have laid siege to his fortress. The client wants seven of *us* to beat the shit out of the seven of *them*. You know the drill, make an example of them, or some such nonsense. Either way, to fulfil the contract, we'll need recruits.'

'Having second thoughts about exploding all the wonderists we knew?'

'Eh?' He paused from stomping through the mud, then chuckled. 'Yeah, too bad about that. Truth be told, the only one of them I liked was Locke. Pity I couldn't have saved him too, but I couldn't be sure he'd go along with the plan – or that he wouldn't try to steal the reward for himself at the end.'

'Fine,' I said with a sigh. 'Tell me about this wondrous artefact.'

'Oh, no.' Corrigan jabbed his finger right up to my nose. 'You pissed all over me earlier for even bringing it up, so now you can just suffer the frustration of ignorance and hope that maybe – *maybe* – I'll let you borrow it when the time comes.'

He set off again, his long-legged stride quickly eating up the distance.

I put a hand on his arm to slow him down. My abused ankle was making it hard for me to keep up. 'Thanks,' I said.

'For what?'

'For believing I was innocent.'

Corrigan stopped again. 'Are you shitting me? You're saying you *didn't* send that shadowy monstrosity to kill Lucien?'

'I told you back at the tavern, that wasn't me.'

'Huh.' Once again, he resumed his march across the camp. 'Wonder which of those pricks killed him, then?'

That Corrigan didn't care one bit about whether I was a murderer or not wasn't much of a surprise to me, but the fact that he'd readily killed the entire squad of wonderists – his comrades-in-arms – because it was the only way to save me? That was harder to reconcile with the man I'd come to know over the past couple of years. It wasn't as if we were childhood friends or sworn brothers. At a guess, Corrigan liked me maybe ten per cent more than he'd liked Locke and the others. I guess that ten per cent was worth more to him than any moral qualms about obliterating them.

Some religious scholars have theorised that violating the natural laws of the universe is a fundamentally perverse and unholy act, leaving the practitioners of such perfidy 'little more than soulless demoniacs whose outward human faces are mere masks to cover their devilry'. Corrigan was pretty solid proof of that theory, but he'd just saved my life, so, you know . . .

'Halt!' shouted the leader of a small squad of soldiers as they surrounded us.

The ash and grit and smoke enveloping the camp were now so thick it was like being caught in a dust storm. Although I could barely make out my hand in front of my face, I counted eight soldiers blocking our path, and occasional glints of steel, not to mention experience, drawn swords and readied spears.

'We'll want two horses each,' Corrigan said, heedless of the armed men all around us. Neither of us were in a state to put up much of a fight. He'd just used the most powerful spell in his arsenal, so he'd need time to recover before he could conjure anything more destructive than a candle flame. As for me, I'd been poisoned by a bat, then hung upside down for nearly an hour. Yet Corrigan kept right on talking to me as if he hadn't even noticed the soldiers. 'We'll be travelling through the Blastlands, so we'll need supplies.'

'Maybe we should deal with these guys first?' I asked, gesturing to the officer striding determinedly towards us.

She was a big woman – or possibly she was a big man; it was hard to be sure when someone was in full armour. One of Lucien's few endearing qualities had been his insistence that there be no discrimination in his army; distinction was *earned* through valour – oh, and flattery. Either way, the silver three-feathered wings on her collar marked her as a lieutenant.

'You'll be coming with us, *wonderists*.' She said that last word as though she had never much liked our kind and was finally being given an opportunity to do something about it.

Corrigan spared her barely a glance – but what a glance it was. I marvelled at the way he could decide in a split-second whether a challenge would best be solved with a few words, a menacing threat or sudden, irredeemable violence. Looking at the lieutenant, I wondered if any part of her was aware that her fate, whatever it would be, was already sealed, and that nothing she would do now could change that.

'By order of the Ascendant—' she began, then staggered slightly as Corrigan backhanded her with stunning brutality, knocking the steel half-helm right off her head.

To her credit, the lieutenant barely shifted an inch. She picked up her helm and gestured at her squad, who instantly raised their weapons in preparation for skewering us.

'The Ascendant's *dead*,' Corrigan snapped, ignoring the sword blades getting perilously close to our necks. 'Now you can either join him in the afterlife to explain your disobedience, or you can go back to doing your jobs.'

'Our . . . jobs?' one of the soldiers asked. He sounded doubtful.

Now that the dust was settling, I was uncomfortably aware of just how young they were. I haven't seen thirty summers myself, yet I felt like an old man in their company.

The lieutenant gave the boy who'd spoken up a withering glance, but even she looked taken aback by Corrigan's effortless intimidation.

'Your *jobs*,' he repeated, not allowing the lieutenant to speak. He swung an arm wide and they all cringed before swiftly recovering their soldierly posture. 'This whole camp is falling apart, in case you haven't noticed! A rogue wonderist murdered the Ascendant and you can bet your cursed arses that even now Archon Belleda – unless she's even dumber than you lot – is preparing to launch a full counteroffensive against this camp.' He leaned closer to the woman in charge and whispered, outrageously loudly, 'She's got wonderists too, you know.'

The soldiers started twisting their heads this way and that in search of the vile and deadly war mages who might even now be stalking them.

'Now,' Corrigan went on, 'as General – oh, what's his fucking name again? Sounds like a genital disease.'

'Kin Vahj?' another soldier offered.

Corrigan pushed the man's sword aside so he could clap him on the shoulder approvingly. 'Right. Kin Vahj. The general's ordered the entire camp be secured, both to keep Belleda's people out and, more importantly, to keep those fucking wonderists *in*. We don't want the assassin escaping now, do we?'

The lieutenant tried to reassert her authority. 'That's what we're—'

Corrigan cut her off by spinning on his heel to face me.

'Mage-Captain Ombra, these pissants are in full dereliction of duty. Take every one of their names down so that when General Kin . . .'

'Vahj,' I offered.

'I know that, you idiot. I was pausing for dramatic effect, in the obviously vain hope of prompting some of these pissants to save their own lives and fulfil the general's orders before he makes us use spells we *should* be using against the wonderist assassin. Do you want to see us waste all that power on separating the heads of these deserters from their necks in the most unpleasant ways possible?'

'Deserters?' another of the young soldiers asked. He looked uncertainly at his lieutenant, who wasn't offering much in the way of help right now.

Corrigan would have made a great con artist – or at least, he would have if he didn't enjoy burning conmen alive quite so much. He turned on the soldier who'd spoken and poked a finger in the man's breastplate as if he could burn his way through. 'Your orders are to secure the camp and challenge any wonderist who isn't already under guard.'

'But sir, that's what we—'

Corrigan gave him a push. 'So go and *do* that! Find anyone who even *looks* like an arse-sniffing wonderist and take them into custody.'

'What should we do if we find one?' the lieutenant asked, apparently having given up trying to understand what was going on, never mind regaining control of the situation.

'Bring them to us for interrogation,' Corrigan replied. 'And then pray to whatever gods or devils you pray to that we're able to get this mess sorted before the Glorians get here and turn all our lives into a living hell.'

The commander mumbled something incoherent.

Actually, it was probably a lot more coherent than the horseshit Corrigan was spouting, but he just went on bellowing right over her, 'The words you're looking for, soldier, are, "As commanded, so obeyed!"'

She hesitated, but I think there must be something in the nature of soldiers that they really like being yelled at. 'As commanded ... so obeyed,' she said at last.

Corrigan stepped back a few feet, forcing the soldiers behind him to scamper out of the way. He stood there until they instinctively got into formation in front of him. He looked as if he were a general himself, ready to inspect their uniforms and weapons.

'Say it,' he directed them all.

'As commanded, so obeyed!'

He put a hand to his ear. 'Hard to hear over the sounds of other soldiers out there doing their jobs and getting ready to be promoted for their diligence.'

'As commanded, so obeyed!' the squad bellowed as one.

Still, Corrigan held them frozen in his glare. The seconds ticked by uncomfortably until at last, his jaw stuck out a little further, he gave them a single approving smile and saluted them.

They saluted back, and I swear the lot of them – their lieutenant included – had big, dumb grins on their faces, the look of soldiers who would, once this was all done, rush back to their tents and write letters home describing how fabulous it was to be in the army.

I give you Corrigan Blight, ladies and gentlemen: a guy who can blast you to bits with fiendish magic one minute and then have you falling all over yourself thanking him for saving your life the next.

Yeah, I know, that describes me, too.

The soldiers dispersed, ready to go and hunt down any wonderists they could find, leaving us to resume our journey back to our tents to collect our gear. We'd got barely twenty yards before yet another contingent of soldiers had caught sight of us and were preparing to take us prisoner. This lot didn't look like they'd fall for the same trick.

'Now where was I?' Corrigan asked me.

'You were saying something about us needing to recruit more wonderists on our way north?'

'Ah, right,' he said, fingers twitching as he smirked at the soldiers, preparing to cast a spell that would leave more piles of ashes on the ground. Evidently, he was feeling much recovered. 'The old bunch were okay, but for this job, we're going to need to recruit some real nasty bastards . . .'

CHAPTER 10

Blood Magic

Darkness still enveloped the encampment by the time Corrigan and I reached my tent. Unease had spread like magefire through the ranks, soldiers and camp followers alike increasingly terrified that this night would be the last for all of them. Rumours about Ascendant Lucien's demise had already begun to give way to reports of Archon Belleda's troops rallying in preparation for an attack. That Lucien's enemy already knew he was dead and his troops in disarray didn't surprise anyone: a camp this big has almost as many spies as it has fleas. The good news for us was that Belleda's invasion would cause all kinds of problems for the justiciars.

Auroral Law is similar to the jurisprudence of your average civilised nation – assuming said nation happens to favour pompous sermonising and a self-defeating morass of criminal procedures. You see, a Glorian Justiciar can't just prosecute any old case in whatever order pleases them. No, they've first got to produce the Hierarchy of Transgressions, in a specific sequence, with those crimes deemed most heinous by the Lords Celestine at the top – things like singing blasphemous songs during consensual orgies or proposing scientific explanations of the universe – and then working down to less egregious offences, like murdering your wife in cold blood.

Where the Glorians would stand on the Lords Celestine's chosen representative's nemesis decimating his now leaderless troops was anyone's guess, but for sure it would keep them busy a while. Things would get even more complicated if Belleda had been smart enough to keep a few of her Auroral wonderists in reserve, as even Glorians aren't immune to Auroral magic.

'Grab your gear and let's leave this shithole to the Devilish,' Corrigan said. 'I'll keep watch.'

I'd pushed aside the flaps and slipped inside before I remembered that I'd set spell knots in place when I'd left earlier that evening. The fire was out and the temperature had plummeted so far that it was even colder inside than out. That was not a great sign. The stench of the recently dead was also a reliable indication that something had gone badly awry.

Damn it all, I thought miserably. *I told them not to leave the tent. What fresh hell have I added to my conscience this time?*

I needed light, but light is a tricky spell to cast if you're not attuned to luxoral magic. Summoning illumination out of thin air may seem trivial, but from a physics standpoint, it's no less a violation of natural law than conjuring fire or lightning. What is easier, however, is binding the radiance of an existing light source to an object whose substance will then, over many weeks, be gradually consumed by the spell. I happened to carry just such an item on my person: a piece of wood no larger than my little finger carved in the shape of a candle. I groped in my pocket, heaving a sigh of relief when my fingers closed around it, thanking the gods it hadn't fallen out back at the tavern or been consumed in the cataclysmic storm Corrigan had summoned.

I flicked my thumbnail over the carved wooden wick to reawaken the spell. It was barely brighter than an actual candle, but that was more than enough to reveal the first pair of bodies lying at my feet.

'Get that away from me,' came a voice out of the darkness. It was female, hoarse, and full of loathing.

'*Galass?*' I peered down at the two dead soldiers on the ground.

81

Their weapons were still in their hands. There were no apparent wounds on their bodies, but even in the dim light I could see the crimson sheen coating their skin, as if someone had dipped their corpses in red paint. Blood was slowly dripping out of their mouths, eyes and ears, and I was willing to bet that if I bothered to look, the rest of their bodily orifices would be similarly leaky.

'What happened?' I asked, holding up the candle.

'I told you to get that light away!'

A wave of sickness passed through me – no, not sickness. Something worse. I turned my hand over and saw tiny droplets of blood oozing up through the pores of my skin.

'Galass, whatever you're doing, stop it *now*.'

'Or what?' she asked scornfully. 'You'll use your demon-bought magic against me? Well, guess what, *Silord*?' The light emanating from the wooden wick in my hand flared, the colour changing from soft yellow to an unnatural scarlet. There were more bodies strewn about the tent like discarded dolls, each one covered in that distinctive patina of drying blood. 'Turns out anyone can make deals with the Devilish.'

I saw her then, some ten feet away from me. She was the same girl I'd left here hours before: young, slim, pretty without being soft. She was still garbed in the pure white obliviate's gown Lucien had dressed his 'gifts' in. There wasn't so much as a drop of blood on the silk. Only Galass' hair had changed, the dark tresses now a radiant scarlet as bright as the flame of my charmed wooden candle.

I should have cast one of my remaining Infernal spells that very instant, something that would maim or kill her before she could take me down. Failing that, I could have shouted for Corrigan so he could blast her and save my conscience the trouble.

Instead, I stood there, trying to imagine what sequence of events had brought us to this calamity.

Part of the explanation was right in front of me: a pair of circles created from the same spell-sand I'd wiped away when I'd ended my communion with Tenebris.

'Oh, Galass, what have you done?'

Someone had managed, without the *years* of training and practice I'd spent developing my skills, to re-form the circle and repeat my ritual.

Inside the first circle lay a pale, perfectly preserved corpse that now looked even younger than its eleven years. Fidick was still breathtakingly beautiful, even in death.

CHAPTER 11

Bad Bargains

I'd once heard it said by a historian of great renown that there was a time when the simple act of lighting a fire was considered a feat of wondrous spellcraft. The earliest humans saw in those flames the breath of the dragons they painted on their cave walls and the majesty of the gods to whom they prayed. Centuries later, the first medicines derived from the sap of a species of tall, graceful trees whose foliage spread wide like verdant wings were believed to be made of the tears of angels. How else to explain the sweet taste that enabled a person to survive the same disease that had killed their neighbours? Magic, this revered scholar had postulated, was merely natural law that experts like himself had not yet had time to decode.

Sensible. Logical. Utterly false.

As I pointed out to my friend the historian – I was, at the time, strapped to a chair while he and his fellow academics were draining blood from several of my limbs and lodging metal devices into parts of my body which, in my admittedly amateur opinion, were quite unsuited for such insertions – natural laws and systems of magic are separated by one incontrovertible fact: while anyone in possession of the necessary substances and following the correct process can replicate scientific *techniques*, only those attuned to the planes from which one wished to derive *unnatural* laws can actually cast spells. That's why the world isn't overrun with wonderists.

The historian, always one for a robust discussion, had countered my fact with his own hypothesis: that since there was no way to prove that such attunement exists at birth, it might perhaps be an ability innate to all human beings, waiting only to be activated through severe psychological or physical trauma. This might explain why most wonderists tend to be more than a little deranged.

I had to admit this did sound like a most intriguing and persuasive avenue of enquiry. Unfortunately, all my subsequent tests upon the historian and his colleagues after I freed myself proved inconclusive, possibly not helped by the excessive amounts of blunt force trauma I'd delivered to their skulls. The insertion of various metal devices into their livers probably hadn't helped, either. Nonetheless, at the very end there, I could have sworn I saw the first traces of a spell manifesting from the historian's still-twitching lips. So maybe he was right all along.

All of which is to say that regardless of where you fall on the born-versus-learned theory of magical ability, it's never a good idea to leave two emotionally scarred children alone in your tent with all your wonderist's tools after they've witnessed you performing a ritual for demoniac summoning.

'He knew just what to do,' Galass said, looking down upon the porcelain remains of the boy she had so desperately tried to protect from the ugliness of the world. 'But how did he know? He just . . . after you left, it was like he was in a trance. He'd memorised every single one of your movements – the way you spread the sand in a circle, all those odd words, every precise step . . .'

'That's how it is with this kind of magic,' I said, cursing myself for never having considered that someone so meek might be harbouring untapped magical potential. 'Those of us attuned to the Infernal realm don't *learn* the incantations. We hear them like whispers all around us. All we need is to find a source to power the spells. It's less a talent than a . . .'

'A calling,' she said.

I'd never heard it called that, but she was absolutely right.

'Galass, what happened? How did Fidick acquire the power to send the hellborn after Lucien? And how did you become—?'

Somehow, Galass had become attuned to the only form of magic derived from our own Mortal plane – the one kind of magic no wonderist ever seeks out, because you can't just buy, borrow or steal the power from somewhere else. You can only strip it from human bodies. The effects – like that very particular, very unsettling shade of scarlet – are unmistakeable.

Remember that Hierarchy of Transgressions I mentioned? By her very existence, Galass had just moved herself to the very top of the justiciars' list.

'He resisted, at first,' Galass said dreamily, her eyes so unfocused that I couldn't be sure if she was even aware she was talking to anyone but herself.

'Who resisted?' I asked. 'Fidick?'

'The diabolic. The one from whom you'd sought to procure your dark spells.'

'Tenebris.' His name came out of my mouth like I was spitting venom. I was already thinking about how best to remove Fidick's corpse so I could summon the demon again and incinerate him slowly, piece by piece, inside my spell circle. There were things even diabolics feared, and when I'd joined this profession, I'd made it my business to learn as many of them as I could.

Galass was watching my face now, tilting her head to examine me as if I were some strange feral animal who'd wandered in from the cold. 'You don't understand. The demon refused to make a deal with Fidick at first. He said . . . he said some evils were worse than others, and that he'd learned from you that all of us must draw the line somewhere.'

A diabolic with a conscience. Now I know for sure the world is ending.

Galass continued, the skin pinching at the corners of her eyes as if the memories were painful to her, 'Fidick copied you when you were trying to bully the demon. He started flicking that pink sand into the circle. It was so cruel. The demon was screaming, trying to refuse him, but Fidick began making these' – her fingers started contorting into unnatural shapes – 'these . . . well, they were just gestures, I guess, but they made me feel really sick. Your demon had it worse – he was in such agony, his cries—' Her hands went up to cover her ears. 'I couldn't stop him. I kept shouting at Fidick, *begging* him, but he wouldn't listen. It wasn't even really for the demon's sake, but because his screams were driving me mad.'

The girl clamped her lips shut and shook her head so hard I worried she'd snap her slender neck. I doubted her psyche would ever be whole again after what she'd witnessed, let alone with what had been done to her. But repressing the experience would only drive the sickness deeper inside her, so ignoring her obvious wish for me to shut up now, I persisted with my enquiry.

'Tell me what happened next.'

Her voice low, she said, 'I grabbed Fidick's legs and tried to pull him down – I hoped that might break his hold on the demon – but something weird was happening inside *me* . . . I don't know how he knew that, but he kept telling me, "It's going to be okay now. We won't have to be scared any more." He was still Fidick, still the boy I pretended was my brother, because I'd always wanted a brother, and he was so *kind*. But there was something happening to *him*, too, because no matter how hard I tried, I couldn't turn away. Fidick wouldn't *let* me turn away. The demoniac had finally stopped screaming, so he must have given in to Fidick's demands, though I couldn't hear the terms because the . . . the blood was rushing in my ears. It was so loud, it was deafening me.' She dropped her head and whispered, 'Then Fidick released the demon and it was all over.'

'What was over?' I asked urgently. I glanced back at the tent flaps, expecting at any moment to see a dozen Glorian Justiciars come striding inside, their hands in those damnably blessed golden gloves of theirs reaching for Galass.

'Fidick threw up.'

I could barely hear her. 'What?'

'He threw up a shadow.' She pointed to the carpet in front of my feet, but there was nothing there. 'He retched, over and over, until a shadow spewed from his throat. Fidick fell to his knees and the shadow moved like it was flowing, right out of the tent.' She walked to the circle, knelt and placed a hand on the boy's pale neck as if searching for a pulse. 'He wouldn't let me move him. I didn't understand why, but he wanted to stay right here. He kept repeating, "It's going to be better now, Galass. I'm so very tired, but I've done what I needed to do. Everything will be all right." But he was wrong. Nothing is ever going to be all right again.'

She began to cry, but the tears were blood, the colour of her hair. 'I must have passed out for a while.' She wiped her cheeks, then unconsciously smeared the blood on her hair when she reached up to touch the long tresses. 'When I woke, my hair had changed. *I* had changed. And when the soldiers came for me . . .'

'They would have killed you,' I said bluntly, because telling her everything was going to be okay would have been a lie, and that, at least, was a truth she might be able to live with.

'What happens now?' She looked around at the dead bodies and shuddered. 'What do I do? Where do I go?'

Corrigan stomped into the tent, shaking a bleeding hand and carrying a bundle of angry fur by the scruff of its neck in the other. 'Does this mutt belong to anyone? Because the little bastard just bit me—'

'Mister Bones!' Galass said, reaching for the jackal.

Then Corrigan caught sight of the blood mage barely six feet from him. The first purple and black sparks of impending calamity danced around his clenched right fist.

'Don't move!' I shouted at him.

'Wasn't planning to,' he said. More sparks drifted down, scorching the shockingly expensive handmade carpet beneath our feet. Corrigan was so intent on Galass that he hadn't noticed the first crimson blush seeping through the pores of his face and neck. The blood from his wounded hand was already floating through the air towards her.

'Kill the bitch, Cade,' Corrigan ordered, with the calm assurance of one who fully expects such commands to be instantly obeyed. I guess he had a point; after all, he had just killed nearly a dozen of our compatriots for me.

'Galass, stop, *please*,' I begged.

But her eyes had gone glassy and I doubted she could hear me. Corrigan was struggling to summon his Tempestoral magic now, and inadvertently squeezing the jackal tighter, until the poor thing began to whine in fright.

I've found over the years that trying to prevent two wonderists from killing each other rarely turns out well. On the other hand, it's terribly bad luck to let an innocent animal die in the process.

I tore open my shirt, revealing the twisted map of ebony sigils covering my chest and stomach. The spells I purchase from Tenebris have to be awakened by tracing the relevant markings with my fingertip before I can cast them. I'd roused a few in preparation for murdering Ascendant Lucien, but they'd gone dormant while I'd been dangling from my ankle in the tavern. I quickly woke the quickest and simplest of the spells.

The sigil for the nightmare bloom appeared in the air before me, a glistening black flower, petals squirming like tethered cockroaches. I snapped off a pair of the hideous little monstrosities, whispered my intent into them, then flicked one at Galass and the other at

Corrigan. He recognised the spell, but he was too slow to get out of the way; it had burrowed into his skull before he could move. Galass was so entranced by her own blood magic that she didn't even notice it entering her mind.

The useful thing about a nightmare bloom is that it conjures up the victim's most paralysing fears. The unpleasant part is that I have to bear witness while the resultant emotional turmoil breaks their concentration, giving me time to do whatever's necessary – usually, killing them. In this case, I just needed Corrigan and Galass to stop what they were doing. My command to the spell had been brief, just enough to bind whatever hellish vision was summoned by their fears to their magic. I'd hoped that would shock them both out of casting their spells before it was too late.

'Gal?' someone called, and we all turned to see Fidick, standing by the spell circle, looking more real than the corpse – *his* corpse – at her feet.

'Fidick?' she asked, her voice full of hope.

The boy smiled, but when he opened his mouth to speak, blood spewed forth – buckets of it, far more than could fit into such a small body. It showered over Galass like a torrent of crimson rain and she screamed . . .

And so did Corrigan.

What he was seeing, however, was a tall woman, a few years older than him, with dark skin and black hair. She was holding her belly and calling out, 'Corry, my love, I felt another kick – I think the baby's coming!'

'No,' Corrigan moaned, 'no, please, don't make me—'

'Look, honey, here it comes—'

The woman took her hands away from her belly. The white wool shift she was wearing began to smoulder, then sparks burned through the fabric into the flesh beneath. When the skin was gone, a lightning storm inside the woman continued slowly eating away at her, even as she smiled up at Corrigan. 'I think it's a boy.'

I clamped my hand over the floating flower sigil, crushing it. Although it felt like squeezing empty air, the spell faded, taking the nightmarish visions with it.

'Before you both kill me,' I said, 'try to remember that there's a full court of Glorian Justiciars making for this camp, and while the mysterious death of an Ascendant Prince will give them plenty to occupy their time, the presence of a blood mage and two renegade wonderists cannot fail to attract their attention.'

Galass shook her head as if to clear her mind of the nightmare. She stared at Fidick's body, lying dead in the spell circle where it had always been. Then she turned back towards Corrigan and raised both her hands.

'Cade, you moron,' he growled, trying once again to summon his Tempestoral magic, 'I told you to kill the crazy bitch and instead yo—'

'Trust me for once, you idiot!' I pleaded with him. 'She's not trying to cast a blood binding on you – she just wants the damned jackal! Put the mutt down – *gently.*'

Corrigan's eyes narrowed in that way he has that suggests he's far too clever to risk his life overreacting to petty grievances against me when he'd much rather take his time concocting a suitable punishment for my various offences against him. On the other hand, he'd never told me he was married, so, you know, there was a debate to be had over which of us had committed the greater offence to our friendship.

No, I didn't think that argument would hold much water, either.

Nonetheless, he set the squirming animal on the ground. It promptly nipped his hand again – the same one it had already bitten, I noticed – before racing to Galass and leaping into her arms. She started sobbing in desperate, manic relief that there was still one tiny part of her world that hasn't been taken away from her.

Sometimes it's the little things that save your soul.

Corrigan's gaze swept over the dead soldiers and paused on the unnatural scarlet hair of the girl hugging the yappy little jackal to her chest. He saw blood on her lower lip: blood that had previously been oozing from the hole in his left hand made by a jackal's tooth.

'Devils fuck me dry,' he said. 'Never thought I'd come across a real live blood mage . . .'

Slowly, so as not to scare either Galass or Corrigan into over-reacting, which would surely end with at least one of them – and certainly me – joining the corpses currently littering my tent, I found a blanket and draped it carefully over Fidick's Mortal remains.

I'm not a religious man, but in my previous profession I'd had to learn a lot of prayers. I spoke the only one I could still tolerate without making myself sick.

> 'There is an end to flesh and spirit.
> The flesh to the ground belongs,
> The spirit to those above,
> But one demesne do Mortals rule,
> Birthed in hearts and smiles and songs,
> For even we who command eternity,
> Hold no dominion over love.'

I tweaked a corner of the blanket, pulling it straight over Fidick's body, then rose and turned to Corrigan.

Not being the sentimental type, he was still staring uneasily at the young blood mage standing less than six feet away from him.

'Cade . . .' he began, almost as if he knew what I was about to say and didn't like it one bit.

'What was it you were telling me earlier? About us needing to recruit some especially nasty war mages?' I asked.

Maybe it comes from being a thunderer, but Corrigan's never been much for debate or negotiation. He makes every decision with the same swift, brutal immediacy of his spells, and he never wastes time second-guessing himself. So it was unusual to see him standing there in silence; he didn't move for so long that I began to wonder if he'd slipped into a trance.

'Ah, fuck it,' he said at last, spinning on his heel to stomp back out of the tent. 'We're taking a job in a shithole so awful they call it Mages' Grave. Gotta figure a little blood magic will come in handy somehow. Besides, she's probably not half as crazy as the guy we're picking up on the Jalbraith Canal.'

I took a deep breath, waiting for my hands to stop shaking, then, deciding that wasn't going to happen any time soon, I grabbed my travelling pack and began filling it with the items I needed most. After a moment, I added a few bits of clothing and kit I thought Galass could use.

Less than ten minutes later, the three of us were ready to head north on a mission about which I knew practically nothing, save that it would supposedly earn us a fortune and would just as surely cost us twice as much. Three outlaw wonderists with a posse of Glorian Justiciars at our back and who the hell knew what waiting ahead.

Well, three wonderists and a yappy, bitey little jackal.

CHAPTER 12

The Canal

Jalbraith Canal is the longest, straightest waterway on the continent. Its high stone embankments were built centuries ago, during an era that wasn't necessarily better than our own, but certainly more optimistic about the future. Sovereign Jalbraith the Beneficent, the former warlord responsible for the canal's construction, had believed that trade was the gateway to peace. The endless stream of would-be tyrants who succeeded old Jalbraith had agreed, though with the intervening steps of a few judicious massacres along the way. In summertime, during what's affectionately called 'Empire Season', when ambitious men like Ascendant Lucien set about fulfilling Jalbraith's promise of a peaceful world in their own violent way, the canal is often clogged for miles with floating corpses.

'I don't like it here,' Galass said, hugging her arms across her chest as she stood at the front of our leaky, single-masted sloop. Despite my offer of a coat and warmer clothes, she'd insisted on wearing her silver-white sublime's gown as if it were a kind of armour protecting her from the truth of what she'd become. Her hair blew in the chill breeze, which would have made for a pretty picture were those long, colourful locks not dancing quite so menacingly. The picture wasn't helped by Mister Bones, either, sitting at her feet and growling at the corpses drifting by, in case they had any ideas about troubling his mistress.

'Don't focus on the bodies,' I urged her, keeping some distance between us in case the blood magic began to overwhelm her again. 'Focus on the river, on the way the water never stops moving. It's like ... think of it as a huge vein filled with blood.'

That might sound creepy, but the thing most people don't understand about blood mages is that the presence of death actually disturbs them. Blood is meant to *flow*, to bring life and vitality. When a body dies and the blood coagulates, it loses the particular form of ecclesiasm from which blood mages draw both power and sustenance.

Galass closed her eyes and extended her hands towards the canal ahead of us. Her fingertips began to sway as if she were conducting an orchestra, her scarlet hair matching each subtle movement.

'I can feel it,' she said. 'The flow of life even amidst all this death, the ... rhythms.' Her eyes were clear when she turned to me. 'I feel a little better now, thank you.'

'You'll want to get into the habit of attuning yourself to the motions of life all around you. Root systems, riverways, ant colonies ... anything but human blood.'

She held up her wrist close to her face, peering at the blue veins on her pale skin as if she could see the crimson currents inside. 'Am I some sort of vampire?'

'No,' I said firmly. 'You don't drink blood or sleep in grave dust. You're a wonderist who happens to be attuned to the wild magic of the Mortal realm rather than the otherworldly planes from which Corrigan and I derive our abilities. You won't be able to cast spells like we do because your magic is more instinctual. You'll be drawn to the flow of life nearby. Blood in particular will make you want to ... play.'

'Play ... yes, that's the word.' She reached out her fingertips towards me, and I felt that strange nausea as the surface of my skin began to redden. She caught herself, thankfully, and closed her fist before dropping her arm by her side. 'You said I can't cast spells. Other than accidentally bleeding people to death, what *can* I do?'

I relaxed my own hands, which had been about to inflict a particularly nasty Infernal binding on her. 'It's hard to guess. Blood magic doesn't obey the usual rules. It's wild and unpredictable – like life itself.'

'Can I bring back the dead?'

I'd known this question would come sooner or later. What she really meant was, *'Can I bring Fidick back to life?'*

'No,' I said. 'You can't resurrect the dead.'

She gave a soft chuckle that didn't quite hide the sob underneath. 'I can only make more of them.'

Lots and lots more, I had the sense not to say out loud.

The sloop tilted backwards from a sudden burst of speed. That was Corrigan using more of his thunder to propel us forward – and to let me know he wanted me to shut the hell up, because to his mind, the more Galass knew about her abilities, the more dangerous she'd become.

'How do you know so much about blood mages?' she asked.

'I know about all forms of wonderism. It's an occupational hazard.'

She shook her head slowly, as if coming out of a trance. 'No, that's not true. I've been subjected to the company of other mages. They like to talk, to brag – always about their particular form of magic. None of those wonderists were like you. You're the only one I've met who—'

I cut her off. 'Just keep focusing on the canal,' I said. We were getting perilously close to topics I didn't want to discuss, especially in front of Corrigan. 'The more you train yourself to sense the movement of life without obsessing about blood, the less you'll feel the urge to . . . tamper with it.'

Sensing Corrigan's glare burning a hole in the back of my azure wonderist's coat, I joined him at the back of the sloop where he was using a spelled barge pole to propel us along the canal. Neither of us were sailors, so we kept the sail furled to the mast. Periodic bursts of thunder beneath the surface of the water lent a pleasant chugging motion to our little vessel.

'She'll develop a thirst for it soon enough,' Corrigan said to me, keeping a wary eye on Galass. 'Brittle thing like her, she'll shatter sharp as glass from the strain if she tries to resist.'

'She's stronger than she looks,' I insisted, though I had no basis for my assertion other than how hard she'd fought to protect Fidick.

Blood mages always go nuts sooner or later. When Corrigan pulls all his different forms of lightning from the Tempestoral demesne, the breach into our realm allows a different set of physical laws to operate. The effects are spectacular, but the violation is only temporary. Any time Galass drew on her blood magic, however, she'd be breaking the natural laws of *this* world, and that, I'm told, does terrible things to the human mind – worse even than trafficking in Infernal magic.

Why had Fidick traded his life and soul to Tenebris in exchange for awakening her attunement to blood magic instead of just buying a few spells? Was it because he knew she wouldn't be able to abide the thought of wielding Infernal magic? Or had he figured that whatever spells he negotiated for that first time would run out sooner or later, leaving her forced to trade away her soul and her conscience, a piece at a time, like he'd seen me doing?

Either way, he'd made a bad deal – for both of them.

Blood mages aren't vampires like in the old stories. They're not undead, for a start. But they do tend to drain their victims dry, so I suppose it's a distinction without a difference. I was still surprised that Corrigan had allowed me to bring her with us. The only alternative would have been destroying her on the spot; leaving her for the justiciars would have been too cruel, even for him. My only hope now was that her indomitable will – the way she'd stood up to me back at my tent, even threatening Tenebris with that little blade of hers – might sustain her longer than most blood mages.

'She can learn to control the urges,' I muttered, more to myself than Corrigan, but my unfounded optimism still had him chuckling darkly as he concentrated on keeping the sloop chugging along the canal. After a while, I asked, 'Any chance you're going to share the details about whatever motley assemblage of moral defectives we're off to recruit for this job?'

His scowl would have curdled milk. 'That depends. Are *you* planning on explaining why a posse of Glorian Justiciars keeps turning up everywhere you happen to be?'

I kept my mouth shut. Corrigan and I had always had this unspoken pact: I don't try to reform him, and he doesn't ask about my past. Not that either of us has ever been particularly good at keeping our sides of the bargain. He emphasised his frustration on this point by taking one hand off the barge pole so he could hurl a bolt of red and black lightning at one of the corpses floating by. The crackling blaze obliterated the swollen sack of rotting flesh and waterlogged bones so thoroughly that all that was left were a few embers sizzling in the water.

'Feeling better?' I asked.

He grinned. 'Yeah. You should try it once in a while. A little pointless destruction and desecration might help you come to grips with the fact that those are the *only* services people hire us for. If you're hoping for some righteous leader to come along and offer you a noble quest with which to assuage your guilty conscience, well, that's never going to happen. That's what scares the hell out of me about you, Cade. It's like you're waiting for old Sovereign Beneficent Jalbraith to rise up from his grave to knight you and give you a mission only you can do.' Corrigan raised one hand to the heavens, lifted his chin and struck the sort of heroic pose you only ever see on marble statues erected outside the palaces of murderous tyrants.

'"Arise, Silord Cade Ombra, take up this righteous sword, bear with honour this unbreakable shield and, in the purity of thine heart, awaken the true magic needed to vanquish the darkness!"'

He started laughing uproariously at his own joke. That's often the case with Corrigan; nobody else finds him particularly funny.

'There are no noble quests for people like us, Cade!' he bellowed, wrapping both hands around the barge pole and sending another burst of his propulsion spell through the sturdy wooden shaft into the water. The sloop lurched forward and I nearly toppled overboard. 'Half the world wants us dead for one spiritual crime or another, while the half who keep us alive and well fed do so only as long as we blow stuff up for them.'

'Yeah,' I agreed. 'Mostly people.'

'Well, a lot of people deserve to get blown up. That's where we come in.' He pulled out the barge pole and balanced it on his shoulder, spread his arms wide, and declared for all the realms in all the universes to hear, 'Everybody works for somebody, and that somebody is usually an arsehole!'

I should pause here a second because there's a danger you might assume the moral dilemma which Corrigan believed to be plaguing me was easily solved.

'But Cade,' I hear you mumbling excitedly, 'don't you see? It's simple! All you have to do is give up your pathological desire for wealth or spells or . . . whatever the fuck it is you want out of life (because you really haven't made that clear thus far), and instead, go and fight on behalf of those brave mummies and daddies rebelling against the baron! You, Corrigan, Galass and whoever else you're about to recruit will surely find spiritual redemption and mend your crooked hearts and—'

Let me stop you right there.

First, as I might have mentioned earlier, Corrigan and I are not the good guys. Like every other wonderist who's managed to acquire powers beyond those of our fellow Mortals, the two of us are absolute human garbage. Our only aim in life is to get rich enough that we can make it hard for those jealous of our magic to torture us, imprison us or, worst of all, deny us the luxurious comforts to which our abilities have accustomed us. I'm not being down on myself here, either; as pieces of human garbage go, I think I'm one of the nicer ones.

I'm trying to be, anyway.

But let's get back to your visions of crusading heroes, shall we?

The Glorian Justiciars are the chosen disciples of the Lords Celestine, who happen to be the apostles of the Auroral Sovereign himself (or herself, or itself – pick whichever pronoun you like). So the beings to whom most people pray have *actual* representatives on earth, following their teachings, spreading their gospels, and being absolute pricks about it.

The Glorians *are* the heroes. They're the ones following the 'will of the eternal', after all. And they want to rip out my toenails before using them to stab me in the eyeballs and testicles.

Keeping one step ahead of the Glorian Justiciars means collecting as much wealth and as many Infernal spells as I can until the day I've either accumulated enough to hire my own army to massacre the bastards, or they've got to me first. In the meantime, I do my best not to make the world an even worse place than I found it. Today that meant keeping a seventeen-year-old blood mage alive in the hope that I could find someone with the esoteric expertise and basic human decency to help her before she woke up with a hangover one morning and drained every drop of my blood through the pores in my skin. Oh, and I'd try to keep the jackal alive, too.

How's that for redemption?

CHAPTER 13

Choosing Sides

'We're nearly there,' Corrigan said, the gruffness of his tone not hiding his weariness.

I leaned on the rail, looking out onto the eastern bank, only now noticing that what had been mostly scrub and dry dirt these past few days had gradually eased into a delightfully wooded glade. Tall trees covered in blue-green leaves stood quiet sentry on either side of the canal, their long, spindly branches towering above us, reaching across the water as if to hold hands. A gentle mist carried the sweet fragrance of sap, while the scent of earthy bark was strong enough to overpower the stench of the floating dead. It was quiet here, and peaceful.

'It's like a cathedral,' Galass marvelled, looking up at the arches formed by the tree branches. 'A cathedral dedicated to nature.' She reached out a hand to brush the spindly lower branches hanging down. Mister Bones jumped up enthusiastically, trying to bite the dangling leaves and instead landing in amiably silly fashion and spitting out his leafy prey.

What neither of them noticed amidst all this pleasant serenity was the absence of any birdsong, the croaking of frogs, or any other life, really, save for the scurrying of tiny feet along the banks and a horde of little grey bodies with beady black eyes and quivering whiskers, pausing frequently to sniff in the direction of our sloop before resuming their dash further down the canal.

'What's going on?' I asked Corrigan.

He began steering the sloop towards the eastern shore. 'That would be our next recruit, I imagine.'

'We're hiring rodents?'

'Not exactly . . .'

Our path was mirroring that of the swarm of rats, and as we negotiated one of the canal's rare bends, I caught sight of their prey: a group of men and women standing near a heap of earth some six feet long. The incantations they were casting upon the mound were probably not helped by the hundreds, maybe even thousands of rodents charging them. They wore long brocaded coats of varying colours and designs (the humans, not the rats, although the latter would have been more interesting). People in our profession don't normally go around advertising our esoteric specialties, as that makes it too easy for our enemies to work out the best way to get past our spells. The exception is when meeting with a prospective employer, when we need to make an impression.

Four of them, three of us, and a job that calls for seven. I shot Corrigan a questioning look. 'You usually have better taste in travelling companions.'

'Currently my travelling companions consist of a soon-to-be-psychotic blood mage, a yappy mutt and you. What the hell gave you the impression I had any taste at all in travelling companions?'

A rumbling roar drew my gaze back to the shore. Judging by her coat, pure black save for the silver tendrils of lightning swirling along her sleeve, the bigger of the two women must have been a Tempestoral mage like Corrigan, and sure enough, bolts of blinding white lightning erupted from her clenched fists as she punched the air between herself and the oncoming rats, scorching a dozen of the frenzied assailants at a time even as the others darted around her to attack from the other side. Tiny, lethal claws and short, sharp teeth were scratching through the four wonderists' clothes to draw blood from the fragile flesh beneath.

Galass suddenly cried out in pain. Time in Lucien's camp might have accustomed her to violence and depravity, but her newly awakened attunement to the flow of blood meant the slaughter of the rats on the shore was a kind of emotional deluge that threatened to drown her.

She needed my attention first. 'Close yourself off from the flow,' I urged her. 'Think of it like holding your breath underwater.'

She shut her eyes, frowning so hard that lines furrowed on her forehead, making her look much older.

'Better?' I asked.

'Shut up,' she replied.

Mister Bones jumped onto the wooden ledge beneath the rail, gnashing his teeth and snarling; I wasn't sure if he was warning off the rats or the mages – or maybe he disliked both. I undid the top buttons of my own coat and shirt and traced a fingertip along one of the more pernicious Infernal runes Tenebris had sold me, warming up the spell in preparation for whatever was going to happen next.

The side of the sloop scraped along the massive stone blocks lining the canal before coming to a reluctant stop.

'Rescue mission?' I asked as I leaped onto the shore. Mister Bones was at my heels, as if the two of us were comrades about to rage into battle together. Nice to know someone had faith in me.

Corrigan tethered our vessel to one of the huge trees lining this stretch of the canal. 'Oh, I wouldn't call it a rescue mission, precisely,' he replied before joining me on the embankment.

As we approached the unfolding chaos, Corrigan's right hand closed into a fist. Sparks began to appear across his knuckles, tiny breaches between our realm and the Tempestoral demesne. The thick grey fog swirling around his right forearm had streaks of unnatural lightning dancing within. I could hear the quiet echoes of the thunder, and the air smelled like the wick of a candle after the flame's been extinguished.

It all looked pretty impressive, but I'd been around thunderers long enough to know that he was having to build up his spell slowly, having exhausted himself being our sole means of propulsion for days on end. Guess we should have worked out how to use the sail after all.

The four mages clustered together some twenty feet away from us had been reasonably successful in fending off the rats, although it did look as if their weary thunderer was responsible for most of the fending. Corrigan grinned slyly as he watched her, which suggested he knew her. I guessed their relationship was probably more carnal than intellectual; Tempestoral mages are prone to particularly stormy sex.

My 'friends with benefits' hypothesis was quickly disproved. Corrigan drew back his arm and opened his fist, readying the raw, destructive energy he'd pulled from the Tempestoral realm. A single bolt of red and black lightning rested on his palm, curled like a sleeping cat. With a grunt, he hurled it at the swarm of rats surrounding what I presumed were our four recruits. The bolt unfurled itself, stretching out leisurely in the air – only to miss the rats entirely.

Well, maybe *miss* is the wrong word.

The bolt struck the other thunderer in the centre of her chest. For an instant, her own web of silvery lightning resisted it, but soon Corrigan's red and black bolt tore away every strand of her magic. She just had time to scream his name – so they *did* know each other – before the sparks ripped across her lovely black coat, eating through fabric and flesh, muscle and bone, until there was nothing left of her but spinning embers that scorched and poisoned the soil as they landed.

There's a reason wonderists try not to batter at each other's spells with their own: conflicting ruptures between esoteric planes have a nasty tendency to result in permanent tears in reality. We call it 'breach dross', and it looks like patches of dead earth upon which nothing grows. Well, that's not entirely true; things do grow, eventually, just not stuff humans should ever ingest.

Not all forms of magic are equally disruptive to nature, of course. Totemic magic often aligns with natural forces on the Mortal demesne, so that's fine. Infernal magic comes and goes with barely a trace, possibly because most of it involves tormenting or otherwise manipulating the psyche rather than, you know, conjuring unearthly forms of lightning and then smashing those against *other* unearthly forms of lightning.

Corrigan, seeing my confused stare, shrugged sheepishly. 'What? I like rats.'

'You *like rats*?' I repeated. 'You just murdered one of your own recruits, you moron! Not that you bothered consulting me on who we were hiring, because if you had, I might have pointed out that two thunderers in a coven is a bad idea, which you've just proven by— Wait.' I glanced at the three remaining mages, who were now cowering behind a glimmering dome shield that wasn't doing a particularly good job of keeping the rats out. Fucking amateur couldn't keep his concentration steady, which made him entirely unsuitable as a war mage, which in turn meant . . .

Corrigan's grin was infectious, kind of like a venereal disease.

Galass came to stand unsteadily alongside us. 'What's happening?' she asked, speaking slowly, as if in a drunken torpor.

Corrigan strode off towards the trio of outraged mages and I followed behind. I traced a teardrop sigil just below my collarbone. The narrowed peak was shaped like an arrow. The other spell I'd warmed up wasn't nearly nasty enough for whatever Corrigan had planned.

'Apparently, we're siding with the rats,' I told Galass.

CHAPTER 14

The Thing About Cosmists

Our arrival brought about a momentary stand-off between the opposing sides, which is always strange when one of those sides is made up entirely of snarling rodents. But the rats ceased their attacks, no longer advancing, just holding their position surrounding the three wonderists. This didn't strike me as typical rat behaviour, since they're usually more of a *Look, the humans have stopped fighting back, let's eat!* sort of species.

'Corrigan, you arsehole!' shouted a short, chubby, pale-faced man of middle years. His fanciful silk coat, which came down below his knees, was repeatedly changing colour, as were his eyes. Luminists have a pretentious air about them at the best of times, but this fellow sported a curled and waxed goatee that made me want to pin him to the ground and let the rats chew it off him. With remarkable indignation, he demanded, 'Why the hell did you just kill Elania Scourge?'

'You mean other than her stupid name?' Corrigan asked.

No one's ever been able to explain to me why Tempestoral mages find it necessary to take on last names like 'Scourge' or 'Bane' or 'Calamity'. I chose not to point out to Corrigan that his last name was 'Blight'.

Standing next to the infuriated luminist was an equally enraged woman whose own coat looked as if it were made entirely out of green and brown leaves. Her skin was a deep mahogany – that's not a metaphor; she had actual bark growing over her skin which enhanced her emerald eyes strikingly. She was currently reaching out, her fingers curling and uncurling as if trying to rouse the trees all around her to life and crush her enemies underfoot – or under *root* might be more accurate. She wasn't having much luck with it.

Before you go laughing at her obvious incompetence, I should mention that floranistic magic – the ability to induce organic but otherwise inanimate matter to come to life and beat the shit out of your enemies – is exceedingly difficult. Just think about it: breaking the laws of physics to summon a storm or trigger nightmares in people is already complicated, but getting trees to start moving around and swatting people? Roots and branches don't have muscles, and I've never managed to work out how the hell floranists manage to make them walk – why doesn't their bark just crack and break off, leaving them in an embarrassing state of undress and unable to survive the winter?

Really, we should be revering floranists as the most marvellous of all mages. But since this one was just crouching there, looking more and more constipated while getting nowhere with rousing the local plant life to her cause, let's skip to the third member of the trio.

'Cade, have you met Chaos Reaping?' Corrigan asked, gesturing to a tall, slender figure whose coat—

You know what? You don't care about the coat. This guy could have been wearing pyjamas dipped in pure gold and you still wouldn't remember a thing about his clothes, not when it was his skin that left such an unforgettable impression. His face and hands were black as the night sky, save for the pinpoints of stars piercing through the veil of darkness. The longer I stared at him, the more convinced I was that I wasn't looking at him so much as *through* him. It was as if his entire body were a window through which you could stare out into space itself.

But okay, fine: his coat was orange. With stripes.

I'd never met an actual cosmist before. The esoteric demesne from which they derive their abilities – specifically, the almost liquid coating of nether-space that covers their flesh and renders them largely immune to things like crossbow bolts or fireballs or what have you – behaves like a portable abyss. A hug from a cosmist is, in effect, a one-way trip to a reality from which you'll never re-emerge. If this sounds like an incredibly dangerous violation of physical laws that risks causing mayhem and destruction on a universal scale, well, you're right.

'We call him "Crap" for short,' Corrigan continued. 'Mostly because "Chaos Reaping" is such a stupid name.'

The cosmist stood a little taller as he faced us – although he didn't have a face *per se*. The face-shaped abyss, however, was pointed in our general direction when he said, 'Corrigan Blight, we have arrived at this place, at this time, to join our strength to yours.'

'You mean you want in on the Blastlands job,' I said, then turned to Corrigan. 'What the fuck is so enticing about this gig, anyway?'

'You don't know?' the floranist asked in a voice rendered distinctly unpleasant to the ears by the bark-like coating that lined the inside of her throat. When she laughed, even her companions looked embarrassed.

The luminist, perhaps excited to find *something* he could do competently, declared, 'Baron Tristmorta, the client, is in possession of' – he paused theatrically here, since that's how they do *everything* – 'the Apparatus!'

I didn't even try to hide my shock and disbelief as I looked up at Corrigan. He gave me a terse nod, along with a faint smirk that said, *'I tried to tell you back at camp, but you were being a prick and acting like you were too good for this job, so now you look like a clueless idiot in front of these even bigger idiots.'*

The Apparatus.

'I see *that's* caught your attention,' the luminist said as he launched into a diatribe about the storied legacy and fearsome capabilities of his quartet of wonderists, periodically forgetting that they were now a trio. I was barely paying attention.

The fucking *Apparatus*.

Scholars of the arcane, steeped in crumbling theological texts and their own convoluted theories of magic, refer to it as 'The Empyrean Physio-Thaumaturgical Device of Attunal Transmutation'. Nobody knows what it looks like, where it comes from or how it works, but if those rarefied accounts passed down through the centuries are true, the Apparatus is the only known instrument in existence that can alter a mage's attunement.

What's that, you say? *'Hardly sounds impressive enough to risk dying for, Cade.'*

Pretend, for a moment, that you're a wonderist trying to make a living, only you're attuned to one of the lame Totemic planes and mostly all you can do is make frogs into your temporary familiars. Try to imagine what it's like to be born with a connection to something as wondrous as magic, only to discover yours is kind of pathetic. It's like there's this hunger inside you that other people don't feel. You're never satisfied, always itching for something you can never have but those around you don't miss.

Or if that doesn't spark your interest, imagine you'd once been attuned to a plane of glorious, wondrous power, only that connection got burned out of you after you'd been cast out and now the only spells you can get have to be purchased from scummy Infernal diabolics at the cost of your own soul. Wouldn't you do just about anything to restore your prior attunement?

Well, get hold of the Empyrian Physio-Thauma— Fuck it; among wonderists we just call it the Apparatus. Anyway, gain possession of this thing and you could give yourself whichever attunement you wanted. It's a one-way ticket to becoming the kind of mage who doesn't have to look over their shoulder every day, or inside the empty chasm of their own soul every night. A miracle in a box, or whatever the Apparatus was contained in. The kind of miracle worth risking everything to acquire. A miracle that might be able to rid Galass of her blood magic and maybe give her an attunement that wouldn't ruin her life and the lives of everyone around her.

The cosmist had taken over from the paunchy luminist and was now addressing Corrigan in equally grandiose terms, only with a deeper voice. 'We came here to form a coven of seven with you, Corrigan Blight, and instead you've murdered one of our own. Your good fortune is that none of us were particularly fond of Elania, but I would choose your next words very ca—'

'Fuck off,' Corrigan said.

It's hard for a figure made up almost entirely of empty space to look confused, but this guy managed it. 'What?'

'I didn't come here to hire any of you amateurs. In fact' – Corrigan gestured to the swarm of rats, who appeared to be waiting patiently for someone to tell them when to renew their attack – 'I'd rather fight alongside any one of these trash-eaters than your entire squad of morons any day of the week. So kindly hit the road before my boy Cade here destroys the lot of you and saves the rats the trouble.'

If you've never heard a cosmist laugh at you, I can tell you it's an unpleasant experience. It's as if an entire universe were chortling at your insignificance. The cosmist spread his arms wide. 'I have borne the assault of a hundred trebuchets, swallowed entire battalions of soldiers. No thunderer's lightning and no blood mage's exsanguination can touch me. So go ahead, Corrigan, let you and your comrades bring forth whatever onslaught you can muster before I—'

'Cade?' Corrigan said, interrupting the cosmist's speech.

'Yeah?'

'Fuck this guy up for me, would you?'

I considered his request for a moment. Not a long moment, mind, just enough to let everyone know I was seriously considering my options. 'Yeah, sure.'

Okay, look, I haven't presented myself or my companions as the most noble exemplars of humanity thus far, but in case you'd somehow missed the point, let me make it clear right up front: we're not indiscriminate murderers. Actually, I guess that's not entirely true, since Corrigan didn't give Elania Scourge the opportunity to surrender – or even let her know we weren't on the same side – before he blasted her from existence. But even that was done for a reason, so let's call it a mitigating factor in our favour, shall we?

Scourge and her little quartet of wonderist arseholes had somehow found out about our job up north, even though Corrigan had picked it up barely an hour after I'd refused Tenebris the first time. I'd assumed he'd brought us here to recruit them, but as he clearly hadn't, that suggested my diabolic agent had been using human shills to pitch this same job to half the wonderists on the continent. But *why*? Since when are the Lords Devilish so interested in some trivial uprising in a part of the world so poisoned from a centuries-old mages' war that almost no one can live there?

Meanwhile, we still had to deal with these three morons who'd apparently decided to muscle in on our gig. That's bad form. That's impolite. That's not how we do things in this business.

Also, it was highly likely that beneath the mound of dirt that had all those rats so riled up was the guy we'd *actually* come to recruit. So, you know, these weren't nice guys we were dealing with here.

Things were now going to play out in an entirely predictable fashion: the remaining trio demanding to join us, knowing we could never trust them and they could never trust us. Corrigan would refuse, of course, so then we'd move on to the threats and entirely wasteful displays of power, until, finally, we start blasting spells at each other, destroying the countryside and probably making it unliveable for the locals. See? Bad manners all around.

But that's not even the worst of it. Corrigan was exhausted from powering our sloop for the past week, Galass hadn't learned to use her magic yet, which meant she was as likely to accidentally exsanguinate us as the other guys, and Mister Bones was just a jackal: a mutt with sharp teeth, and at no point would he be turning into a handsome were-jackal, or whatever the fuck it is you were hoping for. Sorry.

Which left me.

In case you hadn't noticed up until now, my spells tended to be a little slow to cast and frankly, not all that impressive. Any three-on-three fight against a floranist, a cosmist and a . . . okay, so the luminist is probably a waste of space, but you get the point: we'd get our arses handed to us. In fact, the cosmist who was presently standing before us, arms spread wide and waiting to show off how powerful he was, could kill any of us with the merest touch, and since none of Corrigan's thunder could touch him, nor even Galass' blood magic, that meant he was pretty well invulnerable.

Or so he thought.

The cosmist wasn't just a walking void, he was a talking one; he spoke, he laughed, he expressed thoughts and desires, all of which meant he was a conscious being. And a mind is a terribly dangerous thing in the hands of an Infernalist.

That sigil I traced earlier was a weeping arrow. I called on it now, and the black, teardrop-shaped arrowhead not much larger than my thumb appeared in the air before me. I flicked it with my finger and sent it flying towards the cosmist. The weeping arrow doesn't move all that fast – perhaps a touch faster than I could have run the distance on foot. At first the cosmist ignored it, until at the last second he must have understood what was about to happen to him, because he tried to duck. Alas, he'd waited too long. The floranist made an effort to save him by causing the fallen leaves on the ground to swirl up in front of the arrow, but this spell isn't made of matter or normal energy, so it passed right through them. The luminist, meanwhile, decided the safest option was to cower behind his colleagues, which was ironic since any one of his light-shaping illusions would have destroyed the sigil, which was made of shadow.

The weeping arrow isn't an especially impressive incantation. It's just a despair-inducer: it makes you despise yourself. It's good for breaking an enemy's concentration or maybe persuading them to become long-term alcoholics. But if you happen to be someone whose entire body is covered in the vastness of space, you're already constantly reminded of your relative insignificance in the universe. When the weeping arrow struck the cosmist, all those existential anxieties coalesced in a torrent of whimpering self-hatred. He fell to the ground, curled up into a sobbing ball of emptiness – and the pocket universe that had been wrapped around his skin collapsed in on itself.

Hey, it was him or me.

'Okay, now,' Corrigan said, clapping his hands together. 'Anyone else want to play "who's the bloodthirstiest of them all?"' He threw an arm around Galass' shoulder. 'Our blood mage here is a little new at the game, so she could really use the practice, if one of you would care to oblige.'

The floranist and the luminist elected to politely decline the offer, which they communicated by taking off at a fairly athletic pace into the forest and towards a brighter future than the one awaiting them with us. Mister Bones chased them enthusiastically for a few yards, then returned, tail wagging in victory.

'By all that's good and decent in this life,' Galass said, shrugging off Corrigan's arm and turning to me, 'is there nothing of kindness or mercy in your existence?'

'Not usually,' Corrigan replied, tip-toeing past the rats, being careful not to step on any of them. 'But the pay is good.' He stood over the mound of dirt and kicked at it with his foot.

'Was he a friend of yours?' I asked, coming to stand alongside him.

'Hmm?'

I pointed to the mound. 'The dead guy.'

'Oh, he's not dead. He's just buried. Elania and her band of morons were probably just trying to scare him into telling them about the gig so they could bypass us and claim the job for themselves. Even those idiots knew not to kill a guy when torturing him would be more profitable.'

'Don't you think he's been buried rather a long time?' I asked. 'Shouldn't we dig him up?'

'Oh, hell no. I'm not wrecking my nails digging in the dirt.' Corrigan stepped away from the mound and turned to the waiting rodents. 'The enemy's gone. Shouldn't you little bastards be getting to work?'

Just like that, the rats scampered over to the upturned earth and began digging away, kicking up a veritable storm of soil. Mister Bones barked at them angrily, then decided to join in. It was, as exhumations go, a rather festive event.

You're perhaps wondering how Corrigan, a Tempestoral mage with no connection whatsoever to the Totemic demesne, could speak to a bunch of rats. The answer is, of course, that he couldn't; the rats were conveying what their little ears were hearing to the individual whose spell had summoned them in the first place.

Pointing to the rapidly disappearing mound of dirt, I said to Corrigan, 'I can't believe you turned down a thunderer, a floranist, a cosmist and a lumin— Well, the first three, anyway, for one of *them*.'

He grinned, clapping a hand on my shoulder. 'Not just *any*, my friend. The handsomest, most charming of *them* you'll ever have the privilege and pleasure of meeting.'

Soon the rats had carved out the general shape of a person, along with various tiny tunnels underground which I presumed must lead to holes nearby; that explained how a buried man had been able to breathe. The figure pushed up out of the dirt, leaped heroically to his feet and began to brush himself off to reveal a man roughly my own age, a couple of inches shorter and perhaps a trifle slimmer. His long coat was a perfectly even grey, as was the short hair that tickled his collar at the back. His moustache was long and sparse, groomed – once he'd brushed the dirt out of it – to look almost like whiskers. They gave him an oddly debonair appearance, which was complemented by the scabbarded rapier at his side.

'He's beautiful,' Galass breathed.

I wouldn't have gone that far myself, but he was, as Corrigan had promised, handsome, dashing, and with a smile that made you want to follow him anywhere.

I hate rat mages.

CHAPTER 15

The Handsome Rat

The running joke among wonderists regarding practitioners of rat magic is that no one knows whether they're human beings like the rest of us, who happen to be attuned to some Totemic plane ruled by all-powerful rodent gods who grant them magical abilities, or just really big rats who have learned to stand on two legs and dress like dandies while talking about themselves all the time.

'Rat wizardry is, of course, highly misunderstood,' Aradeus informed us as he stood at the front of the sloop. He was apparently unable to speak without one foot on a handy coil of rope and the opposite arm outstretched – all very theatrical, but Galass was entranced. Corrigan and I were doing our best to ignore him.

'How so, Master Mozen?' she asked, sitting on the deck with her back against the mast, staring up at Aradeus while stroking a pair of fat river rats who were making themselves comfortable in her lap. Mister Bones, sulking, took himself off to the back of the sloop, where he periodically lifted his head to snarl at these unexpected competitors for his mistress' affections.

Aradeus took her question as an opportunity to strike yet another devil-may-care pose, placing one fist on his hip, sweeping his rear foot back in a semi-circle and bending at the waist to kiss her hand. 'My dear, please, to you I am merely Aradeus.'

He did it well, I had to admit, if rather too often. I don't know many wonderists who bother with swords, but the swept-hilt rapier with the silver rat's head pommel scabbarded at his side did make for a splendid fashion accessory.

'Hey, Merely Aradeus,' Corrigan called out from the back of the sloop, looking no happier about our current situation than Mister Bones. 'Seeing as how you're hijacking our mission, how about you tell us where the fuck we're going?'

The rat mage turned his gaze to the river ahead of us, right hand shading his eyes as if he were some legendary sea captain leading a dauntless crew to exotic faraway lands. 'Hand steady on the rudder, good Corrigan. Hold fast to the noble heart beating in your breast. We sail now to grand adventure and exalted purpose!'

Okay, first of all, our sloop didn't have a rudder. As I mentioned earlier, it *did* have a sail, but Aradeus, despite living near the world's most famous canal, informed us indignantly, 'Rats may climb masts with consummate skill and swing daringly from ropes, but we never *sail.*'

Second, anyone who uses the words 'good' and 'Corrigan' in the same sentence un-ironically, or who refers to the noble heart beating in his breast, is verifiably demented.

Third . . . well, third was a longer story, but the short version is that Aradeus, who had already demonstrated – repeatedly – his uncanny ability to compose an epic poem on the subject of honour at the drop of a hat, had backed out of the deal he'd made with Corrigan to be our war coven's scout unless we agreed to first join him on a 'brief but gallant errand'.

That our new recruit was blackmailing us into helping him with what would no doubt turn out to be some dangerous and ill-advised grudge against a local princeling didn't bother me nearly so much as the fact that agreeing to do so apparently required listening to him endlessly wax poetic about the nature of rat magic.

'As I was saying, my dear . . .' He turned back to Galass, once again favouring her with a dashing smile that practically glinted off his front teeth, 'ours is a mystical art named not for the physiognomic or any other bodily property of this sublime species, but instead from their superlative moral and cognitive capabilities.'

Yeah, you heard that right: he just claimed that rats are the ethical and intellectual apex species of the animal kingdom.

'The rat,' Aradeus went on, gesturing to the pair rolling around on Galass' lap, 'possesses an unparallelled tactical mind capable of assessing not only the precise nature and magnitude of any threat, but also the most ingenious means of both escape and counter-attack. Thus, a rat mage's foretelling spells – paired with our instincts for daring and the defence of others – often make the difference between glorious victory and ignominious death.'

'Foretelling spells?' Galass asked. 'So your magic is a kind of divination?'

'Astutely intuited, my most sagacious lady, though such scouting spells are only one among our many' – here he felt it necessary to wink at her – 'abilities.'

'I hear the other is eating their own young,' Corrigan shouted from the back.

I thought it was pretty funny, but Aradeus ignored him and Galass was far too caught up in the performance to have even noticed. She scratched behind the ears of one of the rats, prompting a fresh outburst of growling from Mister Bones, who now set to pacing angrily around the boat.

'It's so fascinating,' she said. 'Something people see as dirty and evil can actually be ... virtuous.'

Aradeus knelt down and flashed that charming smile of his again. The long fingers gloved in butter-soft grey leather lifted one of her scarlet tresses. 'My dear, there is not one of us whose nature refutes the potential for goodness. None whom the world can deny the chance for redemption, and not a single one of us unworthy of love.'

Well, fuck me. That, right there – did you see it? The moment when he looked at Galass without a trace of lust or insidious desire? There wasn't an ounce of mockery or self-serving flattery in his tone. Aradeus just saw a heartsick girl. Her fear that she'd become something vile – a creature no better than a rodent herself – was evident in her every word and glance, in the way her shoulders hunched and the trembling of her fingers as she stroked the rats. And it was Aradeus, sincerity cutting through all the nonsense of his foppish clothes and pompous mannerisms, who had given Galass something I wouldn't have thought possible: hope. Hope that becoming a blood mage might be something more than a steady slide into misery and madness. Hope that even if she couldn't yet find it herself, inside, her essential dignity and humanity remained. Hope that her future might be better than her past – and all that with a few words and a kindness born not of self-interest but of something I hadn't seen in a long, long time.

'Ask him how "virtuous" his plague spells are!' Corrigan bellowed from the back. Having none of his own, he was never particularly fond of charm in others.

Me? I just stared at Aradeus Mozen in awe and prayed to whatever deities might take pity on a wretched wonderist like me that he was for real. If that idiot baron up north truly possessed the Apparatus and I could free Galass from her attunement to blood magic and give her something less dire, maybe Aradeus could take her on as an apprentice afterwards, help her see the world in ways I couldn't. Assuming any of us survived that long, of course.

I stepped to the front of the sloop and asked, 'If rats are all so righteous and noble, Aradeus, then surely you won't withhold the nature of our mission from your comrades?'

He smiled at me as if we were old friends, brothers-in-arms, veterans of countless bard-worthy campaigns together. He put a gloved hand on my shoulder and pointed into the distance where

I could just make out the masts of a barge almost as big as a war galleon. 'See you those lascivious red and gold sails, brother Cade? Upon that Infernal vessel, a damsel suffers indignities that would shrivel the souls of demons. She is a princess, or as good a one as can be, if that word holds any meaning beyond petty privilege. The one who holds her captive is a dragon, though without wings or scales or fangs.' He chuckled. 'Though you'd swear the vile beast's breath could wither fortress walls.'

I peered ahead. Our little sloop was travelling far faster under Corrigan's spells than the barge, and now I could make out the gold-trimmed hull and the unusual design of a crown above a bed decorating its sails.

'Is that what I think it is?' I asked Corrigan.

He nodded, his scowl making it clear he'd had no more idea of what Aradeus was intending than I'd had, and that he was even less happy about what was about to happen.

Red sails are the mark of what are politely referred to as 'respite vessels', but which are more commonly known as whoreships. The gold trim and crown above the insignia indicated royalty, which meant this particular pleasure vessel belonged to a prince, and that his clientele would be some of the most powerful nobles in the region – the kind of people you really don't want for enemies.

Corrigan had started swearing to himself. Galass had risen and was staring at the ostentatious ship coming ever closer into view.

Aradeus shook his fist in the air, almost as if doing so would propel our sloop even faster. 'To battle, comrades – in victory or in death do we inscribe our names upon the pages of history!'

Did I mention it's common wisdom among wonderists that one should never get embroiled in the schemes of rat mages?

CHAPTER 16

Beneath Red Sails

Floating brothels are tremendously profitable enterprises. There's the obvious reason, of course: selling someone else's body for a night almost always earns you more coin than it costs to keep them fed and clothed. This is especially true when the clothes are optional. But regular brothels have to deal with the vagaries of the marketplace. For example, let's say *your* bordello starts earning a little too much money. Business is booming and everyone for a hundred miles takes notice. One of three things will happen: a competitor will build their own whorehouse next door and undercut your prices, a local gang will start offering 'protective services' whose primary feature is protecting you from *them*, or someone of high moral purpose will come along and burn your building down – usually with you and your employees inside.

Or what if your town has a few too many bad harvests and no one can afford your services? Or war breaks out in your region and armies run roughshod through the territory? Contrary to what some gullible fools might think, soldiers do not make good customers. They rarely get paid on time, and when their commanders fail to deliver their wages, an easy way to keep them happy is to simply let them have their way with the local prostitutes without paying a cent.

A floating brothel, on the other hand, can travel to wherever the money flows best. Too much local competition? Head on down the river. Local thugs want protection money? Set sail for more welcoming waters. As an added bonus, you can keep your prices high because patrons don't have time to get bored with your employees. Even better? The atmosphere of luxury and adventure aboard a beautiful red-sailed ship makes recruiting comely young men and women to your enterprise as easy as waving them aboard before you leave the dock the next morning.

Pirates won't attack pleasure barges because *other* pirates would retaliate for ruining the only fun available on the high seas. Naval commanders don't attack them because all it takes is for the proprietor to offer the crew a free ride to set off a mutiny that ends with our noble captain hanging from a yardarm – while his sailors toast his health as they enthusiastically sample the pleasures of clean, lovely young men and women his prudishness won them for free.

Seriously, if you're ever in possession of a small fortune, invest in a floating bordello. It's a growth industry.

'Can't believe a fucking prince would own a whoreship,' Corrigan complained, tugging at the collar of his long purple velvet coat, then stroking the satin sleeves inlaid with black bolts of lightning. He'd paid a small fortune for the coat, but whenever he wore it, I thought he looked like a homicidal carnival barker.

My own long blue and silver brocaded coat was more subtle and, in my opinion, more elegant. I'd likely paid three times as much as Corrigan had for his, but that was during better days, when I was still fooling myself that this might be a noble profession, one for which I'd want to look my best when performing heroic deeds. One always wants to dress appropriately for one's portraits, after all.

The more practical reality was that while wonderists typically wear some form of protective leather armour to avoid the embarrassment of getting knifed in the back before we get a spell off, the nature of this business is such that our clients – like those of high-end prostitutes aboard floating brothels – tend to be obscenely wealthy and prefer us to dress magnificently in their presence.

'Damn, but I forgot how much these things itch,' Corrigan groaned, tugging at the back of his striped velvet pantaloons. 'I did wonder why you showed up at our rendezvous dressed like a fop, Aradeus,' he complained to the rat mage. 'This was your plan all along, wasn't it?'

Normally a quartet of wonderists wandering about without the benefit of a patron's army at their backs would dress inconspicuously, to avoid encouraging some local thug or two to make their bones by attempting to kill a war mage. In this instance, however, the only way we were going to be allowed on board a prince's brothel would be by making an impression. And trust me, when you see a thunderer, an Infernalist, a rat mage and a woman in a sublime's silver-white gown with blood-red hair, you are certainly going to leave an impression.

'Silords, you honour us with your presence,' the major domo said, waving an arm as if to point out the assortment of beautiful men and women brought out for our appraisal, currently bathed in dancing coloured lights from the bejewelled lanterns swinging from the massive barge's gleaming masts. Moans of pleasure were seeping up from the floors below, punctuated by a great deal of creaking. 'The Serenity Divine welcomes you.'

'Stupid name,' Corrigan grumbled.

Aradeus shot him a look, but the tall, slender and exquisitely dressed major domo only laughed lightly before walking over and bowing as deeply as he might to any prince. 'The reputation of the great Corrigan Blight precedes him.'

'Does my reputation mention anything about what I like to do with fawning sycophants?'

The major domo chuckled as if the two were old acquaintances sharing a joke, then gave me an apologetic look. 'Forgive me, Silord, that unlearned as I am, I must ask your name?'

'Cade Ombra,' Aradeus said, as though the name should inspire awe, or at least mild panic. 'The Wonderist Supreme: Mage Sovereign of a thousand campaigns, Slayer of Seven Devilish, Keeper of the Lore of the Asters. I present to you the man, the hero, the legend.'

I was literally none of those things, and I was pretty sure he'd invented every single one of those titles on the spot. The major domo, however, made a show of being tremendously impressed, as with a subtle twitch of his fingers, he induced a cadre of beautiful male, female and less conventionally gendered prostitutes to make appreciative *oohs* and *ahhs*, their lashes fluttering and their fingers drifting to their nether regions as if my mere presence had induced them all to mass orgasm.

The major domo turned to Aradeus with significantly less enthusiasm. 'Silord Mozen, I was under the impression you did not approve of our presence in these waters.'

'Really?' the rat mage asked, his neatly trimmed eyebrows rising. 'Whatever gave you that impression, Major Domo?'

The slender man gestured to the rapier at Aradeus' side. 'I believe it was when you challenged Prince Stercus to a duel.'

'A duel which the prince refused.'

'As was his privilege.'

'Yes, but you see, I had been told he was a fencer of surpassing skill. You can imagine my disappointment.'

The major domo spread his long-fingered hands wide as the youthful prostitutes in their beautifully made see-through garments shifted from one seductive pose to the next, just for our benefit. 'Only you, Silord Mozen, could stand upon this deck and speak of disappointment.'

'He makes a convincing argument,' Corrigan whispered to me. He'd already caught the eye of one fetching lass, a grown woman with wide hips and full bosom who was matching him leer for leer.

Is it perverse to say I loved Corrigan Blight for the fact that among this display of barely developed nubile flesh, among whose number Galass would have been considered mature, the big brute had eyes only for the eldest and most confident woman? Monsters, it seems to me, come in all degrees, and however hypocritical it was of me, I took consolation in the fact that the man whose dubious friendship was the last thing of value I possessed was far from the worst of them.

Aradeus spread his hands in surrender. 'I will concede that the pleasures of the flesh are sometimes on a par with those of testing one's skill against a self-styled master of the sword. Further, mages of my speciality are known above all else for our practicality, and this veil of tears in which we live grants the powerful the means to escape the judgement of their betters.'

'Why, Silord Mozen,' the major domo said, 'I do believe that is as near an apology as has ever escaped your notoriously scathing tongue.'

Aradeus bowed. 'It is certainly as close to an apology as the prince will receive from me, Major Domo.'

The man gestured once again to the preening young courtesans, several of whom had accidentally slipped out of their garments. 'And in recognition of such courtesy on your part, the prince has instructed me to offer you and your company the pleasures of our hospitality within our ruby cabins below.'

I guessed that ruby was probably a good thing, although for all I knew, he'd just informed us we'd be doing our rutting in the toilets.

Unbidden, but clearly not unwanted, the voluptuous woman who'd been trading looks with Corrigan came to his side.

Several of her colleagues looked to me, but I shook my head. 'Not for me tonight,' I said, and turned to the major domo. 'I don't suppose you have a library on board?'

'We keep a small collection of books,' he said, disapproval evident in the pursing of his lips. 'Erotic love poetry, mostly.'

'That'll do.'

Aradeus, already arm in arm with a young couple who surely had to be brother and sister, shot me a look that said my taciturn demeanour risked raising suspicion about our purpose here. I shot him a look that told him he could fuck right off if it bothered him. There were far too many lines in my life I'd had to cross lately. I planned to hold to those few I still had some say over.

'And for the lady?' the major domo asked Galass.

'She also prefers to read on deck,' I started. Speaking for another is rarely good form, but given her previous status as a monastic pleasure slave in the Ascendant's collection, I knew she'd never—

'I'll take that one,' she said, pointing to a young woman of seventeen or so, close to her own age.

'You don't have to—'

'That one,' she repeated, and her glare at me made it clear it wasn't the major domo's offer that had affronted her. 'I've only ever known what it is to be another's plaything,' she said. 'Who are you to tell me I can't, for once in my life, experience what it is like to hold that power myself?'

Her words shook me, not because they offended my sensibilities, but because they took me back to another night on a different boat some years ago, and the warning given to me by a woman I'd admired beyond all others just before she'd torn the gold cloak from my shoulders and expelled me from the only life I'd ever hoped to lead. *'You don't understand the ways of ordinary people, Cade. If you did, you'd despise them, and with your despite would come a reckoning I cannot allow.'*

The girl Galass had selected drifted over to her and started stroking the line of her collarbone. 'I am yours,' she said.

'You are mine,' Galass agreed, somewhat more tentatively.

'Then it appears I may turn my attention to my other guests,' the major domo said, indicating the deck below. 'Your companions will take you to your rooms, and I will have someone bring up books for Silord Ombra's more . . . *private* pleasures.'

Yeah, you heard that right; he just implied I was planning to masturbate on deck to a book of erotic love poems.

'Oh, and before I forget,' the major domo said, as if he hadn't been planning on ending with this all along, 'you need have no fears whatsoever for your security aboard our vessel. We happen to have a number of special guests aboard this voyage who, like yourselves, are heading north in pursuit of riches. They have offered to provide additional security for the prince's vessel during their time on board. Should anyone attempt to interrupt your evening – or that of any of our guests – they will quickly meet with the displeasure of our stewards.'

As if on cue, the remaining prostitutes instantly cleared the decks, giving way to a group of nine men and women whose faces I didn't recognise but whose professions were obvious from the raw heat of the magic emanating from them.

'Nine wonderists?' Corrigan whispered to me. 'Who the fuck can afford *nine* wonderists to guard a whoreship?'

A prince, apparently.

How many other wonderists are chasing after this same job in the Blastlands? I wondered.

But it wasn't the competition or their superior numbers that was sending a chill down my spine. Seven of them were dressed much as we were: tailored silks, satins and velvets with subtle runes and sigils embroidered in rich metalic threads on collars and cuffs; ruffled ascots and colourful cravats for both men and women; and a few bejewelled silver or gold arm rings too, like the ones Corrigan wore to make it clear he didn't work cheap. But I was studying the two wonderists who were ever-so-slightly less ostentatiously dressed than their comrades. Their hair, tidily trimmed but unstyled, was a distinctly unimpressive brown – and almost certainly dyed that colour. They sported no braids nor ribbons, no jewels, no make-up of any kind. It was almost as if they weren't entirely comfortable being among such lecherous company, but some greater duty demanded it.

I jabbed Corrigan with my elbow while the major domo was rattling off the almost certainly invented names of the prince's nine protectors. 'Those two,' I whispered.

'The frumpy twins? What about them?'

'Glorian Justiciars. Both of them.'

Corrigan frowned. 'How can you be sure? They look—'

'They look like how justiciars look when they're trying not to look like justiciars.'

'You think they're here for you?'

'Can't be. The way the other wonderists are acting around them, it's too casual, almost companionable. They have to have been on this boat long enough to allay suspicions about their motives for being here, which means they'd have had no way of knowing I was coming this way.'

The typical motive for a Glorian Justiciar to board a pleasure barge, in case you haven't figured this out yet, is to set fire to it in the name of the Auroral Sovereign.

'Then what are they doing here?' Corrigan asked.

I said nothing, having no insight to offer except that nothing pisses off a Glorian Justiciar more than having to stand voluntarily in the vicinity of a bunch of mercenary wonderists – unless, of course, they have their boot heels pressed on said mercenaries' throats.

I peered across the deck at the two justiciars, disguised in as much frippery as their Aurorally infused consciences could tolerate. *Why would the Lords Celestine tolerate you working for a secular prince, esteemed brother and sister, and more importantly, what are you doing for him?*

This wasn't the first time in the past year I'd found Glorians behaving strangely. Hell, backing a warmonger like Ascendant Lucien against his more pacifist neighbours had been a poor choice, spiritually speaking. Come to think of it, why *hadn't* a full court of Glorian Justiciars come hunting me now that Lucien was no longer granting me clemency?

I noticed Galass and Aradeus were leaving the deck with their chosen companions, while our scrutiny was beginning to draw the wonderists' stares. Corrigan gave the curvaceous woman on his arm a playful pinch on the buttocks before he leaned over to me. 'Should have picked a girl, Cade. At least you could have got laid one last time before the bloodshed starts.'

Even Aradeus looked stricken as he allowed the siblings to lead him down the stairs. Apparently this simple rescue wasn't going to be quite as simple as planned after all.

CHAPTER 17

Love Poems

Typically when a wonderist wants something, events play out as follows:

Knock, knock.

'Who's there?' enquires the imposingly armoured captain of the guards at the front gate of whatever castle, fortress or Stygian Hellgate happens to contain the item the wonderists want.

'Mages of surpassing power,' replies the wonderist. 'You have something we want. Kindly hand it over.'

The captain turns to his fellow guards, grins knowingly and motions for any other interested parties nearby to come and join in the anticipated fun of beating up the fool who dared make demands of them into an early grave. There's a lot of laughing, soldiers making a show of gripping the hilts of their weapons, and jokes at the wonderist's expense. The pleasantries eventually come to an end with the captain giving the order to arrest the would-be offender and drag him off to the dungeon in preparation for extensive interrogation, followed by his eventual and inevitable execution.

After that? Explosion, bigger explosion. Lightning. Fire. Rivers of blood. Walls that have stood a thousand years tumbling down. Screams. Prayers. Heads flying off in all directions, until said wonderist is free to saunter into the largely depopulated fortress, secure whatever they came for, and leave with a polite nod to the decapitated corpse of the captain of the guards.

The end.

Here's what *never* happens:

'Hey, the four of us are professional war mages and you have something we want.'

'Really? We have nine of our own. Perhaps you should all fight over it, right here among this civilian population, and see where that leads.'

'Good thinking! Let's begin . . .'

The brutal, unmitigated destruction that comes from wonderists fighting each other outside of a duly declared war – and thus taking place in a location where violence and mayhem are to be expected – tends towards such cataclysmic consequences that every time it's happened in the last five hundred years, that conflict has been followed by the nations of the continent agreeing that a good old-fashioned purge is in order. Purges of this sort are performed with such enthusiasm by the Glorians that I once read an account – a *first-hand* account – that insisted one of the justiciars was seen – briefly – to smile.

Seriously. A Glorian Justiciar *smiled*.

Nobody wants that kind of heat. Wonderists avoid public confrontations with each other at all costs, and if any do break that unwritten rule, others tend to come down so hard on the offenders that nobody feels any particular need for a purge.

Okay, so, Aradeus' righteous rescue mission was cancelled, right? We came, we saw, we ran away.

Except . . .

Aradeus hadn't given the signal to call things off. Corrigan was below, engaging in what sounded like the sexual adventure of a lifetime, and Galass was . . . doing whatever a former sublime does when she's finally the one doing the subjugating. That left me sitting on the largely empty top deck of what I suspected might be the world's most expensive brothel ship, reading an unpleasantly well-worn book of erotic poetry and thinking about the fact that we were entirely fucked.

Well, that's not entirely true: I was also trying to figure out which part of the genitals was represented by the vegetables referenced in one particular poem. I'll spare you the poem, but it was the aubergine that was really confusing me.

Squeak, squeak?

No, that wasn't a reference to the aubergine. A rat at my foot was enquiring about my position on allowing rodents to bite me.

'This again?' I asked.

The rodent appeared to be confused by the question. It squeaked again.

'Oh, for the love of all things Infernal,' I swore, rolling up the cuff of my jacket and exposing my wrist to the rat. 'Fine, but if you try anything funny I'm tossing you over the side.'

The rat gave a somewhat aggrieved twitch of its tail, scampered up my leg and settled on my forearm, from where it proceeded to give an unnecessarily vicious bite to my wrist.

'Cade?' the rat asked with Aradeus Mozen's voice. 'Are you alone?'

I glanced around the deck and saw no one, then closed my eyes and looked again. This time I could see a feminine silhouette sitting cross-legged about twelve feet away. One of the prince's wonderists – not a justiciar, thankfully – was hiding in a patch of Infernal gloom. It's a simple but useful spell that draws shadows from the Infernal demesne. They are impenetrable to human eyes, unless those eyes happen to gaze into that particular realm with regrettable frequency. I pretended not to see her and whispered an old meditational quieting spell I know. It's so subtle you'd have to be watching for it to notice someone casting it on you, since its only purpose is to aid in focusing the mind towards the spiritual and away from the mundane. For the next few minutes, at least, my watcher would be too embroiled in peacefully questioning her own moral peril to notice me talking to a rat.

'Is there literally no other way any of you people know to handle distance conversations?' I asked.

The rat shrugged, although I couldn't tell if that was Aradeus telling me that was just how things are, or the rat saying, 'Hey, you should try being me, buddy.'

'The major domo is having me watched,' Aradeus said. 'Two wonderists are stationed outside my cabin: a lock mage and a felinist.'

I paused to appreciate the cosmic symmetry of our host using a cat mage to watch over a rat mage.

'What about the two prostitutes with you?' I asked.

'I cast a mesmerism on them,' Aradeus replied. The rat on my arm turned its head and shuddered slightly. 'Not sure one was required. They were far more concerned with pleasuring each other than me.'

Having a rodent sitting on your forearm looking offended that a pair of hookers were too busy having sex with each other to pay attention to Aradeus made me almost lose my grip on the spell keeping this conversation from being overheard.

'Regardless,' Aradeus went on, 'my reputation has rendered me too great a risk to go about the barge unwatched. The greater share of our noble quest passes to you, Brother Cade.'

In other words: I got to do the hard part that usually involves getting caught and then beheaded. Somehow I'd known this was going to be the gist of this conversation.

I sighed. 'What do I have to do?'

The rat on my forearm gave me a tiny salute that was in no way inspiring. 'Find a way to the bottom deck near the stern – that's the back. That's where they're keeping her.'

'Keeping who? You've been awfully tight-lipped about this whole operation, Aradeus.'

'Just . . . can I beg your trust in this matter, Cade? On my honour, she is worth the risk, and her plight one that men of valour such as ourselves cannot possibly allow to continue.'

The rat was giving me the rodent equivalent of soul-searching eyes. It was surprisingly effective.

'Fine, but just so you know, Corrigan and I have a deal about murdering the person responsible for either of us getting killed for something really stupid like trying to rescue a rat mage's childhood sweetheart off a damned floating brothel with nine wonderists lurking about.'

The rat nodded. 'Understood. Now, can you find some way to convince the major domo to let you down to the cabin levels?'

'Not if we're trying to keep him from being suspicious. At this point, we'd need divine providence or—'

At that very moment, a man's scream pierced the wooden deck beneath my feet, shaking the very hull of the massive barge. When I looked down, I saw blood oozing up through the surface of the deck.

'Actually,' I said to Aradeus' rat as I took off for the stairs leading below, 'I think I may have just the thing.'

CHAPTER 18

The Price and the Prize

I once heard it said – from an exceedingly reliable source on the subject – that the root of humanity's downfall was not evil, lust, greed or any of the usual sins, but simply hubris: that unique mixture of arrogance, conceit and a distinct lack of foresight of which only human beings are truly capable. Indeed, some have developed it into a fine art.

For example, it was hubristic of Aradeus to think we could casually sneak onto a prince's floating brothel to rescue (or kidnap, for all I knew) whoever it was being kept in the most secret cabin as far below decks as possible. It was hubristic of that same prince to believe his own pet wonderists would keep him safe from war mages like Corrigan and me, or that he could get away with flouting his greatness for all his other noble guests by not just allowing us aboard his magnificent pleasure barge, but actually insisting that we sample his equally magnificent wares.

Corrigan's hubris was his conviction that whatever trouble came our way, he could use brute force to get out of it.

But it was Galass, in her need to – just for one little moment, for one fractured fragment of an existence defined by the desires of others – feel what it was like for her own desires to take charge, who'd shown an entirely different kind of hubris: the kind which had produced the first of many casualties to follow.

As for *my* particular hubris? I've never had a hubristic moment in my life.

'The prince will be displeased,' the major domo said, his voice quavering. His impeccably manicured nails scratched at the back of his hand, although he seemed unconscious of the gesture, for all he was starting to dig tracks into his own skin.

'Who's the victim?' I asked, standing face to face with the body, which was still upright, stiff as a statue against the oak wall of the hallway between cabins, the skin so pale it might have been sculpted from alabaster.

I'd seen plenty of corpses in my time, but never one so perfectly exsanguinated. Every last drop of blood had fled the portly man's flesh and was now defying gravity, spreading out along the low ceiling in search of the gaps between the boards to make their escape.

'Radiance Vejan,' the major domo answered, shaking his head back and forth like a frightened dog wagging his tail in the hope of soothing his master's ire.

The situation wasn't entirely dire, then, for he was a relatively minor noble in these parts, somewhere between a baron and a lesser count. Through the gilded wooden frame of the open doorway of the cabin Galass had been provided, I saw her holding the crying, shivering girl she'd selected, shielding her from the horrific sight of his Radiance's remains – and possibly also from the fact that Galass' scarlet hair was still floating about her head, each lock like a snake poised to strike.

A crowd was forming in the narrow passage between the cabins, staring and muttering and doing the things crowds generally do at times like these. Several middle-aged men and women – adorned in jewels so fine they almost, *almost,* made up for the lack of clothing concealing sagging flesh or the ugliness of their expressions – were demanding to know why the murderess was still living. I counted four of the prince's wonderists among them, no doubt as anxious as I was about what would happen once somebody commanded them to act. I gave the most eager among them a quick look, just to assure him that any conflict between his crew and mine would end with plenty of dead bodies to go around.

'This situation is . . . untenable,' the major domo said, looking at me as if we'd suddenly become lifelong confidants and he figured he could call in the marker on that friendship for me to take care of this mess for him.

I felt like telling him my life story then and there, just so he'd know how very wrong he was.

It took three breaths to take stock of the scene, three more to work out the sequence of events that had led to the radiance's death. Modesty aside, I'm pretty good at it; this used to be my vocation, after all, and some skills stick with you no matter how long you ignore them – kind of like infected scabs.

'The door was left unlocked,' I said, walking over to feel at the latch.

'We always secure the doors for our clients' privacy,' insisted the major domo. 'Discretion is—'

I stepped into the room and pointed to the crying girl.

'Leave her alone,' Galass warned before I could speak, the tips of her floating red tresses darting far too close to my eyes for comfort.

Unfortunately for both of us, I couldn't allow her tendency to think the worst of me to interfere in my handling of the situation, so I gave her *the glare*. I don't mean some dirty look or disapproving side-eye here, but *the glare* I'd learned back in my old job. The one that sometimes comes unbidden when a particular combination of stupidity and injustice conspires to piss me off.

'Don't threaten me, girl,' I warned, employing a calm, effortless grace that made me want to punch myself in the face. 'This is your fault as much as anyone's.' I took the young prostitute by the shoulders and spun her around. 'Sometimes Radiance Vejan liked to watch.' I made sure it wasn't a question.

The girl froze. I shifted my gaze from one which induces hesitancy to one which makes silence distinctly uncomfortable.

'I . . . He sometimes . . .' She glanced over at the body pressed up against the wall outside and started crying again.

It would have been easy to dismiss her reaction as a kind of relief over being rid of him, or terror at what might now happen to her. Had my old mentor been here, she would have tapped me on the shoulder and said, *'You see that, Cade? I'll bet you think those tears are coming from dread or humiliation, don't you?'*

'What else, Master?' I would have asked right back. *'The radiance forced her to do his bidding, to satisfy his own perverse desires. What else could she do but accede to his demands? She has been released from those demands, yet she still fears the consequences to her own life.'*

The old fiend would have shaken her head at me, disappointed as always. *'You can't do this job if you see others only as better or worse versions of yourself. Human beings are complicated. Nuanced.'*

I hated when she talked to me like I was a child. *'I know the world isn't black and white. I can see shades of grey as well as you or anyone else.'*

That's when she would have slapped the back of my head. *'Colours, boy: it's the infinite colours, all those wondrous variations of our humanity, that defy our judgement, that challenge the very idea of the law. Those colours will overwhelm your senses, Cade, if you can't come to grips with them.'*

Would she be pleased with me now? Standing amidst all those people, with their manyfold lusts for sex and violence and pain all intertwined like snakes in a pit, I wondered – would she pat me on the shoulder and nod to me, as if I'd finally proven myself to her now that I could see the fondness – perhaps even the love – the girl felt for the overstuffed dead pervert? In her gaze I had discerned that there had been no abuse between them, only a game that in its own strange way had freed them both from their respective lots in life.

'She unlatched the door for the radiance,' I informed the major domo. 'It was . . .' *No point in the whole truth. He's dead and she's the only one who can suffer now.* 'It was something he expected of her – innocent enough in its way, but when he saw my colleague' – I gestured to Galass, still garbed in the simple silver-white gown worn not only by sublimes, but by recently purchased slaves – 'he mistook her for another of your prince's employees.'

The major domo's look of dismay was almost enough to make me pity him. Almost, but not quite. 'He attempted to force himself on her?'

The easy thing to do would be to say yes, as that would get Galass off the hook completely. But lies, like hubris, are seeds that sprout into weeds whose roots grow in unpredictable ways. 'Likely he merely assumed she would be willing – eager, even, for his patronage. But when he touched her . . . Major Domo, my colleague is new to her abilities. In the throes of passion, instinct would have caused her spells to ignite, without her intention, to the perceived threat. What happened next was . . .'

I reached for a word I could live with – or at least one my old mentor would have tolerated. But what? That this was all an unfortunate *accident*? Ill-fortuned *fate*?

'Tragic hubris,' I said at last.

Relief erupted from the major domo as if I'd just rescued him from falling into a volcano. *'Tragic hubris,'* he repeated, trying on the phrase for size. 'His Radiance, that unfortunate, darling man, was always so beloved of our staff. He mistook your colleague for one of ours, and she, of course, not knowing . . . and really no one is to blame but unhappy destiny.'

Clearly no one had ever taught him the full meaning of the word 'hubris'.

The usual nonsense followed after that: mumbling, questions, assurances from the major domo, promises of free evenings and 'special offers'. The various nobles and their companions left, maybe not quite as satisfied by my explanation as they would

139

have been by further bloodshed, but close enough given they were getting cold standing out in the narrow hallway with little in the way of clothing.

My attention, however, was focused on the other wonderists.

Corrigan gave me a wink as if he'd known all along I'd work things out so that he could get back to bedding his charming new friend. Galass closed the door to her cabin with the girl already in her arms, shooting me a look that dared me to express disapproval of her actions. And Aradeus gave a subtle gesture towards the prince's wonderists, who had apparently decided the occasion didn't call for their intervention, then to the major domo.

Apparently the mission was still on.

'Major Domo,' I said, before the man could slink off to his other duties.

'Yes, Silord Ombra?'

I gave him a sheepish grin. 'I find myself . . . tense . . . from these events. I wonder if I might impose on your generosity.'

He smiled with relief; it was a shame it would soon disappear from his features. 'Why, of course. There are still several lads and lasses available for your—'

'Alas, my personal tastes are highly specific. Some might say . . . *singular*.'

All brothels have that one special girl or boy – the one meant only for the most venerated of guests, those whose rank or wealth is such that not only must they be pleased at all costs, but they expect something precious that will be denied to all others.

The major domo paled, apparently having a much clearer picture of what I was asking for than I had. '*She* is only for the prince.'

I didn't know who '*she*' was, but I've had two professions in my life and both have taught me something of the ways of powerful men. I didn't even bother contradicting the major domo. All it took was arching an eyebrow.

'Well,' he muttered. 'Sometimes his *most* honoured guests are permitted to . . . sample her wares.'

I kept the curl from my lip, forced down the bile and conjured up a smile. 'Surely he wouldn't mind – under these circumstances?' I leaned closer and whispered, 'I can make her forget.'

The major domo tried to look offended, but relief was written in every grateful wrinkle on his forehead. 'I could never condone such a thing.' It was his turn to lean closer. 'But for perhaps an hour, discreetly passed, soon forgotten . . .'

We shook hands, our craven bargain struck. He handed me a key which tingled even as it touched my hand, vibrating so much I had to close my fingers over it for fear it would fly away. That and a gesture sent me through the passage and down a set of very narrow stairs to the bottom-most deck of the vessel. A single red door waited for me. A keyhole was set beneath an ornately carved silver knob shaped like a hand extended in greeting. I could feel the thrumming in the key in my palm as if it longed to open the lock for me. The problem was, I didn't think the key could do much about the two Glorian Justiciars standing in front of that door.

They were both smiling at me.

CHAPTER 19

I Hate Reunions

The most discomforting thing about Glorian Justiciars is the way they look at you. Magic aside – and they have plenty – there's nothing quite so horrifying as staring into the eyes of someone who is absolutely, incontrovertibly convinced of their own righteousness. The silencing glare I'd used on Galass upstairs and the interrogatory gaze to which I had subjected the young prostitute were nothing compared to the sheer spiritual *anguish* that comes from staring into the eyes of true justiciars in the performance of their duties. It's like ... discovering there really is an Auroral Sovereign, that he is all-powerful, and that he loves every living creature.

Except you.

Should you ever have the misfortune of crossing paths with a pair of Glorian Justiciars when your soul is not in perfect harmony with the teachings of the Lords Celestine, I advise you look away, even if the justiciars in question are about to chop your head off with their swords. Trust me, it'll be easier that way.

'Esteemed brethren,' I said, locking eyes with the two of them.

'Renegade,' Dignity said, his deep baritone so pure it was all I could do not to drop to my knees, kiss his hand and beg his forgiveness.

'Apostate,' Fidelity corrected. She always had been a stickler for linguistic precision.

You might be wondering how I knew their names, and if I did, why I hadn't recognised them when they first appeared on the deck. The first is simple: at any time there are only one hundred and twenty-one Glorian Justiciars. That's enough for eleven courts, which is all the Auroral rulers deem necessary to enact their laws upon the Mortal realm. Personally, I always figured it was because the Lords Celestine insist on naming their representatives after moral virtues and they'd got bored after coming up with eleven times eleven of them.

In case you're wondering, my name was—

Well, let's not worry about that.

Anyway, I hadn't recognised Dignity and Fidelity right away because of the muddy brown dye jobs and the fact that they'd been hanging back behind the prince's other wonderists. Also, I'd never been on a court with them, and honestly, it gets hard to tell apart a bunch of people who all have square jaws, piercing eyes and magnificent cheekbones. The Lords Celestine grant their servants many gifts, and they aren't so blind to political concerns that they haven't figured out over the millennia that really good-looking people are perceived as holier than the rest of us.

No kidding: the day I was exiled, my skin lost its lustre and my nose was no longer straight. Mostly that was from the beatings they'd given me on the way out, but still . . .

'You have sunk deeper than we believed possible, fallen one,' Dignity said. He was my height, which wasn't particularly tall for a justiciar, but I always noticed his hands: they were just a little too big for him, like those statues where the sculptor gets a little drunk towards the end and stops paying full attention to his work. I'm pretty sure he was the one who'd broken my nose.

'Not all of us,' Fidelity said. The fingers of her right hand were twitching like she desperately wanted to put on her golden Celestine glove and dish out a little spiritual punishment. 'Some of us knew all along he was a traitor.'

In stature, Fidelity was even less daunting than Dignity, but she made up for it with an outsized sense of self-importance, which, for a justiciar, is hard to imagine.

'It's true,' I admitted, opening my coat and unbuttoning the top of my shirt so they could see the circles of ebony sigils across my chest. 'I'm a vile, treasonous outcast who betrayed every single one of our teachings. I wage war for money, consort with diabolics for my spells and have been known to pleasure myself on holy days.' I leaned in close enough to make it positively painful for them to not rip my throat out and whispered, 'But at least I'm not a fucking glorified bouncer working some petty princeling's whoreship.'

Dignity blanched, his jaw so tight I thought he might actually shatter his own teeth. Fidelity tried to put the stare on me, but I resisted; it's hard to make someone feel morally unworthy when they've done the kinds of shit I've done.

'Oh,' she said, shaking her head without ever taking her eyes off me, 'when at last we purify you, Cade Ombra, it will make the Infernals themselves weep at your torment.'

Now it was my turn to smile. Up until now I'd figured there was a fifty-fifty chance I was about to meet my maker, a fate I had to admit I really wasn't looking forward to. But the thing about Glorians is that once given a mission, they cannot deviate from it, not for any reason. Mind you, this doesn't stop them from smiting the odd heathen along the way, because justiciars are given wide latitude to pursue and prosecute spiritual crimes against their bosses, the Celestines. In case you're wondering, apostasy – my crime – is right near the top of that list.

But while your average justiciar is happy to spend his or her free time hunting apostates with the rampant, single-minded enthusiasm of a dog chasing a squirrel, the Lords Celestine are more obsessed with the bigger picture, which in their case is moving step by step towards the day when they can at last face the Lords Devilish in battle and destroy their eternal enemies once and for all.

Fidelity's use of the phrase *when at last we purify you* told me that her current orders didn't allow for distractions, even getting into a scrap with a renegade like me. Judging by the angry glance at Dignity, she must have caught the relief in my expression. In the back of my head I heard the subtle whisper of the silent voice passing between them. There was a time when I would have been able to make out every word, but even bereft of the sacred tongue, I was pretty sure the conversation went something like:

'Can we please rip this guy's intestines out through his nostrils now?'

'Alas, nay, our mission demands we—'

'C'mon! This is Cade-fucking-Ombra we're talking about here. He's a worthless piece of shit who violated the trust of the Celestines and betrayed our order! You're seriously telling me we can't—'

'Do not let him goad you. Remember always that we walk in the footsteps of the Auroral Sovereign, who instructs us all to blah blah blah blah—'

Okay, maybe that's not *precisely* what they said. I might have got some of the inflections wrong. But I'm a hundred per cent sure about the *blah-blah-blah* part.

'The two of you done yet?' I asked, then gestured towards the door. 'Because I've got an appointment with whoever's inside that cabin.'

Fidelity sneered venomously. She was exceedingly good at it. 'Are you mad, Apostate? You think we would—?'

'The major domo's granted me an hour with whoever's inside,' I reminded her. 'Given that he represents the will of Prince Stercus, and the two of you have been serving the prince, up until now at least, that means those were part of your instructions from the Lords Celestine, and as we both know' – I poked her in the right shoulder where her Celestine's glove would normally have been – 'a good little justiciar always does what she's told, right up until the moment one of the big bosses countermands those orders through a shining golden falcon or a burning bush or whatever they're using these days. And that means you and Dignity here are, at this very moment, in violation of the Auroral Will.'

Okay, a lot of that was conjecture, but I'd been in their faces for the past three minutes and I still had all my limbs, with not even a bruise or a scratch marring my unholy body. There was no way the two of them had free rein over their actions right now.

All of which made me wonder what about protective duty on a pleasure ship could possibly be so important to the Lords Celestine.

Dignity's growl, coming from deep in his belly, would have put Corrigan to shame. He stepped aside from the door and glared at Fidelity until she did the same.

'You may have your hour, Renegade. And some day, very soon, we will have ours.'

I wish I could say that didn't terrify me, but it took every ounce of my own not inconsiderable willpower to keep my hand from shaking as I put the key in the lock, and to keep the quaver from my voice when I opened the door and said to my former brethren, 'Go fuck yourselves. No one else will.'

Petty? Maybe, but pettiness, I promise you, is the least of my sins.

Through that red door was a bare, plain room, with none of the normal pleasure palace décor: no embroidered hangings on the walls to cover the oak boards, no gold-framed erotic paintings, no illustrated engravings of naughty poetry.

There was only her.

The prince's pride and joy, the girl no one was allowed to enjoy but him and those lucky few upon whom he chose to bestow a once-in-a-lifetime honour, was lying on a simple bed made up with plain white sheets. Every step of the way here, I had been turning over in my mind one question: what kind of woman was so special she warranted nine wonderists to keep her from being taken?

Now I had my answer.

CHAPTER 20

The Purpose of Angels

The instand I laid eyes on her I understood the allure she held for princes and lords – for anyone, really. No wonder the Lords Celestine had sent two of their finest justiciars to keep her bound here. No wonder the major domo had looked as if I'd demanded the world of him. I had, in fact, asked for very much more.

After all, how often does a man get to have his way with an angel?

She was, as angelics went, nothing particularly special. Oh, she was beautiful, in that banal way depicted by ladies' boudoir paintings, her pose of graceful wantonness, one arm slightly raised behind her head, the other resting between plump breasts. Her hair was the gold of an illuminated manuscript, the lustrous tresses spread across her pillow like the rays of the sun. Full red lips parted a touch as I entered the cabin and her green eyes watched me as I shut the door.

'Are my innermost desires truly so predictable?' I asked her.

Angelics aren't bound by flesh, which is one of the reasons they're able to enter the Mortal realm. The Lords Celestine created them as heralds. As they were fashioned to be able to speak to all peoples, they were granted the ability to transfigure themselves into whatever form would be most agreeable to those to whom they appeared, which was smart thinking. After all, if everyone on your island has red skin, you're not about to trust someone with green skin who shows up to tell you the Celestines are demanding that you accept a new code of laws. This way, the angelic who stepped upon your shores would be a deeply beautiful version of one of your own people, smoothing the way for the message they'd been sent to deliver.

It had always struck me as a bit of a scam.

On the other hand, if what you wanted was the perfect prostitute, one who could instantly look like whoever the client most desired, well then, who better than the being awaiting me on the bed? Want to sway the local archon to your side? Why not give him the chance to sleep with his wife's sister as she was twenty years ago? The angelic could become your luscious in-law right down to her sparkly toenails. What about the baroness whose armies you desperately need for your next military campaign, who never quite got over her secret longing to bed her own nephew? Invite her aboard, escort her down to the bottom deck, instruct her to allow her secret yearnings to wash over her, and when she steps inside this cabin, her forbidden nephew awaits, eager to enact her carnal fantasies.

Alas, it's not always pleasant to come face to face with your desires.

The angelic gave me a playful smirk. 'What you desire is to see yourself as crass and petty.' She spread her arms wide, inviting, yet not at all enticing. 'And here I am, my lord: beautiful but uninspired; wanton, yet unarousing – an orgasm without release. Do I not please you?'

'I didn't know angelics were capable of spite.'

She leaned up on the bed, one perfect breast flopping less than perfectly to the side. 'The baser emotions are foreign to us, true, but I have discovered that Mortals are remarkably capable teachers.' She arched her back seductively, trying to get a rise out of me.

It worked.

'Now, with which part of my body shall I please you, my lord?'

'I'm not here for that.'

She tapped a finger on her bee-stung lips. 'With my mouth?'

'No – look, if you'll listen a moment—'

Her finger drifted down between her legs. 'Here?'

'Could you just—'

She rolled onto her belly, her hand reaching back to slide between her buttocks. 'Mount me here, my magnificent steed. I can scream with both pain and pleasure as you—'

I slammed my fist against the wall with such force I thought I might have broken my hand. 'Did the Celestines imbue angelics with the ability to shut up for five fucking seconds?'

My cry of pain and frustration neither frightened her nor moved her to sympathy. Instead, she looked up at me from the awkward position into which she'd contorted herself. 'Oh, I know!' she said with feigned enthusiasm, still pouting and batting her eyelashes. 'What you truly yearn for is violence, is that it, my lord? You'll teach the dirty little Auroral whore her place? Here, I'll get us started.'

She slapped her own buttocks, but when I failed to react, she frowned. 'Too meek, my lord? Fragile submissiveness doesn't appeal to you at all, does it?' This time her arm came back and she drove her fist into her hip with such force that it left a large red mark behind. 'How about like this?' She curled her fingers into claws and started digging her nails into her thigh. 'Would you like to see how far I'll go until you at last experience sweet release?'

'Is that truly what you see inside me?' I asked, my throat tight. 'A sick, pathetic bully who gets off on the pain of others? Or have your angelic senses grown so warped and perverted during your sojourn on this barge that you can no longer tell the difference between desire and abuse?'

The angelic sighed and collapsed on the bed like a petulant child overcome with boredom. 'Neither, my lord. I wasn't implying you wanted to hurt someone *else.*' She passed a hand down her leg and the wounds washed away like theatre make-up after a performance. 'How do you feel?' she asked.

'Irritated, which is my usual response when dealing wi—'

'Don't lie to me,' she warned. Closing her eyes, she reached out a hand as if her fingertips could stretch across the cabin to touch my chest. 'You're disgusted, filled with revulsion so thick it's choking you. Doesn't it feel wonderful? Isn't *this* the sensation you crave most? More than sex, more than love, you want *proof*.'

'Proof of what? You're not making sense.'

Her eyes blinked open. They were entirely black now. It was like staring into whatever awaits you after you die.

'Proof that the world is as corrupt as you've always believed, and that you yourself are worthless and vile. What better excuse to ignore accountability for your actions?' Her forefinger curled in the air, beckoning me closer. 'Come, let me taste that bitterness. Let me know your desires, unleashed from your attempts to hide them from yourself. Let me please you.'

The smart thing to do would have been to stay back, keep my mouth shut and close myself off from her. Actually, the *really* smart thing to do would have been to turn around, walk out of that cabin and get off that damned barge. But that crack about bitterness cut a little too close to home, and that pissed me off no end. So I walked towards the angelic, stopping only when her fingertips touched my chest.

'There,' she moaned with pretended ecstasy, 'that's not so bad, is—?'

Her hand jerked away and she recoiled, shaking it as if her fingertips were burning. 'In the name of the Sovereign!' she cried in shock. 'You were . . . You were one of ours! A Glorian Justiciar!'

I opened the buttons of my shirt and tugged it open to reveal the Infernal sigils burned into my chest. 'Not any more.'

'A diabolic's markings—?' Her voice was equal parts disgusted and curious. This was the most genuine emotion I'd seen her display. 'How can this be?'

Oh, what a tale, I thought to myself, *of brave deeds and noble sacrifice, ending in deception, betrayal and tragedy. Sit back and listen well as I recount my life's story to you.*

'I switched sides.'

The angelic swallowed, an oddly human way of conveying her confusion. She transfigured herself once more, but this time more slowly, like an apprentice sculptor attempting a difficult piece for the first time. Her palms passed over her skin, turning it the hideous alabaster much favoured by the Devilish. She tugged at her finger-nails, lengthening and sharpening them, then she traced weaving lines down her cheeks and her neck and between her breasts, leaving behind a texture of ornate diabolic sigils. Next, she brushed a hand through her hair, staining some of the tresses silver, others crimson. Finally, she clenched her fists and pressed them against the sides of her forehead. When she pulled them away, a pair of goat horns had sprouted in their place.

'Can it truly be so simple for one such as us to change our nature?' she asked.

Here's something most people don't know about being in the presence of someone who continuously alters their appearance: it makes you nauseous. While our eyes can handle all kinds of chaotic visions, nothing is more disorienting to human beings than being unable to hold on to an image of a person. The way the angelic kept shifting from one thing to another in her attempt to please her client was making it impossible for me to concentrate. More importantly, it was wasting my time.

I dropped to the floor and sat cross-legged, placed both hands over my heart and, letting my vision blur, I slowed my breathing.

'What are you doing?'

'Trying to concentrate.'

The problem with her kind is that they're meant to be the per-sonification of the Auroral ideal of self-sacrifice. What sublimes like

Galass and Fidick were trained to do – subsuming their own desires so that they could better serve the Lords Celestine – is pretty much baked into an angelic. That this particular angelic was bound to a pleasure vessel and subjected to the continual bombardment of the yearnings of those aboard was making it impossible for either of us to think straight, never mind have a conversation. Trapped between the narrow boundaries of lust to which she'd become accustomed in this cabin, she couldn't stop herself from trying to break through my instinctive repression to attune herself to my sexual desires.

Which very quickly got annoying.

What I needed now were answers, not some momentary sexual diversion. I had to learn what she was doing here, and how some petty local prince had been able to blackmail a pair of Glorian Justiciars to act as her guards. Why would the prince risk everything by desecrating an angelic just to provide salacious entertainment for his guests? Once the Lords Celestine finally got off their heavenly arses long enough to discover what was being done to one of theirs, heads would roll. Lots and lots of heads.

I know what you're thinking. I was thinking it, too. I just wasn't ready to admit it to myself.

Regardless, as questions buzzed around in my head, I was working on slowing the beat of my heart so I could slip into a waking trance – until I was distracted by the sound of writhing flesh and creaking bone. The angelic had twisted into an amorphous, translucent figure, like a sea creature stretching its tentacles in search of prey, in response to the onslaught of contradictory desires seeping through the floorboards from those occupied in their own sexual escapades in the cabins above. My momentary attention caused her body to change back into that of a woman, but even then, she couldn't hold on to a single form. Her hair darkened, then lightened; her breasts swelled, then shrank. The shape of her legs, her belly, even her genitals, constantly changed, thinning, plumping up, lengthening, shortening, as she instinctively struggled to please me.

Apparently, I was making that an impossible task.

'Would you look deeply into my eyes?' I asked.

Amidst the endless transfigurations of her face and body, her voice dived from lilting and musical to deep, almost rumbling. 'Will it hurt?'

'It will be uncomfortable, but it's important.'

Her form stopped shifting, for the most part, although her lips swelled into a sensuous bow and parted softly. 'Will it please you?'

'It won't please either of us, but life isn't always about pleasure.'

Her eyes settled into an almost angular shape, then narrowed, first in suspicion, then in curiosity, as if I'd just said something to her in a foreign tongue and yet she'd understood the meaning. 'Then I will try.'

She abandoned her seductive poses and came to sit at the end of the bed, hugging her knees to her chest. She could have been mistaken for a woman my own age now, pretty, but not overly so, curious about me, even a little attracted, but not overwhelmed with desire. There was more character in her features, which I appreciated: a few lines here and there, the nose not quite straight. She struck me as someone I could have a conversation with, get to know, maybe even come to lo—

Damn it. She was *still* screwing with me.

I kept my eyes locked on hers and started shedding loneliness and sorrow like rainwater off my shoulders, trying to make my will forceful enough to overpower the noise of endless lazy cravings wafting down at her through the rafters.

'What are you doing?' she asked, sensing something changing around us.

'I'm creating space for us to talk.'

'How?'

'Like this.'

I softened my gaze until I could see the weaving strands of desire emanating from those on the decks above us, dangling down from the ceiling, trying to ensnare the angelic. Instead, I knotted them to each other, which kept them away from her. It was slow work, but worth the considerable effort. Together, each of those yearnings formed a thick fog filling the room; once I'd tied them off, they were almost pathetically weak.

'You should not do this,' the angelic warned. 'It is forbidden.'

'Forbidden by whom?' I asked.

'By those who keep me here.'

'Those two arseholes? Dignity and Fidelity?'

She nodded.

Now we were getting somewhere. I found two strands stronger than the others – but they had nothing to do with sexual desire. They were thick as ropes, strong enough to hold a massive galleon to the dock in the midst of a hurricane. I'd assumed all along that the prince must have found some unimaginably ingenious way to bind the angelic to this cabin, and that Dignity and Fidelity had been forced to guard her or risk worse harm coming to her.

I was wrong: they *wanted* the angelic bound to this whoreship. The justiciars hadn't come here to protect her. They were her jailers.

'Why would two Glorians betray their oaths and everything they believe in?'

Yes, thank you. I'm aware of the irony here.

'The justiciars betray no one. They merely enforce my sentence.'

'Who dares punish a spirit incapable of sin?'

'You know the answer.'

I guess I did.

The Infernals would love to corrupt an angelic, just to stick it to the Aurorals, but they could never pull it off; their spells wouldn't work on her. A wonderist – a *really* powerful wonderist – might be able to snare her momentarily, but once she altered her form, any binding would slide off her like shed skin.

That left precisely one possibility.

'Why would a Lord Celestine condemn one of their own angelics to indentured servitude on a pleasure barge?'

'They said I was imperfectly made.'

'By perfect beings?'

Her eyes lowered to the floor, as if she couldn't directly acknowledge the obvious flaw in her argument. 'It is our mission to bring Mortals to the Auroral path.'

'And you failed?'

'Not exactly, but there is a . . . a greater urgency to our cause now. The Lords Celestine have deemed princes and archons more vital to the Great Crusade than Mortals of lesser stature. Prince Stercus has great wealth and a vast army at his disposal.'

None of which is supposed to matter to the Auroral Song, in which each of us is a melody as beautiful as all the others.

'I take it you refused your assignment?' I asked.

'One does not *refuse* the Lords Celestine. I merely . . . questioned.' She lifted her eyes and I saw something briefly flicker there, like a match that sparks but cannot light. Before I could work out what I'd seen, she was back to staring at the floor. 'That which I have become has been deemed more useful to the Auroral Song. My shame provides a warning to other angelics that ours is not to debate, but to do as we are commanded. There must be discipline if we are to defeat the Infernals when the Great Crusade comes.'

'Bullshit. The Great Crusade's always coming, it just never gets here. The Lords Celestine can't invade the Infernal plane any more than the Lords Devilish can breach the Auroral one, and neither can step foot in this one. It's all just posturing so they can keep their people in line.'

I let too much of my own resentment seep through the barrier

I'd been building up between us. The angelic leaned closer, hands gripping the footboard of the bed as if it were the railing of a ship and she'd just spotted a sea monster in the distance. 'How did you survive your apostasy?' she asked. 'How could you not go mad with longing to hear the Auroral Song?'

'I . . .'

I had worked hard to repress the memory of the serene perfection of that voice in my head: comforting beyond words, the most beautiful, heart-wrenching instrument in the universe, played just for me – and then, for a single act of disobedience, I was cut off for ever.

The angelic watched the anguish on my face. Momentarily freed from the desires of others, the natural perceptiveness of her species returned to her. 'Why did you do it? Why did you turn away from the Auroral Song?'

My lips parted, the words and tears long held back threatening to slip from my tongue. I swallowed them back down where they belonged. 'I realised one day that the voice wasn't speaking to me, not really. It was talking *at* me, as it does to you, as it does to all of us.'

Before she could question me further, I held a finger to my lips. '*Shhh*. I need to concentrate.'

She acquiesced, sitting back down on the bed.

I couldn't break Dignity and Fidelity's chains, and if I tried too hard, they'd become aware of my attempts. Instead, I reshaped the space between the angelic and me so that it slid around those unbreakable cords, enabling us to speak to one another as free beings, even if just for a moment.

'*Ahhhh*,' she sighed, her whole body sagging.

'Are you all right?'

She nodded. 'I only felt this once before, this . . . lack of purpose. Another angelic had found a way to this state. She called it the "beautiful unknowing". I am . . . grateful to experience it again, if only briefly.'

Feeling the first brush of the justiciars' wills instinctively trying to reassert themselves over the angelic, I once again slid the space between us around those tendrils to evade them without their becoming aware of us.

'Why did you come here?' the angelic asked.

'A bargain,' I replied. 'I was sent to get you out of here.'

'So you *do* serve another. Who?'

'That doesn't mat—'

She sent her own perceptions rooting through my memories. I tried to hold her back but the suddenness of her attack overwhelmed me. A smile came to her lips, one so unexpected and genuine it nearly broke my heart. 'The swashbuckler,' she said, not with mockery, but admiration. 'The Rat Most Valorous.'

I nodded.

The angelic stood up from the bed, her body changing once again. 'He made love to me like this,' she said, her body now slimmer, a few years older, perhaps thirty, the black hair streaked with grey. I found her entrancing. I guess Aradeus had, too. 'The rat mage had done some great service to the prince, who rewarded him by giving him an entire night with me.' She ran her hands down the curves of her body. 'He delighted in every inch of me, singing to me as we made love, stopping to write poems about me, of which he desperately wanted my opinion. But at the end, just as morning was coming, I think he finally understood what I was, and then he cried and begged my forgiveness. Isn't that strange?'

'It is common decency, so yes, that is strange.'

The angelic laughed, a strange sound for one designed by her creators to witness events through a disinterested haze that separates all of experience into that which conforms to the will of the Lords Celestine and that which does not. That she was able to find mirth in Aradeus' archaic notions of gallantry was as close to a miracle as I had seen in a long time. 'A valorous rat swore to free me from my bonds,' she said, then gestured to me, 'and here he sends me a knight of heresy to be the key that unlocks the shackles of my faith.'

I rose to my feet and extended a hand. 'If we succeed, you can spend the rest of your existence in the beautiful unknowing, if that's what you want. You can be directionless without being lost, for as long as you choose.'

She didn't take my hand.

'You cannot,' she said, and already I could see her retreating into the desires of others. 'Leave here, Merciful Apostate. You came in good faith and fulfilled whatever oath you made to the swashbuckler. But now that you know what I am, and who binds me here, you know too that you must not free me. The Lords Celes—'

'Those pricks already hate me. I doubt this will change anything. Now, give me a moment, would you? I need to see a rat about a man.'

I reached into the pocket of my coat to withdraw the furry, not especially pleasant-smelling occupant who'd been snoozing there for the past hour. I held the rat up to my face. 'I'm assuming Aradeus' spell still lingers over you, so if you'd be so kind as to— Why, you flea-infested bastard—'

The little fucker had bit my nose, breaking the skin. When I yanked him back there was a drop of my blood between his teeth and a self-satisfied smirk on his ratty face. An instant later, the rat's expression grew more serious and he spoke with Aradeus' voice.

'Cade? What's happening? There are two justiciars up here threatening the major domo with purification unless he rescinds his gift of your hour with my most honourable lady.'

My lady. Boy, was he ever scrabbling up the wrong tree. In case it wasn't obvious from all the shape-changing, angelics aren't male or female or anything between. Gender is all pretty much the same to them.

'Find Corrigan and tell him to whip up a distraction of some kind – maybe conjure up a Tempestoral haze over the entire barge. He's lousy at them, but it should keep the prince's wonderists confused long enough for you to get him and Galass down here.'

The rat gave me a disappointed stare. 'Infernal mages are known for their subtlety. I'd hoped you might be able to sneak my lady off the vessel with a minimum of unnecessary violence.'

The anger I'd been failing to completely hold back raged through me like a battering ram splintering a castle door. 'Well, guess what, Aradeus? It turns out the beings that most decent people pray to are bigger arseholes than any of us ever imagined. So I'd say some good old-fashioned unnecessary violence is most definitely called for!'

CHAPTER 21

The Breakout

'You know, Cade,' Corrigan began as he shouldered aside Aradeus and Galass in the cramped cabin, 'I really hope that one day I get to screw you over as badly as you've screwed me lately.'

Mister Bones was sitting on the bed, snarling at the angelic as she grew calico-coloured fur on her body and sprouted a wagging tail. Strangely, that *wasn't* the most distracting thing going at that precise moment. I turned to Corrigan, averting my eyes from his lower half. 'Maybe do up your trousers before you talk about screwing?'

He'd arrived shirtless, the great mop of curly indigo hair covering his torso soaked in the sweat of his apparently relentless efforts to satisfy the appetites of the new love of his life. His striped velvet pantaloons were hanging halfway off his arse and doing an even poorer job of protecting his modesty at the front.

He made an elaborate hand gesture below his waist. 'I feel it's only appropriate that you be reminded both of what you just took me away from *and* my lordly magnificence.'

I ignored the pouting brute and turned to Aradeus. 'What's the tactical situation?'

'Not good.' The rat mage was unsettlingly downcast for someone I'd only ever seen brimming with optimism. 'There's one staircase to the upper decks. They'll know exactly which way we're coming, so they can set any number of spell-traps for us without having to risk their own necks.' He rapped his knuckles on the oak-panelled wall of the cabin. 'We're below the waterline here, so if we breach the hull, we'll have a hellish time trying to swim out – not to mention making ourselves even more vulnerable to enemy spells.'

'I'm assuming that's the good news?' I asked.

Aradeus looked grim. 'While Corrigan's Tempestoral haze was distracting the crew on the top deck, I witnessed one of the major domo's wonderists trying to defend him from the justiciars. The female one – a stunning beauty, I must say – was apparently offended that the major domo had granted you access to this cabin. She lit up the wonderist protecting him with an Auroral remonstration until his internal organs oozed out of his bodily orifices.'

'Isn't that good?' Galass asked. 'If the justiciars start fighting the enemy wonderists, can't w—?'

'Forgive my uncouth interruption, fair Galass,' Aradeus said, unable to stop himself from bowing elaborately and thus defeating the purpose of interrupting her in the first place. 'The justiciar's part-ner – Dignity, I understand – is demanding that command over the six remaining wonderists be ceded to him. He wants to put them all under an Auroral recruitment spell, binding them to his authority. I fear the major domo is about to agree.'

Corrigan guffawed in that way that generally means gruesome death is waiting for you right around the corner and you don't want anyone to know you're about to shit your striped velvet pantaloons. 'Those justiciars must really have a hard-on for you, Cade,' he declared, then stared down at himself. 'Oh, look. I do, too.'

Sometimes the whole *we're about to die so let's make jokes in case anyone's writing all this down for posterity* thing really annoys me.

'You do realise those justiciars are going to rip *you* limb from limb right alongside me, don't you, Corrigan? You and your – Well, since we're likely doomed, it's past time someone told you the truth and it might as well be your only friend: it's a very mediocre cock.'

'Now *that* hurts,' he grumbled. At least he finally yanked up his pantaloons and buckled his belt. 'On the other hand' – he gave that same amiable grin I'd seen right before his Tempestoral spells had torn an ox-sized hole through a twelve-foot-thick castle wall – 'if I were to turn you over to the justiciars myself, I suspect they'd be lenient on me *and* my not-in-the-least-bit-mediocre cock.'

You know you're in real trouble when the voice of reason turns out to be a teenage blood mage who's never more than one glass of sour wine away from a bender that would exsanguinate half the continent.

'This is getting us *nowhere!*' Galass shouted, shoving me back so she could take up position between me and Corrigan. 'Are you both complete fools, or do you just act like it to mask your lack of any coherent plan to get us out of here alive?'

'A little of both,' I mumbled.

'Oh, *I've* got a plan,' Corrigan said. 'Those justiciars want the angelic and Cade, not me or Aradeus. You, they'll torture and kill on principle, what with you being a blood mage – sorry about that, lass. Rough business and all.' He reached over the foot of the bed to scratch the still-snarling Mister Bones around one pointy ear. 'I promise to take care of your dog, though.'

'Jackal,' I corrected.

'Oh, you really are a pair of idiots, aren't you?' Galass asked. She pointed a finger at the angelic, who was still trying to find a form and colour that would convince Mister Bones to stop growling at her. 'The only way the justiciars are getting to her' – Galass' accusing forefinger swung to the rat mage – 'is to get through Aradeus, who, in case you haven't noticed, is both smitten with her and incapable of abandoning her.'

'This is true,' Aradeus confirmed. 'My honour – nay, my very humanity – would not al—'

'Shut up,' Galass said firmly, spinning towards me. Apparently, it was my turn. 'You're supposed to be the smart one – the conniver. The manipulator. The—'

'They get it.'

'—schemer who keeps secrets even from his friends so that he'll never walk into trouble without a trick up his sleeve when the time comes. Well, the time has come, Cade. What's your plan?'

When I stepped back from the onslaught of her fury and collided with the wooden wall of the cramped cabin, I felt my cheeks flush. As I'm neither bashful by nature nor particularly impressed with self-righteous indignation, that meant the blood vessels in my face were swelling because Galass was losing control over the blood magic coursing through her.

I put my hands up in surrender. 'You're right. I *did* conceive a cunning plan before I called you all down here. Brilliantly cunning – in fact, an outstanding plan. Top-notch.'

Corrigan slapped a palm against his forehead. 'We're doomed.'

All right, fine, maybe it wasn't the *most devious or ingenious plan ever devised*, but it wasn't as bad as he was assuming. Let's begin with the hard facts. Roughly seventy crew members were spread out over the pleasure barge, and I'm including the prostitutes, because it's a job, right? Add to that maybe fifty guests currently enjoying their offerings, and twice as many again for the retainers and servants accompanying them to ensure their every need is instantly met. Seven enemy wonderists – no, six now, thanks to Fidelity's propensity for smiting – and two may-all-the-gods-living-and-dead-damn-them Glorian Justiciars.

So, let's say there were somewhere just south of two hundred and fifty souls aboard.

Now let's consider the terrain. We've got one massive barge with four decks, connected by staircases at the bow and stern, except for this one cabin, tucked right at the bottom into the pointy end, which has only one avenue of escape. Breaching the hull wasn't a viable option, as Aradeus had pointed out, since we'd either drown or we'd be easy targets for the enemy.

Finally, there are the time constraints. We couldn't stay there much longer, because that would give the other wonderists time to set spell-traps around us.

All that added up to two choices. We could die quickly, or die slowly.

The solution to most thorny dilemmas, I have discovered after years of experiment, is to introduce a little chaos into the equation. This was the essence of my plan.

Picture this: Corrigan conjures up a particularly nasty Tempestoral bolt, but instead of firing it through the hull, he blasts a hole up through the four decks above us. True, this exposes us to the enemy, but it also provides us with a new means of escape. More importantly, it freaks out the guests and their well-armed retainers, who will inevitably start running around slashing at everything in sight in a bid to show they are protecting their paymasters. Meanwhile, Aradeus uses his Totemic affinity with every rat on the ship (oh, please – don't bother telling me how clean *your* pleasure barge is; there are *always* rodents) to start biting every ankle they can find, which will result in more chaos, and more people drawing weapons without being entirely sure who to attack.

I couldn't risk asking Galass to fight, not just because blood magic has a bad habit of backfiring on the wielder's comrades, but also because I'd decided that since I'd failed to save Fidick, I would at least keep her sane until I could rid her of that lousy mystical attunement. That didn't mean she wasn't crucial to my plan, mind.

No matter how skilfully we distracted the enemy, everything would fall apart if we couldn't keep the angelic stable long enough for us to get her off the barge. Galass had shown herself to possess two qualities rarely found in one person: she was calm under pressure, and she had bucketloads of empathy – well, other than the time she exsanguinated that squad of Ascendant Lucien's soldiers. Regardless, she had the best chance of helping the angelic through the maelstrom of homicidal desires that would be bombarding her as we moved up through the decks.

You're still wondering about the jackal? Just a mutt. Sorry.

And in this ingenious plan, I would be the most important element, because the real danger was still the six wonderists and two justiciars who'd be working together to capture us. Our odds of defeating all of them were nil, but even that wasn't the real problem, because our chances of fighting off just the two justiciars alone was also nil.

But I had a cunning plan . . .

Infernal magic is a despicable cesspool of manipulation and corruption. It's all about giving a middle finger to the natural order of things. Engraved into my chest, just above my third rib on the left, were a pair of sigils for casting what are called reckless abandons. Normally, these wouldn't have much effect on trained wonderists, and they'd do nothing at all against the disciplined minds of Glorian Justiciars. But combined with all that other chaos we were going to set off – the fire and lightning, frantic crew, panicking guests screaming at equally shouty well-armed retainers to get them out of this mess, not to mention the rats – those wonderists would be so confused about what was going on they'd be far more focused on protecting their own skins than hunting us down.

That still left us with our most intractable problem. Dignity and Fidelity were more than enough to defeat us, and now that they'd apparently got permission from On High to break whatever agreement they had with the prince, there would be nothing holding them back from obliterating everything in their way between the angelic and me.

Those reckless abandon spells, when cast on an unprepared mind, induce a state not unlike drunkenness – well, that's assuming that while drunk you also happen to have an almost irresistible desire to blow shit up. The affected wonderists would start firing off every spell they knew, all the while giggling like idiots and probably prancing around with their underpants around their ankles. Yes, I *am* saying that Corrigan's natural state is eerily similar to that of a drunken lunatic.

Fidelity and Dignity might be more powerful than all the other wonderists combined, but even they would be kept off-balance with all those esoteric fireworks going off at once, which should give us time to escape from what any reasonable person would have to agree was an otherwise impossible trap.

Ta-dah!

Now, maybe you're thinking my plan was too cavalier to succeed, but let me assure you, as someone who's had to pull off many such daring escapes in less than ideal circumstances, this one would have come off flawlessly, had it not been for one tiny problem.

'The damned recruitment spell,' I said aloud.

Corrigan, Galass, Aradeus and the angelic stared at me, possibly wondering why I was mumbling to myself while the thumping and thudding of hectic activity on the deck above us were getting considerably louder and more energetic. I reached out to touch the wall behind me and felt the unsettling tingle of various Totemic, sonoral and even luxoral spell-traps being set for us. That last one, well, who gives a shit, but the others might cause us real trouble. But what made my stomach really sink was the buzzing in my ears of two Glorian Justiciars issuing orders to the six wonderists now under their total and absolute control.

That was what was screwing up my ingenious plan.

Had the major domo refused to give up the prince's pet wonderists, my reckless abandon spells would have had a stellar chance. But once granted authority, Dignity would have placed the wonderists under an Auroral recruitment, a binding so powerful that for the next six hours their every action would be governed by his will alone, making any Infernal manipulations on my part utterly irrelevant. The wonderists and justiciars would work together with the efficiency of a well-schooled military squad, methodically and efficiently slaughtering Corrigan and Aradeus first, then they'd take me, Galass and the angelic prisoner for far worse punishments to come.

And Mister Bones would get it, too.

I felt the strangest sensation come over me. It wasn't despair or anger, or even some wonderist's spell messing with my mind. It was sadness.

I could admit to myself that part of me had been craving a confrontation with the justiciars – a fair fight, or as near to it as someone like me would ever get. Maybe I'd always hoped that when my time came, I'd go out in a blaze of ingloriousness, free from my own past, fighting alongside trusted friends.

'Cade, you've got thirty seconds to figure out a way to get us out of here before I turn you over to the justiciars,' Corrigan informed me.

My unease went deeper than that, though. There was a sense of betrayal burning a hole in my gut. The angelic had been right about me. I had always taken a perverse comfort in the idea that I was a failure who'd never lived up to the standards demanded by the Aurorals. For all that I mocked the Lords Celestine and their many hypocrisies, I'd still hoped the Auroral Song was truly as pure and perfect as they claimed, and it was me who had failed.

Except now those same pure and perfect Lords Celestine were selling angelics to petty local princes to use as pleasure slaves. They'd chosen a madman like Ascendant Lucien over rulers just as devout but considerably less power-hungry and bloodthirsty. Meanwhile, Tenebris was discreetly offering every wonderist on the continent the same job up north he'd offered me.

Never before had Aurorals and Infernals so explicitly interfered in human affairs; their 'Great Crusade' against each other had been a war over souls, not territory.

'Someone's changed the game,' I said out loud.

Galass and Aradeus stared at me as if perhaps I'd lost my mind, but Corrigan, for all that he's an insensitive lout, has always been far cannier than most people credit him. He got it: the angelic's enslavement was only the latest in a series of moves by the Lords Celestine that made absolutely no sense.

'None of this "War of the Demesnes" shit has ever been our business,' he reminded me. 'Why should it be now?'

I glanced back at the angelic sitting on the bed, stroking Mister Bones. Apparently they'd come to an uneasy peace, for he was still snarling, even as he tilted his head so she could scratch behind his ear more effectively. With the desires of the other passengers still held at bay by my earlier workings, she looked rather *curious* about the little jackal – and about everything and everyone around her.

'I can't abide it any more,' I told Corrigan. 'I just can't.'

The first red and black sparks of his Tempestoral summonings flickered around his closed right fist. 'Damn you to hell, Cade! You're like a brother to me, but you know the score. Either you tell me how you're getting us all out of here, or I'm making the same trade you'd make in my position.'

I turned away from Corrigan and the others before removing my coat and shirt. I realise it probably looked like an odd occasion for modesty, but I've never much liked people seeing all those circles within circles of Infernal sigils I'd accumulated on my chest these past three years. It was the history of my descent from a Glorian Justiciar to a mercenary Infernalist one bad deal away from being recruited into the damned.

'What are you doing?' Galass asked.

She tried to put a hand on my shoulder, but I shrugged it away.

'Like the man says, I've got to get us out of here or he'll trade us to the justiciars. So that's what I'm going to do.'

'But how?'

'Same way I do everything lately.' I took out the small bag of sand from the pocket of my trousers and began pouring a spell circle onto the cabin floor. 'I'm going to sell a piece of my soul.'

CHAPTER 22

A Whole New Deal

It takes a lot to shock the moral sensibilities of a demon. If angelics are bred to be incapable of conceiving of choices beyond those that fulfil their moral purpose, the diabolics are imbued with a delight in what my old mentor – herself quite a fan of the concept – called *existential perversity*. Simply put, they love seeing the natural order turned upside down.

'You have got to be fucking kidding me,' Tenebris groaned, floating inside the spell circle I'd drawn on the cabin floor. He had one leathery-white hand clapped over his eyes, as if blocking out the view would make us go away. Who knew even a demon's natural affinity for the perverse could be pushed too far?

Outside, two justiciars were banging on the wall, promising that our punishments would be ever-so-slightly less agonising if we gave up rather than forcing them to debase themselves by blasting open the door to get to us. They're bound by their own system of rules to offer perpetrators the chance to find spiritual redemption by accepting their fate rather than fighting it, even if both options are equally horrible. It's all about procedure with justiciars.

'I have better ways to amuse myself than trying to make you laugh,' I told Tenebris. 'Now, do we have a deal or not?'

The demon was swaying wildly inside the spell circle as if caught in a storm, the result of the barely noticeable undulations of the barge on the river causing shifts in the sand forming the circle. 'You want *me*' – Tenebris pointed one clawed finger to the ruffles of the silk shirt he was now wearing beneath a very natty chartreuse silk coat – 'to help' – the finger swung towards the angelic sitting on the bed, '*that?*'

Why must diabolics be such fucking melodramatics? 'What I want is safe passage through the Infernal plane just long enough to get me, Corrigan, Galass, Aradeus—'

Mister Bones barked. Jackals have weird barks, in case I haven't mentioned it up until now.

'—and our jackal—'

While neither Infernals nor any Aurorals save angelics can tread upon the Mortal demesne without disintegrating into non-existence, there's nothing stopping us entering their realms, given permission and a desire to suffer unendurable misery.

'And *her*,' Tenebris corrected me, stabbing his forefinger at the angelic. 'You want me to give *that* passage through one of *our* demesnes! And you want me to do it without six hundred and sixty-six of my brethren getting a taste of what I am sure is her very tasty Auroral flesh.' He let out an exasperated breath. 'Cade, buddy . . . you get what my job is, right? I mean, I do favours for you—'

'You make deals with me,' I corrected. 'And I'm offering you my soul for it. Once this is all done, I'll join your damned. Your bosses can rule over me for the rest of my existence if it pleases them. I'd think at least one of your Lords Devilish would jump at the chance.'

Tenebris bit his lower lip and gazed past the boundary of our realities to look at me with a kind of sympathy you really don't want to see in the eyes of a demon. 'I told you a long time ago, Cade, the more of your soul you give away, the less it's worth to us. You've been playing this game too long. My bosses only let me make deals with you because they think it's kind of funny, what with you once having been a—'

I flicked a grain of sand into the circle and watched him squirm. Sympathy only gets you so far. 'And what did I tell you last time you said it out loud?'

If you're wondering how it was possible that the others didn't know what I'd once been by now, well, take a good look at me and the things I've done and ask yourself if you'd guess in a million years that I'd once been a Glorian Justiciar.

Tenebris threw up his hands in mock surrender, which looks especially mocking when the hands in question have razor-tipped claws growing out of them. 'Whatever. The bottom line is that a diabolic's role among the Infernals is to make deals that advance our interests among humanity. I get away with helping you out from time to time because it pleases the Lords Devilish to know that helping you screws with the Lords Celestine.'

'So help *her*,' I said, gesturing to the angelic, who hadn't spoken a word since I'd summoned Tenebris; she'd been sitting there watching him in confused fascination while Mister Bones nuzzled at her hand, pushing for her to keep stroking him. 'Think how bad that will piss off the Lord Celestine who created her.'

The diabolic groaned. 'We're talking about *an angelic* here, Cade. Anything I do for her is going to get noticed. Questions will be asked. I'll be forced to answer for this, and the people I answer to are going to start wondering if maybe *I'm* the one being corrupted through my association with a former . . . with you.'

I gave that concern all the consideration it deserved. It took me just under a second. 'Maybe you can remind them of what you did to a young sublime named Fidick. After that, you might casually mention how you turned a second sublime from a girl who, despite all the horrors she'd already experienced in her short, unhappy life, wanted only to keep her brother safe and innocent, into a fucking blood mage. That ought to clear up any doubts the Lords Devilish might have about your ethics.'

Tenebris looked stricken. 'Cade ... I swear to you, buddy, the attunement was already part of her. Even so, I didn't want to awaken it. I begged the kid – I *begged* him – to rescind his offer.' The diabolic turned a shoulder to show me the scars where Fidick had cast soul-burned sand through the circle and onto the diabolic's flesh. 'I held out as long as I could, but he didn't give me a choice.'

You would think a demon – a *diabolic*, no less – would have delighted in the destruction of one soul and the corruption of another. So what did it say about the universe that Tenebris managed to look so ... hurt?

'Incredible,' the angelic said.

She stood up and left the bed. As she approached me, I warned, 'Don't break the circle.'

She wasn't listening to me. She came closer and closer, until her toes were practically touching the sand and her face was at the very edge where two planes of reality met. She and Tenebris were practically nose to nose, like two dogs sniffing at each other.

'You know guilt,' she said. 'You know shame.'

'I know nothing of the sort,' the demon said crossly. 'Cade, get this bitch away from me. I told you, we don't do favours for stinking angelics.'

Her head tilted, just a fraction. 'But we are the same, you and I.'

Tenebris gave a hoarse laugh. '*The same?* Sister, we're absolute polar fucking opposites. Built for entirely antithetical purposes. Our respective creations are literally—'

'Angelics cannot feel shame,' she said, cutting him off, her head tilting like a cat's as she watched his face. 'Nor can a diabolic. How could any creature who exists only to serve a purpose defined by others know regret?'

'Ask this fucker,' Tenebris said, jerking a thumb at me. 'He's a terrible influence.'

The angelic turned to me, her eyes narrowing as if she were seeing me for the first time. 'What did you do to him?'

'Nothing,' I replied. 'He's a diabolic. He lies about everything, including this.'

'He isn't lying.' Her golden eyes swivelled back to Tenebris. 'Even as he tries to make light of the truth, he cannot hide that he is ... *changed* from what he was made to be.'

'Sever the spell, Cade,' Tenebris demanded. 'I'm done wasting my time with you and your weird stoned angelic.'

Outside, the banging had stopped. In my head, I felt the buzzing of Auroral whispers, and with my ears I heard the two justiciars chanting the condemnation rite before they blew the door off its hinges and wiped us all out.

Aradeus came to kneel before the angelic. 'My lady, forgive me, but it seems my promises to free you from this place were overly optimistic.' He rose again and drew his rapier, which struck me as both pointless and dangerous in the cramped cabin. 'Should my death grant you one more minute's freedom, I will count it worth the price.'

She reached out a hand and brushed her fingers along his cheek. 'No heart such as yours ought ever break for so small a cause as my freedom, swashbuckler.' With her other hand she gestured to Tenebris in the circle. 'We will all of us escape this place together now.'

'Cade, did you make her deaf as well as insensate when you screwed with all the knotted tendrils of desire I'm seeing dangling around this room? Because she sure ain't good at listening.' The diabolic turned to her, sneering, yet somehow troubled. 'Focus, moron: under no circumstances am I helping some half-witted angeli—'

She put her finger to her lips. '*Shhhh.*'

Tenebris turned to me. 'Did she just shush me, Cade? Did you just make it so that I was shushed by a fucking angelic? Is that what you've brought me to?'

The first crackles of magic made the air shiver inside the cabin.

'One of the wonderists is a thunderer,' Corrigan explained. 'They've got a shield mage, too. The thunderer's brewing up a storm and his friend is keeping it contained to this cabin. In about thirty seconds we're all going to get blasted.'

But the angelic just smiled dreamily. 'No one dies now, don't you understand?' She pointed again to Tenebris. 'He feels shame. He feels guilt. He violates his own nature.'

It occurred to me then that if a Lord Celestine wanted to shatter the mind of an angelic, forcing one to be the plaything of such foul desires as men and women brought to this barge day after day would be the way to do it.

Corrigan turned to me and gave me a look that said this was all my fault and he should've sold me out to the justiciars when he'd first had the chance. Sparks were sliding all along his knuckles. 'I'm going to blow up this whole place. We'll all die, but hopefully, we'll take down a couple of those bastards with us.' Finally he grinned at me. 'Wanna help me kill a couple of guys for old times' sake?'

But my attention was all on the angelic now, because she was leaning right up to the edge of the circle and whispering something to Tenebris that I couldn't hear. And then, just as I could feel the hair rising on my head and forearms from the storm building up inside the cabin, I saw the diabolic's silver eyes go wide.

Then he turned to me and said, 'Looks like we have a deal.'

'What are you—?'

The angelic kicked the sand aside, breaking the barrier between this plane and the diabolic's. Tenebris clasped his hands together as if in prayer and I saw a portal opening behind him: a path into the Infernal demesne.

'What the fuck is he doing?' Corrigan asked.

Tenebris opened his arms wide. 'Corrigan Blight. Cade Ombra.

Galass Idaris. Aradeus Mozen. Ugly dog creature. And . . .' He looked at the angelic.

'Call me Shame,' she said.

'Stupid name. Anyway, yes, and "Shame". On my oath, my vow, my bond, all five of you will pass through the Infernal Lands without harm, free to leave at your will to return to a place of safety in your own world. This bargain has been made, and so will it be fulfilled.'

'No less than three miles up the Jalbraith Canal,' I specified, glancing at Corrigan for confirmation. 'That's where we're meeting our next recruit, right?'

Tenebris groaned. 'Fine, fine. I'll dump you off at least three miles north of this river so you can have a little tea party with your next recruit . Satisfied?'

'Everyone, go through!' I shouted as the first tingles of lightning began crackling all around us.

Galass hesitated. 'But how can we—?'

'Once a diabolic has struck a bargain, they never break it.' I gave her a push towards the portal as the winds inside the cabin began to buffet us. 'Go. *Now!*'

Corrigan and Aradeus went next, followed by the angelic, with me right behind her. Just before I left certain death behind, I hesitated. Everything I had known about the way the world worked told me something worse surely had to be in store for us once the price of safe passage was paid.

'How did you get him to agree?' I asked. 'What bargain could an angelic make to change the mind of a diabolic?'

She took my hand and pulled me into the portal, and as we shifted from one world to another, she whispered in my ear, 'I switched sides.'

CHAPTER 23

Walks in the Dark

We walked one by one behind Tenebris, through horror and chaos, past torment and the tearing-apart of souls. The road upon which we trod was made from the diabolic's own silvery-blue blood. Every few steps, he'd dig one clawed fingernail into his wrist and a few more drops would spurt out before him, pool and expand to provide us with a path above the damned. On either side of the road beneath our feet, an ocean of bodies writhed, limbs splayed unnaturally, mouths gaping one moment, clamping shut the next with such ferocity that we could hear teeth breaking apart inside their mouths. Screams and groans swirled around us, circling like sharks in the water, and all the while we listened to the clank and clang of the Infernal engine.

'Oh, Cade,' Corrigan chuckled, pretending to swoon. 'You always bring me to the nicest places.'

From anyone else, I might have taken heart from those glib words, but in my experience, when the toughest, most fearless and belligerent war mage you've ever met starts nervously making lame jokes, you know you're in trouble. I think even Corrigan recognised how unfunny that one was.

'Don't stray from the path,' Tenebris warned us, not turning to look at us. 'Not even an inch.'

'Aw, can't we?' Corrigan asked. 'Because I was really looking forward to taking a little swim among the damned.'

He twisted his head and caught my gaze expectantly.

I nodded. 'That one was a little better.'

What else was there to do but joke when the nightmares which drove artists mad and stole the voices from poets were staring up at us, eyes wide with anguish, begging for pity – or more likely, longing to drag us down among them?

'Why do they quieten as we pass?' Galass asked. 'They stop moving – only their gaze follows us.'

I came up behind her and pointed to Tenebris, who was digging deeper into his vein to extend the road ahead. 'Diabolic blood, in addition to making excellent paving throughout the Infernal realm, has narcotic properties. It pacifies the damned and keeps them from climbing up to drag us down with them. Instead, they watch us pass and wonder why we're allowed to go free while they suffer.'

'What purpose do such torments serve?' Galass demanded, holding the shivering Mister Bones in her arms. She glared at Tenebris. 'Does Mortal agony so delight you and your kind?'

I really, really wished she hadn't said that. It's not that Tenebris would go back on his promise to guide us through the Infernal realm to somewhere we could leave and be far away from the prince's pleasure barge – breaking contracts is not something diabolics ever do. But now I'd have to listen to him rant the whole rest of the way.

'You know what, little girl?' he began, dropping into his customary patronising tone. 'My people don't give a shit about your suffering. We don't "delight" in your misery. We don't get hard-ons over your emotional angst or the tears you shed after your kitty died or the last fight you had with some farm boy because he danced with a prettier girl at the local . . . hay party.'

'Hay party?' I asked.

'Whatever. I'm sick and tired of listening to Mortals moan on and on about how vile we Infernals are, how we tempt you in times of need and then steal your souls. Fuck me, you actually use the name

179

of our realm as a synonym for evil! How would you like it if we used the word *Mortal* to mean "useless piece of shit who blames all their problems on other people because they're too lazy to sort out their own wasted life"?'

'You do,' I pointed out. 'You *literally* said that to me a few months ago, when referring to a particular Lord Devilish. "Cade, you won't believe what a *Mortal* that guy is. All he does is whine."'

Tenebris paused to sneer at me. 'Using a pal's words against him is a real Mortal thing to do, Cade.' He resumed his steady march through the hellish maelstrom of suffering and said to Galass, 'Listen, lady. You end up in our house? It's because you made a deal to come here. So don't go getting all weepy because you don't like how that deal turned out. You're not our arch-nemeses. You're barely cattle.'

'What Tenebris is trying to say,' I explained to Galass, 'is that each plane of existence has its own physical laws, its own forms of matter. Most of that matter is worthless to those on another plane, but souls are different. They're created from ecclesiasm, the raw essence from which the universe itself first formed.'

'But I still don't understand why they're being tortured!' Galass cried out, which made the jackal in her arms whine. No doubt she was wondering what would happen to her once the blood magic Fidick's deal with Tenebris had awakened in her drove her mad. Would she end up here, among the damned? 'What's the point of all this misery?' she asked. 'Who benefits fr—?'

'Fuel,' I said, cutting her off for fear she'd start talking herself into a panic, which was not an unreasonable concern when someone who spent their entire lives being taught the Lords Celestine would protect them from all spiritual harm was forced to take a stroll through the Infernal plane. 'What the Aurorals claim is a soul and the rest of us refer to as consciousness is ... well, it's elemental. It's not just a bunch of thoughts trapped inside our skulls, but the thing that binds all matter in the universe together. But your soul, my soul, anybody's soul – they're not useful to anyone else until you deconstruct them, until the soul's own internal bonds break, and what's left is a combination of formless spirit, which has no value, and ecclesiasm, which is what gives both the Lords Celestine and Lords Devilish their power.'

'Why not just kill them?' she asked, staring down at one of the open-mouthed ghasts. Its eyes followed hers as she passed it by.

'Because souls aren't like bones or flesh. You can't just grind them up with a mortar and pestle. You have to induce the soul to relinquish its own form, persuade it to break apart on its own.'

'Or torture the soul until it cannot stand to continue its own existence,' Aradeus said with a grimace. 'I like not this place.'

'Well, tough shit,' Tenebris said, picking up the pace. I guess he wasn't getting any more enjoyment out of this conversation than we were. 'There's a war going on, and wars need ammunition. So unless you're wanting the Lords Celestine to take over every single plane of reality and turn every sentient being into one big mass of goody-goodies doing exactly what they're told, the rest of you dumb bastards better start whistling Infernal marching tunes, 'cause *we're* the only ones fighting to keep the universe out of Auroral control.' He gave an imperious sniff. '*Evil*, they call us. We're fucking freedom fighters. We're the *good* guys.'

'What the diabolic says is not entirely false, but it is not entirely true, either,' said the angelic – or Shame, as I guess I'd have to get used to calling her.

Her appearance had changed since we'd left the ship. She was older now, late middle age, maybe. The long golden hair I'd first seen was grey and cropped short, almost a boy's cut. Her torso was thicker, her face jowly, her nose wide and flat. Her eyes were so indistinct in colour and shape as to be noteworthy only for their lack of lustre.

'Are you all right?' I asked. 'Is the Infernal demesne . . . changing you?'

'This place has no more effect on my appearance than would an empty field of grass upon the Mortal realm.' She spread her arms and smiled at me. 'For a very long time I existed only as a reflection of the desires of others. I find now it pleases me to be . . . unmemorable.'

That made sense to me, in a somewhat melancholy way. Most men and women claim that growing older renders them invisible, not only to the young, but to each other, as beauty fades and age has its way with them. But if you've spent your life as an object of someone else's lust, maybe having those gazes turn away from you would be something to cherish.

Aradeus came to interpose himself between us. 'Alas, you fail in your purpose, my lady, for my eyes and heart wander ever towards you, and even more so now you have shed the distractions of false beauty.'

You had to give the rat mage credit, for he managed to sound utterly sincere. Maybe he was. Maybe the Totemic magic which bound him to the source of his abilities freed him from the normal shallow cravings for purely physical attributes. Maybe rats are just better than we are. But I had bigger questions picking at my own thoughts, and none had to do with Shame's new form. It was her allegiance that concerned me.

'*I switched sides*,' she'd told me back on the barge.

The implications of those three simple words made me shudder far more than walking a path only a few inches above a grasping sea of the damned.

'You have to admit,' Corrigan whispered, putting a hand on my shoulder as he leaned closer, 'this is one weird coven you and I have put together. Can't wait to see the client's face when we show up with a blood mage and a fallen angelic.'

Seven, they'd asked for, which meant with me, Corrigan, Galass, Aradeus and now Shame, we still had two more to recruit before we presented ourselves to this baron who was so concerned with holding on to power that he was willing to sacrifice the children of his own subjects just to keep them in line. When I'd agreed to the job back at the Ascendant Lucien's camp, it was from a mixture of gratitude to Corrigan for saving me, concern over how to keep Galass safe and the blissful haze of ignoring, at least for the time being, the grim reality of the services the baron would expect from us. Now, as the ugliness was getting closer and closer, I was becoming less and less prepared for what would come next. It's one thing to take a nasty job; we're nasty people, after all. But something bigger was going on, something set in motion by the Infernals or the Aurorals or maybe both, which left the obvious question: who was really pulling our strings?

I was so consumed by that thought that I nearly walked right into Tenebris. I hadn't even noticed he'd stopped moving.

'What's wrong?' I asked.

He shook his head but didn't reply, just scratched a fingernail into his wrist and shook a few more drops ahead of us. The silvery-blue dribbles drifted in the air for a second before swerving abruptly to the left.

'This isn't right,' the diabolic said. He tried more forcefully, but the droplets ignored him and veered determinedly to the left.

'What the fuck's going on?' Corrigan demanded. His eyes had widened, the way they did when he was in the middle of a storm spell – only he wasn't smiling.

'Someone is trying to draw one of us off the path.' Tenebris took a single drop of blood onto his forefinger and held it out towards each of us. When he got to me, the drop of blood spun in the air in front of my face for a moment and then added itself to the leftward path formed by the others.

'Somebody's inviting you for a meeting, Cade.'

'You have friends down here?' Corrigan asked.

'In the Infernal plane? Other than our current host? Not that I'm aware of.'

Tenebris was chewing on his lip. 'It's not one of the damned – they wouldn't have the power to do this. And it's not one of my kind either. This isn't our style.'

'Who does that leave?' I asked.

'I don't know.'

Corrigan grabbed the diabolic by a spiny shoulder. 'You made a pact to bring us through unharmed.'

'And I will, you big oaf – but if it helps, I don't think whoever's doing this means Cade harm.' He pulled away. 'I think maybe they really do just want to talk.' He turned to me. 'Your call, buddy. I can force the path forward if I have to, but then you'll never know why this mysterious admirer of yours is so determined to meet you.'

I sighed. 'So what happens if I follow the road to the left?'

The diabolic put up his hands. 'Then you're out of my protection. Take one step off the path and you're on your own. I've got no control over what happens next until and unless you return.'

'Then why are we even discussing this?' Galass asked. 'Of course Cade's not going to—'

'I'll go,' I said.

'Why?' she asked. 'Why would you risk it?'

I buttoned up my blue brocade coat and straightened my cuffs. Not sure why, but I felt like whatever was about to happen, I should meet it with as much dignity as I could muster. 'Somebody's going to a lot of trouble to have a chat with me. It would be rude to ignore the invitation.'

Without another word, I stepped to my left, off Tenebris' path and into the Infernal depths.

CHAPTER 24

Voices from the Shadows

I've made a lot of bad decisions in my life. An argument could be made – in fact, it *had* been made, by the kind-hearted woman to whom I was about to be wed, just minutes before she cast a skin binding on me (which really isn't as much fun as it sounds- try to imagine your own skin becoming a straitjacket: you could theoretically get out of it, but you really wouldn't want to) – that I'd never made a *good* decision. Given she subsequently tried to stab me to death with my own sword, I could see her point; deciding to marry her had clearly been one of those bad decisions she'd been so forcefully complaining about. Accepting a mysterious invitation to leave the safety of Tenebris' path, risking certain and no doubt horribly painful death in search of some enigmatic stranger, lent further credence to that particular view.

'Hello?' I called out to the all-encompassing darkness surrounding me.

The tremor in my voice was unflattering. You never want to sound frightened while wandering blindly in the Infernal demesne. That single step off the path had been all it took to lose sight of Corrigan and the others; now I could see no points of reference whatsoever, just endless shadows everywhere, swirling and oozing like thick blots of oil across glass.

Better than walking through the grasping hands of the damned, I supposed.

Though that didn't explain the shaking of my own hands. I felt that uncomfortable itch at the back of my neck that told me I was being watched.

'Why is that which we cannot see so much more terrifying than the horrors we can?' I asked aloud. I hadn't been expecting – or even wanting – an answer.

Alas, that's usually when answers come.

'It's the emptiness we all fear,' said a voice older and slightly higher-pitched than my own. Where it had come from I couldn't tell. 'Death. Pain. Madness. These are all merely gates through which we pass into that void. Do you recall the secret name of that emptiness?'

I called out to the darkness, 'And here I thought I was being lured into a fatal encounter with some hideous demoniac monstrosity planning to feast on my soul for ever and a day. But if my eternal torment is going to involve listening to a philosopher, I'm out of here.' I made a show of turning to leave, despite having not the first idea how I'd get back to Tenebris and my crew.

Whoever it was laughed, as embracing as a warm blanket; light-hearted, if tempered with a touch of old-age wheeze. I remembered that laugh even before I recognized the voice to which it belonged.

From the smothering, swirling void of shadows emerged a figure, at first barely more than the faint tracing of a charcoal line upon a vast black canvas. Her shape grew more distinct with every step, until I could make out her silhouette. She was taller than me, and I wasn't a short man by any means. Older than I remembered, a little crooked at the neck, but still broad in the shoulders. Her walk was a little uneven now, weighted more heavily on the left side, but she had lost none of the strength and purposefulness that had made her so formidable to those like me who would have followed her into battle no matter the odds.

Once she got close enough, the darkness around her dissolved enough that I could make out the silver-grey of her arching eyebrows and short-cropped hair. The scar on her jawline was one I'd been proud to give her during a fencing bout back when she'd insisted I practise with the longsword even though such mundane weapons were barely more than props in our profession.

Of all the people I'd ever imagined meeting in Hell, surely the last was Hazidan Rosh. Once First Paladin of the Glorian Justiciars, she was the woman who'd tried and failed to take an angry, reckless young man and turn him into the sort of hero she so effortlessly embodied. Yet here she stood, looking much as she had five years ago when I'd walked away from her – if you ignored the two black holes in place of the pair of steel blue eyes which had gazed out at the world in amused judgement.

'Cade,' she said, and reached out a hand to give my shoulder a shake. 'You look like shit.'

CHAPTER 25

Friends in Low Places

'Master?' I half expected the blinded figure before me to open her mouth wide and come at me with pointy fangs and a forked tongue. To be honest, that might have been a relief.

'Was I ever that?' she asked, and rubbed the collar of my blue coat between thumb and forefinger as if there were something tawdry about it. 'You seem to have forgotten everything I tried to teach you.'

'Maybe you weren't very good at teaching.'

One eyebrow arched as she looked at me dubiously. I'd always envied her that eyebrow trick.

'You really want me to have to go searching around here for a willow stick with which to beat you?' she asked.

'Hell's a big place,' I replied. 'Might take you a while.'

'I'm a patient woman these days.'

'Smug arseholes usually are.'

It's possible the conversation was getting off on the wrong foot. It's been my experience that reunions between former disappointing students and their disapproving teachers inevitably do. I was trying to ignore an almost overwhelming desire to fall to my knees before her, to kiss her hand and tell her how badly I missed her counsel, how I'd all but forgotten everything she'd taught me and what a ruin I'd made of my life – and I just knew that part of her longed to hug me like a lost child and fill my ears with those platitudes for which she was notorious – the ones that never sounded like platitudes at the time, but instead a kind of spell bestowing upon you the faith you needed to carry on and try again.

Such simple moments of affection should have been the most natural thing in the world between us, and yet, even here in this place where it would mean the most, neither of us could bring ourselves to make the attempt. Idealistic boys become cynical men, gruff women become grouchy codgers and no one is able to stop that progression.

'You've come down in the world, Master,' I observed.

Hazidan *harrumphed*. 'It's not so bad here, actually. They let me bring my books – not that I needed to, as it turned out.' She headed into the darkness, heavy on that left foot, but moving quickly none-theless. 'You can find almost any text ever written somewhere in the endless halls of the Infernal demesne, if you're willing to look hard enough.'

'And pay the price for it,' I said, jogging to catch up with her.

'These amateurs? I've haggled with street urchins selling stolen fruit who were tougher negotiators than these diabolics and demo-niacs and whoever.'

The shadows began to change as we walked through them, or perhaps my own senses were acclimatising. Now I could see that we were in a wide corridor with an arched ceiling stretching further than my eyes could see. I peered into the open doors we passed: here was a bedroom, with a bathing chamber opposite; a dressing room had twenty or more identical white robes, their only ornamentation a simple gold fringe, hanging on a rail – Hazidan was wearing just such a robe. But most of the rooms were filled with shelves packed with books, each with a desk, a low table or a small reading couch crammed in, upon which were piled even more volumes.

Hazidan got a little smile on her face as she passed by each miniature library. 'All in all,' she said, with a contented sigh, 'a perfectly reasonable place to spend one's retirement.'

'I recently noticed several thousands of the damned who'd perhaps argue differently.'

Hazidan's jaw set in that way that told me I'd just pissed her off, which was to say I'd expressed an unfounded philosophical proposition that happened to contradict her own views.

'"Damned" is such a *lazy* word. It implies victimhood. No one can "damn" anyone else, Cade. Surely I taught you better than that. Do you really not remember the answer to the question I posed earlier?'

'I've forgotten already. Remind me.'

Times like these, she'd usually slap me hard around the head, a gentle reminder that the affection of one's teacher was in no way protection against their actual teachings. 'What is the secret name of emptiness?'

The answer was *ourselves*, of course, but I wasn't going to give her the satisfaction of saying it out loud. Nothing in either my former or current professions suggested that Hazidan's almost obsessive convictions about free will were true. Coercion, duress, manipulation, deception – these are the means by which those who desire our moral downfall trick us into it.

She threw up her hands as if we were back in her classroom at the justiciars' training hall and she'd just wasted hours trying to get me to appreciate such a simple axiological precept. 'All these years and you *still* can't get that one lesson through your skull . . .'

'And here's me thinking I took your lessons too much to heart, given you convinced me to betray my oaths to the justiciars and got me excommunicated by the Lords Celestine.'

Hazidan stopped, turned and stared at me through those empty eye sockets. They made it even harder than usual not to shy away from her stare. 'You convinced yourself, Cade – all I did was point

out the obvious inconsistencies in our mission. That you were unable
to reconcile them wi—'

'You were my *teacher*!' I shouted, trying to push her away from
me. It was like trying to shove the hindquarters of a war horse. 'You
were supposed to help strengthen my faith so that I could stand
shoulder to shoulder with our brethren! One day you were praising
me, telling me I might even become a paladin like you, then the
next, you started twisting everything you'd ever told me, until I
doubted *everything*!'

Standing in some forsaken corner of Hell, shouting at a woman
who had apparently consigned herself by choice to the place most
Mortals fear more than any other, it occurred to me that perhaps I
was carrying more pain since our parting than I'd realised.

But Hazidan stood there, weathering my tirade with the same
preternatural calm that had made her so formidable, both as an
Auroral magistrate and a holy warrior.

'Are you done?' she asked, but she didn't bother to wait for an
answer before resuming progress down this apparently endless
hallway.

We passed yet more libraries, but there were other rooms, too,
including a second bedroom. I wondered why Hazidan would need a
second bedroom – perhaps after a hard day's reading, she sometimes
found walking all the way back to the bedroom at the start of the
corridor too onerous? Or maybe on occasion she was allowed house
guests here in the Infernal demesne.

A small study caught my eye. It wasn't another of the little libraries; the bookshelf in the corner didn't have room for much more
than a dozen volumes, and there were no books piled on either the
small desk or the single chair.

But the room that stopped me in my tracks had nothing in it
but a small square carpet in the middle of the stone floor and a
meditation vase suspended from the ceiling above a bronze basin.

I didn't need to examine the huge glass vase to know there'd be a tiny hole in the bottom, just big enough to allow a single drop of water to pass through every second or so. It would make a tiny sound when it struck either the bronze or the water that would gradually pool there. Glorian Justiciars would confine themselves for days on end so they could contemplate particularly thorny moral dilemmas.

I'd stopped, because in all my time with her, I had never seen Hazidan make use of an anchorite chamber.

'What is this place you've built, Master?' I asked. 'What are you doing spending your last days in the Infernal demesne? And don't give me any more nonsense about this being a pleasant place to spend your retirement. It's not. It's fucking *Hell*. It's the last place any sane Glorian Justic—'

Oh shit.

She smiled that faintly patronising smile of hers that said it was nice you'd finally worked out the obvious answer to your own question, but perhaps next time you could try to get there a little quicker.

As she sped up, I trotted behind her, puzzling it out. 'The Infernal demesne is the only place the Lords Celestine couldn't reach you, isn't it? What on earth have you done that's so bad – worse even than turning one of your students against the justiciars – that has you hiding out in Hell? Hazidan, *what have you done?*'

She stopped again, this time in front of a pair of closed double doors. The wood was silvery-white, like the bark of a poplar tree, with carved golden handles that might have been birchwood. I was pretty sure Hazidan had timed our arrival intentionally.

'I asked too many questions,' she said, taking me aback.

'What kind of questions?'

She turned away from the doors and reached out a hand to my face. I almost recoiled – she usually only did that when she was planning to smack me for impertinence – but I was right to hold my nerve, for she only stroked my cheek.

'I demanded answers to the kind of questions you've begun to ask yourself, Cade: the ones that have brought you here to me.'

'What's happened to the Lords Celestine, Master? Why are they trading angelics for the allegiance of small-time princelings? Why are they propping up psychotic dictators like Ascendant Lucien? Why are there Glorian Justiciars following me everywhere I go?'

'Following *you*?' Hazidan asked. Her blatantly feigned surprise clearly meant, *I trained you as an investigator, Cade. You've seen for yourself that questions invite consequences, so why are you still asking the wrong ones?*

Finally, the penny dropped. 'The Glorians haven't been following me at all, have they? They've been *herding* me!'

She clapped her hands.

When Hazidan Rosh tells you that you got something right at last, it's like a glorious golden sun has come out from behind the clouds to shine just for you.

I will admit there might be a small – *very* small – chance I had always been a trifle obsessed with winning my old master's approval.

'Play it through, Cade,' she said, just as if we were back in her classroom. 'Follow the threads, however tenuous they may feel at first, because—'

'"Because sometimes those threads entwine to become a rope strong enough to strangle the truth". Never your best metaphor, Master, if I'm honest.' Before she could conjure up a worse one, I did as she asked. 'Right, so I took the citadel siege job because the Glorians had been getting too close and Ascendant Lucien, whose crusade was blessed by the Lords Celestine, offered me a pardon for all my sins that would bind even the justiciars from arresting me. But then the Celestines granted Lucien permission to slaughter Archon Belleda's surrendering forces.'

'At which point you ... ?'

I didn't appreciate the knowing smirk on Hazidan's face.

'At which point I gave the matter careful consideration,

contemplated all the ethical points in exhaustive detail and decided to murder the son of a bitch.'

'Really?' she asked. Her shocked expression was entirely unconvincing. '*You* of all people decided to go off and do something incredibly reckless because the Ascendant turned out to be a homicidal maniac, and – so much worse – a *hypocritical* homicidal maniac?'

'You're saying the Celestines predicted that I'd lose my shit?'

'I'm saying that given the circumstances, betting that you would "lose your shit" would be easy money.'

I walked up to the door. I was pretty sure that whatever was on the other side would be the punchline to Hazidan's extended joke at my expense, but when I tried the handle, it was locked.

I turned back to face Hazidan. 'The flaw in whichever convoluted theory you're currently pursuing here is that I *wasn't* the one who murdered the Ascendant. If the Lords Celestine were half so clever at mapping the terrain of human behaviour as they claim, how did they fail to predict that Corrigan – just about the most predictable human being alive – was going stop me? Unless—'

Ah, crap, I realised then. *I'm really not going to like how this turns out.*

'Go on,' Hazidan urged.

'Unless they knew Tenebris would refuse to sell me the hellborn conjuration in the first place, because they were already aware that Lucien was as useful to the machinations of the Lords Devilish as to their own.'

'And yet the Lords Celestine clearly wanted Lucien dead, otherwise he would still be alive,' Hazidan pointed out. 'But how to go about it without revealing their hand to the Infernals?'

There was something almost exciting about having her walk me through the case like this, as if we were back in her study at the justiciars' hall, poring over scraps of evidence and challenging each other's assumptions, instead of merely interrogating witnesses with fear and flame, which was what the other trainee justiciars were taught to do.

'What you're implying is just too convoluted, Master. Lucien was killed by a sublime. Fidick was just a little boy – he'd been so mis-used and traumatised that when he saw my ritual, he memorised every bit of it so he could make a deal with Tenebris. But how could the Celestines have predicted Fidick's behaviour? Even if they had prompted Lucien to reward his war mages with the pick of his sublimes, why would—?'

'How did you pick yours?'

'What?'

'You had the choice of any of the Ascendant's sublimes, you said – so how did you pick yours?'

'I . . . I don't know – I didn't want them in the first place. You think I've fallen so low that I'd take to abusing children for my own pleasure?'

She may have had no eyes to roll, but somehow, she still managed to convey the sentiment. 'Can you put your righteous indignation to one side for the moment? Your lack of intention did not stop you from accepting the Ascendant's gift, did it? So *how* did you choose, Cade?'

You'd think it would be hard for an eyeless woman to stare at you with such obvious irritation, willing your slow-witted, plodding pace to reach what should have been the glaringly obvious conclusion.

'I chose the youngest,' I realised suddenly. 'I picked the most terrified-looking, the one I thought would come out the most dam-aged if anyone but Corrigan picked him. Lucien said his captains had to select two each, so I also chose Galass, the girl Fidick was clinging to, because I thought separating them would have made things worse for the kid.'

'So,' Hazidan said, starting to pace around me as if I were a piece of furniture, 'despite your feeble attempts to rebel against your own instincts, turning mercenary, trafficking in Infernal magic to gain work as a petty wonderist, all so you can convince yourself that you're beyond redemption, your actions remain entirely predictable. Continue.'

'I'm not— Fine. So I brought Fidick and Galass to my tent, they witnessed me negotiating with Tenebris, and when I stormed off, the boy apparently repeated my ritual word for word, which, in retrospect, was a remarkable feat, given he'd nev— Oh, shit. The kid was a plant, wasn't he?'

'Given you've just described a terrified little boy performing a demoniac summoning ritual and getting it right on the first try, I'd say that's a reasonable assumption.' Hazidan smacked my head. I knew it was going to happen sooner or later. 'And stop swearing in my presence. Cursing is the lazy man's wit.'

'That's sarcasm.'

She smacked me again. 'Continue. You're almost there.'

It's an uncomfortable feeling, examining events in which you assumed you were in control of your own actions, only to realise you were a puppet blind to his own strings.

'Okay ... so either Ascendant Lucien— No, he was an idiot. It had to be one of the Lords Celestine themselves. So, one of them communes with a young sublime – one who just happens to have a natural affinity for Infernal magic – and teaches him how to focus his will. The ritual itself isn't especially difficult, as long as one knows how to draw on one's attunement to the Infernal plane. Torturing a diabolic using the spell-sand I'd left behind – well, that should have been really hard for an innocent eleven-year-old boy, but if a Lord Celestine was secretly whispering in his ear ...'

The Auroral Voice. It's more than a sound or a whisper. It's a *song* that infuses you with blissful serenity and the *absolute* certainty that you're doing the right thing: the sure and certain knowledge that you are *righteous*.

'So Fidick forced Tenebris to make the deal for a hellborn

conjuration and commanded it to rip Lucien to shreds. The murder gets pinned on me because Cousin Green, the kid who'd begged to become my apprentice when I joined the Ascendant's crusade – also, apparently, in the pocket of the Celestines – tells the other wonderists it was my spell that did the deed. That forces Corrigan to save my life by killing the other wonderists.'

'Such wonderful companions you choose to consort with,' Hazidan said drily.

'With my pardon now in more tatters than Lucien's flesh, I had no choice but to take the first job that would get me away from the justiciars.'

'A job you'd earlier refused, I assume?' Hazidan asked.

'Damned right. No details, no contact with the client, just a bunch of nonsense about needing seven wonderists, without even specifying what attunements were needed . . .'

'Cade?'

A thought had just come to me: a terrible, awful, give-me-somebody-whose-neck-I-can-wring thought. If I'd been dizzy from all the twists and turns of this scheme before, now I felt sick to my stomach.

'Galass,' I said at last.

'The girl?' Hazidan asked. 'The one you said was so protective of the boy?'

'She loved him more than anything in the world.' There was nothing else I could say.

How the hell was I going to explain to her that the second part of Fidick's deal with Tenebris – the sacrifice of his own life in exchange for transforming her into someone who'd never again have to fear being abused by others – was nothing more than a devious scheme by the Lords Celestines to ensure they had *exactly* the right kinds of mages for the job they'd ambushed us into taking on?

'Aurorals can't actually imbue a Mortal with blood magic, can they?' I asked hopefully.

'You know they can't,' Hazidan replied tersely. 'Only diabolics can awaken such an attunement, and only then in someone who already possesses the potential.'

Which meant Fidick had likely met her in the camps, not at whichever sublime abbey had raised them. He'd been ordered to play on her sympathies, cuddle up to her at night, doubtless calming his sobbing only when she held on to him. I'd lay good silver on him having suggested they pretend to be brother and sister so neither would feel so alone.

'Whatever rebellion or war is brewing up north, the Lords Celestine are betting that a blood mage is going to make a difference to the winning side. That's why they needed Galass.'

Hazidan placed her hands on my shoulders. 'And you,' she said. Her voice was oddly quiet, almost tender.

I practically stuttered my next words, so unaccustomed to this kind of affection from her. 'Me? I'm a second-rate Infernalist. I'm not half the mage Corrigan is – or Aradeus, for that matter. He's got real skills.'

'They knew you'd protect her, Cade,' she said, pulling me in close.

Hazidan *never* held *anyone* close. On some level I knew Hazidan cared deeply for me, as I did her, but neither of us would *ever* have dreamed of expressing that love by any means other than rude remarks and the occasional – *very* occasional – approving grunt.

That wasn't *our* way.

Except here I was, enfolded in the strong arms of someone I'd looked up to more than anyone else in the world.

'They knew you'd be overwhelmed with guilt over her fate, that you'd watch over her, help her control her abilities. They knew that no matter what, you'd never abandon her the way I abandoned you.'

'That's not—'

She squeezed me tighter, mostly, I think, to cut off my breath and shut me up. 'I told you before: none of us can be damned by anyone but ourselves. I've made peace with my sins, although not, I'll grant you, in a way you'd approve of.'

I pushed away from her, unable to contend with both the warmth of her affection and the cold shiver of my trepidation over what she'd been keeping from me. 'What's behind the door, Master?'

She reached out a hand, and without even touching the knob, one of the doors began to swing open. She said something then, her voice low, almost a whisper.

I could have sworn the word she'd uttered was *Redemption*.

CHAPTER 26

The Recruit

Hazidan's silver-white doors opened on to a gallery overlooking a huge hall with marble floors broken up by sections of polished hickory. One of these was twenty feet long and six feet wide, looking suspiciously like a fencing piste. Another was circular, maybe thirty feet in diameter, the floor within warped in places to rise up as high as four feet or sinking two feet below ground level: Hazidan's own design, I recalled, for training on treacherous terrain. The twenty-foot-high walls were panelled in a dark oak of almost impossible smoothness. One side was festooned with every type of weapon you could imagine, not to mention a fair few I couldn't even begin to work out what they might be good for. The other side was shelved with row upon row of yet more books.

At the far end, opposite the double doors, was a single chair with a golden nine-pointed star hanging above it. I didn't need to get close enough to examine it; I knew every single line inscribed on every inch. Upon that star were the moral tenets Hazidan had once taught me, with the symbols representing those ideas at each point.

I knew this place. A place almost exactly like this had once been my home.

I looked at her in disbelief. 'You've recreated the justiciars' training hall.'

'I have.'

'In Hell.'

'A lazy word conceived by lazy minds to teach us who to hate, but . . . yes, I've recreated the hall of the Glorian Justiciars in Hell.'

I was half expecting a sudden appearance of horns, fangs and claws, which would doubtless be followed shortly thereafter by a surprisingly quick fall over the railing to break my neck on the marble floor twenty feet below us.

It was worse, somehow, that she was still Hazidan, still the great paladin of the justiciars.

'Please,' I said, 'I am *begging* you, please tell me you aren't training a host of demoniacs to become some sort of private military force to counter the justiciars. Because if, after all this, it turns out you're just some bitter old cow who's been down here plotting a coup d'état against her old bosses, I'm going to be incredibly disappointed.'

She did that eyebrow-raising thing again. It was particularly disconcerting above the empty socket. 'Now, does that sound like something I'd stoop to, Cade?'

'It sounds *exactly* like something you'd conceive, Master. The only difference is that you'd try to find some obscure ethical precept by which to justify what any *sane* person would agree is a completely *insane* thing to do.'

She laughed at that, her deep, thick-as-molasses laugh rising up from the soles of her feet to fill her entire body. She laughed so hard that she had to put a hand on my shoulder to steady herself, while I braced myself for those horns and fangs and claws to appear.

'You're really making me uncomfortable, Master.'

I hadn't thought it possible for her to laugh even harder, but I really should have learned not to underestimate her.

After a few moments, she settled into a kind of satisfied chortling, punctuated by the occasional snort. 'Ah, Cade, you always were my favourite student. You know why?'

'The other apprentices hated you.'

She tilted her head a little. 'I suppose that's true, isn't it? But no, the reason you were my favourite is because of the Two Cades.'

'The two what, now?'

'The Two Cades: the first is perceptive, insightful, almost preternaturally gifted at peeking behind the veil of human self-deception to see the truth underneath.' She reached out a hand and cupped my jaw. Hell had really made her go soft. 'The other is a callow boy who won't stop hiding behind cynicism and a desperate fear that should he ever find something truly worth believing in, he'll be trapped: shackled for the rest of his days beneath the unbearable weight of knowing that the world really is worth defending.'

'Maybe I would have been a better student if you weren't trying so hard to be a poet, Master. What the fuck is any of that supposed to mean?'

She gestured down at the training hall. 'You know what this is about – and don't start up with all that nonsense about me wanting to create my own little demoniac army, because I'll tolerate insubordination from you, but not lazy conjecture.'

I followed her pointing finger, studying that replica of a place that had been the most sacred in all the world to me until, suddenly, it wasn't any more. I understood what Hazidan had been up to here in the Infernal demesne. It wasn't just about hiding from the Celestines, nor about getting revenge on them, although that was surely part of it, despite what she might have liked to believe. This was, I was certain, about the passion that drove Hazidan more than any loyalty or spiritual vocation ever had: proving something which no other Auroral but her had ever believed.

'We all have a choice,' I said, and she grinned, a trifle too manically for my tastes.

'Free will, Cade, the Great Gift. With awareness, with consciousness, comes choice. None of us can be damned by anyone but

ourselves. No one can be forgiven – no one can be *redeemed* – save
by their own heart.'

'You haven't been training an army.'

'No.'

'Because the Infernals would never allow it.'

'Correct.'

'But they *do* have a perverse sense of humour. They enjoy a good
prank, especially at the Aurorals' expense, but even at their own.'

'An admirable quality, in my opinion.'

'Yes, but a joke that hits *both* the Aurorals *and* the Infernals? Now
that would be something truly hilarious.'

'Stop dancing around the question, Cade.'

She was right; I *was* trying to avoid it, maybe because, deep down,
I'd always felt a certain twisted pride in the notion that I was the
only one: Hazidan's one true student. It hurt to think that after
giving up on me, she'd tried with someone else.

'Who is he?' I asked.

'Not "he".'

She took me by the shoulder and spun me around to face the
long corridor we'd come from. A woman was standing a few feet
from the doors, apparently waiting for us. She was lithe and lean,
wearing a leather cuirass the colour of a lion's mane over an ivory
shirt. The wide, fringed sleeves narrowed as they reached her long
golden gloves. Her trousers were a textured midnight-blue leather,
her boots a shade darker than that. Silvery-white hair shorn almost
to the scalp added a striking contrast to her blue-black skin. The
self-inflicted facial scars her people considered fashionable were not
Infernal sigils but the symbols graven into the nine-pointed star
above Hazidan's training hall and representing a set of ideals that
should have been utterly foreign to an Infernal.

'You've lost your mind,' I breathed, staring at the demoniac. She,
in turn, stared right back at me – at my wonderist's coat, specifi-

cally – with far more disdain than one would expect from a being whose favourite food was probably ecclesiasm extracted from dead puppies or something equally horrific.

'I did, in fact, lose my mind,' Hazidan confessed. She walked over to the girl – the demoniac, I should say – and put one arm around her shoulders. My old mentor looked far more comfortable showing affection to an Infernal than she'd ever been with me. 'Meet your sixth recruit.'

CHAPTER 27

Comrades

Her name was Alice, and, even for a demon, she proved to be a real pain in the arse right from the start.

'Could you slow down?' I called up to her as I ran breathlessly along the winding, dizzying path. 'Some of us don't have wings.'

She glanced down just long enough for me to catch a glimpse of the same smirk I'd got the last two times I'd politely requested a little consideration. I was starting to really look forward to the first time she stepped out onto the Mortal plane and discovered that a pair of bat-like wings barely longer than her arms wouldn't provide nearly enough lift for a human-sized body to propel itself through the air. In the meantime, I had to rely on the light cast every time she cracked her steel whip-sword in front of us to split the shadows, allowing me to see the path ahead.

What were you thinking, Master? I wondered despairingly.

Hazidan Rosh had always been eccentric – *unstable*, even – but behind those piercing storm-coloured eyes there had always been a . . . a sagacity. A kind of insight that promised this time for sure she knew what she was doing. I hadn't seen a single sign of that sagacity when she'd informed me that not only had she trained a demoniac in the ways of the justiciars, but that she expected me to recruit her new apprentice into my coven.

'You have to look beyond the old divisions, the old fights,' Hazidan had said as I'd walked away from her cosy private corner of the Infernal demesne. 'The game changed while the rest of us weren't paying attention. The players aren't who we think they are.'

'What's that even supposed to mean?' I exploded. 'Why are you still talking in riddles, saddling me with a fucking *demoniac* who thinks she's a justiciar and expecting me to just blindly go along? What are you keeping from me, Hazidan? What *exactly* is waiting for us in the Blastlands?'

I don't know why I bothered shouting, or asking questions at all. Among the justiciars, Hazidan was without peer at two things: extracting information people didn't want to reveal, and never giving away more than she wanted you to know.

'Take Alice with you,' she said. 'Her calibre of demon was bred to survive the translation to the Mortal plane. She's a rare one; the Lords Devilish killed off most of them because their minds aren't quite right.'

'That's hardly an endorsement for recruitment!'

Actually, given how psychotically zealous most Glorian Justiciars were, maybe derangement *was* a qualification worth considering.

Yet again, Hazidan had placed her hand on my cheek. She was becoming worryingly touchy-feely in her dotage.

'Do it for me, Cade. Do it for an old woman who's been proven wrong so many times that all she's got left is the faith that maybe even her worst mistakes, her most unforgivable errors in judgement, have a purpose. You owe me this much, Cade.'

Her 'most unforgivable errors in judgement', in case you missed it, included me. The old bully might have lost her eyes, but never her nerve.

'Alice' – her proper demonic name was probably the sound one makes when spewing blood and broken teeth – was yet again flying too far ahead.

I started running faster, trying to catch up – until my foot slipped on the glassy blackness of the path. Before I knew it, I was falling into the depths, leaving only my panicked shouts behind. Reaching out around me, I caught only empty space, as if I'd been dropped right in the centre of a canyon with no sides.

If only that had been true.

Without Tenebris' blood to pacify the damned, the nearest grabbed me, pawing at my clothes, trying to rip them from my body, as if wearing them would somehow improve their Infernal existence. I felt teeth biting through my boots at the soles of my feet, and tongues licking at my neck, savouring the fear exuding from my pores.

This is it, I thought. *This is where I've been headed all along, where I'll end up when it's all over.*

Claws sharp as talons dug into my shoulder, piercing through the thick leather of my coat, tearing a second scream from me, and I screamed a third time as I was wrenched upwards, away from the hands and teeth and tongues of the damned, until I was dangling high above the writhing, moaning mass of abandoned humanity.

'You should be more careful,' my rescuer said as she dropped me unceremoniously back on the glassy black path. The gold fringes on her ivory justiciar's shirt swatted me in the face as she ascended once again. I longed for a pair of scissors; I would have enjoyed clipping those stupid things – along with her wings. One thing about demoniacs, though: they can sense emotions, as if each one has its own unique smell. I guess I must have been stinking pretty badly.

'Something you want to say to me, fallen one?' she asked, turning in mid-air before winging back to land less than a foot from where I stood. The steel ribbon of her whip-sword slithered back inside the bone hilt and she sheathed it in the short scabbard she wore in the small of her back.

Fallen one. You know you've screwed up your life when a demon starts referring to you as *'fallen one'*.

I didn't so much resent her for having decided I was the lesser of Hazidan's metaphorical progeny as for implying the two of us had anything in common at all. So I got in her face. 'I'm thinking it's best you and I have it out, here and now, before any confusion sets in.'

An eager and entirely unpleasant smile came to her features, the lines of her ritual scars contorting to add menace to her obvious disdain for me. 'You believe you can best me in a duel?'

She unfurled her wings and took up a stance that had the points twisting towards me. I've no idea why demoniacs think showing off their wings makes them look tough. All it does is remind you that they've got these two flappy appendages that aren't particularly good for combat but sure look pretty when they start flapping madly after you've lit them on fire.

'Couldn't care which of us is the better duellist,' I informed her. 'I've got business to take care of that doesn't involve dealing with the demoniac equivalent of a petulant teenager trying to impress . . . actually, I've no idea who the hell you're trying to impress. Regardless, since you seem determined to get me killed, I figured we could save some time and see if you've got the stones to take me on in a *fair* fight.'

'Trust me, fallen one, when I decide to ki—'

I decked her.

Yeah, it was a dirty move, but why did you think I made a point of asking for a fair fight, if not to use it to catch her off guard? Infernals are more durable than humans, other than the fact that they get sick and die pretty quickly if they set foot on Mortal soil, but Hazidan had made a point of teaching me both fencing and boxing. As effete wonderists go, I've got a pretty good right hook, and Alice nearly took a dive right there and then.

'You hit me!' When she spun back around, she had one hand covering her bleeding nose. 'I think you broke it!'

'Seems only right. You set me up to fall into the depths just so you could haul me back up and laugh in my face. A bloody nose is a fair exchange – and you Infernals are all about square deals, aren't you?'

I kept my gaze soft, watching her wings for the slightest twitch that would tell me she was going to attack. That's another flaw with wings: even the slightest move – like, say, reaching for the hilt of a whip-sword at your back – requires shifting them to keep your balance.

She'll go for a distraction first. Hazidan always said the tongue can be as sharp a weapon as any blade.

Alice squeezed the bridge of her nose, snapping it back into place with a sickening crunch that almost but not quite hid the subsequent twitch of her left wing as her right hand reached back for the hilt of the whip-sword.

I punched her in the nose again, in the exact same spot.

'That's the problem with relying on Hazidan's old tricks,' I said, waiting for Alice to recover and push her nose back into place a second time. 'I know them, too, *demon.*'

She took two steps back, getting out of range so she could draw the sword. I didn't interfere this time. She gave a shake of the foot-long bone hilt and the silvery ribbon slid out once more, hissing in the air like a snake as it snapped back and forth between being flexible as rope and rigid as a steel blade. If you've ever tried fencing against a weapon that changes shape when it thrusts, you'll understand why parrying it with a regular sword is almost impossible. Not that I had a regular sword to parry with.

'Call me a demon again, *human,*' she snarled, 'diminish me with that word once more and see what *that* buys you.'

Yeah, yeah: I spotted the hypocrisy, too. There's a lot of it going around. What did surprise me, however, was the sincerity of her indignity.

'Hazidan really did a number on you, didn't she?' I asked. 'You think just because she dressed you up in a justiciar's mantle and made you memorise a bunch of philosophical nonsense that you're no longer an Infernal bound to the schemes of the Lords Devilish?'

'What I am, *fallen one*, is what I *choose* to be. I am Alice, and you will address me so or face the consequences.'

Stupid name for a demon, by the way, but I didn't say that out loud.

An unexpected sympathy came over me for the young demoniac. Hazidan has always had this talent for convincing people to see themselves as individuals, as unique, even when she was convincing them to join an army as militantly disciplined as the justiciars. That appeal to one's sense of individuality was also how she'd convinced me to betray them.

'Fair enough, Alice,' I said, not bothering to extend my hand so as to avoid having it cut off by a hissing blade. 'My name is Cade Ombra. Not "human", not "fallen one". Cade.'

You'd think what I'd just said would have been the end of it, but the demon girl just tilted her head and looked at me like I was an idiot. 'But you *have* fallen, Cade Ombra. My calling you otherwise won't change that fact. And I do not use the term as an insult, for no man nor woman can rise again, lest first they—'

'If you're going to start spouting the old woman's nonsense about redemption back at me, at least get the quote right. "The measure of a man is not how high he rises, but in how gracefully he falls."'

Alice's features scrunched up in confusion. 'That is . . . not how she told it to me.'

'Well, she's old,' I said, feeling a certain smug satisfaction as I set out on the nearly invisible path before the others got tired of waiting and left me here. 'She's probably senile.'

I heard the rush of air as Alice flew up ahead of me. 'Or perhaps with age she has gained the enlightenment to see that the dignity of women is as worthy of discussion as that of men.'

I do so enjoy getting lessons on bigotry from entities whose inborn disposition is focused on the torture and destruction of all other beings. 'And apparently she thinks a demon can shed their Infernal nature by pretending to be an Auroral justiciar!' I shouted back.

She made a slight, almost insignificant turn in the air to the right;
I followed, and there was Corrigan, barely ten feet ahead, with the
others gathered around him. First thing Alice did when she landed –
the very *first* thing? She started sneering at Galass, Shame, Corrigan
and Aradeus like they were all morally beneath her. I swear, she
even shot the damn jackal a dirty look.

I took Corrigan aside, hoping to explain the odd choice of this
last-minute addition to our crew, but he cut me off before I could
try. 'A flying demoniac with a whip-sword, dressed as a justiciar
apprentice and looking down at the rest of us like we're all pieces
of shit staining her impeccable boot heels? What's to explain, Cade?
That is the most *you* fucking choice of recruit imaginable.'

Tenebris dug a nail into the vein at his wrist again, but this time
he used the blood to trace a six-foot-wide circle in the air before
us that shook and shuddered like the space around the portal was
trying to collapse it. 'Closing time, people,' the diabolic said, ushering us all through. 'You don't have to go home, but you sure as
shit can't stay here.'

Aradeus stood to one side and graciously gestured for Galass,
Corrigan and Shame to go ahead of him. Corrigan grunted something about Hell being overrated, but the angelic paused before she
stepped through, turning to take one last look at the Infernal plane.
I wondered if she was contemplating what would happen to her
the next time she returned. Galass just held tightly to the whining
Mister Bones, but as she stepped through the portal, the drops of
blood forming the circle that held it open wavered, as if trying to
stop being pulled towards her. I shoved Aradeus after her.

'Get a move on, Cade,' Tenebris warned. I was about to do so, but
then the diabolic did something strange. He turned and hugged me.
'Safe travels, buddy. I love you.'

I was so stunned that after he let go of me, I just stood there like
a tree stump. Alice shoved past me, pausing with one foot already

through the portal to give me a grin so smug you'd think she'd just been handed a map of the universe and found a picture of herself right at the centre. 'You were right, fallen one. If Hazidan believes you and this deranged troop of broken souls you've assembled can unwind the corruption that infests the Lords Celestines, she *must* be senile.'

CHAPTER 28

A Deal's a Deal

We stepped out of Hell and into midnight. Our travels through the Infernal demesne had accustomed our eyes to its glassy, almost shimmering darkness, so it took a moment to reacquaint ourselves to the sight of a full moon overhead and the chill of cold air on our skin rather than the bitterness of spiritual unease.

'Where are we?' Galass asked, shivering. The jackal leaped down from her arms, sniffed the dry reddish ground at our feet and growled.

When Corrigan bent down and pried out a chunk of the cracked crimson clay, the cloying stench slithering inside our nostrils set us all to coughing wetly. A pinkish fog rising up from the toxic soil permeated the air. When I gazed skywards, I would have sworn it rose all the way up where the stars fought a losing battle trying to peek through the haze.

'Breach dross,' Aradeus said, batting the red clay from Corrigan's hand. 'I've never seen so much of it before.'

Shocked, I turned to Tenebris. *'You've brought us to the Blastlands?* The deal was for safe passage through the Infernal plane to our own demesne, a few miles up the Jalbraith Canal—'

The diabolic was standing on the other side of his portal, which had settled down now that Galass was through and his blood wasn't trying to follow her. 'Yeah, that's me: Mister Soft Heart. I just shaved nearly two hundred miles off your journey. Don't all thank me at once.'

'I don't understand.' Galass was still staring at the devastation all around us. 'What is this substance? Why is there so much of it here?'

I'd not explained the concept of breach dross to her, which was another sign I was doing a terrible job of preparing her for her new life as a wonderist. Well, never too late to start. 'Magic is a violation of natural laws,' I told her. 'Casting a spell involves someone attuned to the laws of a different plane of reality creating a momentary fissure between their own plane and another. Usually the physics governing the human realm closes those fractures off quickly enough that nature can reassert itself and life goes on as before. However, if too many mages start firing off too many spells too close together, eventually something breaks, and when that happens, the soil, the water, the air – the fundamentals of life itself – get desecrated in a way that can't be repaired.'

'Then why wasn't there any produced by the battles you fought for Ascendant Lucien against the other wonderists?'

'There probably was some,' Corrigan said, still wiping his hands on his trousers. It's unwise to let breach dross touch your skin for too long. 'Mostly we're killing each other off in small numbers, so there isn't enough breach dross produced to have a noticeable impact on the terrain. But a century or two ago, two covens of war ma—'

'*Armies*, you idiot,' Alice corrected him. 'There were nearly a thousand wonderists on each side.'

'Fine, two *armies* of war mages decided to have it out. They set to, kicking the shit out of each other so one side could rule the continent without the other getting in their way. The problem was, they were too evenly matched, which no doubt made for an exciting six-year-long spectacle, but pretty much permanently devastated this part of the world.'

'Which is an excellent reason not to dilly-dally,' Tenebris said. He pointed to the left, deeper into the desolation. 'The picturesque little town of Mages' Grave is just a few miles ahead. If you don't waste the night sitting around explaining long-past historical conflicts to each other, you can get there by morning.'

'What's the catch?' I asked.

'Catch?' Tenebris shook his head mournfully. 'Cade, buddy. Can't a friend do another friend a favour without getting repaid in dirty looks?'

I would have commented on the nature of good deeds and demons, but I realised I rather urgently needed to walk around a bit to settle my stomach; going from canal barge to the Infernal demesne to a completely different part of the continent had left my guts decidedly uneasy.

Corrigan caught my eye. He didn't look any more pleased by our location than I was. Galass, noticing our scowls, asked, 'But isn't this a good thing? We don't need to travel nearly as far now, or buy horses or—'

'A deal is a deal,' Alice said. Her eerie silver eyes, like bottled moonlight, never left Tenebris. I was beginning to think she hated him even more than she hated me, although I couldn't think why. 'But a bargain is *never* a bargain.'

It was the first thing she'd said that I agreed with. Hazidan always had loved a good axiom.

'We're still one short, aren't we?' Aradeus asked. His gloved finger counted us off one by one. 'Corrigan, our thunderer. Galass, our blood mage. The angelic Lady Sha—'

'Shame is sufficient,' she said.

He flashed that gallant smile of his. 'Never to me, my lady.' His finger moved to Alice. 'A demoniac justiciar, our esotericist Cade, and me for rat magic. That's six.' He turned to Corrigan. 'Where is our seventh?'

Corrigan stretched an arm southwards. 'About eight days' ride back that way, waiting for us on the Jalbraith Canal and no doubt wondering why we haven't shown up at the meeting point.'

'No problem,' I said, standing in front of Tenebris. 'My agent here, in the spirit of his new-found generosity, will be happy to do us the favour of taking us back through the Infernal Lands to where we need to go.'

The diabolic shook his head. 'Sorry, Cade. The deal was for a one-way trip. How would it look to the bosses if I went around doing favours for clients?'

I smiled in that way I knew Tenebris would recognise as a sign I'd reached the limit of my amiable disposition. 'Fair enough. Just stick to the original agreement and return us to the riverbank where we left. *That* was the deal, remember?'

'You're being stupid,' he snapped, avoiding my gaze. 'I've brought you closer to the job. You should be grateful!'

'And yet here I am,' I countered, sticking my face up to the portal until we were nose to nose with only the faintest shimmer in the air between us, 'ready to be more ungrateful than you can possibly imagine.'

Tenebris backed up a step. 'Cade, you're getting upset over nothing. Besides, there's really no point in you going back to find whichever lame hack the big purple-haired brute was planning to hire for the job.'

'Why not?' Aradeus asked. He was looking a little snippy himself, perhaps wondering if the derisive view Tenebris held of Corrigan's choice of recruits included him too.

'Because time works differently in the Infernal demesne, rat boy. We're not all caught up in temporal coherency like you lot are. Some planes move slower, others faster. The path we took ... well, let's just say I'd be willing to bet your guy's not waiting for you any more.'

'Oh, you son of a bitch,' I swore, reaching for the bag of spell-sand I keep in my pocket for just such occasions – only to find it was gone.

Tenebris dangled the pouch from his side of the portal. 'Looking for this?'

And here's a lesson worth remembering: when a diabolic hugs you and tells you they love you? Maybe check your pockets immediately afterwards.

'Oh, don't get your tentacles in a twist,' the diabolic said. I was pretty sure he meant testicles. 'You've only been off the Mortal plane for a month or so.'

'Which means half the wonderists on the continent have probably beaten us here to take the job away from us,' Corrigan roared, the first sparks of a Tempestoral spell erupting from his clenched right fist. More worryingly, sparks were dancing along his front teeth. '*And* we're still missing our seventh—'

'Is that all?' Tenebris asked, backing up from his side of the portal. Tempestoral magic is unpredictable – sometimes it can pass through other realms. 'Guys, it's all taken care of, I promise. Head on over to Mages' Grave, get yourselves some breakfast, and your last recruit will appear' – Tenebris brought his clawed fingers together then flicked them apart – '*poof!* Like magic!'

'We want *our* guy,' Corrigan insisted.

'Corrigan,' I said quietly.

'Don't try to stop me, Cade, I'm not fucking—'

I stepped away from the portal. 'Fry his ass.'

The diabolic wiped a non-existent teardrop from his eyes, which aren't able to produce any in the first place. 'After all the good times we've had together, I'm truly disappointed.' Abruptly, he spat right at me. The mottled grey-green fluid never hit me, of course; it couldn't pass through to our realm. Instead, it began collapsing the portal. We could still see through, a little – kind of like staring through a sheet of ice.

Corrigan hurled a bolt of red and black lightning, but it passed harmlessly through to the other side as if nothing was there, instead scorching the already wasted red ground fifty feet away from us. As the glassy remnants of the portal darkened to match the night air, Tenebris held out a fist towards me, palm up, then raised his middle finger. He did that often when our negotiations had come to an end. I think it must be a gesture of farewell among his people.

'Nice friends you have, fallen one,' Alice said with the barely contained smugness of a teenager who's just caught her parents drunk and naked on the floor with the neighbours.

I hate demons.

CHAPTER 29

Travelling Companions

Abandoned by our diabolic escort, the six of us – seven if you wanted to count Mister Bones, who'd been rolling around excitedly on the cracked, dusty ground, only to then race around our legs and rub that reddish clay all over us – set off along the closest thing that passed for a road through the Blastlands, towards the town of Mages' Grave.

I kept looking up into the night sky, hoping to see stars, but finding only the scarlet haze that smothered everything here. The spell-poisoned soil on which we trod was no better. The clay might be hard and dry, but somehow it stuck to our heels, slowing us down, grabbing at us like the hands of the damned. Every exhausting step felt both torturous and treacherous, making me wonder if maybe Hazidan had had a point about Hell being as good a place to retire as anywhere else.

'It's as if too much magic drains away the soul of a place,' Galass said, struggling to keep up. 'I feel like . . .' She reached out a hand in front of her, the hem of her white sublime's gown that had shrugged off the dirt of every other place we'd been now caked in red clay. 'I feel like this land doesn't want us any more.'

'Us?' Corrigan asked dubiously.

'Human beings. Mortals.' She shook her head as if trying to shake her thoughts free. 'I'm sorry. I'm not making sense. I'm just so very tired.'

Mister Bones ran beside her, yapping encouragement. She started to bend down to pet him, then gave up. She looked like she was afraid she wouldn't be able to stand up straight again. The problem with blood mages – I mean, other than the high rates of insanity generally leading to mass murder – is that they're so attuned to the flow of life that any corruption of the natural order has a particularly violent effect on them, leaving them generally confused and weak.

All of which you can fix if you just keep your head down, find the client, kill off the seven heroic gentlemen impeding his oppression of the locals, make him give you the Apparatus in payment, and use it to alter Galass' attunement to something less homicidal. Hey, and maybe if the device works more than once, you can use it to give yourself an attunement that doesn't require kissing the arse of a diabolic every time you need a spell!

Yeah, nothing could possibly go wrong with that plan.

Treading through breach-dross infected terrain was hard on all of us, but Aradeus had a fencer's endurance and Corrigan was too bull-headed and competitive to acknowledge physical hardship. I wasn't sure how an angelic's body even worked, but Shame's form kept changing: she'd be older one minute, younger the next, fat, skinny, male, female, and every shade in between. Maybe all that transforming made the way easier for her, but the creepily placid smile that hadn't left her face since we'd escaped the pleasure barge was making me wonder whether she was celebrating her freedom or working out when best to split open our skulls and start eating our brains.

As for our newest recruit, Alice didn't appear to mind the struggle of trudging through the treacherous clay. It looked like she was blessed with both a justiciar's enthusiasm for deprivation and a demoniac's perverse pleasure in watching others suffer.

'The blood mage won't survive, you know,' she informed me, keeping pace with me when I slowed to let the others go on ahead.

'She has no training, no discipline. Even petty wonderists like you have *some* rudimentary knowledge of how to control your spells. Her mind won't long endure the torments of her attunement. It will burn her out from the inside, and when that happens, she'll kill you all. She'll drain the blood from your bodies and weep useless tears over your corpses.'

'Only if Shame doesn't eat our brains first,' I said, bending over to rest my hands on my knees so I could catch my breath.

'What?'

'Nothing. What were you going on about again?' I held up a finger. 'No, wait, I remember. Galass is a liability and we should get rid of her; the angelic is probably spying on us for the Aurorals; Corrigan's a reckless moron and Aradeus is a rat mage who'll definitely come in handy should one of these seven mystical freedom fighters, or whoever's been pissing off the local despot, offer to settle the dispute over tea after a polite fencing match. Does that about cover it, or do you have any criticism of Mister Bones that you'd like to share?'

'I don't trust him.'

'Who?'

She spoke in a hush. 'The dog.'

Infernals usually get sarcasm, but I suppose I should have anticipated a fanatical demoniac trained by a psychotic old blind woman wouldn't necessarily have a finely tuned sense of humour.

'He has an irritating bark,' Alice went on. 'And his ears are too long. I've seen images of your fauna in books and those ears are completely out of proportion for a dog's head.'

'He's a jackal. They're supposed to have long ears.'

'He looks like one of his progenitors mated with a rabbit.'

'Let's hope that's the biggest of our problems. Anything else?'

Alice glared at me with those daunting, angular demoniac eyes of hers, the tightness of her lips pressed together like she was just waiting for me to mock her so she'd have an excuse to draw that bone-hilted whip-sword of hers from its sheath at her back and disembowel me.

A funny thing happens when somebody stares at you longer than they should: you start wondering if maybe it means something other than what they want you to think. Alice looked frozen in time, this brittle ice sculpture of a smug, disdainful captain preparing to pass judgement on a soldier who'd deserted his troop in the midst of battle. I'd seen that same look a dozen times on other Glorian Justiciars. I think they practise it in the mirror. But Alice held it too long.

'What's wrong?' I asked.

The scowl twisted into a sneer and I braced myself for the inevitable recitation of my own flaws, but then something cracked. She turned away from me quickly and resumed her soldierly march towards the town at a pace that would soon have her overtaking the rest of our crew.

'I don't want to let her down, that's all.'

Girl, I thought, watching the wings on Alice's back twitch as she trudged with violent determination past the others, *Hazidan got to you bad.*

CHAPTER 30

The Blood Soot

The first glimmers of dawn transformed the dusty haze between us and our destination, painting it the colour of rose petals. Technically, 'breach dross' only described the effects of conflicting spells fracturing the barriers between realities on the terrain. But the cloying, ashy fog filling the air the closer we got to Mages' Grave was mixed with the ground-up flakes of skin and bone from two thousand dead wonder-ists and the ecclesiasm left behind by their ruined souls, and it was all bound together by the perversion of nature caused by the breach dross. It settled on everything, strangling most plant life and making seeds and animals sterile, only to then be stirred up and redistributed by the wind so it could begin the process all over again.

That morning, seeing it up close and in daylight for the first time, feeling it on my face and hands, I coined my own term, saying out loud, 'Blood soot,' just to hear how it sounded.

'There's some kind of human settlement up ahead,' Alice called back, ignoring me.

She was now in the lead, always staying a few yards ahead of us, clomping along with a resentful belligerence and a periodic twitching of her wings which, like the rest of her – like all of us – were caked in powdery red. The others had pretty much taken to ignoring her, preferring the aura of sullen silence to having to actually deal with her lousy attitude.

223

Well, all except for Aradeus, of course, who was taking courtesy and comity to unnatural heights. 'You can see through all this fog? Your eyesight is truly magnificent, Alice.'

'Don't be stupid, rodent boy,' she snarled back. 'Sharper eyes don't let you see through particles filling the air.' She tapped a finger to her nostril. 'Can you not detect the stench of your kind coming from up ahead?'

'She's right,' Shame said. The blood soot had turned the irises and whites of her eyes golden, which was far less pretty and a lot more unnerving than you might expect. Her right hand was stretched out before her as if she were walking blind. 'I can feel the vibrations of many human souls from here.'

The physics of that claim struck me as dubious, especially as vibrations don't work that way, but I wasn't in the mood to create any more friction in this unhappy crew.

'How far away are we?' I asked.

The angelic's fingers twitched for a moment. 'No more than a quarter of a mile.'

I breathed a sigh of relief. Actually, *breathing* was a polite word for the incessant hacking; the air in our lungs felt like shards of glass. I was looking forward to leaving this damned and forsaken desert clinging so tightly to my boots that they threatened to come off at every step. 'So it shouldn't take us more than ten or fifteen minutes,' I said.

'Doubt we'll get there before nightfall at this plodding pace,' Alice grumbled.

'You could always fly ahead and scout the place out for us,' Corrigan said, shooting me a grin. 'Go on then, great demon justiciar, flap those resplendent wings of yours and fly away.'

'Don't,' I warned him.

Alice tried to spin to face him, drawing her whip blade as she did. I've no doubt it would have been terribly impressive, had her right boot heel not been trapped in the clay. Her leg twisted awkwardly and she lost her balance. Whip-swords aren't quite so threatening when their wielders have just fallen on their arses in the muck.

'Enough of this, all of you,' Aradeus said pleadingly.

He was walking with one arm around Galass' shoulder, his free hand wiping the blood soot away from her face with a now filthy handkerchief.

She'd been sweating more than the rest of us, and over the past hour had begun to shake uncontrollably. With trembling fingers she wiped again at her lips. 'The ashes keep trying to get inside my mouth,' she murmured. She'd said the same thing at least a dozen times now. 'They want to get inside me.'

Aradeus shot me a questioning look, but all I could offer was a shrug. Breach dross was not one of my specialist subjects. Nothing was going to help Galass until we severed her attunement to blood magic.

I wiped at the muck clinging to my own lips, reminding myself that when people like me try to do the right thing, more often than not we leave only ashes behind.

'We'll be out of this soon,' Aradeus told her soothingly.

I wondered if he knew he was lying. Mages' Grave was close enough to the devastation that the blood soot was probably just a fact of life for those who lived there. In all likelihood, every crop was grown with a red husk, every child born with a racking cough.

Corrigan and I stopped and stared at each other, leaving the others to trudge on.

'You know what I've been thinking, Mister Ombra?'

'No, Mister Blight. What have you been thinking?'

He gestured to the haze ahead of us. 'I'm thinking this is no big deal.'

'The fog?'

'The whole job. I mean, the diabolic told us there's a wonderist waiting to join us in Mages' Grave, right? Someone already committed to the gig?'

'That is what he said, yep.'

'Saves us hours of negotiations, right? No haggling over shares of the money, no special requirements like having to run off and rescue a fucking angelic because a rat mage caught a nasty bout of . . . what's that disease Aradeus has?'

'Conscience?'

'That's the one.'

'You know,' I said, brushing away more of the blood soot from my coat, 'I believe you're right, Mister Blight. Who wants all the hassle of choosing their own crew, anyway?'

'Not us, that's for sure.' He scratched at the ash stuck to his beard. 'When you think about it, the Infernals, the Lords Celestine, that old master of yours, they've all done us a favour.'

'You think?'

His face split into a wide-mouthed grin. 'Easiest job ever. Practically a vacation.'

The two of us resumed our march along the path, sharing the occasional rude comment about our teammates, hanging on to the pretence that any of us had any say in whatever was awaiting us in Mages' Grave. But I couldn't stop watching Galass, the way she stumbled all the time, how she was shaking as if chilled, even when the sun began to beat down on us. I'd made one stupid promise to myself, just one: that whatever happened, I'd keep her alive and sane until this mess was over and I could give her a chance to find a better fate than the one to which she'd been consigned.

So far I wasn't doing so well.

CHAPTER 31

The World's Most Aptly Named Town

Imagine for a moment that you're just a regular person living out near the edge of a desolate, spell-blasted desert. Probably every spring you think about packing up and moving somewhere else. Somewhere more temperate. Somewhere the crops grow a little easier and your skin doesn't prickle every time a southern wind sends the blood soot swirling in the air. You don't leave, though, because, well, you were born here. Your mother and father told you tales of better times and warned you about how things down south are just as bad, and how getting by only gets tougher when you've got no kin, no history there.

So you stay, even though the crops grow more bitter each year, even when the blood soot is getting closer and closer to your own front door. Even when you start to wonder if maybe your neighbours aren't getting a little meaner lately.

'What a shithole,' Corrigan muttered as we walked into the town square.

People stared as we passed, but not nearly as much as we're used to – and not nearly as much as they should have been, given one of us had bat wings protruding from her shoulder blades.

'You the spellers?' a woman asked. She was different from the others, but only because she was striding towards us with a sense of purpose instead of shuffling silently away in any other direction. She stopped a few feet away and gave each of us a glance before answering her own question. 'Guess you must be.'

'We are indeed wonderists,' Aradeus said, offering her a bow and reaching for her hand to kiss it. 'Might we know your name, gracious lady?'

She eyed the rat mage for barely a second, and in that time she'd weighed and measured his attempt at courtesy, decided it was either patronising or sleazy, and turned to me. 'I'm Vidra. Mayor of this town. I suppose you'll be wanting directions to the fortress like all the others?'

'The others?' I asked.

Instead of answering, she turned and headed deeper into town, not bothering to see if we'd follow. I guess she knew we had no choice by now.

I caught up to her, and noted that Vidra was young, probably younger than me, but the skin of her cheeks was dry and cracked like red leather. The others milling around the town square had looked the same. Wind and grit accounted for the roughness of their skin; I guessed the blood soot explained the unusual colouring.

'Have you lived in Mages' Grave your whole life?' I asked.

'Mages' Grave isn't the name of the town.' She pointed towards the hill in the distance. 'It's the name of the fortress. Used to be a proper castle. Had its share of big, powerful men like the baron ruling it. A few women, too, though they never lasted as long. Every time someone new came to take the castle, a little more of it got destroyed. Nobody ever bothers repairing it.'

'How long has Baron Tristmorta been in charge?'

She ignored that question, too, and kept on with her recitation, as if she'd planned out what she was going to say and didn't intend on being derailed now. 'Every couple of years, a little army comes along – no more than two or three hundred soldiers, mostly led by war chiefs from the north. They didn't speak the same language as us, and mostly left us alone.'

'They didn't try to take your land?' Galass asked, jogging to catch up to us. 'Your crops? Your women?'

Vidra gave out a hoarse cough, the local equivalent of a chuckle. 'Didn't need any of it. There's good land on their side of the fortress wall and they'd always bring livestock from their own lands. As to the women, well, some of our young folk would go up to the fortress every now and then, offer their services or their bodies.' Another cough. '*Shishta*, the northerners always said when they sent the girls and boys away.'

'Shishta?' I asked.

'Ugly,' Corrigan translated.

I hadn't known he knew the northern tongue until then. Maybe he was a northerner himself. Funny how you can think of someone as your closest friend and hardly know them at all.

'Can't blame them,' Vidra said, waving at a couple of children who were staring at us as we passed by. 'Up north they're all smooth and pretty. Not like us.'

Aradeus gently took her arm. When she turned, I caught the glint of a small knife held between her thumb and forefinger. The rat mage ignored the threat and said, 'Forgive me, my lady, but it is not in my nature to allow a falsehood to go unchallenged.' With his free hand he gestured to the run-down town all around us, held together with nothing but blood, sweat and raw determination. 'You live in this place, where life is hard. You take care of your people, when others would abandon them. In my travels, I have seen these northern princesses of whom you speak, and my sword will set straight anyone who claims they are more beautiful than you.'

Vidra shot me a look. 'He blind?'

'His eyes work better than most, from what I've seen.'

She smiled at that, but it wasn't the smile of someone who enjoyed flattery, and the blush in her cheeks was only the stain of blood soot. 'Guess a man who can kill his enemies with magic can afford to talk foolish.' She shrugged off Aradeus' hand and resumed her march through town. 'Anyway, the last of the war chiefs decided to call himself "the baron" – nothing else, just "the baron". Didn't even know his name was "Tristmorta" until you said it just now. He's apparently got an interest in southern magic. Guess they don't have much in the way of mages up north.'

'Is it true that he started using your children in his experiments?' Galass asked, holding Mister Bones in her arms to keep him from running off and barking at the townsfolk.

Vidra arched an eyebrow. 'Children? The baron? No, he mostly leaves us alone, same as the others.'

Again Corrigan and I looked at each other. Why lie about the baron's crimes if we were supposed to be coming here to defend him from an uprising? His eyes widened the same time mine did as the answer came to both of us: because suppressing a rebellion against a tyrannical, half-mad sadist was exactly the kind of lousy, soul-crushing job that we'd shrug and take on without asking too many questions.

'Does he have . . .' I hesitated, unsure how to describe an object I'd never seen before. 'Did the baron bring a sort of . . . artefact with him? He might have called it "the Apparatus" or "the Device" or something like that?'

Vidra's narrowed eyes made it plain both how poorly she understood my question and how little she thought of my sanity. 'Why in the world would I know something like that? I told you, we leave them northern invaders alone, they leave us alone.'

'What about these Seven Brothers?' Corrigan asked. 'We heard they were leading a rebellion against him. What are they, freedom fighters? Monks?'

'Don't rightly know,' Vidra replied. 'They're not from the north, though, I can tell you that. Not sure where they're from. Only ever seen them from a distance.' She pointed up past the edge of town to a ridge. 'They stood there a whole day and a night, all seven of them, just watching us. Maybe they weren't looking at us at all, just taking in the majesty of the landscape.' She offered up something between a cough and a laugh.

I turned to stare up past the ridge to the fortress at the top of the hill. It was some two miles distant, and even from all the way down here it looked big enough to have garrisoned Ascendant Lucien's entire army.

'What about the baron's soldiers?' Corrigan asked. 'How many are we talking about?'

Vidra stopped walking a moment. She waved her hand slowly through the ashes drifting amidst the rosy haze. 'Hard to count them, these days.'

Corrigan and I frowned at each other. I guess without meaning to we were silently arguing over who would have to ask the obvious question.

'Where is the baron now?' Galass asked, saving us both the trouble.

'Up ahead,' Vidra said, resuming her march up the main street towards the edge of town. 'He's waiting to have a word with you.'

This time, Corrigan and I didn't need to look at each other.

Everything about this job felt like a set-up: the vague deal terms, the hordes of other wonderists competing for the gig, Tenebris pitching it to me in the first place, only to intentionally delay our arrival . . . all of it was stinking worse than a jackal's farts. And now, after we'd arrived late to the job, this Baron Tristmorta was 'waiting to have a word' with us?

'Perhaps we should reconsider our participation in this endeavour,' Aradeus said.

Given the rat mage's devils-may-care ways, his suggestion gave me pause.

Problem was, the Lords Celestine had already gone to significant lengths – including, it appeared, engineering the horrific sacrifice of an eleven-year-old sublime so that a seventeen-year-old sublime could be condemned to the short and unpleasant life of a blood mage, not to mention manipulating me into coming here with her. What would they do to us if we tried to leave before the job was done?

'The client wants to have a little chat,' I said, following Vidra along the red dirt path towards the northern edge of town. 'Wouldn't be polite to keep him waiting.'

I wasn't as nervous as you might expect. Whatever this Baron Tristmorta was planning, trying to murder six wonderists – even in an ambush – was a bad gamble. Both Corrigan and Aradeus had readied spells of one sort or another, and I'd unbuttoned my coat and shirt and was already tracing a couple of the nastier sigils on my chest to wake them up, in case our client needed remonstration.

Shame, Alice and Galass weren't technically wonderists, but I could see they were preparing their own surprises for whoever was waiting for us. Alice had that whip-sword of hers out. Shame had looked the same for a while, like someone you'd never pick out of a crowd, only her skin had started to change, becoming sleek, hard and shimmering as newly polished steel armour. Galass – well, I've no idea what she was doing except looking like she was sick and tired of holding back the blood magic screaming inside her.

Five minutes later, Vidra arrived at our rendezvous, and we discovered that none of our preparations would make the least bit of difference.

Baron Tristmorta looked younger than I'd expected, late twenties, maybe? Hard to tell when a man's skin and hair has been stripped from his body and he's hanging six feet high from a rope that's attached to nothing but air. He should have been dead – he certainly *looked* dead. Hells, maybe he *was* dead. All I know is that the moment we came within a few yards of him, those lidless eyes started moving to follow our progress and his jaw dropped open.

That's when he started screaming.

CHAPTER 32

The Client

Baron Tristmorta was a man of few words. Even when his tongue reformed inside his mouth, the only ones to come out were, 'Kill me, kill me, please, for pity's sake, kill me!'

'Tell us about the Seven Brothers,' I shouted up at him. It turns out, it's hard to have a conversation with a man screaming in agony while he's hanging several feet off the ground from a rope that doesn't go anywhere.

Okay, yes, I'm aware that the moral thing to do here would have been to put the baron out of his misery, and that, technically speaking, refusing to do so until he shared whatever intelligence he'd gleaned on the Seven Brothers might fit some people's definition of torture. The problem was, I had five other people with me who could end up in the same regrettable position as the baron unless we understood precisely what we were dealing with.

I warned you that we weren't the good guys, right?

'What are their attunements?' I asked.

'You're wasting your time,' Alice informed me. 'His mind is gone, his soul is severed from his body.'

'But he's crying out,' Galass said, trying to use her untested blood magic to put an end to the baron's agony. Her efforts served only to give her a nasty headache and the rest of us bloody noses.

'His brain still functions, but his spirit has been destroyed.' Alice turned to me. 'You should be able to determine as much for yourself, fallen one.'

I softened my gaze and let my awareness shift a fraction. She was right. There was no ecclesiasm suffusing the body. Baron Tristmorta had been reduced to a corpse that couldn't die. He was capable only of eternal suffering.

'Corrigan?'

He shoved us all aside. 'Yeah, all right.'

He squeezed his fist and the familiar red and black sparks appeared around his knuckles. I ostentatiously covered my ears, then pointedly looked at everyone else until they'd done the same. They'd be grateful in about three seconds.

Corrigan drew back his arm and hurled a bolt of lightning dead centre into the baron's chest, blinding us all and shattering the air with deafening thunder.

When the dust had settled, the baron's corpse was nothing but charred bone, creaking as it dangled from the unattached noose.

'What about the other wonderists – the spellers – who came through here before us?' I asked Vidra.

She shrugged. 'Before them brothers left the baron here as a warning, a posse of folks like you turned up in town every couple of days. Always seven at a time. We'd tell them what little we knew and they'd get drunk on our liquor before making a big speech and heading up to the fortress. We never saw them after that.'

'How many different covens – *posses*, I mean?'

'Hard to recall. Maybe six, I guess.'

Seven Brothers. Seven mercenaries in each coven, and thanks entirely to Tenebris' machinations, we were the seventh coven to arrive here.

'Something about this job really stinks,' Corrigan whispered to me.

'*Everything* about this job stinks.'

'And the brothers?' I asked Vidra. 'You only saw them the one time?'

'Some of the younger folks sneak up the hill at night, looking to see what's going on. They come back with stories of beasts on two legs, shadowy men in robes seen through the windows doing things to the spellers who entered the fortress. The kids say that sometimes, when the screams finally stop, they hear a buzzing in their heads, like when a mosquito gets lodged inside your ear.' She shrugged. 'That's about all, though.'

There was something disturbing about the way she spoke, the lassitude in her expression when she described terrors that would have most people fleeing into the night, running as fast and as far as their legs would take them. Vidra, though – maybe all the people in this town, in fact – sounded inured to horror and sorrow.

'Best you get on your way,' she said to me. 'He'll be starting up again soon.'

'Who?'

She pointed up at the baron's corpse.

'By all that's holy,' Galass cried, staring.

She was right to be shocked, for the scorched remains of the hapless baron's skeleton were definitely twitching. It looked like the blood soot was coagulating around his bones, sticking to them like moss on a tree, then thickening into something like sinew and muscle. Soon enough, there was enough of him to start screaming again.

'He'll quiet down again once you're gone,' Vidra explained. 'He only does this when there's a speller nearby.'

'Why do you stay here?' I asked.

She scratched at her cheek, then stuck her finger in her mouth and sucked the powder from it. 'We have thought about leaving,' she said, not even appearing to notice what she'd just done. 'When the baron took over the fortress a couple years back, he came down for a visit. He wasn't like most of them – he knew a little of our language, enough to get me to agree to bring the whole town together. He said something real bad was coming to the Blastlands, that we should maybe all leave. Even offered us money to make the trip easier. Funny thing is, he didn't seem surprised when we refused. Didn't threaten us or kill anybody, just said he'd do his best to keep us out of the ugliness when it came.'

'If this man offered you the means to leave, why did you stay?' Aradeus asked.

Vidra knelt and scratched under her jaw, this time on purpose. She held it out for our inspection. 'You see them red flecks?'

'I've been calling it blood soot,' I said.

The mayor smiled as if I'd said something amusing. 'Fancy name. We just call it "the red".' She stuck out her tongue and licked it. 'Foul stuff – gets in everything. The air. The soil. The food.'

Shame, looking now like one of the townsfolk, young but weathered to an early middle age, came over and scraped some of the flecks off Vidra's hand. She put the stuff on her own tongue – then immediately spat it out.

'Consecrated,' she said.

'"Consecrated"? You mean there's ecclesiasm in it?'

Alice came over and knelt down to pick up a bit of the red soot between her claws. She too spat it out as soon as she tasted it. 'The angelic is right.'

When Alice stood back up, she held out some of the clay soil in her hand. 'In the Infernal demesne, ecclesiasm can be broken down into an even more fundamental element of creation – one that is present in all planes of reality. On its own, it's unusable, but when mixed with the physical matter from our own plane, it promotes life like a kind of . . .'

'Fertiliser?' I asked.

'If I understand the concept, something not dissimilar. It is what attunes crops to our natures, what makes them edible for us.'

'And this?' I asked, pointing to the handful of soil she held.

'I could not eat food raised here.'

Alice turned to Shame, who shook her head. 'Nor could an angelic. I am surprised the humans can tolerate it.'

Vidra gave that hoarse cough of hers again. 'Tolerate it? No, we don't *tolerate* the crops that grow here. We can't live without them. That's why we can't leave.'

'I don't understand,' I said. 'Why would—?'

She cut me off. 'Sometimes folks come through here on their way north to trade. They offer us food to show their goodwill. Stuff tastes fine – good, even. But it don't . . . it's like eating air.' She patted her ribs through her dusty linen shirt. 'Won't stick to us, you follow? We can't get anything from it.'

The baron's screaming was rising in both volume and pitch.

'You all really should get going,' Vidra said. 'He gets louder the longer a speller's nearby.'

I started leading the others away, but Shame moved to stand under the baron's corpse.

'My lady,' Aradeus called out to her gently, 'we should not tarry here. There's nothing we can do for him.'

Ignoring him, the angelic reached up and touched the baron's skinless toe. Tristmorta kept on screaming at first, but something started to change. At first it was just a kind of ripple, travelling up and down the clay-built muscle and bone: flesh sloughed from his bones, only to slither back up, breaking down and reforming, over and over again.

A second scream joined his, which turned out to be Shame herself.

'My lady!' Aradeus cried, and ran to her, but she held out her other hand in warning.

'Stay back!' she shouted in between her agonised screams.

Corrigan started calling up another blast of lightning, though I don't know what he hoped to accomplish with it. 'What the hell's she doing?' he asked.

I was watching in wonder at the suffering Shame was putting herself through. 'She's ... she's trying to transfigure his body so that the spell that keeps giving it life won't recognise it any more. But he's reforming almost as fast as she's breaking him apart.'

'She's going to kill herself!' Aradeus was trying to pull the angelic away from the baron, but she was resisting. 'Cade, use one of your spells to make her stop before it's too late!'

'Silly thing to do,' Vidra said, turning to walk back towards the town, clearly feeling that whatever duty she felt she'd owed us had been delivered in full. 'Girl's going to ruin herself for a body that ain't got no soul any more.'

'The angelic can't abide the desecration,' Alice said to me. For the first time since I'd met her, she sounded sympathetic, almost admiring. 'Desecration affects all who witness it. We are diminished by the unconscionable abuse of another' – her narrowed, angular eyes caught mine – 'even when we prefer to pretend otherwise.'

'Diminished is better than dead,' I said, unbuttoning the collar of my shirt. The nightmare bloom had a decent chance of breaking the angelic's concentration.

'No!' Galass said, seeing what I was planning. She darted to join Shame, who was now shaking all over from the effort of trying to alter the baron's corpse into something the spell reanimating it couldn't overcome.

Galass held out her left hand and almost immediately, red droplets began drifting from the baron's body towards her own. She held up her right hand – and now scarlet drops began to ooze out of her own pores to mingle in mid-air with the baron's blood. 'Try now,' she said.

Shame didn't appear to hear her at first, but then, gritting her teeth, she grabbed hold of the baron's ankle. The ripples increased in intensity, like earth tremors across a mountain ridge. We could see Galass' blood mixture was seeping inside the baron's exposed

239

veins, and at last his screams turned to groans as the spell rean-imating him started to lose its hold. He was about to die, I knew then – die properly, with whatever dignity was left him. The decent thing would have been to let him do so.

'Wait!' I shouted, my fingers tracing the nightmare bloom sigils on my chest. 'Answer my question, or I'll fill your last moments of life with terrors worse than any you've ever known!'

The others stared at me like I was an utter monster, even Corrigan. Fair enough, I suppose.

'Tell me what the Seven Brothers want,' I commanded the baron.

His lidless eyes swivelled to me. He gave a sigh, and I thought his last breath had fled his body. But he actually sounded relieved when he managed to articulate one sentence before Shame and Galass granted him the final peace the Seven Brothers had tried to deny him.

'The red,' he whispered. 'They want the red.'

CHAPTER 33

The Red

Shame collapsed into Aradeus' arms, and when Galass stumbled backwards, I ran to catch her. I wondered what damage the two had done to themselves in order to give some trivial measure of grace to a reanimated corpse.

'We did it,' Galass said to me, smiling with fierce pride as tears streamed down her cheeks. 'We did it.'

She wasn't meant for this world, not when she so adamantly refused to let it corrupt her.

'What did he mean?' Aradeus asked, staring up at the now silent corpse. Had the baron, too, felt proud that he'd managed to defy his tormentors to leave us with that minuscule, meaningless piece of information? 'What would the Seven Brothers want with the blood soot?'

'Perhaps they mean to spread it further south,' Alice suggested. 'Corrupt more and more of the land so that your kind will all end up like the villagers, addicted to their own despair as much as to the poisoned crops grown in their soil.'

Corrigan scooped up a handful of the dry-as-dust clay, sniffed at it, then tossed it away. 'Who cares? We're not fucking farmers, we're mercenaries, and our client' – he jabbed a thumb up at the dead body still hanging in the air – 'is in no condition to pay our fees.' He turned back the way we'd come. 'Let's go, Cade. Maybe we can pick up a little work down the road – blow up a troublesome monastery for the local crime lord or maybe a good old-fashioned kidnapping. Those were always fun. We know how to do kidnappings.'

I kept staring at the dirt at my feet. Corrigan was right; we *weren't* farmers. We certainly weren't lawmen. What did we care if a bunch of robe-wearing weirdos wanted to take over an inhospitable, unfarmable . . .

Oh, shit.

Shit. Shit. Shit.

'What is it?' Aradeus asked.

I bent down to get some of the dust, rubbed it between my hands and let it drift back down to the ground until all that was left was a palmful of sparkling crimson flecks left behind by a mages' war centuries ago: matter that neither Alice nor Shame could tolerate, yet both agreed shared characteristics of the fundamental matter of their respective planes.

'I know why the Seven Brothers picked this place,' I said. 'And I know why both the Aurorals *and* the Infernals have been manipulating bands of wonderists into coming here!'

Corrigan spun on his heel. 'Oh, no,' he warned, holding up his fist so I couldn't miss the sparks erupting from between his clenched fingers. 'Don't you *dare* try and convince me – or any of these other poor saps – that we should do anything other than get the hell out of the Blastlands as fast as possible.'

'Think about it,' I urged him. 'What could possibly motivate the Lords Celestine *and* the Lords Devilish into working together to get the six of us here?'

'Nothing,' Shame and Alice answered at once, and both looked unhappy when they realised they'd simultaneously expressed the same opinion.

'The Devilish and the Celestines despise each other far beyond anything you can imagine,' Alice said. 'There is no one they would rather see obliterated than each other. They would happily watch the entire Mortal plane being wiped out if it allowed them to pursue their "Great Crusade" against one another.'

'More than that,' Shame added, less stridently, but with equal conviction, 'in Celestine prophecy, the Mortal demesne will be the battlefield upon which the Auroral armies at last vanquish the Infernals.'

'Except neither of them has figured out a way to be able to live here,' Corrigan pointed out, his fist still sparking menacingly. 'Come on, Cade, I'm not kidding here. Either come with me, or—'

'But what if somebody else has?' I asked him. 'Somebody who terrifies both the Celestines *and* the Devilish? What if . . .' I glanced around at the town, at this place that felt so unnatural to all of us, at these people who seemed barely human any more. That's the thing about us Mortals: we're good at adapting to change. Push us into inhospitable climates, take away the foods we're accustomed to, somehow we always survive. It's the one thing that gives us an edge over the beings whose realms we breach to steal their magic. Other than angelics, none of them could ever survive on the Mortal plane. 'I think somebody's figured out that the Blastlands, filled with its endless breaches into other planes, has become a kind of no-man's land where other beings *could* survive.'

'You're saying these Seven Brothers were sent here by the rulers of some other realm to become farmers?' Corrigan let out a bitter laugh. 'Man, and here I thought we got all the shitty jobs.'

Me, I wasn't laughing.

'Farming is exactly what they have in mind,' I said. 'Want to know why I'm so sure?'

'Why?'

I turned and set off up the road that led to the fortress. 'Because you can't host an army of invaders from another plane of reality unless you've got something to feed them when they get here.'

CHAPTER 34

Parlay

Nothing good ever comes from talking to your enemies before a battle. I don't know why people waste the time and effort. Tradition, I suppose. As one of the few relatively presentable wonderists who can sit through a formal dinner without getting so twitchy I accidentally blast the hosts and set off a diplomatic catastrophe, I've had occasion to witness several high-stakes negotiations. I've attended princes and generals as they faced one another across a sumptuous table set upon the field, praising each other's virtues and sharing gifts, waxing poetic on the horrors of war and swearing oaths to their own immense desire for peace.

Soon enough – usually right before the dessert – the forces that brought these new-found friends to the precipice of bloodshed are blamed on historical misunderstandings or to the devious schemes of third parties. As the stars twinkle down their blessings, unbreakable bonds of brotherhood are forged and all that's left is to pat each other on the back and bid each other a fond farewell.

By morning, soldiers will be busy slaughtering and being slaughtered on that same field where hours before their commanders had shared wine, until at last only one army is left standing.

Why go to all the trouble of meeting with the adversary when conflict is inevitable? Same reason they agreed to meet with us: the chance to gather intelligence.

We knew nothing about these so-called Seven Brothers – not their attunements, not their plans, not even which plane of existence they came from – and they probably didn't know much more about us. So the only reasonable thing to do was to knock on their door and play the game of talking in circles while gauging each other's weaknesses.

'Beneath a morning sky, I greet you,' said the figure on the other side of the wrought-iron gate. He bore a silver tray in each hand. The one on the left contained an assortment of six pastries – scones, maybe – laden with berries. The tray on the right, my nostrils informed me even before my eyes confirmed it, contained six dollops of shit, each in its own little porcelain bowl.

Isn't it nice when you get to experience the diplomatic traditions of other cultures?

Oh, and the guy bearing these two offerings? He was a goat.

He stood on two legs and was wearing a long grey wool robe, the hem of which didn't quite reach to his hooves. He was bigger than your average goat, with a broad chest and thick-fingered hands that looked like he was wearing gloves made of fur. The curved horns with their wickedly sharp points would be threatening if his head were lowered.

'I am Madrigal,' said the goat, holding out the trays to offer us our choice of scones or shit, or possibly both. 'And you are welcome to this place.'

'Our greeting to you beneath this morning sky, generous Madrigal,' said Aradeus, before executing a deep and convoluted bow. The rat mage took to courtesy like a drunk to an open keg of rum.

'Are you the master of this place?' Galass asked, gazing in wonder at the goat man.

Madrigal looked conspicuously down at the two trays in his hands as if to suggest that someone having to stand out here handing out scones and shit to a bunch of dishevelled bums like us was unlikely to be the boss.

The business with the two trays wasn't that unusual, as it happens. When an enemy arrives at your gates, it's not uncommon for the garrison commander to offer his would-be conquerors a choice of two gifts. One is typically a bag of coins or a silver cloak or possibly even a gold circlet, a promise that in exchange for persuading the enemy general to change sides, the traitor will be elevated to the defender's noble ranks. The second choice was usually a bloody dagger, to symbolise the prospect of war, or possibly the head of one of the general's scouts, to convey his opponent's estimation of how said war would turn out in the end.

Piles of shit were nothing more than a smelly new innovation on an old theme.

'Might I have one of those delicious scones?' I asked.

'Of course,' Madrigal said, looking mildly disappointed by my choice. 'Will you and your company join my masters for more lavish refreshments within the keep? The brothers are very busy with their great endeavour, but when they learned of your approach, they insisted that such impressive beings as yourselves must be offered the hospitality of their home.'

In other words, the Seven Brothers wanted to know what the fuck we were doing on their turf.

'We'd be delighted to join you,' I said.

The goat man gazed past us back towards the road. 'Should we await your other two companions?'

Only Corrigan, Aradeus, Galass and I had come to the fortress. We'd left Shame and Alice behind, because we weren't sure how these Seven Brothers – who, if my theory was correct, came from a different plane of reality – would respond to an Infernal and an Auroral. We'd tried to leave Mister Bones behind, too, but the jackal chased after us anyway. Now he was chewing on the hem of Madrigal's robe and growling. The mutt had no sense of diplomacy.

'What other companions?' I asked innocently.

So they knew there were six of us, which either meant they had some mystical means alerting them to our presence here or – and I had to admit this was far more likely – they had a spy in town.

The goat man opted not to point out my obvious deception, merely bowed his head for a moment – his horns making the gesture more of an implicit threat than an act of obsequiousness – and unlocked the gate.

He led us across the massive open courtyard and beneath a wide arch whose iron-banded doors hung awkwardly from their hinges, looking like they might collapse on anyone who took too long walking through.

'Might I ask you a question, Master Wonderist?' Madrigal said once we were inside the decaying fortress.

'Call me Cade,' I said.

He looked unduly discomfited by that suggestion. 'Well, that is, uh ... Master ... Cade.' He said my name like it was a chunk of grass caught between his front teeth. Then he sniffed the air as if detecting something unpleasant, which was rich coming from a guy who was still holding a silver platter covered in shit. 'You carry the scent of both an Infernal *and* an Auroral on you.'

I was impressed that he could smell such things, and said as much.

'Oh, yes,' he said, nodding vigorously. 'There is an ... *unnaturalness* to their kind. Quite pungent. Can you not detect it yourself?'

'And what about your Seven Brothers?' I asked. 'What do they smell like?'

'Hmm?' He beckoned us to follow him up a wide staircase.

So clearly he wouldn't be divulging any juicy details about his employers.

'To answer your question,' I said, taking hold of the banister because I wasn't at all confident in the solidity of the crumbling stone steps, 'extra-planar beings don't smell unusual to humans. They don't really smell like anything, since most of them can't step onto the Mortal plane. When they manifest within spell circles or other bridging constructs between realities, their physical form within our realm isn't so much flesh and blood as a sort of . . . clothing worn around their spirits.'

'Clothing,' Madrigal repeated. 'Interesting.'

We continued our journey through halls decorated in a patchwork of worn tapestries, old shields and broken weapons, along with various family emblems from northern houses, all of which had been left where they fell and shattered on the dirty floors.

'Can I ask *you* a personal question, Madrigal?'

'Of course.'

'Are you a goat who stands on two legs and speaks as a man, or a being from another plane with the attributes of what we on this demesne would think of as goat-like?'

Madrigal paused, balancing admirably on his hooves despite such appendages not generally being suited for standing on two legs. 'I was a goat,' he said, 'and will be one again some day, I hope. For now, I am Madrigal.'

The wording was carefully considered, and conveyed more than I thought he had intended.

'Are you being held captive in this form?' Galass asked. 'Are you forced to serve the Seven Brothers?'

Madrigal gave a goaty laugh and pressed onwards through the surprisingly dank, decaying hallway. 'We are all captives of our bodies, are we not?'

I didn't find the deflection convincing.

'And we are all servants of someone,' he continued.

'Not so!' Aradeus declared. The rat mage stepped around us to face the goat man. Putting a gloved hand on his shoulder, he said earnestly, 'Freedom is not a play on words, honourable Madrigal. It is *real*. It *matters*. Tell me you are enslaved in this place and by the sword at my side and the spells on my lips, will Aradeus Mozen win your freedom.'

'Oh, for fuck's sake,' Corrigan swore. 'Can you not so much as take a shit without declaring yourself to be on some noble quest?'

Madrigal laughed then, and it really was an endearing laugh, almost a cross between a deep, throaty chuckle and bleating, but when he spoke, it was once again with forced precision. 'My thanks, Lord Mozen, for your generous offer. But I will serve my time, and when I am done, I will return to my mountain. Your kindness has moved me, however, so perhaps one day I will come and set *you* free from your bondage.'

He bleated even more uproariously at his own joke as he motioned for the four of us to pass beneath another archway into a great hall with a large wooden table at the far end. Seven chairs were set on each side. The ones nearest the far wall were occupied by seven figures in grey robes, their heads covered by hoods. The other chairs were empty, if you didn't count the red-brown stains of dried blood, which I could see even from here. Hanging upside down by silvery gossamer threads from the ceiling some thirty feet above our heads were the mad-eyed, gaping-mouthed corpses of dead wonderists . . . *a lot of dead wonderists.*

I counted forty-two of them as I gazed up at their expressions of horror and despair. I saw Fortunal mages and Totemics, Tempestorals, luminists and every other attunement you could name. I even recognised one familiar face.

'Hey, look at that,' Corrigan said, pointing up to the slender fellow whose leather bandolier of keys was dangling from the bloody ruins of his corpse. 'Good old Locke made it out of that tavern before I blasted the others, after all!'

'He's still dead,' I pointed out.

'Yeah, but it wasn't my fault, so I'm okay with that.'

Forty-two bodies, I thought looking up at them. *Six groups of seven wonderists.*

That's how many Vidra said had got here before us. One of the few things the Lords Devilish and Lords Celestine have in common? An abiding fascination with symmetry.

Which makes us the seventh crew of seven wonderists come to face the Seven Brothers.

'If you would be so kind as to take your seats?' Madrigal asked, gesturing to the table where the seven most dangerous men ever to walk the earth awaited us.

CHAPTER 35

Familial Relations

As we approached the table, our hosts removed their hoods, revealing just how unremarkable they were: seven men with dark hair and pasty white skin, neither imposing in stature nor particularly slight. Not young, not old, but somewhere in between, ranging in age, I'd have guessed, from about nineteen to thirty-five or six. It was unusual to find seven male siblings, but not impossible. Maybe it was just a really big family and the women were all off slaughtering someone other than wonderists.

On the whole, though, these seven fellows looked like anyone you might find wandering the streets of your own home town. Admittedly, the crimson irises were a little troubling, but I'd seen worse on chronic drunks and those afflicted with certain blood disorders. The spidery crimson veins creeping over their chalk-white cheeks and foreheads . . . yeah, those were a little unsettling, I suppose, but it wasn't like staring into the abyss of a cosmist's face.

There was nothing about their appearance that explained the unnerving effect the seven men had on us. I knew instantly that they were human, like us, and wonderists as well. Despite the differences between those who make up our profession – different sources of power, approaches to spellcraft and, for want of a better word, *styles* – we all share a sensitivity to individuals attuned to planes beyond the Mortal realm. It's like a tingling on the tips of your fingers or a sudden sharp taste on your tongue, an ache in your bones that differs depending on which plane those who you come into contact with are attuned. That's how I knew the moment I got within ten feet of the Seven Brothers that they weren't like us at all.

Oh, they were mages – of that I was certain – but I'd never encountered whichever realm they drew their spells from. Corrigan had made a far more diligent study of the various forms of wonderism than anyone else I knew (mostly so he could more easily kill his fellow practitioners when the occasion warranted), but his expression when he looked at our hosts betrayed the same mixture of confusion and panic that I was experiencing.

As for the seven gentlemen seated behind the table, they were looking as cool as a winter's morning.

'Will you sit?' one of them asked.

Beyond the red eyes and veiny cheeks, they displayed the similarities and differences you'd expect to find in that many siblings. Most had reasonably strong chins, but a couple were softer. There were aquiline noses all around, although two looked as if they had been broken at some point. One and all were clean-shaven, and their tidy, jaw-length hair was cut alike, but the colour ranged from muddy brown to just this side of black. They shared what you might call boyish good looks, though some wore it better than the others. If I hadn't been so acutely aware of the forty-two dead mercenary wonderists hanging upside down from the ceiling behind us, I would have assumed I was sitting down to a pleasant country brunch.

I strolled up to the middle chair on our side of the table and rested my hand on the back of it. 'Somebody bled on your furniture.'

The brother fourth from the left inclined his head at me, for all the world as if we'd just chosen each other for a duel. 'The remnants of a barbaric ritual,' he said. 'We would never willingly impose such discourtesy on our guests without cause.'

In other words, *sit down, shut up while we tell you how things are going to be, and maybe – maybe – you can walk out of here alive.*

I heard a murmur coming from one of the other brothers that set my inner ear to buzzing. It wasn't quite like the muted paper-crackling sound I could pick up when Aurorals were talking to each other, but close enough that it must have resonated with one of the mystical planes to which I was attuned. A few seconds later, footsteps – or rather, *hoof*steps – echoed from the passage outside the great hall, and through the arched entrance came a group of robed servants, each one bearing a chair that, while clearly not part of a matched set, was at least free of blood. A couple of the servants were goats like Madrigal, but there were other species, too. The donkey looked particularly unhappy to be there, and the one who might have been a mountain cougar – or maybe just a really big house cat – was definitely eyeing up the man-sized rat on two legs, who looked like he was trying to stay as far away from the feline as possible.

Corrigan chuckled. 'Relative of yours, Aradeus?'

'I'm a rat *mage*, you overstuffed idiot,' Aradeus said, 'not an actual rat.'

One of the brothers misunderstood the joke. 'We hope our servants do not make you unduly uncomfortable. We find it more convenient to reshape local animals to our needs rather than contend with the unfortunate eccentricities of human beings.'

In case you're wondering? On the scale of magical abilities one tosses off casually in conversation, transmogrifying animals into walking, talking, *thinking* servants is pretty damned impressive. Actually, *fucking terrifying* would be a better description.

'It's cruel,' Galass said, still holding on to a snarling Mister Bones. Her right hand, extending towards the servants, had started weaving back and forth as if she were holding it under the current of a river. 'They did not consent to be transformed this way.'

'Should they serve us well, they will be returned to their natural state soon enough,' one of the brothers said peaceably.

'As a matter of fact,' I began, sitting down on one of the replacement chairs and resting my elbows on the table, 'we're here to discuss some of those human eccentricities that so trouble you.'

One of the brothers – at a guess, I'd have said he was the oldest, but they were all close enough in age that it was hard to be entirely sure – leaned his own arms on the table as if trying to mirror my casual posture. 'You have concerns about our presence here?'

The brother next to him gestured towards the ceiling at the other side of the hall. 'Perhaps the same concerns as the previous delegations?'

'Our client—'

I stopped myself. Who the fuck *was* our client at this point? Were we working for one of the Lords Devilish for whom Tenebris bartered deals with Mortal wonderists like those dangling from the ceiling? The Lords Celestine who'd sold Shame into sexual slavery? The Glorian Justiciars who had very definitely herded me into this, not to mention who knew how many other jobs since leaving the order?

Whose orders was I following now? Or was I now so accustomed to selling my services – along with my conscience – to the highest bidder that I didn't know what else to do?

Stand up, smile, thank them for their hospitality, and get Corrigan, Galass and Aradeus the fuck out of here. That's the only duty you have left.

I started to rise, but Galass, sitting next to me with Mister Bones snuggled up on her lap, reached over and pulled me back down.

'Our concern,' she started, 'is that you are using magic to poison the land here, making it even worse than it already was, so that the extra-planar beings whom you serve can use the Blastlands as a base from which to invade the Mortal plane.'

So much for subtly guiding our hosts into revealing their intentions.

On my right side, Corrigan hissed between clenched teeth, 'I told you not to bring the crazy girl, Cade.'

During our hike up the hill, the four of us had debated whether to reveal what we knew of the brothers' plans or keep silent. Corrigan and Aradeus had argued that showing your hand to an enemy is never good military strategy. I'd countered that playing dumb when the evidence is obvious to anyone with a brain serves only to convince your opponent that you are, in fact, dumb. Galass hadn't expressed an opinion on which approach we should take. Apparently she'd decided on excessive moral rectitude as a tactic.

'An invasion?' one of the other brothers asked. 'Whoever spoke of—?'

The one two seats down finished for him, '—an invasion?'

I was beginning to wonder how they decided who would speak next, since they never looked at one another, never talked over each other and somehow perpetually finished each other's sentences.

'What are we "invading", precisely?' asked a third.

The younger one next to him replied, 'A place abandoned by its former rulers.'

'Left to rot and decay,' said the slightly plumper-faced brother to his right.

'A graveyard of past misjudgements,' came another.

I was starting to get a sore neck from twisting to meet the gaze of whoever was talking.

'A land already occupied,' Galass said, slamming a fist on the table, which caused the snoozing Mister Bones to awaken just long enough to lend an affirming bark to her anger. 'That they are poor is no reason t—'

'They are not poor,' the brother opposite me corrected, his eyes fixed on mine, as if he'd decided not to deal with Galass any more. 'They are destitute and miserable, despising the desolation that encroaches year after year upon their town, yet unable to leave because their bodies are addicted to the very toxins infecting the soil that make their existences unbearable.'

He rapped his knuckles gently on the table and I heard that same buzzing in my ears from earlier – and suddenly the wooden surface of the table became a living model of the town of Mages' Grave and its surrounding landscape, including this fortress. It even had the blood-red haze that blew across all of it.

'This settlement you seem eager to die for barely sustains the two hundred lives who still cling to it,' said the brother to his left.

The skinnier one to his right asked, 'Do you truly believe the town of Mages' Grave will continue to exist much longer, regardless of our intentions?'

'Could you annoying fuckers talk one at a time?' Corrigan asked.

'This is your idea of diplomacy?' I asked quietly.

He jabbed a thumb at the forty-two dead wonderists hanging from the ceiling. 'They're going to kill us anyway. Do I have to sit here and listen to all this bullshit or can I blast at least one of these fuckers before I die?'

'We mean no harm to anyone,' the brother opposite assured me. He spread his arms wide as if to contain within them the landscape depicted upon the table between us. 'All we ask is to be left in peace within this minuscule, forgotten tract of territory none of you would ever choose to set foot on had not our true enemies tricked you into doing so. I assure you, our intentions are peaceful.'

'Peaceful is my very favourite place in the whole world,' I said. 'I hope to visit it one day, but no one can ever point it out to me on a map. And despite your pleasant talk, I can't help but notice you haven't stated precisely what your intentions are for this admittedly shitty patch of land.'

One of the others began to speak, but I heard that buzzing again and the guy across from me waved him off. 'Let us speak plainly,' he said to me, 'for we are unaccustomed to communicating in this fashion with outsiders and it is . . . irksome to us.'

'We have that effect on people,' Corrigan said. 'It gets even worse when we're blasting their arses out of existence, motherfucker.'

Aradeus had been sitting quietly, watchful and contemplative, but now he intervened. 'You speak as if you are not like us, yet I believe you are human, are you not?'

'We were born as you are,' the fellow opposite me said. I guess he'd be doing all the talking from now on. Of the lot of them, he looked the most normal – you know, despite the red eyes and veiny skin thing. 'Once we were wonderists, like yourselves. However, our attunements were . . . incomplete, our spells so feeble as to be trivial. It was only recently that we understood the cause of our weakness.'

'Let me guess,' I said, finally working through a few details that hadn't made sense until now. 'The seven of you were born attuned to a plane outside the ones with which most mages are familiar?'

He gave me an appreciative smile – kind of like you give a puppy who's just performed his first trick.

If you liked that one, you'll really find this amusing.

'A mystical plane that's in trouble, I presume?' I asked. 'One whose denizens – who also happen to be the source of your remarkable abilities – are slowly dying?'

'Why do you say that?' the heavier-set brother to his left asked, his voice raised both in volume and pitch.

For the first time since we'd arrived, the seven of them looked surprised, and I was reminded that, for all her heretical philosophising, Hazidan Rosh had been one hell of a teacher in the art of investigation.

I shrugged as if the inference was obvious. 'Even presuming you can open a permanent gate between two planes, translation from one realm to another isn't easy. Consciousness – or spirit, as you might call it – can transcend the laws of physics between realities, but it's an unpleasant experience at the best of times. Besides, it's not like the Mortal plane's all that enticing, even on a good day. Your patrons are desperate for a new home, and you're desperate to give it to them.'

That got me a laugh from the one on the far right, who looked to be the youngest. His laughter spread like an infection to the others, one after another, which was exactly as disturbing to watch as you might expect.

'Was that funnier than I thought it was?' Corrigan whispered to me.

The middle brother sitting opposite me took control again. 'We appreciate your . . . candour. Allow us in return to make our own intentions plain. As you've surmised, there is a plane of reality previously unknown to mages, yet closely aligned with this one.'

'Who are these beings?' Galass asked. 'What are they like?'

A tolerant smile appeared on every face. 'The Pandorals are like us, in a way,' replied the middle brother. 'Where the Infernals and Aurorals oppress themselves and their followers with rigid hier-archies, these beings see each other as equals. They have no interest in twisting and manipulating the spiritual beliefs of others' demesnes, for they do not seek war with anyone.'

'If this Pandoral demesne is so close to the Mortal realm, why haven't any of us heard of it?' Corrigan asked. He turned in his chair and glanced up at the forty-two dead wonderists floating above the chamber. 'Why wouldn't there be hordes of mages attuned to it?'

'The Pandorals are . . . quiet beings,' the brother answered. 'Their realm cannot be accessed from without unless a door is opened from their side.'

'But the seven of you have some spiritual connection to this Pandoral plane?' Galass asked.

'As we mentioned earlier, we were born with this most rare and precious of attunements.'

'Why?' Aradeus asked. 'What caused the seven of you to be more innately attuned to their plane than other wonderists?'

'We prefer not to discuss the reasons.'

It's funny how sometimes the strangest beings – the ones least like regular folks – are actually the easiest ones to read. Hazidan would have said it's because we're always more aware of that which is foreign to us.

'They lied earlier,' I said, my gaze never leaving the brother opposite me. 'Or at least, they encouraged my incorrect assumption. The brothers didn't come to the Blastlands solely because of their connection to the Pandoral demesne. They came here because they're attuned to the devastation. That's what's fuelling their powers.' I leaned in close, getting into my counterpart's face with a justiciar's interrogatory gaze. 'Was it one of your ancestors who fought in the mages' war?'

The silence suggested maybe I'd pushed the matter too far. Under the table, my fingers began to trace one of the Infernal symbols I'd prepared on the way here. Then I heard that buzzing in my ears, just for a second, and the tension vanished.

'Our parents, actually,' the eldest said. 'We are older than we appear.' He started to look sheepish – in the sense of being mildly embarrassed, not that he was turning into an actual sheep, although I wouldn't have put it past them.

'Your mother *and* father fought the mages' war?' I asked.

He nodded. 'Against each other.'

Corrigan roared with laughter, so loudly I wondered if he was about to start conjuring thunder right there in the banquet room. 'Now there's a marital argument I would have liked to have witnessed!'

'Their powers were on a scale beyond those of any other wonderists,' the youngest said, defiance clear in his voice.

His reaction sparked my interest, because it had just occurred to me that the longer we were here, the more like normal humans the Seven Brothers were behaving.

'Their conflict tore at the walls of reality, leaving behind millions upon millions of tiny fractures.'

'The red soot,' I said.

One of the brothers nodded and I realised that he was the only one left who hadn't spoken yet. He traced a finger along one of the red veins on his cheek. 'The attunement of which my brother earlier spoke is to those fractures. It is for this reason that our magics were weak, unfocused, until the Pandorals sensed our presence beyond the veil and chose to bless us with the magics of their realm.'

'And in return, they want you to save them.'

'A small price,' he said, spreading his hands. 'Would any of you refuse it for abilities such as ours?'

Other than turning unwilling animals into two-legged servants and murdering wonderists with apparent ease, I wasn't entirely sure what the full extent of their powers were, but I was willing to assume they were formidable.

'So now that the plane of reality from which you derive your magic is collapsing, you want to bring the Pandoral beings here to save them?'

'The Pandoral plane is the smallest of those connected to the Mortal realm,' explained the youngest. 'In terms of physical space, it would be no larger than this keep. Only three hundred conscious beings reside there.'

'And they want to move into the Blastlands?'

'Within the territories covered by the desolation,' he agreed. 'Only here can the soil produce crops that will sustain them. The very thing that makes the desolation untenable for human beings gives them a chance at new life.'

'What about those who already live here?' asked Galass. I noticed she was keeping a steadying hand on the little jackal, who was looking like it was time to jump off her lap and start ripping out the throats of the brothers. 'Will you force them from their homes?'

'Not if they wish to stay,' replied the eldest brother. 'Our patrons are not cruel. Should the citizens of Mages' Grave choose to remain, they may do so. The Pandorals wish only to live in peace.'

'So, on their behalf, you wouldn't mind agreeing to a pact that the Pandorals would never expand their territory?' I asked.

Again I heard the buzzing in my ears and all seven heads bobbed at once. 'Agreed.'

'And you'll recompense the townsfolk for any inconvenience their new neighbours cause?'

Not even a buzzing this time. 'Happily.'

Aradeus started to speak, but I cut him off. 'Well then, friends,' I said, my chair scraping the floor as I rose. 'Sounds like all of this was just a simple misunderstanding.'

Galass stood next, gently placing Mister Bones on the floor. 'We will speak with the townsfolk and explain the situation. Perhaps a pact between both sides might be possible.'

The brothers looked at each other for the first time, then rose to their feet. 'We would be amenable to such a pact. The previous delegations who came were intent only on killing us outright.' He gestured to the bloody consequences of those attempts. 'We hoped perhaps that this gruesome display might help the next delegation to reconsider.'

I had to admit, there were worse reasons for dangling the massacred corpses of your enemies in front of your visitors.

'You'd have to make certain concessions,' I warned. 'We'll expect the local townsfolk to have a say in the management of the territory, to make sure their ancestral rights are preserved.'

'No one likes a noisy neighbour,' Corrigan agreed.

As before, the brothers nodded their assent to our demands. Pretty soon we were all standing. I stuck out a hand. 'To peace, then?'

Awkwardly, the eldest brother took my hand and we shook on our new deal. 'To peace.' I was about to pull away when his grip on my hand grew firmer. 'Allow us to add a small token of our friendship to make this new arrangement of ours all the sweeter.'

As the buzzing started, Madrigal the goat man entered the room with seven other servants, carrying what looked suspiciously like a brass coffin.

'A threat?' I asked, looking down at the eldest brother's fingers, gripped in my right hand. If he thought I couldn't trace the sigils with my left, he really didn't know much about Infernal magic.

He shook his head vigorously as if simultaneously surprised and embarrassed. 'Hardly that, Silord Cade.'

He let go of my hand as the eight animal servants set the ornate casket down in the middle of the chamber. I followed behind him, curious. Was this truly a gift, or a threat, or something in between? On closer inspection, the brass sarcophagus was inlaid with gold and silver, and a third metal that looked like mercury flowed within narrow channels across the lid. Inscribed on the surface was a beautifully rendered outline of a human form, the head adorned with a halo made up of dozens of tiny sigils that I struggled to recognise at first. The eldest brother standing next to me made a soft harrumphing noise as several seconds ticked by, watching me as if confused about why I wasn't already jumping up and down in ecstasy at being shown what looked to be a particularly attractive coffin.

Then I realised why I was having so much trouble making sense of the sigils: while I knew most of them, I'd never seen them all in one place before, because the magics to which they referred belonged to different wonderist attunements.

All the different wonderist attunements.

This wasn't a coffin at all.

CHAPTER 36

The First Offering

Mister Bones leaped from Galass' arms and raced around the seven-foot-long brass casket, making the animal servants distinctly uncomfortable as he darted between their legs, yapping happily all the while.

Galass, Aradeus, and Corrigan approached more cautiously.

'Unholy shit,' I heard Corrigan whisper behind me. 'Is that—?'

'Pretty sure it is,' I replied.

I'd never actually seen it before – almost no wonderist ever had. That's why I'd presumed it was a coffin at first, brought out to warn us against crossing the brothers. I should have known better; the forty-two floating wonderist corpses above our heads were more than sufficient to remind us of their power.

This wasn't a warning at all. It was a bribe – the best bribe imaginable for someone in my profession.

'The Apparatus,' Aradeus murmured.

The eldest of the brothers stepped between us and the casket, frowned down at the puppy-like antics of Mister Bones, and corrected us. 'I believe its proper name is the Empyrean Physio-Thaumaturgical Device of Attunal Transmutation.'

'Only ponces call it that,' Corrigan said.

Me, I wasn't so concerned with semantics. I was too busy staring at the solution to all my problems, past, present and future. I cared not at all about what the Seven Brothers called it – and not much about how they'd come by it.

'That's why you came to Mages' Grave when you did,' my idiot mouth said, too conditioned by Hazidan's training to stop myself from making uncomfortable deductions that shouldn't matter at all to me right now. 'You got word that Baron Tristmorta had acquired the Apparatus. The attunements with which you were born that connected your magics to the Pandoral plane were too weak to achieve your aims.' I pointed to the brass casket with its elaborate gold and silver inlay. 'You laid siege to the baron's fortress for weeks, killing off the mercenary wonderists he kept hiring to protect him, all so you could get your hands on this.'

I heard the light footsteps of the other six brothers coming to join their elder. That faint buzzing in my ear told me they were discussing whether it was going to be necessary to obliterate us after all.

Boy, were they reading the situation wrong.

'I don't care how you got it,' I said.

Galass could be rid of the blood magic that would otherwise drive her to murder anyone crazy enough to be close to her. I could alter my own source of magic to a plane of existence that didn't demand I sell pieces of my soul to a diabolic every time I needed a spell. Hell, if I wanted, I could use this thing to attune myself to the Auroral plane once more, hear the Auroral Song . . .

All this was being offered to us on the proverbial silver platter.

'What's the catch?' I asked.

The brother who looked closest to my age, who'd been sitting opposite me at the table, stepped closer like an old friend come to keep me from making a bad decision. 'Do not let the distrust and suspicion that is the instinct of petty mercenaries overcome you,' he said, going so far as to place a hand on my shoulder. 'As you surmised, we did indeed require the artefact in order to more perfectly attune ourselves to the Pandoral plane. Now that this has been accomplished – now that we can fulfil our mission and rescue the beings whose own realm is slowly collapsing in on them – we have no more need for the device.'

'Power for its own sake holds no sway over us,' one of the others said, the youngest from the sound of his voice. 'Nor do the riches that power can provide interest us.'

'We seek only to give our benefactors a home in this small, wasted territory,' my guy assured me, his hand giving my shoulder a reassuring squeeze. His other hand gestured upwards to the dead wonderists still hanging upside down from the ceiling by invisible tethers. The horror and pain evident in their gaping mouths and widened eyes made them look almost alive – just not any kind of alive you'd want to experience. 'Every time we are forced to defend ourselves,' the brother said sorrowfully, 'our mission is delayed yet again, for we must wait for our strength to be rekindled. All we ask is that you leave this place for a time. Allow us to complete our great work, and tomorrow' – his raised hand descended so slowly it was like watching a feather floating down on the breeze – 'tomorrow the Apparatus and all its wonders will be yours.'

Whether from anticipation at being so close to achieving their ends without further hindrance or simply to let us know the parlay was coming to a close, the Seven Brothers spoke as one. 'Will you accept our terms?'

Galass and Aradeus turned to me, their gazes questioning. My own face wore more of a 'don't start with me' sort of look.

Corrigan, however, wasn't waiting for anyone's permission. 'Are you fucking nuts?' he asked the brothers, arms spread out wide as if he were about to hug all of them at once. 'Of *course* we're accepting your dea—'

'We'll let you know,' I said, cutting him off.

Corrigan's eyes glowed the same purplish-blue as his hair and I was pretty sure he was about to blast me out of existence and take the deal for himself. The only thing that stopped him was the eldest brother's voice when he said, 'Deliver your answer to us by midnight, else we will come seeking you, and then it will be too late for peace.'

Another quick buzzing in my ear was followed by the eight grey-robed animal servants ushering us out of the chamber. Mister Bones yapped belligerently for a second or two, then trotted along behind us. I could tell Corrigan was furious with me, while Galass and Aradeus were wondering why I'd just turned down the most generous offer in the history of 'kindly go fuck yourselves and we'll give you some nice toys to play with' negotiations.

I couldn't have explained my hesitation even if I'd wanted to.

We'd come here presuming some nefarious intentions on the part of these eccentric siblings. Instead, it turned out the people we were working for had lied and manipulated us, and our purported enemies were claiming only to want to save the benevolent beings from another plane of reality, asking for nothing more than a patch of land long ago forsaken by most of our own people. The brothers had promised to never expand their territory, to take care of any civilians who still wanted to remain here, and, asking only that we not interfere, offered us the Apparatus in exchange.

The fucking *Apparatus.*

Now, I know what you're thinking: *'But Cade, some deals are too good to be true!'* And sure, I get that. But look at it from the brothers' perspective: they didn't give a shit about wealth or power or any of the other petty nonsense that occupies virtually every waking moment for people like me. Why *wouldn't* they give us everything we wanted, when they themselves had no interest in any of those things?

Surrounded by the eight servants – two cats, three sheep, that irritated-looking donkey, the anxious-looking rat and Madrigal the goat man – we walked in silence until we reached the gate leading into the courtyard. We'd barely started down the stone stairs to the muddy red ground beyond when a two-foot-tall bundle of overexcited fur raced ahead of us.

'Mister Bones!' Galass called, but the little jackal paid her no heed; instead, he began digging in the soil, yapping enthusiastically all the while.

'What the hell's going on now?' Corrigan grumbled. 'I hate that stupid dog.'

'Jackal,' I corrected reflexively.

I smelled goat breath over my left shoulder before I felt Madrigal's presence behind me. 'The brothers wished me to convey their gratitude for the courteous manner in which you have behaved, as well as their recognition that this appears to be a difficult decision for you to make, Silord Ombra. In the spirit of mutual understanding, they have commanded me to present an . . . alternative gift to you.'

'That'll be the one the jackal's digging up?'

The goat man nodded.

I walked down to the bottom of the steps, keeping a little distance from Mister Bones, who stopped to dance in a little circle a couple of times before resuming his frantic digging. It wasn't long before I saw the 'gift' the brothers had left for me.

Remember when I said the thing about how negotiations often begin with the presentation of two gifts? They sometimes end with a second pair of offerings, and these were just like the platter of delectable scones and bowls of faeces, only instead of the scones, they'd presented us with the Apparatus, and instead of the dollops of shit . . . well, it was certainly an equivalent.

CHAPTER 37

The Second Offering

Mister Bones was doing a masterful job of unwrapping my gift. I assumed the purpose of his frantic leaping from one patch of ground to another, kicking an inch of red clay away here and there, was meant to continue the suspense as long as possible.

'Think I see a nose now,' Corrigan said, looming next to me.

'Two noses,' Aradeus said.

'Two perfectly formed noses,' I corrected. Alice and Shame joined us, drawn by the jackal's frenetic digging.

The angelic reached out a hand towards the mount being steadily unearthed by Mister Bones, her eyes shifting colour back to that unnerving golden hue. 'I can't sense their ecclesiasm,' she said, visibly disturbed. 'Something is hiding their nature from me.'

'That's part of the wrapping,' I said.

I'd had enough of the damned jackal's interminable playing, so I walked over and tried to shoo him away. He growled at me, so I showed him my boot. If you're thinking that was cruel of me – and you're forgetting all the times I'd killed people already – then let me reassure you that the little fucker had it coming. At any rate, he got the idea and ran off to start digging elsewhere.

I knelt down and wiped away the red soil from their faces. Fidelity and Dignity blinked in the sun overhead, so I shifted over a bit to block the glare so they could see me properly.

'Cade?' Dignity asked.

'The fallen one,' Fidelity spat. To be fair, she might have been trying to get the dirt out of her mouth so she could greet me more gracefully. 'Would that I could rise from this foul grave to desecrate this already profane soil with your blood.'

Guess not, then.

'What happened to you?' I asked them, digging lower with my fingers until I discovered there was nothing left of them past the grizzly viscera of their severed necks.

'We were to be the vanguard against the Seven Brothers,' Dignity replied, weeping tears of such sorrow you almost didn't think to wonder where they were coming from since he was basically just a buried head. 'The others were to—'

'The Lords Celestine and Devilish sent a bunch of mercenary war mages to distract the brothers so you could very honourably sneak in and slip a blade in the enemy's back.' I didn't bother making it a question.

'This was a holy quest,' Fidelity insisted. 'We were—'

'Save it,' I said. I stood up and glanced back at the fortress. 'What the hell prompted your bosses to go to all this trouble, only to send two justiciars to fight seven wonderists so powerful they mowed through forty-two war mages without breaking a sweat?'

'Um, Cade?' Corrigan said, tapping me on the shoulder.

He pointed to Mister Bones, who was running from another patch of soil where he'd been digging to start afresh on the next. The little jackal had got the hang of it now, and was making swift work of it. He'd revealed several more beheaded Glorian Justiciars.

'In the name of . . .' Galass faltered. After all, who do you pray to when you're standing on the corpses of the purest, most powerful fighting force of Celestine-blessed warriors ever conceived?

'Guess you won't have to worry about justiciars hunting you any more,' Corrigan murmured.

You'd think at least some small part of me would be relieved. Of all the things I feared in this world – and believe me, there were a great many – topmost was being captured by my former comrades, which I knew was as inevitable as the sunrise. Freed of any restraints, they would have tortured me in ways that would make a diabolic bury his face in his hands and weep.

Somehow, I didn't feel relieved.

'Cade,' Dignity said again. His handsome, otherworldly features were contorted with pain and horror. I'm not sure he'd been aware of what had happened to him until Mister Bones dug him up.

I turned to Shame. 'Can you and Galass do what you did for the baron? Can you give them a proper death?'

'I don't know,' she replied, looking so sad it was as if she'd trans-figured all her features solely for that one expression. 'There are so many, and if we—'

'Fuck this,' Corrigan said. 'We came here like you wanted, Cade. We made the best deal we could for the townsfolk – not to mention ourselves. Now it's time to get the hell out of here.'

'I can't leave them like this.'

He clamped a hand on my shoulder. 'You can, and you *will*. The brothers clearly want them to suffer – which I'm fine with, by the way.'

'Cade!'

I looked down at Dignity, who was still shouting at me.

'What is it?' I asked, kneeling.

I don't know that I've ever seen someone so torn between misery for themselves and mortification over what they were about to say next.

'You must take up our mantle and fight in our name,' he said to me.

'*Fight the brothers*? The seven guys who just killed every wonderist I've ever met *and* an entire division of Glorian Justiciars?'

'You have to fight them,' he repeated stubbornly. His jaw clenched tighter. 'Cade Ombra, Renegade Exile of the Glorian Justiciars, by command of the Lords Celestine and the Auroral Voice, you are hereby recalled for duty and promoted to the rank of Paladin Justiciar. You are to—'

He stopped talking then, mostly because his face was blown off by Corrigan's bolt of black and red lightning. It proved to be a futile gesture, because Fidelity took up the call.

'Cade Ombra, Paladin of the Glorian Justiciars, you mus—'

Corrigan blasted her, too. I guess the Seven Brothers didn't care about keeping them suffering as they had the baron, because her flesh didn't instantly reform. So that was promising, at any rate.

Unfortunately, it turned out that there were dozens more justiciar heads buried just inches beneath the soil, and Mister Bones was doing an excellent job of digging them up.

'Cade Ombra, Paladin and brother to us all, redeem your soul and—'

'Cade Ombra, our holy cause rests with y—'

'Cade Ombra—'

'Cade Ombra—'

Corrigan was running out of lightning, and more importantly, he was tiring himself out, and even he's not so stubborn as to leave himself helpless just to prove a point.

So the six of us stood there, listening to the rest of the dead justiciars telling me my duty, commanding me to defeat the Seven Brothers and protect the Mortal demesne from an invasion by the Pandorals.

When at last they all stopped, Mister Bones walked up to what was left of Dignity's scorched skull and pissed on it.

'Proud of yourself?' I asked the jackal.

He barked in reply, which I took as a yes.

I reached my hands out for the mutt's neck. 'You deceiving son of a bitch.'

'Don't take it out on him!' Galass said, getting in my face.

271

I sidestepped her and stomped over to the mutt, who was now sitting on his haunches, head tilted and looking up at me adoringly. Alice was right. Those ears were too fucking long.

'The game's over,' I said. 'Time to show yourself.'

'What are you—?'

I held up a hand to forestall Galass' objections. 'Go on,' I told the jackal. 'Make your big entrance.'

He rolled onto his back and at first I thought he was still screwing with me, but then the jackal spasmed and I heard the crack of bone breaking.

'Mister Bones!' Galass cried, but I grabbed her arms to keep her away from him.

There were more cracking sounds, and a kind of stench like the smoke from a candle being blown out, over and over again. The little canine form stretched out, the fur shedding in some places, lengthening in others, changing from silver-grey to blond, the muzzle pushing back into his face even as the head grew to the size and shape of a man's.

Well, not a *man's*, exactly. More of a boy's.

'*Fidick?*' Galass asked.

Guess I was wrong about Mister Bones not being anything more than a jackal.

CHAPTER 38

The Revenant

I had any number of reasons to be afraid of the naked eleven-year-old boy smiling at me over Galass' shoulder as she hugged the breath right out of him. Most of these stemmed from having covered up his corpse on the floor of my tent not so long ago.

There's nothing overly impressive about reanimating the recently departed; a body is just a body, after all. A collection of parts. Bones, muscles, sinew, veins – they're all just bits and pieces of matter with needs that magic can provide. Fluids need to replenish and flow. Skin needs to grow and die and grow again. Is it complicated? Sure – and expensive as . . . well, expensive as hell. But it can be done.

Even the problem of the mind can be solved, assuming you're feeling a driving need to have the corpse in question talk back to you. Some wonderists have been known to use a spell to reconstruct the original consciousness from a gestalt of those memories and instincts still present in the dead flesh of the brain. The result is gruesome, of course, but if you want to spend the equivalent cost of recruiting, housing and feeding an army just to acquire one shambling, drooling slave to be at your beck and call, people like me can get the job done.

Fidick, however, wasn't reanimated. Not only had his spiritual essence – the unknowable mixture of his consciousness and the ecclesiasm that housed it – been removed from his body the instant he'd traded it to Tenebris and then swapped bodies with Mister Bones, but the fundamental design of his body had been implanted into the poor jackal as well. To add insult to injury, the mutt's body had been reshaped to look like that of a dead eleven-year-old boy.

Fidick wasn't a revenant. He was a miracle.

And there's only one way to make a miracle.

Shame came up beside me and I could tell the same question banging furiously at the inside of my skull was doing likewise to hers.

'What the *fuck* were the Lords Celestine thinking?' I asked her. 'Infernals can't pull off resurrections on their own, which means your old bosses participated in this atrocity.'

She let the wide-eyed gaze and furrowed brow speak for her.

Corrigan, marching up on my left, had a more practical question. 'How do we kill it?'

He'd spoken quietly but his words sent ripples through our little company. Galass spun around, scarlet hair whipping up around her head like a bloody halo, hands already outstretched. I could feel the veins rising on my neck. Alice summoned her mystical whip-sword and added her own snarl to the hissing of the blade writhing in her grip. She was on our side, though, which improved our odds considerably – until Aradeus, principled piece of shit that he was, drew his rapier and took up position beside Galass and Fidick.

'I'll not be party to the butchery of children,' he said.

Fuck you for being so honourable, I thought, *and fuck you twice for reminding me I'm not.*

The cause of our mutiny decided it was time for more enlightened minds to prevail. 'You're all scared,' Fidick said, gently pushing aside the hand Galass was using to keep him behind her. 'Please, there's no need.'

'My mother used to tell me not to be scared,' Corrigan said, one of his more catastrophic Tempestoral spells igniting around his clenched fist, 'every time Grandfather turned up in the middle of the night to beat the two of us half to death until he finally passed out. He always looked so peaceful after he was done. Serene. Like you.'

Fidick looked down and shook his head sadly. I couldn't say for sure whether it was from staring at the bodiless heads of the dead and desecrated Glorian Justiciars, or perhaps because he'd been hoping his genitals would have come back with somewhat more impressive dimensions. 'I'm not here to hurt you, Corrigan Blight. I'm not here to hurt any of you.'

Damn straight, you aren't, I thought. I brought my fingers back out from my open shirt. I had enough mind-and-soul-crushing Infernal spells ready to make this kid *wish* he'd ended up in Hell instead of crossing me. Shame made an awkward gesture with her open left hand. At first I thought it might be a spell, then I recognised it as a very old sign of prayer. It struck me as funny that even exiled angelics turned religious when things got tough.

'What is your mission here, Abomination?' she asked, repeating the gesture of prayer a second time and then a third. 'Why did the Lords Celestine violate their own edicts to grant you this unholy life?'

Fidick smiled benignly at her, as though she were a child raising a nervous hand in the classroom because she was worried her question was so silly it would get her in trouble. Her question wasn't silly, though – but it wasn't complete, either.

'Why did the Lords *Devilish* allow it?' I asked.

Alice and Shame, both of whom understood the broad principles of Auroral revivification better than any of us, stared at me aghast.

'The kid's deal with Tenebris included his soul,' I told them. 'That was the price for the murder spell he used to execute Ascendant Lucien, and for the blood magic awakened in Galass so she could protect herself.'

'But if the Lords Devilish bought his soul . . .' Aradeus began, his glance now shifting to the boy. No doubt he was now wondering if he'd put himself on the wrong side.

'He couldn't have been swapped with the jackal without the express consent – no, the *collaboration* of the Lords Devilish,' Alice said, her upper lip curled in a snarl that made me nostalgic for Mister Bones.

'Care to explain why the Infernals have become so cooperative?' I asked Fidick.

The boy folded his arms across his chest. It was almost endearing. 'Come on, Cade,' he said. 'The Lords Celestine kept going on about how clever you were. Hazidan Rosh's finest student – the keenest investigator of all the Glorian Justiciars. Is such a simple question truly beyond you?'

The others were watching me again. I, in turn, stared at the charred heads of my former comrades. Poor bastards. They'd truly believed the forty-two wonderists who'd gone ahead of them had been decoys to give the Seven Brothers a false sense of security. But a con – a really good con – always misdirects the target *twice*. Fidelity, Dignity and the rest of their justiciar squad had been the second misdirect.

And us? We were both the endgame and the biggest suckers of all.

When I turned around, I could see Madrigal, the goat chamberlain, was still standing at the top of the stone stairs leading into the fortress. When I walked back up to him, he flinched, but stood his ground.

'How many like you are inside the keep?' I asked.

'However many the brothers need. Sometimes they create more of us from among the creatures of the hills. When they have no more use of us, they send us away.'

'Are they kind to you?' Galass asked from below.

The goat man looked unsure how to answer that. 'They are masters, we are servants,' he said finally.

I did a stupid thing then: I reached out a hand to him. With no less awkwardness than the brothers had, he shook it, and as he did so, I leaned in and whispered, 'Find an excuse to get the other servants out of the keep tonight.'

Corrigan shot me a look that would have killed me on the spot, if such a thing were possible.

Madrigal's lips parted, revealing great big clenched teeth. 'You'll die,' he said. 'And our circumstances will not improve.'

'Good thing I'm not dying for your sake, then,' I replied.

He walked backwards into the fortress and closed the doors shut. For the next several minutes, Aradeus and Alice were occupied holding back Corrigan to stop him from punching me in the face with a fistful of lightning. Once he'd stomped off, Galass said, 'I don't understand what's going on. You heard the brothers: the Pandorals only need a place to live. This land is barely used and they agreed to every single one of your demands, even going so far as to offer you this "Apparatus" you're all so mesmerised by. Why are you acting as if they've already betrayed their promises?'

I walked down the stairs and headed back along the path towards town, my mind already trying to work out a plan that had almost no chance of success.

'Because they agreed to every single one of our demands,' I explained.

CHAPTER 39

The Thunder

Wonderists tend to spend their last hours before a big fight sitting cross-legged in a dark room, meditating silently, attempting to gather the inner calm and focus that spellcasters need to survive the mayhem of battle. I found Corrigan in one of the abandoned cottages at the edge of town Vidra had offered us, slumped over a battered wooden table. The dusty green-glass bottle in his hand stank of a liquid whose alcoholic benefits had likely been achieved through festering rather than fermentation. At least half the remaining six bottles lined up on the table had been drunk dry.

'So, you really are one of them,' he said when he caught sight of me in the doorway. 'Not just some guy who ran afoul of a bunch of Glorians, but an actual fucking justiciar.'

The obvious response was, *Don't pretend to be surprised. You knew. You always knew. You just pretended you didn't so we could remain friends.*

'I *was* a justiciar,' I corrected instead. 'Past tense.'

He shook his head, turning to stare at the cottage wall, refusing to meet my eyes. 'Except that's not true, either, is it? One of those golden-haired chisel-jawed disembodied heads *deputised* you. So now you're not just a lying ex-Glorian Justiciar, you're a *current* Glorian Paladin Justiciar.' He made a show of holding up his hands. 'You here to arrest me on a charge of blasphemous sorcery, *Glorian Paladin Justiciar?*'

'Look, it was a long time ago. I was a kid, barely older than Galass, when I was recruited by the most remarkable woman I'd ever met. She convinced me I could be something more than a . . . You know what? It doesn't matter any more.'

Corrigan took a long swig from the bottle, ignoring the dribble of thick brown liquid oozing into his beard. 'Makes no difference. Once a lunatic religious wonderist hunter, *always* a lunatic religious wonderist hunter.'

I couldn't argue with that.

'Should've killed you back at Lucien's camp,' he added with renewed spite, 'let Locke and Narghan and Smoke and the others have their way with you. Instead, I killed them to protect you – killed all of them. I liked Lady Farts, you know – liked all of them. They were family.'

'You hated them,' I reminded him. 'Half of them had tried to kill you on previous jobs, and Lady Smoke tried to do it on that one, as I recall.'

Corrigan scrunched up his mouth in a drunkard's scowl, shaking his head. 'Jus' a misunderstanding. She was a good comrade. They were all good comrades.'

'Even Zyphis?'

Corrigan took another swig, swishing the foul-smelling liquor in his mouth. Finally he swallowed, then winced. 'Now *that* reedy little snake was going to have to die either way, so I'll give you Zyphis.'

This was as much of an invitation as I was going to get. Slowly, keeping my hands loose in case things got ugly faster than I expected, I stepped over debris and sand to pick up a battered chair lying on its side. I set it upright and took a seat.

'None of them were good guys, Corrigan. Good guys don't survive in this profession.'

He gave a soundless snarl, then slammed the bottle on the table and slid it over to me. 'Except you. Fucking Glorian Paladin Justiciar.

Best of the best. Don't you have to be, like, inhumanly holy to get that job?'

I felt certain the rancid booze was a test of some kind, so I drank it, and regretted my decision instantly. 'I used to believe that – it's what we told ourselves, anyway. But after a while, I couldn't keep doing the job.'

'What happened? You get an erection one day and they kicked you out for having illicit desires?'

'I refused an assignment.'

'Why?'

I slid the bottle back to him. 'It's a long story.'

He slid the bottle right back over to me. 'Give me the short version. You might not have time for a longer one.'

How do you explain something like this to someone who's never been part of the order? How do you share what it's like to hear the Auroral Voice – which, by the way, hadn't returned to me even though I'd been 'deputised' – singing inside your skull, inside your very soul? What words can describe the sense of belonging, the absolute, unassailable conviction that you're fighting for a great cause rather than selling yourself for money or more magic? How do you make someone understand what it feels like when all that gets taken away?

'I thought the Celestines were the most noble, compassionate, loving beings in the universe,' I said at last. 'I believed our cause was righteous.'

'So what happened?'

I took another drink of the wine. Sometimes a bad taste in your mouth makes some things easier to say. 'Hazidan, the woman I mentioned who recruited me? She . . . she started to ask me questions.'

'Questions?'

When I set the bottle back on the table, I noticed my hand was shaking. Usually I'd have assumed Corrigan had poisoned me, but

I recognised this trembling. I got it every time I remembered those days.

'A Paladin Justiciar's job is to investigate supernatural atrocities. We go in, figure out what happened and track down the perpetrator.'

'And execute them without a trial,' Corrigan said bitterly.

'There's always a trial. We're just not the ones who set the verdict.'

'Who does?'

'Technically a Glorian Arbitrator, but they just do whatever the Lords Celestine tells them. Whenever one of us apprehended a rogue wonderist, we'd bring them to an arbitrator, who would pray for guidance. But it wasn't like sitting there watching someone mumble to themselves with their eyes closed and their hands making silly prayer gestures. We could hear the voice of whichever Lord Celestine they were talking to. That voice ... Corrigan, it's not like *anything* you've ever heard. Every word is a poem, every inflection a melody. It's as if the universe itself is revealing its own inner workings to you. There's no questioning that verdict, not whether it's too lenient or too harsh, because you know – you *know* – the sentence is perfectly just.'

Corrigan was staring at my face now, eyes narrowed. He looked perplexed. Troubled. 'Except you *did* start to question.'

'It was Hazidan's fault. She started going over recent cases with me – not just mine, but those of other justiciars. We noticed that some of the worst perpetrators were being set free by the arbitrators, and others, whose crimes were nowhere near as vile, we were being ordered to execute.'

Corrigan's lip curled. 'You're saying the Lords Celestine *weren't* delivering perfect justice to our sad little world?' But though he tried to mask it under his usual biting cynicism, I could tell that even he was shaken by the possibility that the Glorian Justiciars could have been corrupted.

'Deals were being made,' I said, and paused to down another

mouthful of the foul liquor. Turned out, it really did help. 'Some of the wonderists we caught entered into contracts with the Lords Celestine, and I thought they must have some hidden potential for redemption that I couldn't see yet. I didn't notice the pattern until it was too late.'

'What the fuck would a Lord Celestine want with a wonderist who commits the kind of massacres that attract the attention of the justiciars in the first place?'

I turned the nondescript green-glass bottle in my hand, suddenly feeling an urge to smash it against the table, to let the shards cut into my hands, to watch the blood seeping from wounds in my palms, an all-too-familiar feeling.

'Well, it turns out, not all massacres are created equal.'

'By all the pink-arsed perverts in the hell—?'

'There's a war going on, Corrigan, and it's been going on for a long time. Everyone knows that. What I hadn't understood is the first thing you discover the day you walk onto a battlefield where two armies are doing everything they can to slaughter each other.'

Corrigan grabbed the empty bottle and hurled it against the wall, sending shards of glass all over the cottage floor. Then he picked up the next one, tore the wax seal from the top and took a long drink. 'There's no such thing as justice in wartime.' He set the bottle down between us as if he were planting a flag in the ground. 'So you start getting queasy about the job and one day they send you to kill some dumb wonderist going about his business and you refuse?'

'Pretty much.'

'Who was it?'

Reflexes born from years on the battlefield brought both our hands up, spells on our lips even before either of us realised we were reacting to the sound of footsteps approaching the open door to the cottage.

'Hello?' Galass asked, peaking her head inside.

Corrigan and I both breathed in deeply at the same time, forcing our hands to relax back down to our laps. We chuckled at each other.

'Is this a bad time?' she asked.

'It's fine,' I said. 'What can I do for you?'

She glanced from me to Corrigan, then back again. 'I was hoping I might have a private word with you, before ... before we go back to the fortress.'

'Sure. I'll come see you in a little while.'

She smiled, and for a moment looked almost like the seventeen-year-old girl I'd met mere weeks ago rather than the blood mage with whom I was about to go into battle.

'What's that all about?' Corrigan asked, arching an eyebrow.

'Nothing like what you're thinking. She just wants to tell me that when the fight starts, when people start dying, that if it comes down to a choice, if I can only protect one of them, she wants me to save Fidick instead of her.'

'How can you know that?'

I shrugged. 'I was a professional inquisitor. You think they name just any idiot to the Glorian Justiciars?'

He chewed on that a while, then asked, 'Cade, just how good at this investigation business were you?'

The chair creaked in complaint as I levered myself to my feet, as if it was already missing my company. 'Good enough to know that we've been set up, and not just by the Lords Celestine and Devilish. The Seven Brothers are both as righteous as they believe themselves to be, and as vile as we expected. If they win the fight, these Pandorals of theirs are going to bring more pain and suffering to the Mortal realm than you or I have ever seen.'

'So you're saying the fate of all humanity is down to you, me and the most pathetic bunch of unstable wonderists ever assembled?' He stared at the bottle in his hand, brought it to his lips, but then pulled it away. 'Can we beat them?'

'Of course.'

'How can you be so sure?'

I took the bottle from him and drained what little remained so I could hold the glass up to the fading light of the sun coming through the cottage door. Hazidan used to do that – hold up a filthy glass to the sun or a lantern. She liked to see the way the light became distorted, and in that distortion, she said, a more honest vision of the universe could be found.

'The Lords Celestine and the Lords Devilish conspired to get you and me here because we're good at leading a small crew. They allowed us to recruit Aradeus because they wanted us to feel comfortable enough that we'd still commit to the job even after they made sure we'd end up with Galass – who became a blood mage through their machinations.'

'And the boy?'

'I can't tell you how, but I'm absolutely positive he's the key to the entire operation. He's how we're going to win.'

'Given you've just declared victory, Cade, I'm curious why you're scowling like that.'

'Because winning and surviving aren't the same thing. They've given us the tools to destroy the gates, Corrigan, but not to escape the battle. They're expecting us to win, but not live.'

'Why? Why would they . . . ?' His question drifted off into nothingness as he worked out the answer for himself. Corrigan might have made a passable justiciar himself, if he weren't so fond of criminality. 'They don't want witnesses.'

'These sorts of jobs, would you want anyone knowing what happened?'

I headed for the door. I'd still need to talk to the others, make sure they knew the plan, such as it was. More importantly, I needed to make sure they were committed.

'Cade, wait.'

I stopped, already knowing the question that was coming. 'Yeah?'

'The guy you refused to kill – the wonderist. Who was it?'

'Nobody,' I said. 'Just some big, loud-mouthed thunderer who was guilty of a hundred sins, just not of the crime for which I'd been sent to drag him to a sham trial followed by a swift execution.' I couldn't help but smile then. 'Dumbest, most corrupt son of a bitch you ever saw, but underneath all that bluster and lightning was a soul the Lords Celestine knew would never bend to their wills. When the time came, I couldn't bring myself to kill him.'

He didn't make a sound, but I swear I could hear Corrigan's mouth drop open. 'Wait . . . you mean . . . ?'

I left him to ponder that last thought as I headed out into the early evening. I imagine it must've made him feel a little better about all the times he'd saved my life to believe that, just maybe, he was the reason why I'd abandoned the Glorian Justiciars.

Would have been a nice story, right?

CHAPTER 40

The Girl and the Boy

I spent the next couple of hours going from cottage to cottage, spending what time I could with our misbegotten little crew. Every profession has its traditions, and among us wonderists, it's basic courtesy to say something rude and hurtful to each of your comrades before heading into battle. The logic – if there is such a thing in this sorry business – is that since such despicable insults could never be intended as last words, they instead convey your conviction that both of you will survive to laugh at such ill-chosen sentiment . . .

I never said this was a rational way to make a living.

'You spoke to Galass?' Fidick asked.

'I did.'

I could see how hurt she'd been when the boy had insisted on having his own cottage, so I'd made some nonsense up about how those who have beheld the Lords Celestine often need periods of solitude to make sense of the experience, lest it overwhelm them. Technically that's true, although I knew it didn't apply in this case.

'She tried so hard to keep me safe back in the camps,' Fidick said, wandering barefoot around the filthy floor of the cottage, gazing up at the spiderwebs festooning the rotten beams as if they were great works of art. 'Did she ask that you protect me during the battle? I expect she told you to trade her life for mine if it came to it, and reminded you that I am the only innocent one of all of us?'

286

'Something like that.'

'And will you heed her request?'

I considered that a moment, as I had when she'd been pleading with me with the kind of agonised intensity of which only teenagers are truly capable. I wandered over to join Fidick as he stared up at the mouldy ceiling. 'If I have any say over what happens tonight, I'm going to do everything in my power to make sure she lives a long and happy life, and that you die as horrifically as possible.'

That won me an enigmatic smile. This kid really had been in the presence of the Celestines. 'You'd sacrifice an eleven-year-old child for a blood mage? You must know what she'll become as the years wear away her humanity. Don't tell me you bought that nonsense about the Seven Brothers turning over the Apparatus to you?'

'I'd sacrifice you if I thought it would bring the jackal back, never mind cure Galass. You stopped being a child the moment you forced Tenebris to make your deal with the Lords Devilish. Actually, no, even before that – when you tricked Galass into protecting you, pretending you were her brother.' I ruffled his hair as if he were the boy he still appeared to be. 'And speak of her "humanity" as if it were a soiled nappy one more time and you'll be fulfilling your destiny tonight with two black eyes and a split lip.'

He pulled away from me, and when he looked up at me, there were tears in his eyes. 'Cade, I—'

'If you were planning a career as an actor, you'll need more practice.'

He laughed at that, the bright melody of a church bell at morning service. 'You are exactly as they described you.'

I didn't take the bait. 'Be ready at midnight,' I said, and headed for the door.

'I was scared, you know,' he said, evidently not done with me. 'After you'd left our tent, I was terrified. That part was real. I wanted to protect Galass and that part was real, too. I didn't know it would mean—'

'Most people don't know this about the Infernals,' I said, cutting him off, 'but when they make a deal for another's soul, they never lie. They don't hide the terms of the deal, or the consequences.'

Fidick gave me a tut-tut. 'You make them sound almost honourable, Cade. Is it possible that after all this time away from the Glorians, your moral compass has broken?'

'It's got nothing to do with morality or decency or any other human concern. A soul that realises it's been deceived fights to hold itself together, even in the Infernal plane. Those who gave up their souls in the full knowledge of what it would mean deliver purer ecclesiasm. You knew exactly what the spell you bought would do to Ascendant Lucien, just like you knew exactly what price Galass would pay to become a blood mage.'

'She needed power to survive in this world.'

'She needed power to do the job your bosses expect her to do.'

'They're your bosses too. You just forgot for a while. There's no leaving the Glorians. They just let you . . . take a little vacation, that's all.' He rose and followed me to the door, not a trace of fear in those young eyes of his. Maybe part of him still was an eleven-year-old kid, with an eleven-year-old's trust that the world was a good place, filled mostly with good people. 'You're going to do what the Celestines need you to do and so is Galass. That's how these things work. But I wasn't lying about wanting to protect her like she'd protected me. I hope she survives. I really do.'

He was too sure of himself, too filled with that self-righteousness that comes from hearing the Auroral Voice in your head, knowing that song is sung just for you. Mostly, though, he was standing too close.

So I decked him.

It was no kiddy love-tap, either – I drove my fist into that saintly little fucker's face with all I had. He must've stumbled six feet back before he finally fell on his arse and looked up at me, broken nose bloody and eyes wide.

'Smile, kid,' I told him. 'You say you want Galass to live? I'm going to see that you get your wish.'

CHAPTER 41

The Angel and the Rat

My time with Shame was mostly spent in silence. Angelics have an inborn sense of when a person's lying to them. Justiciars learn that talent the hard way. Two people being straight with each other when our prospects were as miserable as ours were would have depressed us both.

Shame did ask one question before I left.

'What did it feel like after you betrayed the justiciars?'

She'd found a cracked mirror inside her dilapidated little cottage and was staring into it, her fingers probing at the jowls of her cheeks, the wrinkly folds of flesh under her neck. She looked pleased with what she was seeing.

'Disgraced,' I replied. 'I'd never felt so much guilt before. My actions let down every one of my brothers and sisters in the order.' Of its own accord, my hand reached up to rest on my right shoulder where the golden glove of my office used to be pinned. 'The Celestines . . . you never realise how reassuring their touch can be until it's taken away from you.'

'But . . . ?'

The word hung in the air.

'But what?'

'But you felt something else, too, didn't you?'

'What makes you say that?'

She shrugged, still apparently obsessed with her own reflection. 'Because you didn't try to go back.'

How much of this interrogation was curiosity and how much was trying to make sense of her own decision to – as she put it – 'switch sides', I wondered. I still didn't know what deal she'd made with Tenebris, and as she'd made it clear she had no intention of telling me, really, what did I owe her?

'I felt free,' I said at last. 'For a while. The feeling didn't last.'

She pursed her lips and at first I thought she was posing in front of the mirror, but then realised she was thinking about my words. 'All that you gave up – purpose, companionship, the love of the Celestines – all for a fleeting sense of self-determination. I wonder, was it worth it?'

I noticed suddenly that she was not studying her own image in the mirror, but looking at me, watching my expression.

I left her with a gambler's grin and four words. 'You bet your arse.'

My visit with Aradeus was more entertaining, if only because watching a rat mage shadow-fencing in a dark, dirty cottage before a fight in which a blade would almost certainly prove useless is kind of funny.

'Cade!' he shouted at my arrival, greeting me with the sort of enthusiasm normally reserved for a long-lost friend.

I found myself wishing that I'd met the rat mage sooner. Maybe life would have gone a little differently for me if I'd had more experience of the way his debonaire idealism could hold even in the face of the wretched world in which we lived. Aradeus embodied what Hazidan used to call 'the sublime contradiction' – she hadn't been referring to the sublime orders, but to the way human beings could embody contrary notions and make them somehow beautiful. Aradeus was a wonderist who modelled his magic after rats, which everyone with any brains despises as plague-spreaders and corpse-eaters. Yet he took from those loathsome rodents all those qualities that others missed, and in so doing, not only made himself admirable, but somehow managed to ennoble all rats in the process.

'Have we a daring plan with which to defeat these vile brothers and their insidious patrons?' he asked me after a moment or two.

I smiled. 'We have two, in fact.'

'Excellent!' He launched into a series of parries and ripostes against an invisible attacker, brandishing his rapier with consummate skill and grace.

'You don't want to know the details?' I asked.

He performed a pair of long, lightning-fast lunges, punctuating each one with a bizarre 'huzzah!' before pausing long enough to say, 'You'll tell me when I need to know. You're a good leader, Cade.'

'You met me barely a month ago. Besides, Corrigan was supposed to be in charge.'

He grinned, and made a few more swipes in the air with his rapier. 'I've an instinct about such things. Rats are excellent judges of character. You'll see us through the dangers to come, and by morning we'll be celebrating our victory and spreading tales of our adventures far and wide.'

He said all this with a certainty that convinced even me, if only for a moment.

Aradeus Mozen, rat mage and swashbuckler, really was a remarkable human being. He would have made a lousy justiciar.

CHAPTER 42

The Demon and the Diabolic

I decided to leave Alice for last, mostly because I disliked her company almost as much as she disliked mine. It wasn't just because she was an Infernal, either. I'd had more than my share of dealings with them and your average demon is no more nor less pleasant to spend time with than a human being. But Alice had that look in her eyes I'd seen on far too many of my fellow justiciars: a warning that every word you ever said would be weighed to judge its righteous holiness. Who wants to spend what may well be their last hours of life in the company of a zealot? Especially one of the smirking, snarling, 'aren't my bat wings so very impressive?' variety.

There were altogether too many demons in my life at that moment, and there was one I needed to see far more importantly before I got down to her.

'Cade, brother!' Tenebris said excitedly as I summoned him inside the circle of spell-sand. I'd spread it in the middle of the main road that ran from the edge of town up to the fortress on the hill. One of the cottages would have been safer, but I wanted to be outside.

'Kind of a risky spot for a meeting, don't you think?' the diabolic asked, looking around. 'What if one of those townies sees us together and gets the wrong idea about you?'

'What would the wrong idea about me be?' I asked.

'That you consort with the Infernal, of course.'

'I think the cat's out of the bag on that one.'

I sat down cross-legged on the dirt road and took out the pipe I'd found on the floor of Galass' cottage. The bowl was cracked but intact, and the stem was broken off near the end, but you could still suck air through it. The previous resident had thoughtfully left a little satchel of the local pipe-weed that hadn't looked too mouldy. Now I just needed a light.

'Would you mind?' I asked Tenebris.

He looked down at the pipe from where he floated inside the circle. 'You know I can't cast spells on your world from here, Cade. I can only grant them to you.'

He was expecting me to ask for a flame spell for free, but instead, I reached out a finger and brushed a line in the sand, creating a one-inch gap in the outer circle. Tenebris gasped – which, interestingly, in a demon creates a truly disturbing sound. In all the years he'd been my agent, I'd never once broken the barrier between us without a deal in place to ensure my protection.

'Cade, buddy,' he said, 'I'm touched.'

I stuck the bowl of the pipe up to the gap. 'Spare a fellow a light?'

He extended a clawed finger and a tiny flame erupted briefly inside the pipe bowl. A second later it settled into a pleasant little plume of smoke. Corrigan always claimed demon-fire was the best way to cook a steak for the most flavour. I was hoping the same applied to mouldy pipe-weed.

'Aren't you scared I'll use this little portal you've given to have my way with you?' Tenebris asked. 'There's no rule that says I can't cast a recruitment spell on you and make you my unwilling slave.'

'Funny you should bring that up.' I sucked in smoke through the broken stem of the pipe. It wasn't bad – it reminded me of being in an old-growth forest just after a storm, or some other stupid metaphor like that. 'You and your pals have already screwed me over pretty thoroughly,' I went on, letting a blue-grey cloud of smoke escape from my lips. 'Which means there's not much more you can do to me.'

'Never took you for an optimist, Cade.'

'No, but you did take me for a fool.'

'Hey now—'

I waved away his objection with the pipe, wisps of smoke flittering from the bowl as if it were a censer and I a holy man. 'Not as big a fool as Ascendant Lucien, of course. Can't imagine what the Celestines you're secretly working for had to promise that pompous arsehole to get him to declare he was going to massacre the surrendering soldiers, just to get me to come to you and ask for an assassination spell.'

'And *I* refused to sell you that spell, remember?'

I nodded as I sucked in another mouthful of smoke. On second puff, the stuff was actually quite foul. 'You needed me for other things, though, which is why you suggested to the Lords Celestine that they order Ascendant Lucien to make sure I took two of his pleasure slaves with me, knowing I'd have to have them in the tent when I summoned you.'

Tenebris gave me his sincerest fake chuckle. 'Just because two kids see you summon a demon doesn't necessarily mean one of them is going to follow suit and sell their soul the second you leave your tent.'

'That's what I thought, too. For a while.'

'And?'

I figured I'd give the pipe-weed one more try. Add that to the long list of bad decisions I keep making. 'And then I remembered the horrors those two kids had already lived through. Given the chance not just to escape those awful lives, but to actually be given even an ounce of power over others? Who in those circumstances could turn that down?'

I flicked away a little of the excess weed in the bowl, in the hope that it might lighten the increasingly unpleasant fragrance a little.

'The girl didn't try to summon me,' Tenebris argued. 'She tried to stop the boy.'

'Galass is different. She *was* different, anyway.'

Tenebris folded his arms across his chest. He wasn't above shows of petulance if it was in service to a lie. 'The problem with your little conspiracy theory, Cade, is that very few humans have the ability to work Infernal magic, which means—'

'Which means Lucien was a better actor than I would have expected, and his slavering over Fidick – which was what made me pick the boy as one of my prizes in the first place – was also part of the act. But you knew all that, Tenebris, because you were the one pulling Lucien's strings. The Lords Celestine owned him, but they're not nearly subtle enough to have played me so smoothly.'

I tried one more draw on the pipe, decided there were faster and more pleasant ways of killing myself. I flipped the bowl over to bang it against the hard ground, sending tiny embers of still-burning weed skittering along the ground like wingless fireflies. Tenebris was watching me. The uncertainty in his gaze might as well have been a book of all his most intimate thoughts.

'They didn't understand you, Cade,' the diabolic said, almost affectionately. 'Not the way I do. They think you betrayed the justiciars because you couldn't hack the job. They thought you lacked ...' He paused and thought for a moment, one long claw tapping his lower lip.

'Faith?' I suggested.

Tenebris snapped his fingers. 'That's the one. All they saw was a young justiciar corrupted by a bitter old paladin slowly going deaf to the Auroral Song. The Lords Celestine never understood that beneath all your self-hatred and cynicism, the problem wasn't that you weren't pure enough for them, it was that *they* weren't pure enough for you.'

'But you saw through to my shining golden soul?'

Tenebris didn't laugh, didn't smile. 'That's the only reason why I was able to manipulate you into coming here, Cade, to take on this fight that no one else alive could win. I had faith in you. I *have* faith in you.'

Without doubt, that was the nicest thing anybody had ever said to me. Too bad it had come from a diabolic.

I didn't bother thanking him. I stared at my little pipe for a moment, contemplating keeping it as a souvenir just in case we survived the battle tonight. I started to toss it away, then found I couldn't. There was something about the existence of something so mundane – so lacking in purpose either glorious or vile – that felt reassuring right then.

'I'm going to need a few spells for tonight,' I said at last.

The diabolic looked a little hurt. No doubt he'd been expecting that the two of us would bare our souls to each other – figuratively, rather than literally – and talk about how we were just two half-decent beings caught in the machinations of the great powers. But I had business to conduct up in that fortress on the hill, where seven wonderists who were far more powerful than my ragtag little gang were putting the finishing touches to whatever gate would enable the Pandorals to enter this plane and make themselves gods or slavers or whatever they'd decided they'd be. Who knows? Maybe I should have been asking myself whether humanity might not be a bit better off with someone else guiding our affairs.

'So about those spells?' I said.

Tenebris nodded, and for the next half an hour we went back and forth over my particular needs. The diabolic made a show of trying to negotiate me down from my demands, but a show is all it was. We both knew I was doing the bidding of this little alliance between the Lords Devilish and Celestine, so there wasn't really any point in denying me what I needed.

'Cade?' he started as I turned to go. 'Good luck tonight.'

One of the things you learn becoming a justiciar is to listen for the things people say that don't need to be said: the extra word here, the repetition of something they already told you, the forced smile or awkward handshake. I guess I should have been flattered that both my training and my instincts told me that his parting words were signs that he really was my friend, and that some part of his diabolical heart wished things could be different.

'No such thing as luck,' I told him. 'Just angels and demons putting their thumbs on the scale.'

They weren't bad words to part on. Just because you're heading off to meet your doom doesn't mean you can't do it with a dash of style.

That's why it was too bad that by the time I got to Alice's cottage there were tears streaming down my face, and the moment I stepped inside, I dropped to my knees and wept like a child.

'What is it?' she asked, wings twitching in awkward discomfort. 'Has someone injured you?'

I didn't know how to answer that question. How do you explain to a demon that you've come to realise nothing you ever did mattered – that all your petty efforts at freedom have served only to make you a more valuable slave?

She came closer, and I took her hand and pressed it to my cheek. The hard, leathery feel of her skin was a reassuring proof that life was exactly as callused as I'd come to believe. I clung to her as though she were a rope tied to the shore, keeping me from being swept away by the tide.

'Why have you come to me?' she asked. 'If you seek comfort, why not go to Corrigan or the girl – or even the angelic?'

'Please,' I cried, 'please, tell me Hazidan sent you here for a reason. Tell me the old woman saw all of this coming, that somehow it all

298

fits into one of her damned conspiracy theories. Tell me our mentor had a plan.'

The demon girl stopped pulling away and instead just stood there a while listening to me weep. At last she rested her other hand on top of my head as if in blessing.

'Oh, Cade,' she said. 'She warned me you'd get like this.'

CHAPTER 43

The Tunnel

Midnight came and the seven of us set out on a mission that could either have been described as a noble quest to protect all humanity from supernatural forces of unimaginable power, or just plain old-fashioned murder. One thing it would never be described as, however, was pleasant.

'How did I not call this?' Corrigan grumbled as we trudged up the treacherous stony slope of the sewer tunnel, stooped over like old men to keep from bashing our skulls on the rough-hewn rock overhead. 'Follow a rat, wind up knee-deep in shit.'

'Follow a rat *mage*,' corrected Aradeus with what even I considered unseemly joviality, 'and you find the surest way to penetrate a fortress undetected.'

'Surest way to drown,' Corrigan countered. 'In *shit*.'

I was no happier with our surroundings than he was, but my deeper concern was that none of us could detect any spells preventing our passage. There were no mystical barriers, no aetheric alarms. Was Pandoral magic so foreign to the multitude of planes to which the seven of us were attuned that *none* of us could sense its effects? Whatever saga was written to commemorate our daring crusade was going to be awfully short if we snuck all the way up a sewer tunnel only to find ourselves surrounded by battle-ready mages with nothing to fight them off with but the stench emanating from our clothes.

'My deepest apologies,' Aradeus told Galass, who was stumbling a little drunkenly through the malodorous river of filth. 'I promise we haven't much further to travel along this admittedly unpleasant path I've selected for us.'

'I don't mind,' she said, gazing absently around the tunnel. Her features were unnaturally pale under the faint glow of Alice's whip-sword. The blade was now only a few inches long, illuminating our way forward as it weaved in the air like a candle flame. 'The sewer carries the scents of all those who once lived in the fortress. It's . . . intoxicating.'

She's not a vampire, I reminded myself. *She's just confused by the aftershocks of her blood magic. She won't suddenly switch sides in the middle of the fight to drink your blood.*

Corrigan shot me a look that told me he knew what I was thinking and wasn't nearly so optimistic.

'Quiet now,' Aradeus said, turning to face us. He looked down at the palm of his gloved hand, where even now multiple lines were appearing, marking the routes of half a dozen rats scurrying along the passages of the keep. Their trails were becoming a map on Aradeus' gloved hand. 'My little spies are seeking out these gates to the Pandoral realm the brothers have been constructing.'

'How does a rat know what a mystical gate looks like?' Fidick asked. His curious expression made him look like the innocent child I'd first met in the Ascendant's camp – almost. The broken nose I'd left him with helped remind me that he knew more than any of us what was really happening here, and the fact that he was still keeping his knowledge and his part in this a secret meant he would surely betray us before the night was out.

Aradeus took his customary delight in explaining the marvels of rodents. 'Our furry cartographers are following lines of magical force to their source. Rats, you see, are the most sensitive of all animals to magical emanations. A gate between planes will emit waves of mystical force that they can track. Once they've found the most potent—'

He froze.

'What is it?' I asked, staring at his hand.

Aradeus pointed to several red dots on the grey leather. They were twitching and hopping about like tiny fleas. 'These are living beings.'

'Seven of them,' Alice said, leaning past me to peer closer. 'Must be the brothers.'

'Yes,' Aradeus said, but he looked confused. 'But see the lines . . .? They're changing.'

He was right. The little trails left by the rats were becoming concentric spirals that were twisting tighter and tighter around the red dots.

'Does that mean what I think it means?' Corrigan asked.

Aradeus nodded. 'The rats are . . . they're converging on the Seven Brothers.'

Galass came closer. 'But won't the brothers notice a dozen rats so close to th—?'

Tiny flames erupted all over Aradeus' glove. He howled in pain and tore off the glove, waving his hand wildly as he dropped the still-burning glove into the sewage below us.

'What happened?' I asked.

Aradeus' hung his head in sorrow, his shoulders slumping. 'They slaughtered the scouts I sent to find the gates. Every last one of them.'

'I'm so sorry,' Galass said, putting a hand on the rat mage's shoulder.

'Oh, for fuck's sake,' Corrigan swore. 'They were *rats*. Besides, the stupid little bastards didn't even find the gates – they just ran up to the nearest humans. Probably got blasted begging for cheese.'

Aradeus spun on his heel and cocked his fist, but before he could punch Corrigan in the face, Alice and I pulled the two of them apart.

'Don't,' I told Corrigan. 'We haven't time for this. We need a new plan to find the gates if we want to—'

'We've already found the gates,' Shame said.

She'd been standing off by herself, looking so uninterested in our affairs that I'd wondered how much use she was actually going to be. But now she was staring up the tunnel ahead of us, an unmistakeable look of wonder in her golden angelic eyes.

'What do you mean?' I asked.

'The rats – they did exactly as Aradeus asked them: they found the breaches between this realm and that of the Pandorals.' She turned to me and her golden eyes turned black; an involuntary instinct of angelics when their preternatural senses warn them that things are about to go very badly. 'The Seven Brothers were never *building* the gates. They were *becoming* them.'

I gaped, trying to make sense of what this meant, and how in any hell we were supposed to stop living portals to a magical realm.

'Good,' Fidick said, and skipped ahead of us, gleefully splashing his way through the river of filth and decay into the darkness that led up to the fortress. 'The fun part's about to begin.'

CHAPTER 44

Complications

We abandoned our previous plodding, methodical pace and all caution as we ran up the sewer tunnel. We didn't bother with even cursory checks for traps and barriers, mystical or mundane. Time was of the essence, now, even if we didn't all agree which direction we should be running.

'This is absolutely nuts,' Corrigan said, swearing savagely as he grabbed for my arm, trying to hold me back. 'You can't expect us to fight the brothers any more. Didn't you hear the angelic? *They're the fucking gates!*'

'I don't understand,' Galass said, gripping the hem of her long silver gown to keep it from trailing in the muck. Not that it really mattered; she was as soaked in sewage as the rest of us. 'What difference does it matter whether the gates exist inside or outside the Seven Brothers?'

Yet another example of what a piss-poor job you've done teaching her the fundamentals of what it means to be a wonderist.

I slowed my pace just enough that everyone would be able to hear me. 'If the brothers were building gates outside themselves, they'd be draining their own attunements to do so. They'd be at their weakest now, and we'd have the advantage.'

'But even if the gates are within them, aren't they still weakened?' asked Galass.

'Weak is a relative term,' Shame explained, sloshing alongside us. 'Every wonderist – even an angelic like me – is, in a sense, a gate. Spells are momentary fractures between two planes: they allow the physical laws of one to leak through into the other, under the control of the wonderist. That is how a wonderist is able to enact their will in ways that would otherwise contradict the laws of nature. Even though such leaks are like tiny cracks in a huge dam, allowing only a feeble drip to pass from one side to the other, that drip is still enough to summon forth magics as powerful as any army.'

Galass paled. 'So if the brothers . . .'

Shame looked at her. 'Indeed. The brothers will *become* the dam, and should they unleash the river within them, our own magics will be as nothing but the smattering of raindrops flung against a raging sea.'

Poetry aside, the angelic had the right of it. The situation was actually worse than she described, but I decided not to point that out, in case my brave companions lost their nerve. I wasn't sure how much more some of them could take. I wasn't sure how much more *I* could take.

For all the flashy spells we throw around, a duel between mages isn't really about magic. It's about the body. Fire spells, drowning spells, agony spells – they all rely on the physical laws of *this* plane to weaken or destroy the opponent's body. Your enemies, in turn, will use magic to deflect or evade the effects of your attacks, creating shields or using transubstantiation or even illusion, which they can then follow up with their own attack against your physical form. It's a bit like a fencing match, with thrusts and counter-thrusts, parries and ripostes.

But how, I wondered, *do we attack a living gate into a magical plane? What physical laws apply to them?* Corrigan could hurl all the lightning and fire he wanted, Galass could attempt to exsanguinate every drop of the brothers' blood, but it was likely their 'bodies' wouldn't be affected, because they were now governed by a completely different set of physical laws – laws we didn't understand.

In other words, we were pretty much—

'Fucked!' Corrigan shouted, finally catching up to me.

He spun me around and got his face so close to mine that even the sewer smell couldn't block out the stench of rancid liquor escaping his lips. 'We can't fight these bastards, Cade, you know that. Whatever it is they're planning to do, they're going to succeed. We don't have the means to stop them.'

I turned my gaze to Fidick, hoping – praying, really – that the boy really did have some secret knowledge about how to defeat the brothers that he would now reveal.

'Mister Corrigan's right,' the boy said, smiling placidly. 'What comes now cannot be stopped.'

'See?' Corrigan said, jabbing a finger into my chest. 'Even the creepy little freak agrees. We've got to turn back, Cade, now – we need to get the hell out of this tunnel and as far away from this place as we can.'

'And where will you go, Mortal?' Alice spat. 'Three hundred beings from the Pandoral realm do the brothers seek to bring here, and with them such supernatural power as to be like gods to your people. *Three hundred gods.*'

Corrigan was shaken, but he tried to cover it up. 'Well, then, all hail our new shitty gods,' he said. 'Can't be any worse than the old ones.'

'The Lords Devilish and Celestine have left you alone for the most part,' Shame said. 'They have never been able to physically cross over into your world. You Mortals have had it easy. Until now.'

Not, perhaps, how I would have described the situation, but I figured even Corrigan had to take her point. 'We can't allow this,' I told him, gripping his arms, ignoring the bruising pain where his thumbs and fingers were pressing forcefully into mine. Locked in this strange sort of embrace, neither of us were willing to give in or let the other go. 'It's down to you and me now, Corrigan: no more pretending we're just two self-serving pieces of shit who don't give a damn about the rest of the world—'

'I *don't* give a damn about the rest of the world.'

'Stop it!' I shouted in his face. 'Don't you get it yet? There's no one else left to fix this – what little freedom humanity has ever had in this life, it's going to be taken away from them unless you and I stop the Seven Brothers before it's too late.'

'*Freedom?* That's what you want me to die over? There's *never been* any freedom, you idiot! I've been trying to teach you that simple truth since the day we met. Life is a river of filth, just like this sewer. You either go with the current and enjoy the ride as long as you can, or you push against it and drown in shit.'

He shoved me away and I slipped and landed on my arse in the muck, which I guess was his way of emphasising his point. When I tried to stand, he shoved me back down again, twice as hard.

'I don't know what rubbish has been bubbling around inside your head all this time, Cade. Maybe that crazy old mentor of yours filled you up with stories of humanity's contradictions being its own redemption or some nonsense like that, but those are *just words*. It's all fairy tales – and I *refuse* to die for a fucking fairy tale!'

'Then go,' I shouted back at him, 'follow the river of shit downstream and pretend you're enjoying the ride.'

'No.'

'No?'

I had a bad feeling I knew *exactly* what he was about to do; I'd known it even before we learned what the brothers were really up to.

'I've been a good comrade to you, Cade,' he said, grabbing me by my lapels and hauling me back up to my feet. Shaking me like a doll, he went on, 'You, on the other hand, have mostly been a pain in my arse. But you're the only friend I've got, and I'm

307

not letting you kill yourself for this. You're coming with me.' He turned to the others. 'So are the rest of you, if you ever want to see another sunrise.'

I tried to pull away, but Corrigan was strong and he held me fast. In the corner of my eye, I saw Aradeus preparing to draw his sword. Alice had already summoned hers; I could hear it hissing.

'Nobody move,' I ordered them, hoping I could somehow keep them out of it.

'Sorry to do it this way, Cade,' Corrigan began, preparing his spell. Thunderers are mostly all about destructive forces, but Corrigan was one of the best, and I knew he had a few other tricks up his sleeve.

'You'd use magic against me?' I asked him. 'You'd force me to come with you against my will?'

He rolled his eyes. 'Oh, stop being so fucking melodramatic. It's just a little bludgeon spell to knock you out until you come to your senses – trust me, you'll be thanking me for this tomorrow.'

'In that case . . .' I took in a breath, trying to calm myself. I hadn't done this in a while. 'Corrigan Blight, by your deeds and words have you proven yourself guilty, and I do judge you for it.'

His jaw hung open for a moment. 'You *what*? You *judge* me? You fucking *judge* me? *Me*? You think you can pull that justiciar bullshit on me, Cade? I'm not some . . .'

His voice tailed off, he went quiet and his eyes went wide as he realised he hadn't been watching my hands for several seconds. He looked down at the glowing black sigils in the air between us and noticed he couldn't move his feet any more. 'Oh, shit . . . you bastard.'

He'd already got us into position for the spell, which would otherwise have been the hard part. I'd had the binding ready ever since I'd made Tenebris give it to me. With just a few words from my lips, Corrigan Blight, my best friend, was now my slave.

'What have you done to him?' Aradeus asked.

I didn't answer. Technically it's called a 'recruitment' spell, which

I suppose is as accurate a name as any; after all, when an army recruits you, you don't have much in the way of choice either.

A pale, blueish sheen had fallen across Corrigan's features; only his eyes remained fully under his own control, and they spoke volumes. 'You treacherous son of a bitch,' he said, but only because I allowed him to do so.

'You enslaved your own comrade,' Alice remarked. She didn't sound particularly judgemental about it.

Galass, on the other hand, had set her scarlet hair swirling all around her. She looked as if she was one wrong word away from killing me. 'How could you do something like that to him? Would you try it on me, too, knowing what I've—?'

'Shut up,' I said, letting go of Corrigan's arms. He stood there, looking exactly as he always did, apart from the blue-grey tint to his skin: belligerent, arrogant – ready to kill someone for the sheer hell of it. The only difference was that now he would be doing those things for me.

I turned and spoke to the others, all of whom had come here by choice and were now wondering whether I would betray them too. I doubt any of them considered the fact that Corrigan had been intent on denying me *my* choice. I doubted that justification would have made them feel any better. It certainly hadn't worked for me.

'I'm going to make this very simple for you all.' I jerked a thumb at the tunnel ahead of us. 'Seven wonderists with a lot more power than any of us have ever seen are about to create a permanent bridge between this plane and that of the Pandorals. Are they monsters? I don't know. Maybe they're lovely souls. Maybe they just want what's best for everyone. A hundred years from now, the whole world might be some garden paradise under their benevolent rule. I. Don't. Give. A. Shit.'

I bent down to pick up Aradeus' glove. The charred lines provided our only map to where his rats had died. The sleek grey velvet was covered in filth now, so I wiped it off against my trousers before handing it back to him. 'Unless we kill the brothers, this world is lost, and it's the only one we've got. We can argue all day about whether human beings truly have free will or just a choice between survival and death, but there are countless millions out there who haven't been given the privilege of debating that question. They don't even know any of this is happening. Their freedom is about to be taken away and they don't even get the choice of whether to fight or not. So, on their behalf, the seven of us are going to go up into that fortress, and we're going to throw our lives away in the vain hope that we can stop the Pandoral gates from opening. And have no doubt: if I have to choose between all of our deaths and eternal damnation, in exchange for even one hopeless shot at taking those bastards down? I'm taking the shot.'

I shut up just long enough to realise I was out of breath and my hands were trembling. I spun on my heel and started up the tunnel, Corrigan close behind like a dog on a short leash.

One by one I heard them follow behind. Fidick caught up with me first.

'Nice speech,' he said.

CHAPTER 45

The Walls

To the omnipresent stench of the sewer was added a tingling in the hairs on the back of my neck as we entered the fortress. I'd been curious why the Seven Brothers had bothered to set up shop inside the old keep. With all their power, it wasn't likely that they feared an attack from the outside world. I'd come to the conclusion that they were simply avoiding the trouble of having to blast aside hordes of pitchfork-wielding townsfolk who might have taken exception to someone constructing supernatural gates on their land.

I was dead wrong.

'By all that's good in this world,' Aradeus breathed. 'What's happening to the walls?'

Fortifications like this fortress are generally built with stone walls more than fifteen feet thick. Normally, a wonderist would work on wearing them down over time, but this was something completely different. The huge stone blocks were actively *rippling* as we watched – and it wasn't just the walls: the worn carpet beneath our feet was undulating like a snake slithering across the sand. We struggled to keep our balance as we were tossed left and right.

'All this weaving around is making me nauseous,' Corrigan said; being bound inside a recruitment spell wasn't stopping his complaints about all the things that were currently displeasing him. I hadn't had the heart to take that away from him, too.

'It's not the motion of the floor that's making you sick,' Alice said, her largely useless bat wings reflexively twitching as they tried in vain to keep her upright. 'The barriers between the Pandoral plane and this one are weakening, so the physical laws of both realms are clashing against each other. Our own bones and flesh are absorbing these infinitesimally small fractures, losing coherence with the laws of this plane of existence.'

'That . . . does not sound like the kind of thing one recovers from,' Aradeus said.

'It isn't,' the demon girl replied. 'The brothers picked this place to perform their rites because stone withstands the effects better than weaker forms of matter, and that includes flesh.' She turned to me. 'Before long, we'll all be too weak to cast spells or fight.'

I watched the floor in front of me trembling like a dog shaking its fur. 'How long do we have?' I asked.

'Hard to say. The breeding that allowed me to survive the trans-lation from the Infernal realm into the Mortal plane gives me a certain resilience. I'll last perhaps another hour.' She gestured to Shame, who was watching the fortress shifting all around us with a distinct lack of interest. 'The angelic's form is inherently malleable, so it's possible she'll endure longer.'

'What about the rest of us?' Aradeus asked.

Alice shrugged. 'Humans are brittle things with delicate forms and fragile minds. I suspect your bodies will begin to fail you within the next half an hour or so. Within minutes, you'll become puddles of flesh upon the floor.'

'So what do we do?' Galass asked. She was holding on to Fidick as if somehow her body could protect him from the onslaught of tiny fractures in reality currently destroying our skin and bones.

I stared at the boy a moment, wondering whether his connection to the Celestines would provide him with protection Corrigan, Galass, Aradeus and I didn't have, but the boy was the slightest of all of us, and he was looking increasingly weak now. I wasn't sure whether that disappointed or reassured me.

'We keep going,' I said, running up the latest undulation of the floor in front of me, trying to ride the crest of the wave as it flung itself down the corridor. 'Fifteen minutes should be plenty of time to save the world.'

CHAPTER 46

The Thunderer's Choice

I tried to keep track of time, but we were making such unbearably slow progress, fighting down nausea as we battled the motion of the floors all around us, that I gave up. After all, no one was likely to be awarding us posthumous medals for having died slightly later than Alice had predicted.

The distortions got worse the higher we went, until we found ourselves combatting the weather itself, which shouldn't even have been possible inside a roofed fortress. Halfway down the second corridor, a sudden downpour – without the benefit of any clouds, I noticed in passing – drenched us to the bone. When we turned the next corner, we were pelted by hailstones the size of apples, then enveloped in a fog so thick we had to hold hands to avoid losing one another. Only Aradeus knew where we were going as he followed as best he could the lines that had been inscribed on the palm of his glove by the rats which had died, nobly or otherwise, in our cause.

'There's a large open area up ahead,' he said, his words echoing confusingly around us as if he'd spoken them minutes earlier and they were only now reaching us. 'It could be a foyer or hall of some type. There's a narrow passageway beyond.'

'And after that?' I asked.

His voice was grim. 'After that, I believe we will have our reckoning with the Seven Brothers.'

Those last few feet of corridor became even more treacherous as a pounding hurricane took hold, hurling us against walls that shivered and shook us off. The wind was so strong we had to close our eyes and feel our way ahead with our hands, until suddenly we were clear of the gale and could see again.

I almost wished we'd remained trapped by the weather.

'What have they done?' Aradeus demanded, striding forward.

There were doors on three sides of the space, and between them, walls that at first looked as if they'd been decorated with the trophies of some sort of big game hunter. Only I couldn't imagine any hunter being as cruel as this.

'The servants . . .' Galass' voice shook. 'The animals the brothers transformed . . . why would they do this to them?'

There had to be more than a dozen of the poor creatures, all buried within the walls, almost as if they had fallen into melted candle wax which had then hardened around them. Their heads were sticking out, as if in their last moments they'd desperately stretched their necks to keep from drowning in the stone. There were paws and hooves poking out here and there too, reaching for something they would never find.

'Why did they have to kill the animals?' Fidick asked, for once sounding like an eleven-year-old boy.

It was Shame who answered. 'The creatures must have sensed what their masters were doing. They are of this world, and this realm belongs as much to them as it does to humankind. I would guess they tried to stop the brothers, and paid the price for their defiance.'

'But the brothers could have just turned them back into animals,' Fidick insisted. 'They didn't have to kill them . . .'

The angelic's reply was flat, emotionless. 'When the slave displeases the master, the master punishes them neither for convenience nor justice, but as a warning to others that disobedience comes with a price.'

I walked over to the far wall, where Madrigal the goat man was imprisoned for ever. His dead eyes seemed to follow me, as if to warn me away from this place, as I had tried to warn him just a few hours earlier.

'How did you know?' Galass asked, coming up to stand beside me.

'Know what?'

'The brothers. They were so . . . reasonable. The way they described the Pandorals sounded almost noble. But you knew the whole time, didn't you? You knew right away that they were callous and cruel. How?'

I felt like telling Galass that my predictions came down to assuming the very worst imaginable about someone and then waiting to be disappointed. But as there was a high chance none of us were getting out of here, instead, I told her the truth.

'They gave him the power of speech,' I said, reaching out a hand to touch one of Madrigal's horns. I knew nothing about him, about his life or what it had meant to exist as a goat and then a man. Yet somehow I felt a kinship with him. Was that empathy, or vanity? I wondered. 'But they never once spoke to him in our presence, just commanded him with their thoughts.'

I felt sick again, but I chalked it up to the nausea that came with feeling the very essence of my body gradually falling part.

'Cade, we have a problem,' Aradeus said. He was standing next to the door that I was assuming led us further towards our destination.

'What is it?' I asked.

'I . . . I think there's a storm behind this door.'

'So what?' Alice asked. 'We just came through three of them.'

'I'm pretty sure this one is different,' Aradeus said, and carefully pulled open the door.

First we heard the thunder, like the roar of a dozen cannon firing all at once in that narrow corridor. The bolts of blue lightning zigging everywhere were blasting chunks out of the floor and walls, sending shards of shattered stone whizzing through the air. There was no way any shield spell could protect us from that much concentrated power.

'Can we go around?' I asked, gesturing at the two corridors on either side of us.

Aradeus shook his head. 'According to the rats, this is the only way through.'

I turned to Corrigan. 'You're a thunderer. Is there any way you know of to walk safely through a lightning storm?'

'Go fuck yourself,' he replied, which was probably to be expected, but we really didn't have time for his sulking.

Hating myself, I pushed harder on the recruitment spell. Corrigan grimaced at me, gritting his teeth, but finally he admitted, 'I can't end the storm, but I can redirect the lightning.'

'Where?'

'Into myself.'

It must have taken a supreme act of will – and even then, it could only have been possible because of the nausea overwhelming me – but somehow, Corrigan resisted the recruitment spell for long enough to mutter one of his own incantations and walk right into the storm.

'Wait!' I called to him, trying not to let anyone hear my panic, 'You could die in there!'

He laughed at that, and somehow his voice sounded over the booming of the thunder. 'Fine fucking time you pick to start worrying about my life, Cade.'

317

CHAPTER 47

The Lightning

Corrigan took his first step into the corridor and was immediately struck by a massive bolt of lightning. He swallowed an agonised growl but kept moving, his body bathed in blue sparks as he took the next step. Another bolt struck him, then a third. I'd heard tales of thunderers who showed off their strength by climbing to the top of a hill during a storm and allowing themselves to be deliberately struck by lightning – but I'd never heard of any of them surviving three hits.

'How much more can he take?' Alice asked, a note of something that sounded suspiciously like admiration in her voice.

'I don't know,' I said. 'Not much, I don't think.'

When the next bolt struck, this time Corrigan screamed. In the blue glow, we could all see the steam rising from his skin.

'Hurry, you dumb fuckers!' he shouted. 'I'm drawing the lightning to me, but I can't keep it up for ever.'

I ran into the corridor, careful to stay a few feet behind Corrigan. I could feel my hair filling with static electricity, rising up from the top of my head, and my mouth tasted like copper. But I wasn't being hit.

'Come on, Galass, Fidick,' I said reassuringly, fully aware I sounded like an idiot. 'Alice and Shame next. Aradeus, would you be kind enough to bring up the rear?'

Step by step, we made our way down that endless corridor. I doubt it was more than ten yards long, but that journey took an eternity. Corrigan's howls were becoming increasingly desperate, and at last I had to cover my ears with my hands because I couldn't stand to listen to my best friend's pain any more.

He was stumbling by the time he reached the end of the corridor, but he stopped inside the door and stood there, being hit over and over by the lightning.

'Corrigan, move!' I shouted, coming up behind him and readying myself to push him through, but he was shaking his head.

'You have to go *around* me, idiot! If I walk past the end of the storm, the lightning will attack the rest of you!'

I really was losing it. *'Quickly!'* I screamed, and one by one, we squirmed past Corrigan as fast as we could without touching him, and when we were all safely on the other side, I turned, expecting him to be right behind me. But he was still standing in the corridor.

'What are you doing?' I called out. 'Get the hell out of that place—'

I could see Corrigan's jaw was clenched tight. It took a real effort, but at last he managed, 'I can't seem to move.'

I pushed with the recruitment spell, commanding his legs to walk him towards us, but nothing happened. It wasn't his will resisting me, but the inability of his muscles to follow the dictates of his mind. The lightning struck again, and this time his scream was hoarse, barely more than a whimper. He looked as if his body wanted to collapse, but the storm wouldn't allow it.

'We've got to get him out of there!' Galass shouted.

I ran back to the edge of the storm and prepared to grab him by the belt and haul him through.

'No,' he said, 'not you!'

'What? Why not?'

'Make one of the others do it.'

'Why?' I couldn't believe he didn't trust me enough to get him out of there.

'I don't want you touching me.'

'We don't have time for this,' Alice said, shoving me aside, then she stood there, doing nothing.

'What the hell's wrong with you?' I demanded. 'Pull him through!'

'Not yet,' she said, staring at the roof.

'Why . . . ?' I suddenly realised what she was doing: if she grabbed him when the next bolt hit, she'd be killed and he'd still be stuck in the corridor.

Counting the seconds, watching the fear in Corrigan's eyes, was a whole new kind of hell – then the lightning struck, and just as the flash faded, Alice grabbed hold of his belt and yanked him out of that corridor, away from the storm. I slammed the door shut, but Corrigan had already collapsed onto the floor; he would have crushed Alice beneath him, had she not rolled nimbly out of the way.

She stood up and stared at her hand. The skin of her palm was charred black.

I dropped to the ground to examine Corrigan, searching for some sign that he was breathing, but Aradeus placed a hand on my shoulder, preventing me from touching him.

'Cade,' he said, his voice kind, 'we have other duties right now. We need to figure out how to get through that final door. It's too strong to break, and neither my spells nor Shame's will be able to get through—'

'In a moment, damn it! I'm trying to—'

The rat mage knocked my hand out of the way before I could touch Corrigan. 'Look at him, Cade! His body's glowing: all the lightning he absorbed is still inside him – and he's a Tempestoral! You'll burn to a crisp the instant you touch him.'

Stupidly, I tried reaching for him again – maybe this is what your mind makes you do when you've betrayed your best friend and don't want to watch him die in front of you. But Alice and Aradeus had taken hold of my arms and were pulling me back.

'Cade, we need to get through that door!' the rat mage shouted in my ear. 'The brothers are on the other side—'

'Shut up!' I said, trying to listen for Corrigan's breathing, but I couldn't hear anything – until his body spasmed and he coughed so loudly it was like a thunderclap. He spat out blood, and when he lifted his head, his eyes were bright red where the blood vessels had burst. The rest of us watched in awe as he pushed his hands against the roiling stone floor and slowly, agonisingly, rose to his feet. He stumbled towards me and I wondered whether he'd absorbed so much lightning that he'd broken the recruitment spell and was now coming to kill me. I watched as his trembling hands rose up above his shoulders, sparks dancing across his forearms. Alice yanked me out of the way just as a bolt of lightning so massive it was like every bolt he'd absorbed had come out of him all at once struck the door Aradeus had told us was impregnable.

We all turned to look.

There was nothing was left but smoke and tiny embers floating in the air.

As Corrigan stumbled past me into the final corridor, he croaked, 'Have I pleased you, Master?'

CHAPTER 48

Doorways

The chamber we entered was seven-sided, with twenty-foot-high walls curving together at the top like a cathedral dome. At first I thought we must be in one of the towers, then I realised the shape had been altered for whatever use the brothers intended to make of this place. There were windows on three sides, tall as a man but only the width of a hand. The glass undulated as if it were a slow-moving waterfall. The high-pitched crack of panes shattering every few seconds was followed by a sound like the grinding of teeth as they reformed once again. But my attention was drawn to the walls: every inch of stone from floor to ceiling was covered in esoteric sigils, the kind used for ceremonial magic, although I couldn't recognise any of them. This was a ritual utterly beyond any I'd ever witnessed.

All the while, the walls and floor continued to undulate around us, rippling this way and that as if following the tides of an unseen ocean. So unstable had physical reality become in this temple to their Pandoral masters that even our exhalations echoed around the chamber in such odd ways that I could no longer tell whose breathing I was hearing.

As for our enemies, the Seven Brothers were waiting for us, each of them standing like slack-jawed statues in front of one of the room's seven walls – including the one with the door we'd just

322

blasted through on our way inside. Their eyes were closed, but their mouths hung open, drool dribbling down their chins.

'What are they doing?' Galass asked.

'Perhaps the gate failed,' Aradeus suggested, 'and now they're frozen in some kind of mystical sleep?'

Corrigan strode forward, my recruitment spell barely holding him any more – although whether that was because of the lightning that had nearly killed him or my own guilt, I couldn't be sure. 'Good,' he said, sticking his face so close to the tallest of the brothers their noses almost touched. 'Let's kill them all and be done with it.' He glanced in my direction, but didn't meet my eye as he added, 'Unless my master has other plans?'

I carefully navigated the shifting floor until I was standing in front of the brother I'd sat opposite at our previous meeting. He looked so still, so ... uninterested. These bastards had tried to give over the realm of their birth to the Pandorals, and now they just slouched there like drunks without even the decency to float above the floor?

Alice joined me, but when she reached out a clawed hand towards the brother nearest her, I grabbed her wrist.

'Never touch me, human,' she snarled. 'Not without my consent.'

I let go of her wrist. 'You appear to be fine with the idea of touching *them* without their consent,' I pointed out.

I reached into the pocket of my coat in search of something I could afford to lose, and found the pipe I'd used in the village. I tried to press the broken stem into the chest of the brother in front of me, but it was like pushing a toothpick against diamond.

'A shield spell of some sort?' Aradeus asked.

I tapped the stem against the loose robes, with the same result. 'Stronger than anything I've ever seen cast,' I said.

'So what now?' Galass asked. 'Is it over? Have we ... won?'

I didn't have an answer, partly because the floor was rippling again and I had to concentrate on not falling. I was having diffi-

323

culty not throwing up too; the nausea was getting worse and my hands were trembling. Soon I wouldn't have the coordination to cast spells. Alice had predicted we had about half an hour before our feeble human bodies fell apart from the effects of the warping magic all around us – who would have thought the demon was an optimist?

'What if Corrigan hits them with lightning?' Galass suggested.

'Finally, someone has an idea worth trying,' he said, stepping back several feet before unleashing enough aetheric lightning to obliterate a mountain. When that failed, he tried again, and again – but it had no effect. He might as well have been trying to drown the brothers by spitting at them repeatedly.

Alice went next, striking them with her whip blade, which I was pretty sure could cut through any normal substance. She had no luck, either.

With some considerable effort, Shame pushed open one of the tall glass windows. 'The grounds around the fortress are shifting, too,' she reported. 'The effects are starting to spread.'

'But how?' Aradeus asked. I noticed his hand was reaching for the hilt of his rapier, only to pull back again, as if aware a blade wouldn't serve any purpose here, yet unsure what else to do with himself. 'The brothers clearly haven't finished the gate, so why is their magic still affecting this place?'

Fidick cried out, and we turned away from the window to see him doubled over, the fingers of his hands pressing into his skull.

'What's wrong?' Galass demanded, running to him.

'My head hurts. I think . . . I think someone's coming—'

I spun around again, expecting to see the brothers suddenly awake and some sort of magical gate appearing in the air, but they hadn't moved. They were just standing there, as they had been since we'd entered the ever-shifting room, eyes closed and mouths hanging open. I stepped closer, searching, I suppose, for some sign of emotion on their faces – despair or satisfaction, or anything. Then I peered inside inside the eldest brother's open jaws – and saw something crawling on the back of his tongue.

'Get back!' I cried, jumping to one side. I felt a deep chill inside me that I couldn't blame on the sickness assailing us.

'What is it?' Aradeus asked. Now he had drawn his rapier and was waving it around, searching for the new threat.

'The brothers *did* finish building the gates,' I whispered. 'We were just looking in the wrong place.'

First I saw the little antennae, like those of a locust, peeking out from behind the brother's front teeth, then the segmented eyes and twig-like limbs, each one no longer than a fingernail. An insect, its translucent wings pressed to the back of its coppery shell, crawled across the brother's tongue before dropping from his mouth to the floor. The creature turned left and right, as if finding its bearings, then just lay there.

'What is it?' Galass asked. 'Is that one of the Pandorals?'

I remembered how I'd heard a buzzing in my ears whenever the brothers were casting their spells.

'There's another one,' Alice warned as another insect identical to the first crawled out of the next brother's mouth. This one stood with its front legs on his lips for a moment before it too jumped.

'There are more,' Shame said, but she didn't need to tell us, for the insects were appearing from all of the brothers' mouths now, first one at a time, then by the dozen, crawling over each other to get out more quickly, then joining their brethren on the ground.

Corrigan, unbidden by me, blasted the insects with a fire spell, nearly singeing the rest of us in the process, but the bugs showed no sign of distress, and the flames did them no harm.

Our fear turned to horror when the insects began to crawl all over each other, making a heap, as bugs continued to pour from the brothers' gaping mouths. The growing mound of insects began to writhe as it rose higher and higher, like dust caught in a whirlwind. All the while, a buzzing sound filled the seven-sided chamber, rising in pitch and volume like a cross between a lover's voice coming to the final point of ecstasy and a massive nest of wasps we'd had the misfortune to disturb.

'They're turning into something,' Galass said, 'but . . .'

The question died on her lips as the buzzing dropped, almost to a sigh, and the transformation completed. Before us now stood a being who might have been mistaken for a man, were it not for the twelve eyes circling his head like a crown, and the way his gleaming, coppery flesh was made from thousands of crawling insects.

We had just met our first Pandoral.

Aradeus, ever the diplomat, slid his rapier back in its scabbard and gave a short, courteous bow. 'Greetings, my friend. You have just accomplished something wondrous, something never before achieved. You are the first Pandoral being to set foot upon the Mortal demesne.' The rat mage extended a hand. 'You and I have an opportunity, one heretofore unknown to two entities as different as we are from one another. We could, with a single choice, a single act of decency and dignity, put aside violence and distrust and set a course for both our peoples towards understanding and peace.'

The glittering being stared down at the proffered hand, so still that even the bugs comprising his body stopped fluttering and twitching. Two of the twelve eyes looked down to meet the rat mage's gaze, then the other eyes studied each of us in turn, as if trying to decide what to make of the bizarre creatures before him.

At last he smiled, and in a voice formed of the beating of thousands of wings, perfectly modulated to create pitch and tone, said, 'You will serve.'

CHAPTER 49

The Pandoral

You will serve. The first words ever spoken by the inhabitants of a neighbouring plane of existence to those of ours: a proclamation meant to instil terror and subservience.

This guy didn't understand who he was dealing with at all.

'Alas, great Pandoral,' I said, offering our visitor a bow even deeper and more elaborate than the one Aradeus had given moments before, 'I got out of the servant business some time ago. And you, I'm afraid, have already outstayed your welcome.'

As I stood back up, I blasted him with the desecration spell I'd negotiated from a very perturbed Tenebris hours before.

'You can't be serious,' the diabolic had said. *'Do you not have the phrase "the cure is worse than the disease" in your realm?'*

But I'd been implacable in my demands, and despite all his warnings, he'd eventually relented.

The desecration spell is a particularly destructive form of Infernal magic. It's built on the aspect of the physical laws of their realm that splits consciousness from ecclesiasm. Basically, it tears your spirit – or the thousands of tiny bug souls that make up your spirit – into infinitesimal fragments of self-destructive misery. The desecration is the undisputed king of unmaking spells; the hellborn conjuration that shredded Ascendant Lucien in his tent and the weeping arrow I used on that idiot cosmist back at the

Jalbraith Canal both look like candle flames trying to outshine the sun next to a desecration spell.

Black, green and red gobs glimmering like vomit-shaped chunks of onyx, emeralds and rubies spewed from my outstretched hands to spray all over the Pandoral. The onyx bits splintered like tiny knives, separating the individual bugs making up his form from one another. The gleaming rubies exploded into thousands of tiny fireballs while the green stuff was busy poisoning minuscule aspects of the Pandoral's consciousness and spirit, not that you could see that bit. And it was happening all at once.

Thousands upon thousands of little screams echoed around the seven-sided chamber as the bugs fell apart onto the floor, until at last, silence returned. Then, after a decent pause to let me think I'd won, they skittered back together, climbing over each other once again until the Pandoral stood before us once more.

'You will se—'

'Yeah, a moment if you please,' I said, then turned to Corrigan. 'You're up.'

It occurs to me that I might have made Tempestoral spells all sound the same, like it's all just one big pile of loud, blinding bolts of fire and lightning and whatever the hell other disasters emerge from that plane of reality when you open a breach into it. But I'm sure Corrigan – and all Tempestoral mages, really – would want me to tell you that it's not all noisy blasts. There's nuance. Subtlety. Texture.

'Burn, you motherfucking bug piece of shit arsehole!' Corrigan bellowed, and unleashed enough raw destructive force to make every previous spell I'd ever seen him cast look like a butterfly kiss. Somebody – maybe it was Shame or Alice – had the sense to wrap the rest of us in some kind of preservation spell to keep us from being turned to ash. I'm not sure Corrigan was particularly concerned either way; he just wanted to obliterate the Pandoral, no matter who else died in the process.

The walls all around us started to fall apart. Individual stones that had been rippling from whatever reality-warping spells the Seven Brothers had been using to prepare the way for the Pandorals were now separating from their mortar and catapulting towards us like a giant spitting out broken teeth.

'And *that's* how you take care of business,' Corrigan said when it was over. At least, I'm imagining that's what he said, as I was pretty much deaf by that point, so I couldn't hear him any better than I could the Pandoral, who was busy assembling himself out of the swarm of bugs again before repeating, 'You will serve.'

Alice tried slicing him with her whip blade, but it passed right through his body and the swarm came back together unharmed. Aradeus stabbed the Pandoral with his rapier – yeah, I know how stupid that sounds, but rat mages have their own destructive spells, and he wasn't letting anybody take over the Mortal realm without a fight. Shards of grey magic, like tiny claws, erupted from the tip of his sword, each one tearing at one of the insects holding the invader's body together.

Galass, teeth gritted and eyes bleeding tears, summoned up the blood magic she so despised and turned it on the Pandoral, drawing oozing red droplets from the insects. Shame reached out with her hands and began distorting the swarm's shape, weakening its cohesion, leaving it vulnerable to the attacks of the others. Fidick's young, beautiful face became even more stunning as alabaster skin glowed with golden light. When he spoke, the Auroral Song emerged from between his lips, a vibration that shook the Pandoral's form, causing dozens of insects to fall apart from the others, landing like raindrops on the stone floor.

Together, the seven of us gave the Pandoral a good taste of what happens when you go around trying to conquer the Mortal realm.

Corrigan caught my eye and he grinned like we were back at the Ascendant's camp, laying siege to some citadel or castle. He looked almost happy – and proud, actually. All this time, I'd been so focused on the machinations of those who'd brought the seven of us together – the Lords Celestine, the Devilish, Hazidan Rosh, even our own apparently insignificant choices – that I'd never realised that there was something marvellously messed up about this little coven of ours: Corrigan, with his thunderer's conjurations of lightning and fire and just about every other destructive force you can imagine; Galass, with her blood magic, able to tamper with the essence of life itself; Aradeus, the dashing rat mage, his spells a mixture of trickster magic and daring. Even I was no slouch, with my complement of Infernal spells meant to poison minds and summon any number of ugly things to the world. Add to that we had an angelic and a demoniac on our side – never before, to my knowledge, brought together. And finally Fidick, the beautiful boy in whose radiance you could sense the hands of both Lords Celestine and Devilish resting gently upon his shoulders.

Fighting together like that, blending our disparate abilities into an utterly insane combination of tactics and assaults as we gave our all to a humanity none of us had ever really felt a part of? It was like . . . it was like being part of a family.

And it was fucking glorious.

. . . right up until we discovered *nothing* we'd done had hurt the Pandoral one little bit.

'He's not even bothering to fight back,' Galass reported, slumped against Aradeus, exhausted from the effort of trying to bleed the swarm dry. What blood she'd been able to draw out of them was a thimbleful compared to the ocean that remained.

I heard a buzzing like the one the brothers had used to communicate, then Corrigan cried out, followed at once by Galass, Shame, Alice and Aradeus as their ears were assaulted by the insidious sound.

'What is it *doing*?' Alice asked, hands pressed against the sides of her head.

I didn't need to know whatever language the Pandorals spoke to work out what was going on. 'I think he must be the advance scout,' I shouted to the others. 'He's telling the others in his realm that it's safe here – there's nothing we can do to harm them.'

Sure enough, another insect crawled out from one of the brothers' gaping mouths.

Corrigan and Alice tried turning their attacks on the brothers, but the barrier protecting them was too strong.

When all our attempts failed once again and we stopped for a breather, the Pandoral scout appeared to have reached a decision.

'You are poorly made,' he said, his voice the buzzing of insect wings. 'You will be transformed to better serve us.' His gaze fell upon Alice. 'But not you,' he said. An arm made of writhing bugs reached out and grabbed the demon girl's throat, effortlessly lifting her up off the ground. 'You are Infernal. You disgust us.'

I heard a sizzling sound and saw burns appearing around the leathery skin of her neck. Aradeus sliced into the Pandoral's arm, but his rapier blade passed harmlessly through the skittering bugs. Alice's tongue was lolling from her mouth as the creature tightened its grip, choking the life from her.

'He's killing Alice!' Galass shouted redundantly. 'Cade, *do* something!'

Calling on me to play the hero seemed like a poor choice, given I was probably the weakest of all of us. On the other hand, since none of our powers had had the slightest effect, I supposed strength had become a redundant concept anyway.

Besides, cowardly accommodation had always been more my thing.

'Wise Master,' I said, kneeling before the Pandoral, 'why do you waste your time on an Infernal when you could be sampling the sweetness this land can provide?' I gestured to the narrow window. 'The fertile lands for which you have risked so much await you.'

The creature turned to me, and in his gaze, my justiciar's training saw that the Pandoral knew this was a pathetic ploy on my part to get him away from Alice, that he felt no need to tell me so, that he was, indeed, hungry for what this realm had to offer, and was unconcerned with revealing this fact.

In essence, we didn't matter to him at all.

He let go of Alice and she fell to the ground, gasping.

'I suppose I should inspect the soil from which the crops will grow that will allow our numbers to swell.'

He turned and walked straight into the wall, breaking apart as he hit the stone. The insects making up his body flew up in a great buzzing cloud, then spread out and disappeared. Some found cracks in the walls to crawl through; others went flying out through the narrow window. A second later, they had reformed outside, and I watched him floating through the air down to the red ground below.

CHAPTER 50

The Gates Within

'*That* was your heroic stand?' Alice demanded, coughing as she rose to her feet. 'Better you had let me die than make me an accomplice to your cowardice, fallen one.'

Corrigan shoved her away. 'Aw, did he offend your scruples? Because he made *me* his fucking *slave*, so if you're hoping to get some righteous revenge on this prick, the line starts behind *me*.'

'Thanks to him, I'm a blood mage,' Galass pointed out.

Corrigan's sneer came and went faster than a flash of lightning. 'Fine. The line forms behind you. But I'm second.'

'Well, this is going great,' I muttered.

Fidick tapped on my arm. 'More of the Pandorals are coming through,' he said, and pointed to a bug crawling out of another brother's mouth.

'It's starting again,' Aradeus said unnecessarily. 'Cade, we must close the gates!'

Why does everybody insist on stating the obvious? On the other hand, Aradeus hadn't thus far blamed me for ruining his life, so he got priority.

Okay, so we couldn't defeat the Pandorals when they came through the gates, and we couldn't destroy the mages who *were* the gates – what options did that leave us?

I stared at the brother nearest me, wondering who he'd been before

333

he had turned himself into a conduit into another realm. Had he been the favourite of his other siblings, or had they mostly resented some flaw in his character? Was he the 'funny' one? The 'sensitive' one? Did he like beer and fornication on his days off from plotting the overthrow of the entire Mortal realm?

I stepped closer now. There was no discernible expression on his pale, veiny, slack-jawed face. Was he in ecstasy now? Was incomparable bliss suffusing every part of his being? Or had he been deceived by the Pandorals, expecting some sort of godlike beings to appear before him, only to now suffer the eternal torment of knowing he'd helped unleash a plague on the world of his birth?

'Cade?' Galass asked. 'I don't think we have long left.'

Again with the obvious.

When I turned to her, I could see she was having trouble standing. Her gaze was unfocused and her skin was nearly as pale as that of the brothers. All the while, the walls around us were continuing to swirl and shift, almost as if they were oozing. What must this barrage of abominations have felt like to someone attuned to the very essence of life?

'If there's anything you need from me,' she said, slurring her words like a drunk, 'you'd better have me do it now.'

I wanted to reassure her somehow. Teenagers shouldn't have to bear witness to the end of humanity. But I couldn't because the warping spells all around us were slowly killing me too, and what little strength I had to offer, I would use for this final task of my life.

We can't defeat the enemy and we can't blow up the bridges bringing them here. Our spells are useless and our strength inconsequential. Power, therefore, can't be the answer.

I found myself absently fumbling with the pipe I'd found in town, finding odd comfort in the smoothness of the bowl, the way it was so utterly mundane. Almost as a joke, I held it up to the mouth of the brother nearest me. 'Care for a smoke?' I asked.

He chose not to humour me with a reply.

Then I found myself staring at my own shaking hand, and at the stem of the pipe I'd poked inside the brother's mouth.

Oh, hell, I thought. *That really wasn't the answer I'd been hoping for . . .*

'We can't bring down the gate from our side,' I announced. 'We have to do it from theirs!'

'How?' Galass asked.

'How about we just reach inside and rip their fucking lungs out?' Corrigan suggested. He extended his arm, but I grabbed hold of it.

'Don't,' I said, and showed him the pipe.

I'm not sure I'd ever seen Corrigan Blight look quite so shocked – not that I blamed him. The stem of the pipe which had entered the brother's mouth had turned from ebony wood into some kind of glittering stone.

'The matter translated as it entered the Pandoral realm,' Alice said. 'I doubt flesh can long survive such a change.'

'But it wasn't instant,' Aradeus said, stepping in front of me. 'If I reach inside the brother's mouth quickly enough, I might have time to cast a spell before the effect takes hold—'

'And do what?' Alice asked. 'There are seven of them. Even if your spell killed one, the others would still be alive.'

'Then we all do it,' Galass said, with the desperate enthusiasm only seventeen-year-olds on the verge of dying a miserable and pointless death can muster. 'Seven of them, seven of us. We each stick a hand inside one of their mouths and—'

I cut her off. 'We don't all have the same kind of magic. Some spells can be cast quickly, others take longer – and we're running out of time. How much do you reckon we have left? A minute? A few seconds? It won't work. The only way this could have worked would have been if we'd come here prepared with a way to—'

I found myself staring at the walls rippling fluidly: the same effect that was killing us, because human beings weren't meant to be turned into malleable things.

'Shame,' I said, turning to the angelic, 'that thing you did with the baron, altering his form so the curse couldn't take hold of it . . . can you do that to us as well?'

Her golden eyes narrowed. 'It is forbidden, as well you know, Justiciar. I broke that law to grant peace to a tormented soul.'

'Probably a little late to be getting uppity about morality. Besides, I'm not asking you to *change* us, but the opposite. I'm asking you to use your angelic transfiguration to keep us the same.'

'What are you talking about?'

I was about to shoot her a look that said that for an avatar of the all-knowing Celestines, she was a little slow on the uptake, but then I recalled that not everybody spends their lives trying to conceive devious ways to use magic to catastrophically destroy other people's existences.

Corrigan, on the other hand, got it right away. 'Yes – yes, bloody *yes*! The angelic uses her power to keep our bodies from translating on the other side so that we can cast our spells, blast the brothers from the inside out and sever their connection to the Pandoral realm!'

Shame clearly didn't share his enthusiasm. There was a terror in her expression I'd never seen before that I found particularly dis- comfiting in an otherwise preternaturally placid Auroral being.

'What's wrong?' I asked.

'To be . . . enmeshed with so many others at the same time . . . I will lose myself in your flesh, in your petty lusts and loathings! I have known the freedom to explore my own nature for such a brief time – now you would take that away from me? There may be nothing left of me afterwards!'

More insects were crawling out of the brothers' mouths.

'I'm sorry,' I said, feeling dreadful. Such a feat would be horren- dously intimate for anyone, but for an angelic who'd already been

336

abused by the desires and hatreds of so many others? It would be tantamount to spiritual suicide. Then again, maybe my guilt was just nausea from my body slowly being destroyed by the exposure to so much raw extra-planar magic. 'Shame, this is it. We're at the end of our road. Here in this lousy fortress in the shittiest part of the entire continent. The seven of us have been tricked, manipulated, lied to, and now we're probably all going to die. Am I to blame because I let myself be suckered by an Ascendant, a sublime, a diabolic, the Lords Celestine and Devilish, and even my old master? Maybe, but I think if you factor everything together, it's really more Corrigan's fault than mine.'

'Hey! I'm not th—'

'But it's not about blame.' I jabbed a finger at the nearest of the brothers. 'It's about killing these pricks before their bug-faced masters can take over what's left of this world. The Mortal realm might be one giant shithole to an angelic – hell, it's a giant shithole to me, and I was born here – but it's the only home left to any of us. This is our one shot, and we can't make it without you.'

You know how usually a speech sounds good in your head and then falls flat when you blurt it out loud? This time it happened in reverse, because I seriously didn't think I'd made a persuasive argument for personal sacrifice. And yet . . .

Shame smiled weakly at me. 'Then I will try.'

'Good, then let's—'

She ignored me, went to Aradeus and took his hand. 'There is something I would say to you, Aradeus Mozen. You came to me on that ship, you risked everything for a stranger. The Celestines teach us that humanity is all weakness and corruption. They do not despise you for it, but reason that this is why you must be guided.' She lifted up his hand and kissed it. 'Thank you for teaching me that even the gods can be wrong sometimes.'

'My lady . . .' he said.

It was a nice moment, and I wished I could have allowed it to continue, but I couldn't be sure how many insects it would take to form another Pandoral on our side of the gates.

'How will you make this work, though?' Fidick asked. 'You assume that killing the brothers will close the gates, but what if you're wrong? Surely just blasting away at their insides is too simple a solution?'

I looked at Fidick and he stared back up at me with that same guileless expression. I've hated a lot of people in my time, but never as much as I hated that eleven-year-old boy in that moment, because I knew his question wasn't musing but guidance. He was making sure I knew that our plan wouldn't work – that we needed something else.

So why is it so important that he not just tell us?

But I had to set that aside for the moment, because right now what we needed was a plan. I stared at the others, looking for the key to unlock this puzzle.

By my reckoning, there were only two possibilities here: either we were seven random people brought together by malice and happenstance, or each of us had been necessary to get to this place at this moment – and we did have it within us to destroy the gates. This wasn't a problem of spellcraft, but of alchemy: how did we all fit together? How were a bunch of wonderists, an angel and a demon supposed to cure what was destroying our world?

A cloud of the reddish haze that periodically blew across this terrain came through the window, making us cough as we inhaled its poisonous . . .

Poison, I realised then. *We don't need a cure or even a weapon – we need to become the poison that makes* them *sick.*

'Quickly,' I said, 'everyone, gather round. Aradeus, we're going to need your rapier.'

Without a word, he proffered the hilt.

I held out the palm of my hand. 'Cut me – cut all of us, especially Alice.'

'Why me?' the demoniac asked. Her leathery wings were shuddering as they tried to keep her balanced. The room was swirling around us and the creak of shifting stones in the walls and ceiling was so loud I had to shout to be heard.

'Because the rest of us don't disgust the Pandorals so much that they'd bother wanting to kill us. It's *your* existence that sickens them, and right now, I want to make them very fucking sick indeed.'

It took her a moment to work it out. 'My blood? You believe they can't tolerate that which comes from the Infernal plane?'

I would have taken some pleasure in the look of surprise on her face, but I had other things to deal with. 'Galass, we're going to need your magic.'

'How?' she asked. 'I barely know what I'm doing.'

'This will be easy,' I lied as one by one they allowed Aradeus to make incisions on their palms with the tip of his rapier. 'Everybody join hands. We need our blood to mingle.'

The others complied, and soon the seven of us were standing in a circle like a bunch of religious zealots about to pray – only we were facing outwards, towards the Seven Brothers, our hands clasped together tightly, the shallow wounds on our palms touching. They were as dull-eyed and slack-jawed as ever, but I would have sworn the one in front of me was trying to smirk.

Let's see how funny you find this next part, you fucker.

'Galass, can you feel the blood in each of us?' I shouted over the din.

She was visibly trembling and would have fallen down, had she not had Aradeus on one side and Shame on the other, supporting her.

'There's so much,' she whispered, 'and it's all so different . . . you, Shame, Corrigan, Alice—'

'Alice! Just focus on Alice. I need you to make some of her blood – her *essence* – flow through each of us.'

'How? What am I—?'

'It's just like when your magic exsanguinated those soldiers back in the camp, the ones who were attacking you. Only now I need you to make the blood pass through into each of us through our veins. Remember the way you could sense the shifting movements of life in the canal? Let your perception shift to the flow of blood, take that feeling and let it guide you so that you're binding our essences to each other.'

Galass closed her eyes, her brow furrowing with effort. I could see sweat begin to glisten on her forehead. 'I think . . . I think I can touch it now, move it from her to—'

'Not so much!' Shame warned.

Her shout roused me and I realised I'd started to pass out from sudden blood loss. Corrigan and Aradeus looked no better, and Alice's face was ashen, her eyes glazed.

'I'm sorry!' Galass cried. 'I'm sorry, I just—'

'It's okay,' I said, 'just share a little from each of us, that's all we need.'

Please, if there's any justice to this world, let a little be enough.

Galass' hair whipped about her face in the opposite direction from the winds pelting us. Unlike the rest of us, she was looking stronger than ever. When she opened her eyes, they were blood-red. 'It's done, I think.'

I let go of Fidick and Shame's hands and walked on unsteady legs to the brother in front of me. Copper-shelled insects were still pouring from his mouth; all too soon there would be enough to build another Pandoral. That one would either kill us outright or simply delay us long enough that the poisonous effects of the gates would leave us too sick to fight. Either way, our last chance to save our miserable little corner of the universe would be gone.

I lifted my still-bleeding hand. 'Is everyone ready?' I asked.

Each one had taken up position opposite one of the brothers. Our faces were grim, determined; no one needed to state the obvious; we all knew that the odds were against us. Five seconds from now, most likely all of us would be dead and this would all have been for naught – and yet not one of them hesitated.

Looking at them was . . . it was like that feeling I'd longed for so badly when I'd joined the Glorian Justiciars, the one promised to me by the Auroral Song and yet never fulfilled until this moment. The seven of us had started out with nothing in common. Hell, we could barely tolerate each other's company most of the time. But in that instant, as we abandoned all our petty and selfish impulses so that we could share in one tragic, glorious act of defiance . . . we became our own army, our own family.

And brother, we were a sight to see.

'Hey, Corrigan?' I asked.

'Go fuck yourself, Cade,' he said, but he was smiling.

'Fair enough. Everyone, it's time to wave hello to our would-be conquerors.'

As one, we drove our hands inside the mouths of the Seven Brothers, whose bodies were being used as gateways between our plane and that of the beings who would enslave us to rework our world to their design. I saw the eyes of the man before me flicker open, just for a moment.

And then the world exploded.

CHAPTER 51

Blood and Guts

Something very hard struck me in the back of the head. It turned out to be a great chunk of rock from the fortress wall. Normally, such things aren't much of a cause for celebration, but the wall was no longer undulating, so I took that as a good sign.

I reached back to feel how bad the injury was, but when my hand came back all bloody, I had no idea if it was mine, since I was at present covered head to toe in the flesh and bodily fluids of what had once been the Seven Brothers, the greatest wonderists of our generation.

Well, I suppose technically, *we* were now the seven greatest wonderists of our generation, and all of us were similarly smothered in the blood, skin and organs of our newly obliterated hosts. I don't think I had ever seen anything quite so disgusting in my life as Corrigan, Galass, Aradeus, Shame, Fidick and Alice, drenched head to foot in stinking gore.

For some reason, I suddenly realised that hideous, stomach-churning sight was the funniest thing I'd ever seen.

'What are you laughing at, fallen one?' Alice demanded, and that made me laugh even more, because I couldn't figure out how to explain exactly why it was so funny. Aradeus opened his mouth to attempt an explanation, but instead, the normally urbane rat-mage started sniggering uncontrollably, which turned out to be a very un-debonair look for him. Corrigan's great belly-laugh rang out, and now Galass was giggling wildly, until even Alice found herself laughing wildly at the mess of guts hanging off her hands. The whole chamber was echoing with our preposterous mirth, as if it were its own breach between the planes, with its own laws of physics altering the world around it.

And for a while, we all just laughed at each other.

All except for Shame.

'What's wrong?' Aradeus asked, suddenly seeing she was not reacting. He reached over to touch her hand, and when she pulled away, it occurred to me that keeping our bodies from altering as we'd reached into the Pandoral plane might have been too much for her.

'I'm sorry,' she said.

'Sorry about what?' Galass erupted, a mixture of awe and disbelief in her voice. 'You did it – you held us together. You saved all of us, Shame. You saved the entire Mortal realm!'

The angel ignored the praise. The others were confounded by her expression of misery, all except for Alice. Unlike the two of us, they hadn't studied under the legendary Hazidan Rosh, hadn't been trained to discern the subtlest signs of guilt in the expressions of others. Shame's gaze met mine, and for the first time since she'd chosen that name for herself, she embodied it fully.

No . . .

'You bi—' Alice tried to say. I'd never heard her swear before, nor had she succeeded in doing so now. The others had stopped laughing, and moving. I myself tried to resist, only for my body to betray me, just the way I'd made Corrigan's betray him.

A recruitment spell, cast by an angelic, in payment for her freedom.

Too late I recalled how our path through the Infernal demesne had been purchased, and Shame's words as we'd left that cabin beneath the pleasure barge.

I switched sides.

CHAPTER 52

That Which is Holy

I lost time then – not a lot, but you don't need to lose much for everything to change. Corrigan, Alice, Galass, Aradeus and I were all frozen in place. Shame was kneeling on the floor, crying. Fidick was kissing the top of her head.

'Bless you, sister,' he said. 'You have helped me to bring holiness to this world.'

'What the fuck are you doing, Fidick?' I demanded, gratified to find my mouth was working again. At least I was able to swear at the little bastard. Then again, maybe it amused him, listening to us vent our futile rage.

Fidick didn't answer me, but knelt down next to the weeping angelic and scooped up some of the gore that had been the Seven Brothers before we obliterated them. He frowned at the gooey mess in his palm. 'Well, this won't do.' Turning back to Shame, he asked, 'If you wouldn't mind?'

She rose to her feet and held out her hands.

He poured the noxious mess from his hands to hers, and as if drawn to itself, more lumps began to slide along the floor towards her. I felt an awful slithering sensation as gobs of blood and brains and intestines slid over my own skin, making their way to the angelic, who was soon surrounded by oozing, bloody piles. She blinked her eyes and the whole mass turned a glorious shimmering gold – then the dead flesh and bone at her feet began to coagulate, binding together, at first just inchoate masses, until they began to take on the shapes of men.

Seven men.

'Shame, what are you doing?' I shouted. '*Don't* – you *can't* bring them back!'

'Betrayer!' Alice spat. 'You claimed to have switched sides, yet now you do the bidding of the Lords Celestine?'

'Don't be so hard on her,' Fidick said, and I could almost see the golden shadow of the hand of a Lord Celestine on his right shoulder, as if he were a Glorian Justiciar now.

Then I saw a second hand, on his left shoulder, this one the scarlet of a Lord Devilish.

'There was an agreement,' Fidick explained, as if he was doing us all a tremendous favour by sharing the truth. 'A pact, of sorts: the angelic saved your lives on the pleasure barge by submitting herself to the command of the Lords Devilish. However, they have come to their own accord with the Celestines.'

'I never agreed to this,' Shame sobbed, staring at her moving hands as if they were nothing to do with her.

I guessed from the agonised look on her face that this was without her consent, an unwilling sculptor birthing works of art at the cost of her own soul. The seven bubbling masses of rendered flesh were becoming more distinct now, taking on the subtle variations of height and build of the different brothers.

'Please,' she begged Fidick, 'don't *violate* me like this. My soul won't bear it!'

'Oh, don't get me started on what happens when you make pacts with Infernals and Aurorals,' the boy said. 'It's never quite the deal you expected. Besides, you're an angelic. What makes you think you even have a soul?'

The tears falling from her golden eyes looked heartbreakingly human to me. We stared silently as her unwilling body methodically completed its hideous work.

It took just a few more minutes before the Seven Brothers we'd destroyed so utterly less than ten minutes ago were once again standing before us, gasping.

'What . . . what have you done to us?' the eldest asked, the dread in his voice almost enough to make me pity him.

'Oh, tut tut,' Fidick said, and gestured at Shame. He didn't even bother to look at her as he passed on his order: the subtle disdain of a master for his slave. It brought back that moment on the prince's barge when Galass had chosen one of the pleasure girls for herself.

'I've only ever known what it is to be another's plaything,' she had said. *'Who are you to tell me I can't, for once in my life, experience what it is like to hold that power myself?'*

But Galass had been tentative, almost deferential to the girl she had chosen for herself, while Fidick dominated Shame without the slightest hesitation, as if subjugating another were the most natural thing in the world to him.

On his unspoken command, Shame's fingers twitched. How she knew what he wanted, I had no idea; maybe he was speaking directly in her mind.

The Seven Brothers' eyes widened in horror. When they opened their mouths, their tongues were gone.

'Much better,' Fidick said with a contented sigh. 'I much prefer not having the architecture scolding me.'

'Architecture?' Galass demanded. 'Fidick, how can you—?'

'They made themselves into gates, Galass. They chose to become doorways between this realm and another. Who are we to deny them the destiny they themselves chose?'

The brothers were lined up now. It looked as if all our efforts – all the sacrifices we'd made – had changed nothing at all. But that wasn't true. It turned out we'd changed *everything*.

Fidick walked along the row, a general inspecting his unwilling troops. 'Now,' he said, 'we have a little problem with the size of our portals: the beings who rule the Infernal and Auroral planes are quite a bit bigger than insects.' Again without looking at Shame, he ordered, 'By my hand be guided.'

I didn't understand what he was doing at first, until he reached up and slid his fingers into the mouth of the youngest of the brothers. Slowly, he prised open the unwilling jaws, pulling them as wide as they would go – and then wider and wider yet, and as he did so, Shame's transfiguration magic altered the brother's face until it was just a hideous parody of a human being. The poor bastard needed no tongue to scream.

'Fidick, stop this!' Galass shouted. 'This isn't you – it's wrong! *It's evil!*'

'Don't be silly,' he replied, patiently continuing his monstrous work. 'You and I have witnessed true evil, Galass. We experienced it in the Ascendant's camp – what they did to us there, remember? What right does humanity have to govern their own affairs when men like Lucien can rip the innocence from children?'

The boy stopped and stepped back to inspect his handiwork. The brother's mouth was now a gaping maw stretching down to the floor: more than enough space for a grown man to walk through.

'There, that's better,' said Fidick with satisfaction.

He moved to the next brother, and as we stood there, paralysed with terror and shock, he transformed one after another, until only the brother in the middle – the one I'd locked eyes with a lifetime ago – remained unchanged.

'I'm afraid seven is an odd number,' the boy informed him, 'and it wouldn't be right to give one side more than the other. I'm sure you understand.' He turned to us, smiling as if he'd only just remembered we were still there. 'Would any of you like to kill this one again? I don't mind which way you choose to do it. Corrigan? Aradeus?'

When none of us spoke, he shrugged. 'Fine, then, I'll do it myself.'

He reached up and pressed the brother's nose closed, holding it firm with one small hand while with the other, he pushed the man's mouth shut. He might have looked like an eleven-year-old, but he clearly had an adult's strength, for he held firm even as the man struggled to free himself.

The brother's body was shaking violently now, but he still wasn't able to move more than a fraction of an inch, no matter how hard he fought. In just a minute or two, the spasms became less frequent, and soon stopped completely.

He might have been dead, released from life, but he was still in bondage, for his corpse remained frozen like an anguished statue.

'What happens now?' I asked, trying to hide the tremor in my voice.

Fidick turned to me and smiled. 'But you already know, Cade – you figured it out before we even began, didn't you?'

'I was a little busy trying and apparently failing to save the world. I didn't have time to work out all the details of your complete and utter betrayal of humanity.'

Fidick clapped his hands excitedly. 'And you *did* save the world, Cade, you and the others! All of us, really! We should all be very proud of ourselves.' He frowned. 'But there's a problem, see? We didn't *really* save the world because all that was going to happen was that the Mortal demesne would go back to being the awful place it's always been – a place where cruel men and women get to have their way with little boys and girls.' He wagged a finger at us. 'And you wonderists have far too much unchecked power, you can surely see that. You could have fought for us, but instead, all you've ever done is to sell your magic to the highest bidders, no matter how evil they are. You must see it's long past time we did something about *that*, surely?'

As if on cue, a bright light suddenly shone from the gaping mouth of the first brother.

A figure stepped forth, dipping his head to avoid mussing his hair on the top row of teeth.

I'd never seen a Lord Celestine in person before – no one has, since their essences aren't supposed to be able to enter the Mortal plane. Yet here he stood, as tall and beautiful and golden as I always imagined they'd be. The brother began to bleed at the gums; the skin inside his mouth started smouldering, charring like pig's meat on a spit, and as we stared, his body turned to ash, collapsing into a pile of grey-black dust on the floor.

Shuddering, I tore my eyes away from the little heap that was the last remains of the portal and looked at the other brothers. On the other side of the room, a Lord Devilish was emerging in the same way. His ivory-white flesh, accented in scarlet, was clad in shadow. As he stepped into the room, he gave a small bow to the Celestine, who replied in kind.

Others followed, two more from each realm, until six beings – until now refused entry by the natural laws of our universe – stood upon the ashes of their human gates, staring into the faces of their erstwhile allies.

'The bargain is fulfilled,' one of the Celestines said, his voice ringing out like a trumpet. 'As we leave this place, so our pact comes to an end.'

One of the Devilish smiled tolerantly, as if dealing with an inexperienced gambler who hasn't yet realised he's holding all the wrong cards. 'And so the war begins,' he responded.

They left then, the six of them, like three pairs of newlyweds gearing up for one hell of a honeymoon. For all their magnificence, they might have been mistaken for Mortal emperors and empresses, and only we seven knew any different. Our world had something now that it had never had before.

We had gods.

CHAPTER 53

Farewell

When it was done and the Lords Celestine and Devilish had departed to transform the world into a board upon which they would play their murderous games, Fidick turned to Shame and said, 'You are released.'

She looked up at him from where she was still kneeling on the floor, glaring at him with a fire in her eyes that would have set me running, were my legs able to move.

The boy was unimpressed. 'You have no idea what I've had done to me, angelic one,' he said. 'Even Galass doesn't know. I kept it from her, because she did so like to believe she had protected me from the worst of what life had to offer. So kill me if you wish, but it will make no difference. I will die knowing I made the right choice. Men of wealth and power have ruined this world because they lacked someone to fear. I have given them gods, and now they will be very afraid indeed.'

'Go,' Shame told him. Her eyes had turned an unnatural polished silver, and even from where I stood paralysed, I could see Fidick's image was being reflected back at him in her gaze. 'Leave here now, child of hate, child of spite. If you are wise, you will fade away into the world, never to be heard from again. But know this: should I hear your name uttered, I *will* find you, and I will make your death a memorable one.'

The boy chuckled, as if he hadn't really understood her threat. As he walked away, Galass called out, struggling against the hidden bonds that held us all, 'Fidick, wait! Where are you going?'

He stopped, looking almost surprised. You'd think he'd never given the matter any thought until now. But I knew that for pretence. Whatever else drove the little bastard, he loved to put on a show.

'At first I thought I might like a little power for myself,' he said, a slender, childlike hand rising lazily to gesture towards the door through which we'd come. 'The Apparatus awaits inside the room where the Seven Brothers offered it to us. They weren't entirely honest, of course. They used up almost all its power enhancing their own attunements. But it's probably good for one last transformation.' He pursed his lips then blew out a bubbly breath between them. 'But no. I think I'm done with all this wonderism business. Maybe I can find a nice couple to adopt me, maybe with an older daughter who can be a sister to me. Maybe a dog.'

Watching his little performance, I wondered if he understood even now, even after all he'd done to her, how deeply he was wounding the girl who'd been willing to give up everything to protect him.

'It doesn't have to be like this!' Galass cried. 'The Celestines and the Devilish – they manipulated you! They—'

Before he left us there, he turned back to her and said sadly, 'Oh, Gal. I do so wish you would grow up.'

CHAPTER 54

The Apparatus

Shame released us then, ending both our bondage and the debt that had bound her to the Infernals. I recalled something Galass said to me when we first met, that not all shackles are visible to the naked eye, nor are they made of iron. I thought the angelic had suddenly found herself at the bottom of a pit where the walls were made of guilt and far too high to climb.

For a moment, I watched her weep, wondering whether some expression of sympathy or offer of absolution on my part would do her any good. To save our lives, she had become her name and betrayed everything she believed in. But Aradeus was already there, and with what comfort a gentle yet daring heart could provide, he set himself to the task of climbing down into the depths of her despair in the hope of someday helping her to climb back out.

It's the sort of thing rats do, I guess.

Now I just needed to put an end to as much of my own despair as circumstances would allow.

'Come with me,' I said to Galass.

'Where?'

I pointed to the arched doorway that led back into the maze of passageways, and from there to the chamber where the corpses of forty-two slain wonderists awaited us, along with a large, coffin-shaped brass box that for once would bring life rather than more death. 'Fidick said the Apparatus might work one last time. We're going to use it on you.'

I'd reached the door before I noticed she wasn't following me.

'Don't you get it?' I asked, turning on her with more anger than I'd even been aware was churning inside me. 'You don't have to be a blood mage any more. You can give yourself a different attunement, become a totemist or an echoist, or even a damned floranist if you want. Anything but a luminist.'

'She could become a thunderer,' Corrigan suggested.

'Not that, either,' I said.

Galass still hadn't moved. She was standing there in the tatters of her now filthy silver sublime's gown, the red locks of her hair dancing around her face as they generally did before she accidentally bled people to death.

'No,' she said.

I've never so badly wanted to choke someone with my bare hands before. 'No? *No?* I'm offering you a cure, Galass. A future. A *life.*' I jabbed a finger towards the hallway. 'The Apparatus is the most precious artefact ever lusted after by wonderists everywhere, and you're *refusing?* Have you lost your mind? Why am I even asking myself that? Of course you've gone nuts. You're a fucking blood mage and that happens to all of you sooner or later!'

Still she hadn't budged.

'Are you done yelling at me?' she asked.

'Not even close.'

'How many have you known?'

'What?'

'Blood mages. How many have you known?'

'Not many,' I admitted. 'But the ones I did are all dead, as are all the ones any other wonderists have ever heard of.'

Her eyes went to the floor, and she bit her lower lip. For a moment, I thought maybe I'd got through to her. As in so many things, I was wrong. When her gaze rose to meet mine again, I knew I'd lost the fight.

'How many blood mages spent their childhoods training to be sublimes?' she asked, though it was obvious she wasn't expecting an answer. 'How many have gone through the things I've gone through? Suffered the way I have?'

'I . . . I doubt any of them.'

On light footsteps she ran to me, coming to stand before me as if she wanted me to see her fully – not as the fragile, brittle girl I'd met in the Ascendant's camp, but as the woman she was and perhaps always had been. 'Cade, I can do this.'

'Do what?'

She held up her hands, reached out with one slender finger and held it close to my cheek. I felt the slightest flush rise in my skin, but nothing more than that. 'These abilities, as strange and awful as they are, they're part of me now. Without them, we all would have died. You said that blood magic is the only kind whose power is born of *this* realm. Why would nature allow some of us to be attuned to it if nothing can come from it but horror?'

'Because it's a shitty world?'

She placed her palm against my chest. I felt my heart beating faster, but only because of the unexpected intimacy of another human being's touch that wasn't them pummelling me or trying to kill me. It didn't feel so bad, actually. I guess it must've been written on my face, because Galass rose up on tip-toes, kissed me on the cheek and whispered, 'For a bitter, cynical wonderist who consorts with Infernals for his spells, you're not such a terrible person, you know that?'

Someone coughed. Or maybe gagged. It was Alice.

'Are we done here?' the demoniac asked, her wings twitching with irritation. 'I'd like to leave this fortress before it collapses on us.'

'How about you?' I asked. 'There's no reason the Apparatus

shouldn't work on a demoniac. You could attune yourself to the magic of the Aurorals if you wanted, maybe become a proper Glorian Justiciar. You'd hear the Auroral Song everywhere you go. I imagine the Lords Celestine will be hiring now that all their other justiciars have been slaughtered.'

Her stare could have wilted an entire garden. 'I *am* a proper Glorian Justiciar.' She tapped a finger to where the heart would have been on a human. Who knows what Infernal organ demons have there. 'And the song of my teacher plays inside me all the time.'

Good grief. Hazidan really did a number on her.

'Well, somebody had better use the Apparatus before some wandering arsehole wonderist we don't like gets to it.' I turned to Aradeus. 'You could get a real attunement instead of that rat nonsense.'

He gave me one of those hideously graceful bows. 'A generous offer, brother Cade, but I will decline.'

'As will I,' Shame said, holding on to him for support. 'Whatever the penance for my crimes, I will face it as I am, not as I wish myself to be.'

Corrigan gave a yawn. 'Don't look at me. Tempestoral magic is the best kind anyway.' He made a flowery gesture towards himself that somehow ended at his crotch. 'Why mess with perfection?'

'Seriously?' I asked, turning to stare out into the hallway that led to the chamber where the Apparatus was waiting. 'The most precious artefact in existence and *nobody* wants to use it?'

The others were silent a while, but eventually Corrigan said what they were no doubt all thinking. 'Go on, Cade. You're the one who's never been comfortable with your own attunements. Besides, I doubt you're going to find diabolics willing to sell you Infernal spells any more. It won't be any fun killing you for using that recruitment spell on me if you've got nothing to fight back with but your lousy personality.'

He had a point there.

Funny how I hadn't even considered using the Apparatus myself until now. I guess maybe it was because a quieter, wiser part of me already knew what attunement I would choose when I lay down inside of it.

'See you all on the other side,' I said as I walked through the door.

CHAPTER 55

The Virtue of Malevolence

An hour later, I stumbled out of the fortress, which now looked more like a poorly made child's toy shaped out of clay that hadn't set right. Someone was waiting for me outside.

'If you're going to hit me,' Tenebris said, 'I should warn you I've got a bit of a glass jaw.'

The diabolic walking freely on the Mortal plane was the first sign that our realm had changed. We were no longer its masters.

'It's not like you to gloat,' I said.

He smiled. 'That's just about the nicest thing you've ever said to me.' He breathed in deeply, then let it out all at once. 'Damn, but the air smells like rotting arsehole out here. How do you stand it?'

'It's not so bad. I imagine you'll learn to appreciate it after a while.'

He apparently took that as licence to come closer and brush some of the dust off my shoulder. 'If you say so. Anyway, look, buddy. I just came to say I'm sorry for how things turned out.'

'You mean for having manipulated me and my friends into murdering the Seven Brothers, not to protect our world from the Pandorals but so your bosses and the Celestines could turn it into one big fucking battlefield?'

'Hey, no need for false modesty, man. You also killed off most of the Pandorals for us.' The little shudder that went through him seemed genuine, for once. 'If I'm being honest, Pandoral magic freaks my employers out. Too unpredictable. Also, it's gross.' He sniffed the air, curled his lip in disgust, then sighed as if overcome with unavoidable sadness. 'Anyway, I've got some bad news.'

'What's that?'

'I can't be your agent any more.'

'Yeah, I figured.'

The diabolic hugged me and proceeded to pat me awkwardly on the back. 'Buck up, old pal. You've always been resourceful. You'll figure something out.' He let me go and took a step back, wagging a finger in the air at me like I'd just been caught with my hand in the cookie jar. 'Word to the wise, though, Cade: don't fuck with us. The Celestines and the Devilish rule this world now. They're finally getting the Crusade-To-End-All-Crusades they've dreamed about for millennia. You guys had your chance, you screwed it up and now we're in charge. So do yourself a favour, okay? Either pick a side, or find someplace quiet to hide out for the next century or so while my bosses figure out how to win this war.'

'Good advice,' I said. Since the world had turned utterly perverse on me, I grabbed the diabolic and returned his hug, whispering into his ear, 'Thanks for everything, old buddy.'

As we parted, he gave me a quizzical smile like he couldn't tell whether I was being snide or not. That gave me a little hope, at least.

'See you around, Cade,' he said, and headed down the path that led towards the town.

I waved goodbye. Hopefully someone would stick a pitchfork in him. If not, the bag of spell-sand I'd snatched from the pocket of his coat – which had been in his possession long enough to be attuned to him – would come in handy the next time we met and I tortured him to death.

The heavy thump of familiar footsteps made me turn.

Corrigan came to face me. 'So what did you pick?' he asked, then, as was typical for him, stopped me from answering. 'No, let me guess. While lying there in the most potent magical device ever built, knowing you could attune yourself to any plane you wanted – like the Tempestoral plane, for example – you chose something feeble.' He jabbed an accusing finger into my chest. 'You went with Fortunal magic, didn't you? All those jobs where you pretended to be a chance mage, and now you've gone and made yourself one.'

I coughed. 'Seems to me we could use all the luck we can get, don't you think?'

He threw his hands up in the air. 'You're so predictably sentimental it almost makes me sad to think you're not long for this world, Cade.'

I started coughing again. I'd probably be doing a lot of that, given what I'd just done to myself.

Corrigan thumped me so hard on the back I nearly choked on my own tongue. 'I didn't see you get injured during the fight,' he said. 'What's the matter with you?'

'Nothing. Bug in my throat. Speaking of injuries, you still planning on killing me?'

'Abso-fucking-lutely.' He sat down heavily on the stone steps to the keep's main doors. 'Not yet, though. I'm a little tired at the moment, and I've already taken one unwanted bath in some guy's blood and guts.'

I sat down next to him. Not too close, just in case. 'You're not going to give a shit about this, but I'm sorry for what I did to you. It was ... I've done a lot of awful things in my life, Corrigan, but none of them ever made me so sick to m—'

He leaned over and backhanded me – not as hard as usual, so that was something. 'Don't get all melodramatic on me, Cade. If I'd had a recruitment spell I would have used it on you ages ago. Only difference is, I would have made you dance naked in front of the others, instead of forcing you to help save the world.'

'Save the world?' I peered through the reddish haze at the road and the town beyond, at all the places that would now have to live with gods and devils fighting a war that benefitted only them – not to mention the one Pandoral lord who was probably already figuring out how to use the blood soot all around us to breed more of himself. 'I don't think we saved anything at all.'

'Well, not that I want to interfere with your sacred right to feel guilty, but I really hated those Pandoral bastards. They were made of bugs, which is gross, and whatever motivated them, it wasn't greed or lust or bloodthirstiness or—'

'—any of the good stuff.'

'Exactly. If it had to come down to those pricks or the devils we know, well, it's like I keep telling you: nothing that moves gets to stay clean for long. All you *do* get to do is decide which river of shit you're going to swim in on the way to oblivion, and do your best not to drown in it on the way there.'

I thought about that for a while as we sat there. 'I'm pretty sure you've never said that before. Did you just make it up?'

'Too much? With the river of shit thing?'

'Actually, it's not bad.'

Galass came out of the fortress, followed by Alice, and soon the six of us were sitting companionably on the steps together gazing out at the pinkish dawn.

'What now?' Galass asked.

I thought about that, but all that came to me was something Tenebris had said. 'Pick a side, I guess.'

'Which one?' Aradeus had his arm around Shame, who was looking almost as miserable as I felt. But she was leaning into the rat mage's embrace, which gave me a little hope for her.

'I'll not fight for the Infernals,' Alice said. 'Nor the Aurorals, not now that I've seen what bastards they are.'

'Bad news, sister,' Corrigan said. 'Those are the only two sides left.'

Two sides.

There was this fight I'd had with Hazidan, years back, when she was first making me question the teachings of the justiciars. I was shouting at her about treason, and how there were only two sides and we all had to choose one or the other. I don't remember exactly what she said, but I'll never forget what she *did*.

I pulled myself a little shakily to my feet and walked down the stone steps. I picked up a stick and drew a line in the reddish dirt. 'Corrigan's right. There *are* only two sides. But nobody gets to tell me what those sides are. So that one' – I tapped the stick on the ground on the other side of the line I'd just drawn. 'That one there is for everyone who thinks that gods and devils have the right to rule this world, to decide for the rest of us what good and evil mean.' I lifted my stick like a banner, then drove it into the ground on my side of the line. 'And this one is for everybody who plans to make the lives of those self-righteous pricks a living nightmare.' I looked around at my dishevelled, debilitated, and disreputable fellow wonderists. 'Anyone care to join me?'

Aradeus was the first to step forward, of course. I'm not sure if it was because he believed in me, or because rat mages can't resist a call to arms, however suicidal. But Shame stood alongside him, and beneath the tears, I would have sworn something new was awakening in her. Galass followed, scarlet curls swirling around her head as if even her hair was itching for a fight. Alice was next, shooting me a look that said she'd heard *exactly* the same speech from Hazidan, and the old bag did it better. But she came to my side all the same.

'Well?' I asked Corrigan.

The thunderer grumbled to himself, not meeting my eyes, but then finally stomped down the steps and joined us. 'Oh, look,' he said snidely, 'here we all are, standing on one side of a stupid line in the dirt. I feel so magnificent now. It's like all the pain and suffering we're sure to endure before our inevitable deaths won't be so bad now because we're all standing on one side of this pathetic little line that you couldn't even draw straight.'

Sparks suddenly erupted from the knuckles of his clenched right fist as he raised it over his shoulder, then drove it down towards the ground as if he was punching the earth itself. The light was blinding, but when we could all see again, there was a ten-foot-long charred ditch in front of us.

'There's your fucking *line*.'

'Feel better now?' I asked.

He sniffed. 'As a matter of fact, I do.'

'Good. Then can we—?'

Corrigan leaped across the ditch, then spun on his heel to face us. 'I've changed my mind.'

'*What?*' Galass demanded. 'You'd side with those who would ensla—?'

He interrupted her, snarling, 'Don't get uppity with me, little girl. You're still a fucking blood mage. Probably going to drain me dry in my sleep. No, before I commit myself to spending what's left of my life on a futile, doomed quest against the most powerful beings in the universe, I have demands.'

'Demands?' Aradeus asked.

'Demands, plural. Two, in fact.'

Alice sneered, 'Even with the freedom of your own realm at stake, you're still just a filthy mercenary at heart, aren't you? Looking to take advantage of every situation for your own gain.'

'Stop flirting with me, girl,' Corrigan warned. 'You're making me hard.'

'Well, no one wants that,' I said. 'So, what exactly are your demands?' I had a bad feeling about this.

'First,' Corrigan said, and promptly dropped his trousers, 'everyone here has to admit that I have a truly magnificent cock. Aradeus, stop turning away! Come on, Galass, get a good look. I want you all to take as much time as you need, then tell me this is truly the finest instrument ever forged by gods nobler than the Aurorals and perverts fouler than the Infernals for bringing those most deserving to unimaginable ecstasy.'

Corrigan Blight, unhinged thunderer, unrelenting degenerate, and the best friend one could ever hope for in a world like this one, stood there with his dubious manhood on display until each and every one of us had vowed that it was surely the finest in the land.

'Dare I ask about your second demand?'

'Hmm?'

'You said you had two demands.'

'I did?' He looked down at his crotch. 'Was I wanting one of you to—? Oh, no, I remember now! We have to hire another wonderist for our coven.'

Galass looked confused. 'Why?'

'Because if I'm going to get myself killed fighting some insane war against the Celestines *and* the Devilish *and* all their minions, then I damn well want the world to know who we are.' Corrigan grinned from ear to ear as he declared, 'And the "Malevolent Six" just doesn't have the same ring to it.'

CHAPTER 56

Real Heroes Don't Name Their Swords

Picture a hero.

Go ahead, close your eyes if you need to.

There he is, see? Broad shoulders, chiselled jaw, the high cheek-bones and bright blue eyes that give artists spontaneous wet dreams. Bet he's holding a gleaming sword up high. Probably calls it 'Daunt-less Light' or 'Blade of Valour' – because shiny pointy weapons work better when you give them cool names, obviously. The cloak's a must, too, right? Long, flowing mantle that's just perfect for tripping over when you're attacking, and just the right length for your enemy to grab hold of and choke you to death when you're trying to run away.

Does he wield magic, this paragon of virtue? Sure, but none of those shitty Infernal spells that everyone knows are bad for the soul. No, our boy hurls balls of brilliant blue flame – because setting fire to your enemies is so much more noble than messing with their heads. Most of all, though, this is the guy you call when your quest is righteous in every possible way. Don't waste his time if you're not so nice yourself – if you're a, you know, regular human being with all the nasty foibles that actually make us human in the first place. Damsels in distress need apply only if they're virgins.

Behold your valiant hero: a self-important, sermonising poser who'd never stoop to getting down in the mud where the real fight's about to start because he might have to get his hands dirty and that would make him 'no better than the bad guys'.

Well, guess what? There's a whole lot of mud down here, and we're all neck-deep in it. Maybe it's time somebody came along who's ready to be *worse* than the bad guys.

So, go ahead, open your eyes.

I'll show you a fucking hero.

Acknowledgements

Regarding the Various Realms of Magic and their Practitioners

Two perennial truths dominate a fantasy novelist's career: first, readers will always want a detailed listing of the magic systems in the book, and second, nobody likes to read acknowledgments. I've made it my mission, therefore, to deviously intertwine the two so as to ensure that the many wonderful people who help bring my books to store shelves and libraries get their due.

Behold, therefore, the only existing list of all mystical attunements mentioned within the pages of *The Malevolent Seven*, and a few fine people whose magic was integral to putting this book in your hands.

Auroralists
Auroral magic comes in the form of blessings granted by the Lords Celestine themselves, heavenly beings who each embody a specific virtue such as justice, devotion or serenity. These blessings operate continuously, thus granting the receiver a channel to that particular form of power. This makes Auroral magic exceptionally potent and desirable. Alas, such blessings can be taken away for even the slightest perceived offence against the Lords Celestine.

While no Auroralist myself, I've certainly received more than my share of blessings from the Lords Celestine of Publishing. Thanks, therefore, to Jon Butler of Quercus who kindly agreed to let Jo Fletcher buy this book despite the other four books under contract with me having not yet been released. Thanks also to Jo herself, fantasy's finest editor, for her supportive words on acquiring the manuscript, which were, I believe, 'Well, I don't want anyone else to publish it.'

Infernalists

Infernal spells are imparted to the wonderist from various Lords Devilish through the negotiations of a conniving and often manipulative Demonic (commonly referred to as an 'agent'). The transmission of each Infernal spell produces a tingling ink-black sigil on the flesh of the recipient. When awakened through the specified gestures and paired with the bearer's emotional impulse, these spells can be cast only once before the markings fade to a kind of unsightly charring of the skin. Infernal magic focuses most potently on the alteration of consciousness, thus enabling the caster to manipulate the minds and souls of others.

My years as a touring musician, though far from remarkable, were nonetheless filled with wonderful adventures. Many of the best occurred thanks to the cunning negotiations of music agents (Infernalists one and all) who regularly sold my soul – along with my mediocre guitar, keyboard and vocal talents – to various clubs, bars, festivals and wedding planners around the world. One agent in particular will always be close to my heart, if only because he ended so many of our calls by shouting into the phone, 'Burn my number, you asshole! Burn my number!!' before slamming it down on the receiver.

Literary agents seem a much kinder breed. However, it must be noted that both my first agent, Heather Adams, and my current one, Jon Wood, insisted that this book should be published despite my repeated attempts to convince them it was too violent, mean-spirited and cruel to small, carrion-feeding canines. Complaints regarding emotional harm suffered due to the fate of Mister Bones should be directed to the RCW Literary Agency.

Tempestoralists (a.k.a. Thunderers)

The Tempestoral plane is filled with endless, raging mystical storms composed of every kind of destructive energy imaginable. Tempestoral mages, often called 'Thunderers', have the ability to channel various Tempestoral blasts into our realm without harming themselves. Some scholars – along with anyone who has ever met a Thunderer in person – suspect that the violent nature of Tempestoral magic induces a tendency in those attuned to it to go berserk on a regular basis.

Anyone who's ever worked with Jo Fletcher knows she's a magical hurricane waiting to happen. Some people – nasty, mean-spirited ones, mostly – might accuse this author of sharing a similar temperament. Fortunately, a skilled tempestoralist by the name of Ajebowale Roberts, assistant editor, kept all our frantic thunderbolts from blowing up the book. Thanks to Anne Perry, publishing director, for tolerating the many ensuing lightning storms and channelling all that mayhem into a successful launch.

Echoists

The Sonoral Realm's mystical gifts go beyond the mere amplification of sound or even creating new ones out of thin air. An Echoist can lend tremendous potency to their words or those of others, transforming mere verbal statements into almost irresistible commandments. Even the most awkward of speeches can become spiritual testaments of such inspirational force as to rouse armies.

Thank goodness that my books have been repeatedly blessed by one of the great voice talents of our age, namely the one and only Joe Jameson, who narrated the Greatcoats Quartet, the Spellslinger series, and many of my Tales of the Greatcoats short stories. His dulcet tones are brought to the audiobook editions courtesy of Dom Gribben and Hannah Cawse from the Hachette Audio team.

Luminists

Coloured light and the spectacular images that can be conjured with provide a source of wonder and awe. While some wonderists doubt the potency of

Luxoral magic, those who appreciate its power to entrance and amaze will pay a great deal to have one in their coven.

Book covers are something I take very seriously. They often make the difference between potential readers picking up a book versus leaving it to languish on the shelves unpurchased. The job is all the more complex when some idiot author insists on having seven different characters on the cover. Thanks to Patrick Carpenter and Keith Banbury, and the team at Head Design, for bringing the seven together.

Floranists

The physical laws of the Floranistic plane imbue all plant matter with psycho-kinetic properties. Thus, a Floranist using their attunement to create breaches between that realm and our own can induce trees and other forms of plant life to obey their will and take any shape the wonderist desires.

Much floranistic magic went into making the former trees that now make up the pages of this book look sensible, for which we have type-setter Ian Binnie and Amy Knight, the production director, to thank.

Portalists

The ability to open a door in one place that leads to one halfway across the world is surely one of the most desirable sources of magic for any wonderist . . . or criminal.

While certainly not criminals (at least insofar as my investigations have uncovered), the following individuals have cast many a porta-tionalist spell to get this book into places all around the world: sales directors David Murphy and Chris Keith-Wright, Jessica Dryburgh of Special Sales, Mobius' Rachael Hum and Giuliana Caranante, export sales directors Eleanor Wood, Jemimah James and Matt Cowdery, digital mastermind Frances Doyle and, of course, rights director Emma Thawley, whose portational magic is so potent it even gets the book translated into other languages.

Totemists

The laws of the Totemic realm bind animal forms to sets of archetypal charac-teristics which, when summoned by a totemist, behave like a toolkit of magical spells aligned with the nature of a particular animal. Thus a felinist can display cat-like grace and resilience, or a chiropteranist can navigate through sound while also communicating through bats. Every Totemist is attuned to a single animal form, and they all thing their animal is the most noble and impressive.

Publishing houses always seem like they're full of strange animals, so my gratitude to totemists Emma Capron, editorial director, and Georgina Difford, managing editor, for keeping the zoo intact as the novel went through the publishing process. Thanks as well to Peter McNulty, whose role is so mysterious that Jo Fletcher couldn't even tell me what it was, but assured me his spells are vital indeed.

Cosmists

Those attuned to the Abyssal plane are by far the deadliest of wonderists. Their entire existence is a continuous breach between our realm and that of endless space. Covered by a thin layer of abyssal matter, a Cosmist's entire body becomes a portal into a void from which no one ever returns. Fortunately, the constant, unyielding awareness of the vastness of eternity and the insignificance of any individual tends to cause Cosmists to off themselves before they can get up the will to actually destroy the world.

Books are a bit like cosmists, filled with the potential for un-imaginable power until they somehow collapse in on themselves at the last moment and disappear from the store shelves as if they'd never been there at all. Hopefully the efforts of publicist Ella Patel and Lipfon Tang, marketeer for this novel, will keep our seven troubled wonderists from suffering such a dire fate.

Sanguinalists

Blood magic is the only form of wonderism entirely native to our world. It is the fundamental wildness of nature itself: the same force that first caused groups of molecules to become the fluid of life. Drawn to the flow of blood around them, Sanguinal Mages are especially dangerous when the hunger to play with the lives of other beings overwhelms them.

Nobody makes my books bleed like my friends and first readers Kim Tough, Eric Torin, Peter Darbyshire, Jim Hull, Brad Dehnert and Wil Arndt.

Fortunalists (a.k.a. Chancers)

Chance is merely an illusion in our own world, for in reality all events are subject to the laws of cause and effect. Those attuned to the Fortunal plane, however, can summon breaches that momentarily sever the natural connection between cause and effect. The breaches alter outcomes of events while still appearing to follow physical laws.

Whenever you publish a book, it always feels like the outcome is preordained – as if success or failure can't be influenced one way or another. And yet, there seem to be some mages out there who can alter the odds for a book's success and give it a second chance. I've been lucky (ha – see what I did there?) to have so many wonderful Fortunalists turn their magic on my books. Apologies that I can't name you all here, but special thanks to Jade of Jadeyraereads, Allen Walker of the Library of Allenxandria, and L'Ours Inculte, who is not a cartoon bear as his Twitter picture would suggest, but a wonderful French book blogger.

Pandoralists

Little is known of the Pandoral realm save that it's physical dimensions are far smaller than our own and that the few beings who live there are possessed of the ability to warp and reshape matter and even bodies within our world, making those attuned to that form of magic incredibly dangerous. Rumour has it that the Pandoral realm is collapsing in on itself, but can such raw power every truly disappear?

We come to the end of our list of mystical realms to the most powerful of all, which is the one possessed by readers around the world. It may appear that the world of books is slowly collapsing from the pressures of movies, video games and other forms of entertainment, but nothing could be further from the truth. In fact, the power of individual readers to affect the future through their reviews, recommendations and sharing of books may be greater than ever. I am, as always, eternally grateful for the support readers have shown my books, and I always delight in receiving your letters and e-mails at decastell.com/contact.

Wonderists Mysterialis

So rare is this type of mage that neither the plane of reality from which their spells derive nor any description of their enigmatic abilities appear in any known text, including this one. Their power, however, in unquestionable.

There is no form of magic grand enough or potent enough to describe my favourite wonderist of all. Love always to Christina de Castell. Marrying you was surely the greatest spell I could ever hope to cast.

Sebastien de Castell
September, 2022
Vancouver, Canada